LAST NIGHT
AT THE
TELEGRAPH
CLUB

by Malinda Lo

DUTTON BOOKS

DUTTON BOOKS

An imprint of Penguin Random House LLC, New York

First published in the United States of America by Dutton Books,
an imprint of Penguin Random House LLC, 2021
First paperback edition published 2021

Visit us online at penguinrandomhouse.com.

LIBRARY OF CONGRESS CATALOGING-IN-PUBLICATION DATA IS AVAILABLE.

Printed in the United States of America

ISBN 9780525555278

3   5   7   9   10   8   6   4   2

BRR
Design by Anna Booth
Text set in Sabon LT Std

To all the butches and femmes,
past, present, and future

"A sweeping and romantic page-turner, the heart of this rich and ambitious historical novel is a love story that thrums with passion and self-discovery."
—**Laura Ruby, two-time National Book Award Finalist
and Printz Award–winning author of** *Bone Gap*

"An absolute masterpiece."
—**Randy Ribay, author of** *Patron Saints of Nothing*, **a National Book Award finalist**

"Malinda Lo turns her masterful talent toward an under-covered period of San Francisco history. *Last Night at the Telegraph Club* is by turns gut-wrenching, utterly compelling, and deeply tender. I loved Lily fiercely, and you will too."
—**Rebecca Kim Wells, author of** *Shatter the Sky*

"A lovely, affirming, layered, and deft coming-of-queer-age novel."
—*New York Times* **bestselling author Kate Elliott**

"Lo has really outdone herself here. I don't think I can overstate how refreshing it is to read queer historical fiction that is so complex, nuanced, and tender. It's my opinion that this book will quickly become a new touchstone of the genre of queer literature. What an accomplishment." —**Sarah Gailey, award-winning author of** *Magic for Liars* **and** *Upright Women Wanted*

"The writing is so atmospheric and detailed that I am convinced I have lived in San Francisco in the 1950s. It's a passionate, smoldering romance that perfectly captures the feelings of falling in love for the first time."
—**Christina Soontornvat,** *New York Times* **bestselling author and Newbery Honoree**

"Malinda Lo was, for so many of us who write and read books about queer girlhood, the first introduction to seeing ourselves on the page. Her latest book continues that legacy with this startlingly beautiful historical coming-of-age."
—**Leah Johnson for Reese's Book Club**

"A must-read." —*Us Weekly*

"*The Price of Salt* meets *Saving Face* in this gripping historical thriller from the celebrated author of *Ash*. . . . *Last Night at the Telegraph Club* is proof of Lo's skill at creating darkly romantic tales of love in the face of danger."
—*O, The Oprah Magazine*

"Lush, ambitious and layered, Malinda Lo's sweeping historical novel is the queer romance we've been waiting for." —*Ms. Magazine*

"A vivid must-read." —*Bay Area Reporter*

"Lo taps into the evocative San Francisco of yesteryear while deftly navigating McCarthyism, ethnicity, sexuality, and the 'Lavender Scare' in this striking novel that holds some unnerving contemporary parallels." —*Toledo Blade*

"A journey of self-discovery that's as necessary as it is dangerous." —**PopSugar.com**

"An enthralling historical lesbian romance." —**WBUR**

"Malinda Lo is an absolute icon." —**BuzzFeed**

"A joy to read." —*The Advocate*

"A gripping novel where historical fiction meets romance, *Last Night at the Telegraph Club* is a whirlwind read set in San Francisco's Chinatown during the Red Scare. Immersive and creative, Lo gets wrapped up in her fictitious world of adventure and adrenaline and follows Lily Hu as she seeks out the woman she loves." —*Gay Times*

★ "Finally, the intersectional, lesbian, historical teen novel so many readers have been waiting for." —*Kirkus*, **starred review**

★ "A must-read love story . . . alternately heart-wrenching and satisfying." —*Booklist*, **starred review**

★ "*Last Night at the Telegraph Club* is a work of historical fiction that's as meticulously researched as it is full of raw, authentic emotion. . . . Shout it from the highest hills: This is a beautiful, brave story, and Lily is a heroine that readers will love." —*BookPage*, **starred review**

★ "This immersive, powerful coming-of-age novel tackles perceptions, expectations, and identity while sweeping readers into smoky lesbian nightclubs and '50s culture." —*BCCB*, **starred review**

★ "Smoothly referencing cultural touchstones and places with historic Chinese American significance, Lo conjures 1950s San Francisco adeptly while transcending historicity through a sincere exploration of identity and love." —*Publishers Weekly*, **starred review**

★ "Historically accurate and well-researched." —*SLC*, **starred review**

★ "A riveting, emotionally stirring tale. . . . *Last Night at the Telegraph Club*— focused on unapologetically embracing one's true self—is a spectacular addition to the young adult historical fiction genre." —**Shelf Awareness**, **starred review**

★ "This standout work of historical fiction combines meticulous research with tender romance to create a riveting bildungsroman." —*Horn Book*, **starred review**

LAST NIGHT
AT THE
TELEGRAPH
CLUB

1950 — Senator Joseph McCarthy produces a list of alleged Communists working in the State Department.

— The Korean War begins.

— Judy Hu marries Francis Fong.

July 4, 1950 — **LILY attends the third annual Chinese American Citizens Alliance Independence Day Picnic and Miss Chinatown Contest.**

1951 — Dr. Hsue-shen Tsien is placed under house arrest on suspicion of being a Communist and a sympathizer to the People's Republic of China.

— Judy takes Lily to Playland at the Beach.

— In *Stoumen v. Reilly*, the California Supreme Court rules that homosexuals have the right to public assembly, for example, in a bar.

PROLOGUE

The Miss Chinatown contestants were clustered together behind a canvas screen near the stage. They hadn't been there when Lily Hu walked past the same area fifteen minutes earlier on her way to the bathrooms, and there was something startling about their sudden appearance.

Lily was thirteen, and she couldn't remember if she'd seen a group of Chinese girls like this before: in bathing suits and high heels, their hair and makeup perfectly done. They looked so American.

She slowed down. The pageant was about to start, and she'd miss the introductions if she lingered here. She should go back to her family's picnic blanket on the lawn in front of the stage, but she dawdled, trying not to appear as if she was staring.

There were a dozen girls, and their bathing suits were white or black, sea green or forest green, one piece or two. Their arms and legs were bare beneath the hot noonday sun, their gleaming black hair curled and pinned in place. Bright red lipstick on their mouths; scarlet polish on their fingernails; smooth, tanned skin. Each girl a variation on a theme.

Their high-heeled shoes were sinking into the grassy ground. Every so often one of them lifted her foot to make sure her heel wasn't stuck in the damp earth, like the slender-legged foals in *Bambi* learning to walk. The girl in the black two-piece bathing suit wore particularly tall black heels, and as she shifted in place, the right heel stuck in the ground. Her foot rose out of the shoe, revealing an ugly red mark where the back of the shoe had rubbed against her Achilles tendon. The girl frowned, tugging again at the shoe with her toes, but this time her entire foot slipped out. The round pinkness of her bare heel; the intimate arch of her foot; toes flexing in midair. Lily had to avert her eyes, as if she were watching a woman take off her dress in public.

A microphone hummed on, and a man declared in English, "Welcome to the third annual Chinese American Citizens Alliance Independence Day Picnic and Miss Chinatown Contest!"

Applause and cheers rose from the audience gathered on the lawn. An older woman carrying a clipboard began to herd the girls into a line behind the screen, preparing them to climb the stairs onto the stage. Lily turned away and hurried down the path to the lawn.

She spotted her family toward the middle of the crowd, gathered together on the scratchy old army blanket stenciled with her father's name—CAPT. JOSEPH HU—in white paint. They were surrounded by other families, all lazing beneath the clear blue sky, all facing the stage set up in front of the main lodge.

Lily saw her mother stand, pulling four-year-old Frankie to his feet. Her father, still sitting on the blanket, handed Mama her bag, and then she and Frankie began to make their way to the path along the edge of the lawn. Uncle Francis and Aunt Judy, seated next to Lily's father, watched the stage with mixed expressions. Uncle Francis was absorbed; Aunt Judy looked skeptical. There was no sign of Lily's other brother, Eddie, and she guessed that he was still off playing with his friends.

Lily met her mother on the path.

"I'm taking Frankie to the bathroom," Mama said. "There's still some fried chicken left."

Someone set off firecrackers as Lily headed across the lawn. The summer sun was sinking hot and dry into her black hair. It was real summertime weather here in Los Altos—Popsicle weather, unlike cool and foggy San Francisco. All day Lily had been shedding the layers she put on that morning in their Chinatown flat, and by now she was wearing only a short-sleeved blouse and cotton skirt, and wishing she had worn sandals instead of shoes and socks.

When she reached her family, she knelt down to claim the last piece of fried chicken from the basket. Her friend Shirley Lum was seated nearby with her family, and she gestured at Lily to join them. "Can I go sit with Shirley?" Lily asked her father, who nodded as the emcee started to introduce all the pageant contestants. Their names rang out over the lawn as Lily straightened up, drumstick in hand.

"Miss Elizabeth Ding!"

"Miss May Chinn Eng!"

Lily joined Shirley on their blanket—an old white tablecloth—and curled her legs to one side, tucking her skirt over her knees like a lady.

Shirley leaned toward her and said, "I like the third one best—the one in the yellow two-piece."

"Miss Violet Toy!"

"Miss Naomi Woo!"

Lily took a bite of the chicken. The skin was still crispy, the meat juicy and salty. She cupped her hand beneath it to catch the crumbs that fell. Onstage, the girls were walking across one by one. They sashayed in their heels, causing their hips to sway back and forth. A few whistles rose from the audience, followed by laughter.

"I think the girl in the black bathing suit is a little too flashy," Shirley said.

"What do you mean?" Lily asked.

"Look at her! She's acting like she's a Hollywood star or something. The way she's standing."

"But they're all standing like that."

"No, she's doing it more, as if she thinks she's perfect."

The girl in black didn't look any different from the others to Lily, but she remembered the sight of her naked foot in the air, and she was strangely embarrassed for her. The contestants were all smiling, hands cocked on their hips, shoulders proudly held back. The emcee explained that they had to circle the stage again for the judges to assess their face and figure, and the audience clapped some more.

The judges were seated at a table on the ground in front of the stage. Lily couldn't see them, but she had heard all about them. Two were Chinatown leaders, one was a prominent local Caucasian businessman, and one was a woman—the Narcissus Queen from Honolulu, Hawaii. Lily had seen her taking photographs with fans earlier; she was wearing a pretty floral-print dress and a big pink flower in her hair.

"Look—my favorite's going around now," Shirley said.

The girl in the yellow two-piece was taller than the others, and her figure was curvier. She had wavy black hair pulled back with combs, revealing sparkling drop earrings. As she crossed the front of the stage, whistles rose from the audience. When she reached the far side she paused, bending one knee and glancing back over her shoulder coquettishly. The audience erupted in applause, and Shirley joined in enthusiastically.

Lily, still holding her half-eaten drumstick, looked away from the stage uncomfortably. She didn't understand the shrinking feeling inside her, as if she shouldn't be caught looking at those girls. She saw a group of older Chinatown men nearby, sitting casually and smoking as they studied the contestants. One grinned at another, and there was something off-putting about the expression on his face. He made an odd gesture with his left hand, as if he were squeezing something, and the other man chuckled. Lily dropped her gaze to her fried chicken, and the bone of the drumstick reminded her of the girl in black's Achilles tendon, rubbed red from the hard edge of her shoe.

"Let's go up on the stage," Shirley said conspiratorially, taking Lily's hand to pull her across the lawn.

"We shouldn't—"

"Don't you want to see what it's like?"

It felt dangerous, rebellious—but only moderately so. The afternoon sunlight was golden and heavy now; the show was over; and the spectators were packing up and preparing to go home.

"All right," Lily agreed, and Shirley squealed in response.

They almost ran the last few yards, and then they were at the bottom of the steps and Shirley came to an abrupt stop. Lily bumped into her.

"Just imagine," Shirley said dreamily, "what it must be like to be Miss Chinatown."

There had been controversy when the judges declared the winner today. Lily had heard a faint chorus of boos amid the applause, and she saw the winning girl's face go pink with both pride and dismay. A man had shouted at the stage in English: "She looks like a pinup, not like a Chinese girl!"

Lily had eyed him surreptitiously; he was sitting near the man who had made the lewd gesture, who then leaned toward him and slapped him on the shoulder. They had begun an animated conversation that

Lily couldn't quite understand—they were speaking Toishanese—though she made out the words for *beauty* and *woman*.

"Lily, aren't you coming?"

Shirley had bounded up the steps, and Lily realized she had fallen behind. She put a hand on the railing—it wobbled—and quickly went up the stairs. The microphone and its stand had been removed, leaving the stage entirely bare. Shirley walked toward the center, sashaying like the contestants as she pretended to be a beauty queen.

Lily hesitated, watching her friend turn to face the broad, emptying lawn. Someone whistled, and Shirley flushed with pleasure as she bobbed a curtsy.

"Next time it'll be you!" a disembodied voice called out.

Shirley giggled and glanced over her shoulder at Lily. "Come on! Come and see the view."

Lily joined Shirley at the front of the stage just as a raft of firecrackers popped in the distance. The afternoon sun was behind them, casting their shadows across the ground, and as Shirley raised her hand to wave, queenlike, Lily watched her shadow stretch dark and thin over the grass. The ground was dotted with empty glass bottles and crumpled paper sacks, and the grass was flattened into the irregular impressions of blankets and bodies.

"Lily!"

The voice came from the left, slightly behind the stage. She stepped back to get a better look and saw Aunt Judy coming up the path from the parking lot, waving at her.

"It's time to go!" her aunt called.

Lily waved in response and tugged at Shirley's arm. "We should go."

"Just a minute," Shirley insisted.

Lily retreated to the stairs, then turned back to see Shirley still standing at the edge, gazing out over the lawn. The back of her head was crowned in sunlight, casting her face in shadow. The profile of her nose and mouth was still sweet and girlish. But there was a modest swell to her breast, and she had cinched in the waist of her dress to emphasize the slight curve of her hips. Lily wondered if this was what a Chinese girl should look like.

PART I

I Can Dream, Can't I?

August–September 1954

1

"That woman is so glamorous," Shirley said, nudging Lily to look. Two Caucasian women were seated across the restaurant at the table in the alcove. "I wonder if she's going to a show."

It was Friday night in the middle of the dinner rush, and the Eastern Pearl was almost full, but Lily knew immediately who Shirley was talking about. The red paper lanterns hanging overhead shed a warm glow over the woman's blond hair; it was pulled up in a twist and pinned with something glittering that matched the droplets in her ears. She wore a royal-blue satin sleeveless dress with a scoop neckline, which showed off her creamy skin, and a matching blue bolero jacket hung over the back of her seat. Her companion was dressed much less glamorously. In fact, she wore trousers—gray flannel ones, with a soft-collared white blouse tucked in at the waist. Her hair was cut short in the current style, but on her it looked a bit less gamine than mannish, which drew Lily's attention. There was something about her posture that felt subtly masculine. Lily couldn't put her finger on it, but it intrigued her.

Lily realized she was staring and turned her attention back to the messy pile of napkins in front of her. Beside her, Shirley was moving rapidly through her own stack, transforming them into crisp swans. Lily had spent countless hours in the restaurant with Shirley since they were little, and over the years she'd helped out with various small tasks as needed. Now they were about to start their senior year in high school, but she still couldn't fold a napkin into a decent swan. She picked apart the one she had been working on and started over.

On weekend nights, the Eastern Pearl mainly attracted tourists rather than local Chinese. Shirley said it was because one of the tour companies that brought people to Chinatown recommended it, which led to good business for the restaurant. Lily wondered if the women in the alcove were tourists, and she snuck another glance at them.

The blonde was removing a silver cigarette case from her handbag, and her companion pulled a matchbook from her trouser pocket, leaning toward her as she struck a match. The blonde cupped her hand around the flame, drawing her friend's hand close to her face as she inhaled. Afterward, she sat back and offered the case to her friend, who removed a cigarette and lit it quickly, pulling the cigarette away from her mouth with her thumb and index finger. Smoke curled up into the red-lit ceiling.

"You're making a mess of those," Shirley said, glancing at Lily's poorly folded swans. "Ma won't like them."

"Sorry," Lily said. "I'm no good at this."

Shirley shook her head, but she wasn't annoyed. This was the way it always was. "I'll redo yours," Shirley said as she pulled Lily's napkins toward her.

Lily sat there for a moment, watching Shirley shake out her messy swan, and then she reached for the *Chronicle*. She always enjoyed the theater and film reviews and society columns, with their photographs of women in furs and diamonds, and she wondered idly if the blonde had ever been in the paper.

"Maybe she's an heiress," Lily said to Shirley. "The blonde over there."

Shirley glanced across the restaurant again, briefly. "An heiress to a gold mine?"

"Yes. And her father recently died and left her with a fortune—"

"But she's discovered that she has a half brother—"

"—who's fighting her for the inheritance—"

"—so she hired a private investigator to seduce him!"

Lily shot Shirley a confused glance. "What?"

"Well, who do you think that other woman is? She looks like a female private investigator. Only a female PI would look like that. She was probably undercover."

Lily was amused. "Undercover where?"

"Oh, who knows."

They had played this game since they were children—inventing stories for strangers they saw in the restaurant—but Shirley tended to lose interest in their inventions before Lily did.

"Did you see the new ad my parents placed?" Shirley asked, setting the latest napkin swan next to the others, all lined up like a funny little army.

"No."

"It's in there—I saw it earlier. Keep going. It's on the same page as the nightclub reviews."

Lily obediently flipped the pages of the *Chronicle* to the "After Night Falls" column, which took up half of the page. The other half was filled with ads for restaurants and nightclubs. She skimmed them, hunting for the Eastern Pearl ad. MEET ME AT JULIAN'S XO-CHIMILCO: SERVING THE BEST MEXICAN DINNER. ALL-CHINESE FLOOR SHOWS—SUPERB FULL-COURSE CHINESE OR AMERICAN DINNER—FORBIDDEN CITY. An illustration of four faces—father, mother, son, and daughter with a bow in her hair—advertised GOOD FOOD! GOOD LIVING INCLUDES DINING AT GRANT'S.

"There it is," Shirley said, pointing to an ad near the bottom of the page. A simple black rectangle with the type in bold white read: EXPERIENCE THE FINEST ORIENTAL CUISINE AT THE EASTERN PEARL—THE BEST OF CHINATOWN.

But Lily's eye was drawn to a square box directly above the Eastern Pearl ad. It read: TOMMY ANDREWS MALE IMPERSONATOR— WORLD PREMIERE! THE TELEGRAPH CLUB. 462 BROADWAY. It was a relatively large ad that included a photo of a person who looked like a handsome man with his hair slicked back, dressed in a tuxedo. Something went still inside Lily, as if her heart had taken a breath before it continued beating.

"It's not very big, but Pa thinks it will get noticed," Shirley said. "What do you think?"

"Oh, I—I'm sure it'll get noticed," Lily said.

"People read that page, don't they? They always want to know what stars are in town."

"You're right. I'm sure people will see it."

Shirley nodded, satisfied, and Lily forced herself to look up from the photo of Tommy Andrews. Across the restaurant the two women were paying their bill. The woman in the blue dress took a wallet out of her handbag, while the woman with the short hair unexpectedly pulled a billfold out of her trouser pocket. Their dollars tumbled limply onto the table.

Behind the counter, the swinging door to the kitchen opened. Shirley's mother poked her head out and called, "Shirley, come help me for a minute."

"Yes, Ma," Shirley answered. She gave Lily an exasperated glance. "Don't touch the napkins. I'll finish them when I get back."

The bell attached to the restaurant's front door jingled, and Lily saw the two women leaving. The short-haired woman held the door open for her friend, and then they were gone, and Lily was staring down at the ad for the Telegraph Club again.

Four-sixty-two Broadway must be only a few blocks from the Eastern Pearl. There were several nightclubs on Broadway, just east of Columbus. Lily's parents always told her to avoid those blocks;

they were for adults, they said, and for tourists. Not for good Chinese girls. Not for girls at all. Lily understood that she was supposed to think the clubs were tawdry, but every time she crossed Broadway (always during the day, of course) she'd look down the wide street toward the Bay Bridge in the distance, her gaze lingering on those closed doorways, wondering what they hid from view.

Her palms were a little damp. She glanced over her shoulder, but no one was behind the counter. She quickly tore out the page with the Telegraph Club ad, folded it into a neat, small square, and tucked it deep into the pocket of her skirt. She closed the newspaper and slid it back into the pile of *Chronicle*s beneath the counter. As she straightened the stack, she realized her fingertips were smudged with newsprint. She ran to the bathroom and turned on the sink, scrubbing at her fingers with the harsh pink soap until no trace of ink remained.

2

The Eastern Pearl was only a ten-minute walk from the Hu family flat, but that night the journey home seemed to take Lily forever. As soon as she left the restaurant, she had to spend several minutes talking to old Mr. Wong, who was locking up his imports store next door. Then, as she rounded the corner onto Grant Avenue, Charlie Yip at the concession stand called out to her, saying he had her favorite wa mooi[1] on discount. She bought a small bag to share with her brothers, and as she slid the candy into her skirt pocket, she took care not to crush the folded newspaper.

Outside the Shanghai Palace, a clump of Caucasian tourists blocked the sidewalk. They were dressed up for their night out in Chinatown, and Lily could tell they'd had a few cocktails. None of them noticed her as she slipped around them into the street, dodging a cigarette butt flung by a woman in a fur stole. Lily shot an irritated glance at the woman's back as a car honked at her, causing Lily to jump out of the way. Now pinned between the tourists and a parked Buick, she was forced to wait for the traffic light to turn red before she could finally cross the street, darting impatiently between idling cars.

When she reached the opposite sidewalk, she glanced back up Grant toward Broadway and North Beach, wondering where the Telegraph Club was exactly. She imagined a tall neon sign over an awning-covered door. She remembered the two women she'd seen at

---

1. · Salty dried plums; a snack.

the Eastern Pearl, and she pictured them going to the Telegraph Club. She imagined them taking a seat at a small, round table near the stage, where Tommy Andrews would emerge, dressed to the nines, to sing.

She wanted to take out the newspaper ad right then and there to see Tommy's face again, but she resisted. Clay Street was right ahead; she was only a couple of blocks from home. She walked faster.

Lily unlocked the front door and hurried up the long wooden stairs to the third-floor landing. The flat was quiet and dark to the left, where the kitchen was, but down the hall to the right the living room door spilled light into the hallway. She hung her jacket on the coatrack, took off her shoes, put on her slippers, and padded toward the living room, passing the closed door to her parents' bedroom.

Her father was seated on the sofa, reading the newspaper and smoking his pipe. Her younger brothers, Eddie and Frankie, were sprawled on the rug reading comic books. When she entered, her father looked up and smiled. The lenses of his round glasses reflected the lamplight.

"Have you had dinner?" he asked. "How was Shirley?"

"She's fine. I ate with her. Where's Mama?"

"She went to bed early. If you're still hungry there are leftovers in the kitchen."

Eddie looked over his shoulder at her. "Also some cake. There was a bake sale at Cameron House."

This reminded Lily of the wa mooi, and she pulled them out of her pocket. "Do you want some of these? I got them from Charlie Yip."

Frankie jumped up to take them from her, while Papa said, "Not too many—it's almost time for bed."

Lily could predict how the rest of the night would go. Her father would stay up until he finished reading the paper—perhaps another half hour. Her brothers would argue that they should be able to stay up later, but they would be forced into bed by ten o'clock. She could sit in the living room with them, impatiently reading a novel, but she already knew she wouldn't be able to concentrate. Instead she went into the kitchen and put the kettle on to boil. While she waited she stood at the window over the sink, gazing at the city lights, each a glowing ember marking someone else's life: bedroom and living room windows, headlights crawling up the steep streets. She wondered where those two women from the restaurant lived and what their homes looked like. She slid her hand into her pocket and touched the folded newspaper.

She made a cup of jasmine tea and took it to her bedroom, which wasn't really a bedroom but an alcove off the living room behind pocket doors. She left them open for now. Her father had used the space as an office until Frankie had turned four, when Lily had argued her way out of sharing a room with her brothers. Now she had her own tiny hideaway, into which she had crammed her narrow bed, an old bureau with drawers that never closed properly, and several tall stacks of books that created a precarious nightstand for her bedside lamp. The small window in the wall above the foot of her bed was covered with a short curtain made of blue velvet, dotted with tiny sequins. Lily had sewn it herself in home economics class in junior high school. The stitches had begun unraveling almost as soon as she hung it up, but she still liked it. It reminded her of the science fiction novels she liked to read, with their covers depicting outer space.

While she waited for her father and brothers to go to bed, she went to brush her teeth and then puttered around her little room. She folded some laundry she had left on her bed; she shuffled through her notes from last year's math class to see what could be discarded. All the while she was acutely aware of the piece of newspaper in her skirt pocket: the soft whispering sound it made when she knelt down to put away her clothes; the way its edges nudged against her hip when she sat on her bed.

It felt like hours before her father and brothers left the living room. When they were finally gone, Lily closed the pocket doors to her alcove and changed into her nightgown. She pulled out the newspaper ad and set it on top of the books that made her nightstand. She had folded it into a small square, but now it began to open of its own accord, parting like the wings of a butterfly.

Startled, she watched it until it stopped moving. Outside, the cable car rumbled as it came up nearby Powell Street, and the bell seemed to clang in time with the beating of her heart. She began to unstack one of the piles of books beside her bed, and pulled out Arthur C. Clarke's *The Exploration of Space*, which had been a gift from Aunt Judy. She laid the book on her bed, then pushed her pillow against the wall and sat back against it, reaching at last for the ad.

She unfolded it carefully. There was Tommy Andrews gazing into the distance like a movie star, a halo of light around Tommy's gleaming hair. TOMMY ANDREWS MALE IMPERSONATOR. Some time ago, she had seen an advertisement for a show at a different nightclub that read: JERRY BOUCHARD, WORLD'S FOREMOST MALE IMPERSONATOR! It had been accompanied by an illustration of a woman (her curves were apparent) in a top hat and tails, with the curls of her hair poufing out beneath her hat. The illustration had seemed wrong—comical, somehow. Not like this photo. Tommy was handsome, debonair. The photo wouldn't be out of place on Shirley's bedroom wall, alongside her pictures of Tab Hunter and Marlon Brando.

Once, Lily had torn an illustration of a moon colony out of *Popular Science* magazine (which her father sometimes purchased for Eddie) and taped it on the wall above her bureau. When Shirley had seen it, she had teased her for having a boy's tastes, and after Shirley went home, Lily had taken it down. If she were exceptionally daring, she would cut away the words TOMMY ANDREWS MALE IMPERSONATOR from this ad and pin up the picture in the space left by the moon colony. She doubted that anyone—even Shirley—would realize that the photo was not of a man.

But she knew that she did not dare. She set the ad down on her bed and opened *The Exploration of Space.* Hidden between the pages were two other folded clippings. She had torn the first one out of an old *Life* magazine that had been left in a box outside the Chinese Hospital. It depicted a young Katharine Hepburn lounging in a chair, legs casually draped over one of the arms. She wore widelegged trousers and a blazer and held a cigarette in one hand while gazing off to her left. There was a knowing confidence in her expression, a hint of masculine attitude in her shoulders.

Lily distinctly remembered coming across the photo while she was flipping through the magazine on the sidewalk. It had been September, and the sun had been bright on her head. She had stopped at the photo and stared at it until her hair began to burn from the heat, and then—before she could second-guess herself—she ripped it out of the magazine. Someone had been walking past at the time and Lily saw them look at her in surprise, but by then it was too late, and she pretended as if she hadn't noticed their glance at all. She had quickly folded the page in two, slid it into her book bag, and dropped the magazine back in the box.

The other clipping was an article about two former Women Airforce Service Pilots who had opened their own airfield after the war. It included a small photo of them sitting close to each other, looking up at the sky. They were dressed in matching sunglasses, collared shirts, and trousers, and the woman on the right, who had tousled, short hair, protectively held the hand of the woman on the left. The short-haired woman worked as a mechanic; her companion was a flight instructor. They weren't as dashing as Katharine Hepburn, but there was something compelling about their casual closeness.

The article had come from an issue of the magazine *Flying* that Lily found at the public library last spring while researching a report on the WASPs. She vividly remembered sneaking the magazine into the emptiest, farthest corner of the library and tearing the article out beneath the table as quietly as possible. She knew she shouldn't, but she had needed to have the picture in a way she didn't consciously understand. She'd surreptitiously left a nickel on the library's circulation desk as if that might make up for her defacement of library property.

Now she laid the women pilots on the bed next to Katharine Hepburn and Tommy Andrews and looked at them all in succession. She couldn't put into words why she had gathered these photos together, but she could feel it in her bones: a hot and restless urge to look—and, by looking, to know.

3

The elevator girl at Macy's was a young Chinese woman wearing a sky-blue cheongsam[1] embroidered with yellow flowers. "Good morning," she said to Lily and her mother. "What floor, please?"

"Good morning," Lily's mother said. "The junior miss department, please."

"Yes, ma'am." The elevator girl pressed the button for the third floor. She looked barely older than Lily herself, but Lily didn't recognize her, which suggested she hadn't grown up in San Francisco.

"Are you Mrs. Low's granddaughter?" Lily's mother asked. "Mrs. Wing Kut Low, on Jackson Street?"

As the wood-paneled elevator passed the second floor, the girl answered, "No. I'm from Sacramento."

An uncomfortable-looking stool was bolted to the floor in front of the control panel. Lily imagined the girl sinking onto the stool to rest her feet, slipping them out of her black pumps between elevator rides. The idea of being trapped in this moving box all day—doors opening and closing, but never able to leave—seemed like a suffocating way to earn a paycheck.

"Sacramento!" Lily's mother exclaimed, as if that were the far side of the moon. The gears creaked slightly as the elevator slowed down, approaching the third floor. "Are you alone here in San Francisco?"

1. A traditional Chinese dress.

"I have an uncle in Chinatown."

"I see."

The tone of her mother's voice told Lily that she did not think much of this arrangement. When the elevator stopped at the third floor, the doors slid open with an accompanying *ding*. Lily's mother paused in the doorway. "If you are ever in need of feminine aid," she said to the girl, "I work at the Chinese Hospital. I'm a nurse in the obstetrics department. Mrs. Grace Hu."

The elevator girl seemed uncomfortable. "Thank you, ma'am. That's very generous."

Lily cast a glance of furtive sympathy at the girl before she stepped out of the elevator.

"I worry about girls like that," her mother said in a low voice as the door closed behind them. "She's too young to be on her own. I can't imagine her uncle takes good care of her."

Lily glanced around to make sure nobody else had overheard. Directly ahead, the junior miss department sprawled beneath fluorescent lights. The floor was dotted with other shoppers, making their way from one glass display case to another. There was a mother-daughter pair near a case of hats, and the teenage girl giggled as her mother pinned a blue pillbox on her curled blond hair. They glanced at Lily and her mother as they passed, and then their gazes slid away dismissively. There were no other Chinese on the floor this morning, and Lily became self-conscious of the way she and her mother stood out. Her mother was wearing an out-of-date, square-shouldered brown suit and a matching brown hat, something that Lily had only ever seen her wear to church. And Lily's cheap skirt and blouse, acquired on sale, were far from the height of fashion.

She slowed down to let her mother go ahead of her, as if that might make others think they weren't together. When that thought made her flinch with guilt, she allowed herself to be distracted by the jewelry—silver button earrings and gleaming pearl chokers and cubic zirconia bracelets—and then by a framed advertisement on top of an apparel counter. It showed a trio of girls in mix-and-match suit separates. The middle girl wore a tuxedo-style jerkin over a white mandarin-collar blouse with a slim, dark skirt. She stood with one hand on her hip, one shoulder angled down, looking directly at the camera with a flirtatiously raised eyebrow. One gloved hand dangled next to the hand of the girl next to her, so close their pinkie fingers were almost touching. All three girls wore knowing smiles, as if they shared a secret.

"Would you like to try something on?"

Lily looked up from the ad to see a salesgirl approaching. "I was just looking," Lily said awkwardly.

The salesgirl had a friendly, open face, and her light brown hair was cut in a Peter Pan style. Her name tag identified her as MISS STEVENS. "These separates are very versatile," she said, moving the framed advertisement aside to show Lily the clothes in the case. "You can wear the blouse with these lovely A-line skirts as well."

"Oh, I—I don't know," Lily stammered, but she took a step closer to the case. The tuxedo jerkin was in a navy blue fabric with notched black lapels.

Miss Stevens took out the jerkin and laid it on the glass. "And it's hand washable. Very smart."

Lily reached out and touched it, her fingers running lightly over the crisply pressed texture.

"I can bring an appropriate size to the fitting room if you'd like," Miss Stevens said.

"Lily! There you are."

Lily jerked her hand away and looked up. Her mother was walking toward her, boxy black handbag slung over her arm, a blond salesgirl following with an armful of shirtwaists and skirts.

"I've found some things for you to try on," her mother said. She glanced down at the tuxedo jerkin and raised her eyebrows. "What's this?"

"A wonderful collection of mix-and-match separates, ma'am," Miss Stevens said. Her gaze flickered briefly to the blond salesgirl and then back to Lily's mother, who went to the case and examined the jerkin and the ad.

"Where would you wear this, Lily?" Her mother's tone was short and critical.

Lily was embarrassed. "I don't know. I was just looking."

"It's perfect for parties," Miss Stevens said. "If Miss Marshall is preparing a fitting room for you, she could bring this ensemble too."

The blond salesgirl—Miss Marshall—stepped forward with her armful of clothes, her face blandly expectant, but Lily's mother shook her head.

"Thank you, but I don't believe this is right for my daughter. Come to the fitting room, Lily. I have some school clothes for you to try on."

Lily gave Miss Stevens an apologetic look before hurrying after her mother and Miss Marshall. Miss Stevens returned her glance with a thin smile as she folded the jerkin to put it away.

In the dressing room, the salesgirl hung a row of dresses, shirtwaists, skirts, and matching jackets on the wall-mounted rail. Lily's mother took a seat on the bench inside the room. "Try on the brown dress first," her mother said. "That one, with the black buttons."

There was a succession of brown and gray dresses and skirts, with pale pink or baby blue cotton shirtwaists featuring demure round collars or cuffed three-quarter-length sleeves. They were the teenage version of her mother's church suit, inoffensive but boring. Lily thought longingly of the tuxedo jerkin, but as she made her way through the clothes her mother had chosen, the idea of it became increasingly outlandish. Maybe her mother was right. Where would she wear such a thing? It would cause a sensation at the fall dance, but she wasn't the kind of girl who caused sensations.

"The jacket is too big for you," her mother said, studying the latest suit Lily had tried on.

It was taupe-colored and boxy, and Lily thought it was old-fashioned. "I don't like it," she said.

"You're going to be a senior," her mother said. "You need to have the right look." She opened the dressing room door, but the corridor outside was empty. "Where's that salesgirl?" She glanced back at Lily. "Wait here. I'll be right back."

After her mother left, Lily gazed at her reflection in the mirror. *You need to have the right look.* Lily knew what her mother meant. She needed to look respectable and serious. The girl in the mirror looked like a schoolgirl dressing up in her mother's clothes. Her mouth was pinched shut and her forehead was creased, her body swallowed by the jacket's padded shoulders. If her mother could see her now, she would tell her to stop being ungrateful. They hardly ever shopped upstairs at Macy's unless there was a major sale, but here she was in the junior miss department with all the latest fashions, not the bargain basement with its odds and ends from last season.

Lily remembered a different visit to Macy's when she was a child—nine or ten—with Eddie clinging to Mama's hand as she pushed the buggy with baby Frankie in it through the heavy doors onto the first floor. It had been a struggle to get all of them into the elevator and up to the fourth floor where Santa's workshop was located. Lily remembered silver snowflakes hanging from the ceiling, tinsel strung over the display cases, and boxes and boxes of toy cars and airplanes stacked on the shelves. An electric train circled a miniature Christmas village, and Eddie knelt to stare at it, transfixed, while

Lily was drawn to a table-top chemistry set. There were test tubes in a stand, and a tiny Bunsen burner, and strangely colored liquids housed in little glass vials. The box that the chemistry set came in had an illustration of two boys playing together, and over their blond heads were the words DISCOVER THE FUTURE TODAY!

She didn't know how long she examined the chemistry set, but suddenly her mother appeared with Eddie and Frankie in tow, exclaiming that she had lost her, and what had she been doing? Lily had pointed to the chemistry set and asked, "Can I have this for Christmas?"

Her mother gazed at her for a moment, and then said, "Don't you want a doll instead?"

Lily had been too old for tantrums, but something about her mother's response made her angry, and she fisted her hands by her sides and announced, "I don't want a doll!"

Her mother's face had hardened instantly, and Lily saw her hand jerk as if she were about to strike her, but she couldn't let go of either Eddie or Frankie. Instead, she snapped, "You're in Macy's, for goodness' sake. Be quiet."

Her mother's cutting tone had stunned her, and Lily had burst into tears.

Now, the dressing room door opened and her mother returned, Miss Marshall in tow, with another two suit jackets. "Try this one on," her mother said, handing over a smaller size.

Lily complied. The smaller jacket fit much better. When she buttoned it, the waist nipped in as it was supposed to, rather than ballooning out around her hips. Her mother adjusted the jacket's drape. Over her mother's shoulder, Lily saw Miss Marshall carefully plucking a stray black hair from the lapel of the larger jacket and surreptitiously dropping it on the floor.

"Better," Lily's mother said, stepping back and blocking Lily's view of the salesgirl. There was an unusual expression on her face, and it took a moment for Lily to realize that her mother was satisfied.

"唔錯,"[2] her mother said in Cantonese. "幾好."[3]

Lily turned to the mirror. She saw a Chinese girl in a characterless gray suit—blank faced, nothing special, even a little boring. *Respectable.* The word felt square, immovable, like a sturdy box with all four corners equally weighted. A respectable girl was easily categorized, her motivations clear. She wanted a college degree, and then a husband, and then a nice home and adorable children, in that order. She saw her mother smile tightly, as if conscious of the salesgirl hovering behind them, and then Lily understood why her mother had worn the church suit to Macy's. Even if it was ugly, it declared her investment in respectability. Her mother was a real American wife and mother, not a China doll in a cheongsam, relegated to operating the elevator.

"It's so professional, but also very ladylike," said Miss Marshall. "Would you like me to ring it up for you?"

---

2. Not bad.
3. Pretty good.

4

This year we're going on a journey to better understand ourselves and our goals for life after high school," Miss Weiland
announced, standing at the blackboard at the front of the classroom. She was petite, with a heart-shaped face framed by a halo of
light brown curls. She was also one of the youngest teachers at Galileo High School, and half the boys in Lily's class had a crush on her.
Today she was wearing a checked gray pencil skirt and a form-fitting
pink blouse that accentuated her curves in a way that Lily had heard
the boys murmuring about as soon as they got to class.

Every senior had to take Senior Goals, taught by either Mr. Ste-
venson (he had a reputation for being a bit lecherous with the girls)
or Miss Weiland (Lily was glad she'd gotten her). The class was officially about preparing for life after high school, but it was widely
known to be an easy A that involved watching a lot of filmstrips
about etiquette and dating.

"We'll be covering three major units," Miss Weiland said. "Personal Growth and Family Living, Vocational Adjustment, and Con-
sumer Education. Today we'll begin with a personal assessment of
where you are right now. I'd like you to divide up into groups of four
and discuss a few questions with one another that I'm going to write
on the board. You will work with the people in your row—the four
toward the front and the four in the back. Go ahead and move your
chairs together."

Chair legs scraped across the floor as everyone formed their groups. Lily's group included Will Chan, who was in front of her; Shirley, who was behind her; and Kathleen Miller, who was behind Shirley. Lily, Shirley, and Will had known each other since they were children, having gone to Commodore Stockton Elementary together. They had known Kathleen since junior high, though they had never been real friends. Kathleen wasn't the kind of girl who would be part of their group. She was Caucasian, for one thing, and Lily's close friends were all Chinatown kids. But Kathleen and Lily had been in the same math classes together since eighth grade, and Lily had always thought Kathleen was perfectly nice—quiet, but smart.

She scooted over to make room for Kathleen's desk beside her, and as she repositioned her chair she noticed Will sharing a grin with Hanson Wong, who was in a group nearby. The boys rather obviously glanced toward Miss Weiland, who had her back to the classroom while she wrote several questions on the board. With her arm raised, her blouse was tugging up slightly out of the waistband of her skirt, and the skirt's darts led Lily's eyes over the curve of her backside and down the length of her legs. The back seams of her stockings were decorated, just above her heels, with a diamond pattern.

"Stop gawking," Shirley whispered.

Lily started guiltily, only to realize that Shirley was aiming her pointed whispers at Will. He turned back to Shirley with a falsely innocent smile. Lily dropped her gaze to her notebook, picking up her pencil and trying to pretend that she hadn't seen anything.

"All right, these are the things I want you to discuss," Miss Weiland announced. "What was your childhood dream? What is your dream now? And what are three steps you can take to achieve that dream? I'd like you to appoint a chairman for your group, and that chairman will make a report at the end of class about your discussion. You'll have twenty minutes to talk over the questions, and then you'll share your reports. I'll come around to check on your progress."

The classroom immediately erupted into discussion. Shirley flipped open her notebook and said, "Will, obviously you should be our chairman."

"Sure, I'll give the report."

Kathleen had taken out her notebook and was dutifully copying down the questions from the blackboard.

"I think Lily should take notes," Shirley said. "Her handwriting is the best." Kathleen's pencil wavered for a moment, and then she put it down.

"All right," Kathleen agreed.

"Fine," Lily said. "Who wants to begin? Childhood dreams?"

"I wanted to be a basketball player," Will said.

"I wanted to be a movie star," Shirley said, leaning back in her chair and patting her hair. She'd gotten a permanent wave at a Chinatown salon last week, and she was proud of her curls.

Will grinned. "I could see you in Hollywood."

Shirley preened. "Because I'm beautiful?"

"Because you're so dramatic," Lily said, and Will laughed.

"Well, I know what *your* dream was," Shirley said to Lily.

"What?"

"Didn't you want to go to the moon? What a funny dream!"

"It's not funny," Lily objected, feeling faintly stung. "Sure, I wanted to go to the moon. I still do. Wouldn't you?"

"Heavens no," Shirley said. "There's nothing to do there."

"I'd want to go," Kathleen said.

They all turned in surprise to look at her, and she looked back at Shirley.

"Was that your dream too?" Shirley asked, her tone faintly condescending. "Make a note of it, Lily, for the report."

"No, my dream when I was a child was to be Amelia Earhart. But going to the moon is a great dream."

"Have you ever been in an airplane?" Lily asked.

"Yep. When I was in eighth grade my Wing Scout troop got to fly. We weren't up there for very long—we had to take turns—but it was amazing." Kathleen's face lit up when she talked about the flight.

"What was it like?" Lily asked. "Was it scary?"

Kathleen smiled. "A little at first, but as soon as we left the ground I wasn't scared anymore. There was too much to look at."

Lily was about to ask more—she wanted to know all about the flight—but Shirley said, "Let's move on. We only have twenty minutes. Next question is what's your dream now. Will? What about you?"

Kathleen's smile disappeared. Lily frowned at Shirley, but Shirley was looking at Will.

"Well, I don't want to be a basketball player anymore. That's kid stuff. I'm going to be a lawyer. Do you still want to be an actress?"

Shirley laughed a little self-consciously. "Don't be silly. I want to get married and have a family, obviously." She looked at Lily. "You're next. What do you want now?"

Lily couldn't decide whether Shirley was goading her or not. Her tone was politely interested, but whenever Shirley sounded that way, it usually meant she was up to something. "Well, I guess I want to find a job like my Aunt Judy's," Lily said. "She works at the Jet Propulsion Laboratory as a computer," she explained to Kathleen.

"Really?" Kathleen brightened up again. "What exactly does she do?"

"Oh, she does math. They design rockets there—not my aunt, but the engineers."

"Are you taking Advanced Math with Mr. Burke?" Kathleen asked. "Next period?"

"Yes, are you?"

"Yep. I heard he only gives one A each semester." Kathleen leaned back in her chair and pointed her pencil at Lily. "I bet you'll get it."

"Oh no. If that's true, the A will go to Michael Reid—"

"Girls, you're getting off track," Shirley interrupted. "What's the next question? Oh, name three steps you can take to achieve your dream."

"But Kathleen hasn't said what her current dream is," Lily objected.

Shirley's expression tightened. "So what's your *current* dream, Kathleen?"

Kathleen's eyebrows lifted slightly at the curtness of Shirley's tone, but she didn't comment on it. "I still want to be a pilot."

"And how will you achieve your dream?" Shirley asked.

"Well, step one is to go to college, maybe major in aeronautics or engineering. Step two—"

"I didn't think you were college material," Shirley said.

Lily stared at her friend in shock. She had no idea what had gotten into her, but Kathleen didn't seem entirely surprised. She merely smiled slightly before she responded.

"Cal takes anyone in the top fifteen percent of their graduating class," Kathleen said. "I'm not going to have a problem. Neither will Lily. But I don't think we'll see you there."

Shirley's cheeks turned pink, but before Lily could do anything to defuse the situation, Miss Weiland arrived at their group. She smiled benignly and asked, "How are you doing? Any questions?"

"We're fine," Kathleen said. "Lily's taking excellent notes, and Will's going to be our chairman."

"That's good to hear," Miss Weiland said. "I'm glad you're working so well together."

After Miss Weiland moved on to the next group, the four of them sat in silence for a moment. Will looked slightly stunned. Shirley was still red-faced, while Kathleen was the only one who looked calm. Lily was strangely thrilled by what had just happened. No one ever stood up to Shirley like that.

After school, Shirley waylaid Lily at her locker and asked, "What are you doing Saturday?"

"I don't know, why?" Lily asked as she packed up her book bag.

Shirley leaned against the wall next to Lily's locker. "Will invited us to a picnic in Golden Gate Park. I think Hanson and Flora are coming, too. You should come."

"I have to study," Lily hedged. She and Kathleen had been the only girls in Advanced Math, and she'd gotten the distinct sense that the teacher anticipated neither of them would last long. She was determined to prove him wrong.

"You can study before the picnic. Come on, don't make me go alone."

"You just said Hanson and Flora are going."

Shirley pouted. "If it's just the four of us, Will's going to think it's a double date or something. You have to come."

Shirley had always been demanding this way, almost like a boy in her assertiveness. Sometimes her insistence was flattering—it could make Lily feel like she was the only friend who mattered—but it wasn't quite working on her today.

Shirley suddenly linked their arms together, pulling her close, conspiratorially. "Lily, you *have* to come. I've already told Will that you would. His brother's cultural group is throwing the picnic—we don't have to do anything except be there for Will."

"So it's not just the four of you," Lily said.

Shirley looked at her entreatingly. "*Please* come. It won't be any fun without you."

Lily sighed, but even as she pretended to be exasperated, she felt an incriminating little buzz of pleasure. "All right, fine, I'll go with you."

Shirley squeezed her arm in excitement. "Wonderful! I'll come by your house Saturday just before noon and we can walk over together. I have to go to student council now. Are you going home?"

"Yes, I—"

"All right, then I'll see you tomorrow!"

Lily watched Shirley rush off down the hallway. She thought she saw Kathleen Miller crossing the hall over by the athletic trophies, and it occurred to her that the two of them could study for math together. She quickly finished packing her book bag and hurried in Kathleen's direction, but by the time she got to the trophy case, there was no sign of her.

5

Almost every morning, Lily and Eddie met Shirley and her younger brother on the corner of Grant and Washington to walk to school. Along the way, they'd pick up Hanson and Will in front of Dupont Market, and then Flora and Linda Soo a block north, and by the time they reached Broadway there would be a whole gang of them, proceeding up Columbus Avenue through North Beach in a kind of Chinatown parade. The younger kids would split off at Francisco Street to go east to the junior high, and the older ones would head west up and over Russian Hill to Galileo High School.

Lily liked walking to school with her friends, but she secretly enjoyed walking home alone even more. She could take the quieter side streets with narrower sidewalks, and she could linger over a pretty view if she wanted. Today she climbed the Chestnut Street steps up Russian Hill, and at the top she turned around to catch her breath while looking out toward the Presidio. She'd always thought there was something magical about the city, with its steep stairways and sudden glimpses of the bay between tall, narrow buildings. It felt expansive and full of promise, each half-hidden opening a reminder that the city she had been born in still held mysteries to discover.

She continued up Larkin and down Lombard until she was absorbed by the tourists who were always loitering on the crookedest part, taking snapshots of Coit Tower perched on Telegraph Hill in the distance. The view reminded her of the Telegraph Club ad, and she thought about it all the way down Columbus until she reached the stoplight at Broadway.

The club must be on that block to her left. She couldn't see it, but if she crossed the intersection and walked a little way down, she might pass it. The thought made her heartbeat quicken, and she almost turned in its direction, but then she caught sight of Thrifty Drug Store down the street, past Vesuvio Café on Columbus. She checked her watch; she had a little time before Frankie got out of Chinese school. When the light turned green, she hurried across the intersection.

The first time Lily had gone to Thrifty had been sometime last year. She had ducked in to buy a box of Kotex, because she hadn't wanted to get them at the pharmacy in Chinatown, where she'd risk running into people she knew. Thrifty was just outside the neighborhood, so her friends didn't usually go there. She had soon discovered that Thrifty had another advantage over the Chinatown pharmacy: it had a very good selection of paperback novels. There were several rotating racks of them in a sheltered alcove beyond the sanitary napkin aisle. One was full of thrillers with lurid covers depicting scantily clad women in the embrace of swarthy men. Lily normally bypassed that rack but today she paused, drawn in by *The Castle of Blood*, on which the blonde's red gown seemed about to slip off her substantial bosom, nipples straining against the thin fabric.

The book rack alcove was normally deserted, but even so, Lily spun the rack self-consciously, retreating behind it so that she was hidden from view. The women on these book covers seemed to have a lot of trouble keeping their clothes on. The men loomed behind them or clutched them in muscular arms, bending the women's bodies backward so that their breasts pointed up.

There was something disturbing about the illustrations—and it wasn't the leering men. It was the women's pliant bodies, their bare legs and lush breasts, mouths like shiny red candies. One of the books had two women on the cover, a blonde and a brunette. The blonde wore a pink negligee and knelt on the ground, eyes cast down demurely while the shapely brunette lurked behind her. The title was *Strange Season*, and the tagline read, "She couldn't escape the unnatural desires of her heart."

An electric thrill went through Lily. She glanced around the edge of the book rack, sharply conscious that she was still in public, but although she could hear the ringing of the cash register at the front of the store, she didn't see anyone approaching her corner. She went back to the book, opening it carefully so that she didn't crease the spine, and began to read. The book was about two women in New York City: a young and inexperienced blonde, Patrice; and an older brunette, Maxine. When Patrice was jilted by her boyfriend in public, Maxine took pity on her and helped her get home. Thus began their somewhat confusing relationship, which veered from Maxine setting up Patrice with new men, to strangely suggestive conversations between the two women.

About halfway through the book, things took a turn. Patrice arrived unexpectedly at Maxine's Fifth Avenue penthouse, distraught after a bad date, and Maxine began to comfort her.

> *"Why do I want to kiss you?" Patrice whispered as Maxine stroked her long blond hair.*
>
> *Maxine's fingers jerked, but then she resumed the rhythmic petting. "I don't know, Patty, why do you?"*
>
> *Patrice twisted around on the couch, rising to her knees. "Max, I'd rather be here with you than on any date!"*

Lily turned the page, her heart racing, and she could barely believe what she read next.

Maxine pushed Patrice back against the velvet cushions, lowering her mouth to the girl's creamy skin. "You're like me, Patrice. Stop fighting the possibility." Patrice whimpered as Maxine pressed her lips to her neck.

"Max, what are you doing?" Patrice gasped. "This is shameful."

"You know what I'm doing," Maxine whispered. She unbuttoned Patrice's blouse and slid the fabric over Patrice's shoulder, stroking her breasts. Patrice let out a sigh of pure pleasure.

"Kiss me now," Patrice whispered.

Maxine obeyed, and the sensation of Patrice's mouth against hers was a delight far beyond shame.

Lily heard the creak of wheels rolling in her direction, and she quickly peeked around the book rack, her skin flushed. A clerk was pushing a metal cart stacked with boxes of Kleenex past the shelves of Modess and Kotex. She hurriedly closed the book and stuffed it into the rack behind the novel *Framed in Guilt*. She sidled over to the next rack—science fiction—and pretended to peruse the books.

Her position enabled her to keep an eye on the clerk, who was restocking the shelves at the end of the aisle. She itched to return to *Strange Season*, but she didn't dare read it while the clerk was so nearby—and she could never, ever buy it. The clerk was moving so slowly she felt as if she might jump out of her skin. Usually the science fiction rack was her favorite, but today her eyes skipped over the cover illustrations of planets and rocket ships without registering them. She couldn't stop imagining Patrice and Maxine on that couch together. She wanted to know—she *needed* to know—what happened next, but as the minutes ticked past, she realized she wouldn't find out today. She had to go get Frankie from school. She cast one last look at the rack that held *Strange Season*, and left.

For the rest of that day—as she met Frankie and walked home with him, as she did her homework, as she ate dinner with her family— all she could think about was that book. She knew that what she had read in *Strange Season* was not only scandalous, it was perverse. She should feel dirtied by reading it; she should feel guilty for being thrilled by it.

The problem was, she didn't. She felt as if she had finally cracked the last part of a code she had been puzzling over for so long that she couldn't remember when she had started deciphering it. She felt exhilarated.

She went to bed imagining Maxine's hand on the buttons of Patrice's blouse, unbuttoning it. She slid her own hand beneath the placket of her nightgown; she felt her own warm skin beneath her fingertips. In the quiet darkness of her bedroom she felt the faint but insistent beating of her heart, and she felt its quickening. She imagined the blouse sliding off Patrice's shoulders, the pale swell of her breasts. Lily's whole body went hot. She felt the need to cross her legs against the hungry ache at the center of her body. She imagined them kissing the way Marlon Brando had kissed Mary Murphy in *The Wild One*, which she and Shirley had snuck into last February. ("Don't be such a square," Shirley had said when Lily had worried about getting caught.) But now, in Lily's imagination, Marlon Brando became Max, crushing Patrice bonelessly in her arms. And then their lips pressed together, and Lily tugged up the hem of her nightgown and pressed her fingers between her thighs, and pressed, and pressed.

6

s this the right place?" Lily asked.

The address that Will had given them was a basement on Stock-ton Street. The metal bulkhead doors were open, tied to waist-high barriers on either side, and stairs led down from the sidewalk to a closed door.

"There's a sign," Shirley said, pointing.

A placard tied to the barriers was printed in both Chinese and English. Lily understood only about half of the Chinese characters, but the English read: CHINESE AMERICAN DEMOCRATIC YOUTH LEAGUE.

The door at the bottom of the stairs suddenly opened, and an unfamiliar young Chinese woman with a pouf of short curled hair bounded up the steps. When she saw Lily and Shirley, she asked in Mandarin Chinese, "你們是來參加聚會的嗎?"[1]

Lily could speak Cantonese relatively fluently, but her Mandarin was much worse; she only knew a little of it because her father spoke Mandarin. She decided to respond in English. "We're here to meet Will Chan. Do you know him?"

The girl beamed at them. "Oh, they're coming," she said in Mandarin-accented English. "They went to get his brother's car." She extended her hand. "Edna Yang. Are you coming to the picnic too?"

Lily shook her hand; Edna's grip was firm and no-nonsense. "Yes, we are. I'm Lily Hu."

---

1. Are you here for the picnic?

"Shirley Lum," Shirley said, shaking Edna's hand as well.

Behind Edna, a stream of people had begun coming up the stairs—girls in skirts and sweaters, boys in chinos and athletic jackets—carrying foil-covered plates and white pastry boxes tied with red string.

Lily and Shirley stepped aside for them, and now the basement entrance seemed like the door to a clown car. The honking of a horn drew Lily's attention to the street, where a green Plymouth sedan had pulled up, double-parked, and Will leaned out the front passenger window and waved. "Lily! Shirley!" he called.

A young man emerged from the driver's side of the car, running around to open the trunk, and Lily recognized him as Will's brother, Calvin. Will got out while the youth group members packed the trunk with picnic supplies. They argued, laughingly, over whether the boxes should be stacked or not, and whether the bottles of soda would be too shaken up by the trip, and then Shirley volunteered to hold the pot of soy sauce chicken on her lap so that it wouldn't spill. When the trunk was finally closed, the driver of the car came around to the passenger side, and Will said, "Calvin, you remember Shirley and Lily." Shirley gave him a sort of curtsy because her hands were full with the chicken pot.

"Sure I do," Calvin said. He had Will's face, but leaner and more defined, and he smiled at Shirley as he asked, "You really want to carry that pot?"

Shirley laughed. "I'm happy to."

Calvin had never made much of an impression on Lily, though she had seen enough of him over the years to recognize him. He'd always had his own friends, a couple of years older than Lily and Shirley's group. Now he was a student at San Francisco State, and Lily couldn't recall the last time she'd seen him. She noticed Shirley giving him a grateful smile as he helped her into the front seat of the car, then carefully handed her the pot. When he closed the door, he lightly slapped the roof twice, then leaned into the window with an easy smile and said, "You're all set."

"We'll sit in the back," Will said, opening the rear door for Lily.

"But where are Hanson and Flora?" Lily asked.

"They couldn't make it," Shirley called back. "Sorry about that, Will. Get in, Lily."

There was something about Shirley's breezy tone that made Lily suspicious, but Shirley had already turned away.

"Lily?" Will said, prompting her.

"Sorry." She got into the car, sliding across the wide bench seat, and Will climbed in beside her. Lily's position gave her a good view of Shirley, and now Lily recognized the smile Shirley had turned on Calvin. It was the one she put on when she wanted to impress someone. Lily understood, then, the real reason Shirley had wanted to come on this picnic.

They parked the car along Main Drive in Golden Gate Park, near the glass Conservatory. Calvin was gallant and insisted on taking the chicken pot himself, while Shirley carried the picnic blanket. Lily and Will followed, laden with bags and boxes. They chose a stretch of grass on which to lay out their things, weighting down the blanket's four corners with the chicken pot, a basket of dishes and utensils, and bottles of soda.

It was a beautiful day, still and warm beneath a clear blue sky, and before long Shirley took off her pink cardigan to reveal a matching pink sweater shell beneath. Lily realized she had never seen this pink twinset before, nor the baby-blue-checked capri pants her friend wore. Shirley always took care with her appearance, but Lily thought Shirley had made a special effort today. She was wearing clip-on earrings of pink flowers with rhinestone centers that glittered in the sunlight, and her hair was carefully pulled back to show them off.

Lily had no opportunity to ask Shirley about her new clothes, however, because Calvin and Will were always going back and forth from the car with more picnic supplies, and Shirley was busily acting as hostess, arranging and rearranging the dishes and napkins and asking Calvin to open a soda for her.

Finally, the bus that the other members of the youth group had taken arrived up on Main Drive. They spilled out, carrying boxes of pastries and a long duffel bag that contained volleyball equipment. Once they had all gathered together, Lily counted about two dozen people in total—a relatively even mix of girls and boys—almost all in college, though a few were in high school. The college students seemed so much older to Lily; they were friendly to her, but they treated her like a little sister. Several of them spoke Mandarin, which was uncommon in Chinatown, where people mostly spoke Cantonese. Lily soon learned that the Mandarin speakers were students from China—exiles now, unable to go home because of the political situation.

Lily was curious about them. Although they dressed like any other American, there was something faintly foreign about the way they carried themselves that seemed, if not un-American, then less American. She wanted to ask if any of them were from Shanghai, but she felt shy around them—she felt un-Chinese—and besides, they had to eat.

They helped themselves to the chicken, warning each other that the soy sauce would soak through the paper plates unless they ate it immediately. There were hard-boiled eggs in the pot too, marinated to a rich brown color. Lily fished out one, cut it in half, and shared it with Shirley. Lily ate her egg in two quick bites, and then she ate a drumstick more slowly, finally depositing the bone in a paper sack that was being used for garbage. The white boxes contained pastries that someone had bought from a Chinatown bakery: sesame seed balls and egg tarts, and a dozen soft white barbecue pork buns that they split apart so everyone could have some. One of the girls had made a batch of fried dumplings that she called chiao-tzu, stuffed with chopped pork and Napa cabbage, and Lily dipped hers in the drippings from her chicken leg and then licked her fingers to get the last of the sauce.

Afterward, drowsy and full, Lily lay down on the grass and threw an arm over her eyes to block the sun. She began to doze off, feeling as if she were sinking slowly into the warm ground, the voices of the youth group members growing ever more distant. Someone was talking about how China was moving forward into the future, and Lily imagined a Chinese man in a space suit, his face blurry behind his round helmet, standing on a red planet. Behind him, an army of similarly space-suited explorers blinked into existence: hundreds, thousands of Chinese, and the man in the lead now held a Red China flag, its five gold stars on the red cloth blending into the Martian landscape.

She must have fallen asleep, because when she woke up, blinking slowly at the bright blue sky above, she was alone on the picnic blanket. She heard laughter nearby, and the *thunk* of a volleyball. She rolled onto her side, and green blades of grass poked against her cheek. The volleyball net had been strung between two poles, and the youth group members divided into two teams, while others watched from the sidelines.

She pillowed her head on her arm to make herself more comfortable, but she didn't get up. Shirley was actually playing in the game, which was somewhat unusual. When they were children, Shirley had been quite good at sports; she was always getting chosen first in gym class and dominated the basketball games they played on the courts behind Cameron House. It had been a long time, though, since Lily had seen Shirley dust off her athletic skills. Now she saw Shirley standing with her knees slightly bent, eyes up as she followed the trajectory of the ball, hands clasped in front of her. The ball came at the player beside her, who bumped it with his forearms, and then Shirley jumped up, arm outstretched to smack the ball down over the net, where it struck the ground between two players.

Shirley's team broke into cheers, and Lily saw Calvin run up beside her, patting her on the back. If his hand lingered a bit longer than necessary, nobody noticed except Shirley—and Lily, who saw her friend lean into his hand, tilting her head up to smile at him.

"You like him, don't you?" Lily asked Shirley as they walked home from Stockton Street.

Shirley, who always played it cool, couldn't prevent a slight flush from coloring her face. "Everyone was very nice."

Lily laughed. "Yes. Everyone. But Calvin was especially nice to you."

Shirley shook her head. "I don't know what you're talking about," she said loftily. "I noticed that Will was especially nice to *you.*"

"What? Will was just . . . Will."

Shirley gave Lily an incredulous look.

Lily frowned. "He was just being nice. As usual. Why do you always see things that aren't there?"

"Why don't you ever see what *is* there? You can be so oblivious sometimes. If you don't pay more attention, you'll never have a boyfriend."

Lily almost retorted, *I don't want a boyfriend*, but she stopped herself just in time. Instead she said, "My parents won't let me have one until I go to college, anyway. So it doesn't matter."

They saw their friend Mary Kwok coming up the street then and dropped the topic, but later that night as Lily climbed into bed, she realized Shirley had succeeded in distracting her from her original subject: Shirley's interest in Calvin. It was strange that Shirley didn't want to talk about it, but the whole day had been somewhat unusual. Spending it with two dozen strangers, for one thing. Lily and Shirley had had the same group of friends for as long as Lily could remember. Although there were always new immigrants from China showing up at school, they were relegated to Americanization classes and didn't interact much with the American-born Chinese kids. And this was the first time Lily had spent so much time with college students. She couldn't quite believe that she'd be one of them in less than a year. Their lives seemed so different from hers, both freer and more weighted with responsibilities. Lily also noticed that Shirley had inserted herself deliberately into the college students' conversations in addition to their volleyball game. She had been charming, too, in a way that she normally wasn't. She'd kept a lid on her bossier tendencies and instead played the part of modest, cheerful guest.

All of that had gone out the window as soon as they left Calvin and Will on Stockton Street, of course. *You can be so oblivious sometimes*, she had said. It had irritated Lily that afternoon, and now the feeling flared into frustration at the way Shirley saw her—or didn't see her.

The sheets felt hot and scratchy tonight, and she threw them off, kicking her legs free. She had opened the little window in her room, but the air was still and didn't circulate. She heard the sounds of the city floating through the window: car engines chugging up and down hills, the distant sound of someone laughing. She punched her pillow and flipped it over to the cool side, and wondered if what Shirley had said about Will was true.

She called up Will's face in her mind's eye, but she didn't feel anything special for him. She tried to imagine what it would be like to kiss him, but the idea felt distinctly embarrassing and oddly repugnant. He was just Will. Ordinary, same old Will from Commodore Stockton, perfectly nice, who used to want to be a basketball player but now wanted to be a lawyer. She began to imagine Will throwing the basketball through the hoop in the Cameron House yard.

One, two, three, four.

Finally, she was sleepy.

7

On Monday at school, Shirley seemed more distracted than usual, as if she were constantly being dragged back to prosaic reality from some much more interesting place in her imagination.

On Tuesday, when Lily finally commented on it, Shirley said, "Don't be silly. I'm just busy. The fall dance is coming up soon and my dance committee has so much work to do. I wish you'd joined it. We could really use you."

"I have a lot of math homework this semester," Lily replied.

"Typical," Shirley said, but she sounded more amused than upset.

On Wednesday, Lily stayed late after school to use the library. She wanted to look up the V-2 rocket, which Arthur C. Clarke mentioned in *The Exploration of Space*. As she was leaving, she ran into Will by the athletic trophy cases.

"I'm surprised you're still here," Lily said to him. Most of the after-school rush was over by now and the hallway was largely empty.

"I had science club, but I'm glad I saw you," he said. "I wanted to talk to you."

"About what?"

He looked nervous then, and he shifted the strap of his book bag on his shoulder. "Well, you know the fall dance that Shirley's working on . . ."

When he trailed off and looked past her shoulder rather than directly at her, she grew puzzled. "Yes, why? Did she send you to convince me to join her committee?"

"No, I . . ." He stepped into the shadow of the trophy case and reached for her elbow, drawing her with him. "Lily," he said hesitantly.

She knew, in that instant, that he was going to ask her to the dance, and even before he spoke the words, a horrified heat crept up her neck.

"Lily," he said again, "I was wondering if you would like to come with me to the dance. As my date." And then, to make matters worse, he looked her in the eye, and she saw a startlingly poignant hope in them.

"Oh," she said, and then words failed her. She had to look away. Over his shoulder she saw the baseball trophies lined up all in a row, each miniature bronze boy holding a bat raised and ready to strike a ball that would never come. Out of the corner of her eye she saw movement through the doorway to a classroom: the suggestion of boys' lanky limbs folding into chairs. It was Mr. Wright's room, she realized; he was the teacher who led the science club.

"Lily?" Will said again.

She had to answer him. A voice inside her mind that sounded an awful lot like Shirley asked, *what harm will it do to go with him?* But she couldn't bring herself to say yes. The word was stuck in her throat like a tiny fish bone. It scratched.

"I'm not allowed to—" she began, but he interrupted.

"There'll be a group of us. Flora and Hanson, and some others, I'm not sure who yet. We're going to do a special pre-dance dinner at Cameron House."

"A group?" She clung to this. If it was a group, then it wouldn't be a real date.

"Yes, but it'll be all couples. So, I'm hoping you'll go as my date."

Her stomach churned. He was too close to her, looking eagerly down at her face, and she had to work so hard to keep her expression neutral. She took a step back. "Please excuse me for—for a minute. I have to—I need to go to the girls' room. I'm sorry."

She turned and walked away from him, trying not to run.

"Are you all right?" he called.

"I'm sorry," she called back, and sped up. Her book bag bounced painfully against her hip. The girls' restroom was down the hall and around the corner, and it had never seemed so far away before. When she finally arrived, she rushed inside, plunging into a stall and leaning her forehead against the closed door. The wood was cool against her flushed skin. Her pulse throbbed in her temple, and she rubbed at it to ease the pressure.

The door to the bathroom opened, and someone entered the stall next to hers. She froze. She saw the edge of the girl's brown-and-white saddle shoes beneath the wall. She realized that meant the girl could probably see her feet too, and given where she was standing, she obviously wasn't using the toilet. Lily hung her book bag on the hook behind the door and sat tensely on the edge of the toilet seat, deciding to wait until the other girl was finished. It seemed to take forever, but finally the other toilet flushed. The door of the other stall banged open, and the girl went to wash her hands.

At that moment, Lily's book bag slipped off the hook. She saw it all in a split second that seemed to last much longer. The hook wasn't properly secured to the door. The bag's strap had only been partially looped around the hook, and the weight of the books had dragged it to the tip. And then it slid right off. As the bag smashed against the black-and-white tiles, her math notebook tumbled out, followed by *The Exploration of Space*. Three pieces of paper fluttered free, and she glimpsed the photo of Tommy Andrews just before it floated out of sight beyond the stall door.

Lily heard footsteps crossing the bathroom floor, and then they stopped. There was a rustle of paper. A moment later the girl said, "Lily? Is that you in there?"

Lily froze. How had the girl known who she was? The voice sounded familiar, but she didn't quite recognize it.

"Lily? Are you all right?"

"Yes, sorry," Lily said, heart racing. She bent down to pick up her bag, and even more items spilled from it: a pencil case; a math textbook; her Senior Goals notebook; a Kotex pad that slid across the floor.

She opened the stall door. Kathleen Miller stood in the middle of the bathroom with the Tommy Andrews ad in one hand and Lily's math notebook in the other. Lily's name was written across the front in her neat cursive script.

"My—my bag fell," Lily said. Hurriedly she began to gather her things, picking up the two magazine clippings first, which had come to rest between her stall and Kathleen's feet.

Kathleen helped her, chasing after a stray pencil that went under the sink, rounding up the notebooks while Lily collected the pad. Lily stuffed everything into her book bag, then straightened up and held out her hand for the newspaper clipping, which Kathleen had retained. The words MALE IMPERSONATOR seemed to scream out in bold black type.

"I was just . . . using it for a bookmark," Lily said, and blushed.

Kathleen seemed reluctant to give it back to her. There was an odd expression on her face, but after a silent, awkward moment in which Lily began to fear that Kathleen knew what that ad meant, Kathleen wordlessly handed it over. Lily found *The Exploration of Space* again and quickly slid the newspaper back inside.

There was a knock on the girls' bathroom door. Will's voice called, "Lily? Are you in there? Is everything all right?"

Lily looked at the closed door in shock.

"Are you sick?" Kathleen asked, concerned. "You don't look so good."

Lily tried to latch her book bag closed. "He asked me—he asked me to the dance," she said in a low voice, hoping he couldn't hear her. She couldn't get her book bag closed. "He wants an answer, but I—I can't." The bag lolled open, its contents exposed.

The concern on Kathleen's face cleared. She gave a quick nod and said, "I'll tell him you're not feeling well. You don't have to give him an answer right now."

It wasn't a question. The calm certainty of Kathleen's statement filled Lily with sudden relief. "I don't," she agreed.

Kathleen immediately left the girls' restroom to talk to Will. Lily was too stunned to intervene. When Kathleen returned a moment later, she had a briskness to her, a determination.

"What happened?" Lily asked.

"I told him you were having, you know, girl problems." Kathleen gave her a small smile. "He didn't want to hear anything more."

Lily knew she should be embarrassed by what Kathleen had told Will, but instead she wanted to laugh. "Oh my goodness. Thank you."

"You're welcome." Kathleen gave Lily that determined look again. "You know, I've seen Tommy Andrews before."

The words were spoken softly, but to Lily they sounded like fire-crackers. "What?"

"Tommy Andrews. I've seen her before." Now Kathleen's face went a little pink. "At the Telegraph Club." Her jaw tightened, and she dropped her eyes to the floor as she said, "My friend Jean and I went over the summer."

The bathroom was so quiet Lily heard the drip of the faucet on the left-hand sink, a tiny *plink* against the porcelain. Kathleen raised her eyes to meet hers, and in that gaze Lily saw that Kathleen knew what she had given her: an opening.

The water dripped again. A question hovered in the back of her throat, tangled up with the paralyzing sensation of being on the cusp of connection. She couldn't put it into words.

Finally Kathleen said, with a faint look of disappointment, "I have to go home. I'm supposed to babysit." She started to head toward the door.

"Wait," Lily said. The moment was about to slip from her grasp, and she couldn't let that happen. She finally latched her book bag closed. She slung the bag over her shoulder, and it came to rest against her hip like a nudge. "I'll walk with you. I mean, can I walk out with you?"

Kathleen turned back with a surprised smile. "Sure."

Kathleen lived in North Beach near Washington Square. She was half Italian and Catholic on her mother's side; she had three siblings—one older, two younger; and most days after school she had to babysit her younger sister and brother, although her sister was twelve and could've managed on her own. She spoke about her siblings with a mixture of exasperation and love that Lily found quite endearing. As they walked down Columbus together, talking about their families and math class, Lily wondered why she hadn't gotten to know Kathleen before. They had been in the same classes together for years, but it was as if they had been figurines in an automated diorama, moving on mechanical tracks that approached each other but never intersected until now. Today they had broken free from those prescribed grooves, and Lily was acutely aware of the unprecedented nature of their new friendliness.

At the corner of Columbus and Filbert, where Washington Square Park occupied a flat green expanse of North Beach, Kathleen said, "I have to turn here."

They stopped at the intersection, and Lily wondered if this was the moment she would ask the unspoken question still caught in her throat—but no, Kathleen was moving on, and Lily said hastily, "Thanks, Kathleen. Thanks for helping me out with Will."

"You're welcome." Kathleen paused, then asked, "Do you mind—will you call me Kath? My friends call me Kath, not Kathleen."

She seemed a little abashed; a shyness flickered across her face, which turned the palest shade of pink. Her cheeks, Lily noticed, were now the same color as her lips: that delicate shade of blush, like a peony.

"Of course," Lily said. "I'll see you at school, Kath."

When they parted, Kath walked east toward the Gothic towers of Saints Peter and Paul Church, and Lily headed south toward Chinatown. The word *friends* echoed in Lily's memory like the chime of water dripping into the bathroom sink.

8

What did you do?" Shirley demanded in a whisper. She had cornered Lily at her locker in the ten minutes between the end of school and the start of student council. "Will is acting so uptight about the dance. Did he ask you to go with him?"

Ever since that afternoon by the trophy case, Will had avoided being alone with Lily, and when they were with their other friends, he carefully did not meet her eyes. She had been happy to accept this delicate distancing because it absolved her of having to give him an answer. She was disappointed that Shirley had noticed.

"I didn't do anything," Lily said a bit sharply. "But, yes, he asked me."

"What did you say? You didn't say no, did you?" Shirley sounded aghast.

Lily sighed. "I didn't say anything. I didn't know what to say."

Shirley's eyebrows rose. "Yes! You should have said *yes.*"

"But I don't—why can't we all go together in a group, like always? He said there was going to be a group dinner at Cameron House before the dance. Are you going?"

"No, I have to be at school early to set up. You should go with him."

Beyond Shirley down the hall, Lily saw Kath hovering by the main doors. They had taken to walking home together, but during school hours they also made sure to act like they barely knew each other. They hadn't discussed this strategy, but had fallen into it so naturally that only now, with Shirley pressing her about Will, did Lily notice how strange it was.

"Don't you like him?" Shirley asked, bewildered. "You two make the perfect couple. I know you can be shy about these things. Do you want me to talk to him?"

Lily couldn't tell if Shirley was being kind or condescending. It was probably a little of both. "No, don't talk to him," Lily said. She saw Kath take a seat on a bench near the main office, waiting for her.

"Well, you'd better talk to him, then," Shirley said. "It's not right to make him wait for an answer like that." She glanced at her watch and said, "I have to go now. Talk to him, Lily." She hurried off down the hallway toward the student council room.

Lily finished packing her book bag and went to meet Kath, who stood up as she approached.

"What's going on?" Kath asked as they exited the building together. "You don't look happy."

"It's nothing." Lily didn't want to talk about Will; she didn't even want to think about him. It made her antsy, as if she didn't quite fit in her skin. "Do you have to babysit today?" she asked Kath.

"Not right away. My brother and sister are at our nonna's today. I'm supposed to go get them in a couple of hours, though."

"Let's do something," Lily said impulsively. The sky was bright blue above and the scent of the ocean nearby made her restless. She had to distract herself from that conversation with Shirley.

"What do you want to do?" Kath asked, sounding amused. "Don't you have to go pick up Frankie today?"

Lily had nearly forgotten her own plans. She groaned and looked at her watch. "Yes, but not for a little while—not if we hurry. Let's get ice cream."

"Where?"

They discussed the possibilities as they walked up Francisco and down the steps at Leavenworth, and finally decided on Ciros in Washington Square Park, where Kath promised her fancy Italian flavors. When they arrived at the park, it was full of young mothers pushing babies in strollers, old men in fedoras dozing on benches, and children chasing each other with their ice cream cones dripping onto the grass.

Inside Ciros, the stainless-steel-and-glass ice cream counter took up half the small space, and two Italian men in white aprons and caps were doing a brisk business with those young mothers and children. Behind the glass were gallons of chocolate and vanilla, strawberry and mint, and long rectangular tubs of gelato in flavors that Lily hadn't tried before: bacio and hazelnut, stracciatella and fior di latte. Along the right was a rainbow of pastel sorbetti in lemon yellow and mandarin orange and pale lime green.

After consultation with Kath, Lily settled on a cup of lemon and strawberry sorbetti, and Kath ordered a hazelnut gelato cone, which they took back out to the park. They found an empty patch of grass beneath a tree, and Lily ate her sorbetti with a tiny wooden spoon while Kath licked her gelato with a slurping sound that made them both giggle.

"I've never had sorbetti before," Lily said, carefully pronouncing the unfamiliar word. "There's an ice cream shop in Chinatown, Fong Fong's. They have ginger ice cream. That's my favorite."

"Ginger! How does that taste?"

"It's delicious. Little bits of candied ginger are mixed into the ice cream. You should come to Fong Fong's with me sometime and try it."

When Kath finished her cone, she leaned back on her elbows, stretching her legs into the sun. Her shins were bare between the hem of her skirt and her short white socks. "Sure, I'll come."

There was a distant droning sound, and Lily saw Kath look up at the sky. A wistful expression came over her face, and Lily followed Kath's gaze upward until she spotted an airplane flying overhead.

"Have you only been up in an airplane once?" Lily asked.

"Yes. But I've gone out to the airfield in Oakland with my cousin a few times. She was a WASP during the war, and afterward for a while she worked as an airplane mechanic."

"Really?" Lily remembered the *Flying* article about the two women who owned their own airfield. "Does she still do that?"

Kath made a face. "Nah, she got married and moved to Mountain View. Now she has children and no time to fly. Sounds like a raw deal to me."

Lily laughed. "I take it you wouldn't have gotten married and moved to Mountain View?"

"Are you kidding? When I get my pilot's license, I'm never giving it up. I've only gone up that one time and it was the best thing I've ever done."

"Why?" Lily asked curiously.

Kath sat up and looked Lily in the eye. "Haven't you ever wondered what it would be like to have nothing keeping you attached to the ground? When we were taking off, the plane was rolling along the runway on its wheels, right? You could feel every bump and every jolt. And it went faster and faster and then all of a sudden—*nothing*." Kath snapped her fingers, the excitement of the memory suffusing her face in a rosy glow. "The wheels lift off the ground, and you don't feel it anymore. There are no more bumps. Everything is miraculously smooth. You feel like—well, like a bird! Nothing's holding you down. You're floating. You're *flying*. And the ground just falls away below you, and you look out the window and everything becomes more and more distant, and none of it matters anymore. You're up in the air. You leave everything else on the ground. It's just you and the wind."

Lily was transfixed by the expression on Kath's face: the sheer joy of her memory, the longing to fly again. "That sounds . . . incredible," Lily said, her voice hushed.

Kath seemed to come back to herself all of a sudden, and she ducked her face shyly, plucking at the blades of grass on the ground. "Sorry, I didn't mean to go on like that. My brother's always telling me I talk too much about airplanes."

"No," Lily said quickly. "No, you don't. I loved hearing about it. You can talk to me about it anytime."

Kath smiled and shrugged self-consciously. "Well, you might be sorry you said that."

"I won't be."

They looked at each other, Kath with her shy half smile and Lily with her earnestness, and there was such an unexpected feeling of openness between them—a flying kind of feeling, as if they had lifted off from the ground right then and there. But then Kath flushed and looked away, and Lily was flooded with self-consciousness. She shifted her gaze toward the edge of the park, where pedestrians were making their way around the grass. There were children running ahead of their mothers; there were a few couples. She was sharply aware of her heart beating in her chest, the air catching in her lungs when she breathed.

A group of four young women—probably in their early twenties—came walking down the sidewalk toward them, two of them in slacks, one pair arm in arm. Three of them were Caucasian, and one was possibly Mexican. One of the women in slacks had a debonair style to her in the way she walked, with her hands in her pockets and her eyes hidden behind sunglasses. The woman beside her—the darker one, with a head of glossy black curls—was looking at her with a pleased expression, but Lily couldn't tell if the woman was pleased with herself or admiring her companion. And then she slipped her hand around her friend's arm, their hips softly bumping together, and the woman in sunglasses turned her head and gave her a flirty little grin that struck Lily as shockingly bold. They were in public!

Lily glanced surreptitiously at Kath to see if she had noticed. Kath seemed to be watching the girls too, and there was something particularly studied about the bland expression on her face. Lily wondered if this was the moment they would finally talk about the Telegraph Club, but Kath seemed content to stay quiet. Was there something significant, then, in her silence? Lily felt as if the newspaper clipping and Kath's acknowledgment that she had gone to the club made an invisible chain linking her and Kath together, and every once in a while she heard the chain clink like silver against glass: a faint, resonant ring. Did Kath hear it? How could she not? And yet Lily couldn't bring herself to speak of it. What would she even say?

The moment was slipping away again. She watched the four young women disappear around the corner, and when they were gone, she felt a peculiar sense of loss. She said, "I should be getting home."

"Me too," Kath said.

Lily got up from the ground and offered a hand to Kath. Kath hesitated for a moment, but then let Lily pull her to her feet. Kath's hand was cooler than Lily expected, and for one second, two, neither of them let go. Lily felt a sudden rush of heat in her face, and Kath dropped her hand. They both spoke at the same time.

"I'll see you tomorrow."

"Goodbye."

Lily turned away, walking briskly toward Columbus, not letting herself look back even though she wanted to.

9

At the intersection of Broadway and Columbus, Lily saw the Thrifty Drug Store sign across the street. She wondered if that novel was still there. The last time she'd gone, she had read through almost to the end before she had to leave, and she was dying to know what happened. She glanced at her watch. The light turned green, and she was halfway across the street before she knew she'd given into her impulse, and then she began to hurry so that she'd have as much time as possible to read. She was almost there— twenty feet, fifteen—when she saw one of her mother's friends from the Chinese Hospital, Mrs. Mok, hurrying toward the drug store. She had an anxious scowl on her face, and she pulled open the door to Thrifty and plunged inside as if she too were racing against the clock. She hadn't seen Lily.

Lily sighed in disappointment and turned back toward Grant Avenue. She glanced at her watch. She was still a little early to pick up Frankie, so she decided to head home first. Perhaps one afternoon she should bring Kath to Thrifty and show the book to her. The thought was startling, and she began to imagine the two of them in that alcove in the back of Thrifty, spinning through the book racks. She pictured herself finding the book and plucking it out of the rack, handing it to Kath. She wondered what Kath might say upon seeing the cover with those two women. An excited thrill went through her.

Lost in thought, Lily barely noticed when she reached Clay Street.

She climbed the last uphill block automatically, and then she inserted her key into the front door. Inside it was cool and dim, and voices floated down the wooden staircase. It sounded like her parents were home early, which was unusual. She climbed the stairs, and as she approached the top floor she heard someone come out of the kitchen— her father. He stood waiting for her on the landing, and he was still wearing his doctor's coat, as if he'd come straight from the hospital and forgotten to take it off.

"Is something wrong?" she asked.

He studied her almost clinically, and she paused a few steps from the top, wondering for a terrifying moment if somehow he knew she had been thinking about that book.

"Put down your things and come into the kitchen," he said. "Your mother and I need to talk to you."

The tone of his voice was grave. She left her book bag on the bench and hurriedly slipped off her shoes, following him into the kitchen. Her mother was sitting at the table, holding a water glass. She was still wearing her nurse's uniform; she hadn't even taken off her shoes. Her father leaned against the counter and crossed his arms.

"Sit down," he said.

She pulled out a chair and took a seat. Her mind raced. "Is it Eddie? Or Frankie?" she asked.

"No, they're fine," her mother said.

"Two FBI agents pulled me out of work today," her father said. "They wanted to interview me about a young man I treated last week. They think he's a member of a Communist organization in Chinatown."

His words were so unexpected that at first she simply stared at him, dumbfounded. Finally she said, "But why would they ask you?"

"The FBI and the immigration service are very worried about Communists." Her mother spoke almost primly, sitting ramrod straight in her chair. She made no move to drink her water, only kept her fingers squeezed around the glass as if it were a safety railing. "When they find someone they think is a Communist, they interview that person's acquaintances as part of the investigation."

Her father put his hand on her mother's shoulder briefly, pressing down. Her mother's fingers twitched around the glass. "The agents asked me if I knew anything about this man—my patient—but I said no," her father said. "I only knew him as a patient. And then they said that he was part of an organization that was known to harbor Communist sympathies, the Chinese American Democratic Youth League. The members call it the Man Ts'ing."

A small shock went through her. "They're a Communist group?"

"That's what the agents said," her father answered.

Lily wondered which of the boys at the picnic was her father's patient.

"They're leftists," her mother said, spitting out the word as if it were dirty. "They're young, and they don't know what they're doing."

"The FBI agents said that you were seen with the Man Ts'ing," her father said. "You and Shirley. You were seen at their headquarters and again at Golden Gate Park."

Her mouth dropped open. "Someone *saw* me? It was only a picnic! I went to the picnic because—because Will Chan invited me." The idea of Will being a Communist was ridiculous, and she almost laughed, but the expressions on her parents' faces smothered her laughter. "Does this mean Will is in trouble? He's not a Communist. *Will Chan?*"

Her father seemed to stiffen slightly.

"I think that this group, the Man Ts'ing, has someone on the inside telling the FBI these things," her mother said.

The statement sounded like something out of a movie, and Lily gaped at her mother. "Really?"

Her mother frowned. "Lily, you need to pay more attention. You spend too much time in some kind of dream world. Fantasizing about rocket ships! You're exactly the kind of girl they would try to recruit. You don't notice they're putting ideas into your head."

"What ideas?" Lily asked indignantly. "I only went to a picnic. One picnic! They played volleyball, that's all."

"That's how they do it," her mother shot back. "They make you think they're harmless and then they brainwash you."

"Grace," Lily's father said warningly.

Her mother's mouth pressed together into a thin line, but she subsided. Lily crossed her arms angrily. *Fantasizing about rocket ships.* Her heart pounded as if she had been running.

Her father took off his glasses and rubbed his eyes, then sat down at the kitchen table. "We can't be sure what their motivations are, but it's best to steer clear of the group." He put his glasses back on and gave Lily a look that was surprisingly frank, as if she were an adult rather than his daughter. "I don't believe you had any bad intentions. You've never shown any interest in politics, but the things you do can reflect badly on others. We're living in a complicated time. People are afraid of things they don't understand, and we need to show that we're Americans first. Do you understand?"

The seriousness of his tone scared her. "Yes, Papa," she said, although she didn't entirely understand.

A couple of years ago, during the Korean War, she remembered Chinatown kids marching in the Chinese New Year parade holding signs that declared DOWN WITH COMMUNISM. Eddie had been one of them; she had cheered him on by waving a miniature American flag from the sidelines. She remembered her father and Aunt Judy watching the parade with such odd expressions on their faces, as if they were both proud of Eddie and a bit frightened by the spectacle. Now she was confused, as if she'd been reading a book that had several pages removed, but hadn't realized the pages were gone until this moment.

Her father still looked concerned, so she said, "I didn't even want to go to the picnic, Papa. I didn't mean to . . ." She trailed off. She wasn't sure what she had done.

He nodded and said, "And you won't go again."

"What about Shirley? And Will?"

"We'll talk to their parents." Her father stood, pushing his chair back. "And now I have to go back to work. You should go do your homework. Your mother will be home the rest of the day, so you don't need to pick up Frankie from Chinese school."

Lily had more questions, but her parents were standing, sorting out dinner plans, moving on. She felt as if she had been ejected from a movie theater in the middle of the film. Disconcerted, she left the kitchen, picked up her book bag, and took it back to her room. She opened her math book and sat down on her bed to look over the problem sets that had been assigned, but the numbers and letters swam in front of her eyes. A couple of minutes later she heard her father leaving, his footsteps receding down the stairs. She thought about Shirley and her interest in Calvin, and wondered whether that would end now.

"Lily."

Her mother was standing in the doorway. She came into the room and sat down on the foot of the bed, and the mattress sank toward her so that Lily's pencil rolled across the coverlet and lodged itself against her mother's hip.

"What?" Lily said a bit defensively.

"Your father didn't want me to tell you, but I think you're old enough to know the truth. The FBI took his citizenship papers."

Lily sat up, and her math book slid off her lap onto the bed. "Why would they do that?"

Her mother's face was pale, her lipstick too red in contrast to the whiteness of her skin. "They wanted him to sign a statement admitting that Calvin—his patient is a Communist, but your father wouldn't do it."

Calvin. Her mother had clearly not intended to say his name. She seemed a bit nervous now and fiddled with the name tag still pinned to her uniform. MRS. GRACE HU, R.N.

"Your father would never comment on a patient without their permission, and he refused to lie to the agents. So they took his papers as punishment."

"But why would the FBI punish Papa for—for not lying?"

"They aren't looking for the truth. They're looking for scapegoats. Your father should know this. He should have just told them what they wanted. Now he's protecting a boy he barely even knows—all because he refuses to tell them what they want. And that has put your father in danger, which means it's put you and me and your brothers in danger."

"How is he in danger? He's an American citizen. He was a captain in the army!"

"They're using these investigations as an excuse to deport Chinese," Lily's mother explained. "They took his papers, so now he has no record of his citizenship. And he has family in China—*you* have family in China. You've never met them, but that doesn't mean anything to the FBI. And you were at the picnic, even if you had no idea who the Man Ts'ing are. It doesn't look good."

"But . . . they'll give him back his papers once they realize he hasn't done anything wrong, won't they? They can't deport him, can they?" Even as she asked the question, she knew the answer. Every so often Lily overheard talk in Chinatown about how so-and-so had been interrogated by the immigration service, or was about to be sent back to China because they had come here under false documents.

And she remembered Aunt Judy talking about how the FBI had detained the Chinese-born founder of the Jet Propulsion Lab under suspicion of Communist ties, even though he had supported the United States during the war.

"All we can do is cooperate with them," her mother said. "I'm trying to persuade him to sign the statement."

"What will happen if he doesn't?" She instantly wished she hadn't asked; she felt as if saying it out loud would make it come true.

Her mother looked worried. "Let's not think about that now. What we need to do is make sure we show we're a proper American family—because we are. That means you study hard, and you don't have anything to do with the Man Ts'ing." Her mother stood up. "I'm going to get Frankie, and after Eddie comes home I'm going to talk to both of them about this. You focus on your homework."

Her mother paused in the doorway and added, "If you suspect that Shirley or any of your friends are still involved with that group, you tell me right away."

She thought about how Shirley had denied being interested in Calvin. She wondered whether Shirley knew about the Communist connection. The possibility was unsettling.

"Lily, will you tell me?"

She looked up at her mother and said, "I will."

1931	Japan invades Manchuria.
1932	Joseph Hu arrives in San Francisco to attend the Stanford School of Medicine.
Sept. 23, 1934	**GRACE WING meets her future husband, Joseph Hu.**
1936	Grace Wing marries Joseph Hu.
	Chinese graduate student Hsue-shen Tsien joins the "Suicide Squad," a group of rocket scientists at the California Institute of Technology.
1937	Lily Hu (胡麗麗) is born.
	Japan invades China.
1940	Edward Chen-te Hu (胡振德) is born.
1941	United States enters World War II.

GRACE

Twenty Years Earlier

The first time Grace Wing noticed him, she accidentally caught his eye while she was waiting to pour herself a cup of coffee in the fellowship hall after the Sunday service. He was standing halfway across the room, eating a sandwich. He didn't look like the other Chinese men she knew. His shiny black hair had a Clark Gable–like wave at the front, and he wore a gold signet ring on the little finger of his right hand. She thought he was handsome.

When their eyes met, he was still chewing, and Grace was embarrassed to be caught watching. She turned away immediately, wondering who he was. She didn't think she had seen him during the service. She focused on fixing her cup of coffee, pouring in extra milk and two spoonfuls of sugar, and then took her time selecting a sandwich for herself. As she settled on egg salad on white bread, Mrs. B. Y. Woo waylaid her to ask advice about an ailment she had been experiencing. Grace was only a twenty-two-year-old nursing student, but Mrs. Woo always enjoyed sharing her complaints while Grace listened sympathetically and offered suggestions for treatment, which Mrs. Woo inevitably refused because she didn't trust Western medicine. Grace was about to launch into her advice when Reverend Hubbard came over to greet them. That wasn't surprising, but he also had the strange new man in tow. He had finished his sandwich, but Grace noticed a stray crumb clinging to the lapel of his gray flannel suit. Her fingers itched to brush it off.

"Miss Wing, Mrs. Woo, I want to introduce you to one of our newcomers," Reverend Hubbard said. He was a middle-aged Caucasian man with a balding pate; the skin of the top of his head was particularly bright and shiny that day. "This is Mr. Joseph Hu, newly arrived from China. Mr. Hu is a medical student at Stanford. Miss Grace Wing is a nursing student, so you have something in common."

"I'm honored, Miss Wing," Joseph said, and extended his hand to Grace in the American way.

"Welcome to San Francisco," she said, shaking his hand.

"Thank you," Joseph said. "It's wonderful to be here at last. I've heard so much about your city."

"Oh, I'm not a San Francisco native," Grace replied. "I only arrived here myself a few months ago. Mrs. Woo has been here much longer."

"Almost my whole life," Mrs. Woo said. "I came here as a girl from Kwangtung. Where are you from?"

"Shanghai."

Mrs. Woo looked at him more curiously. "Shanghai! Is your family all there?"

"Yes. My father is a friend of one of Reverend Hubbard's acquaintances."

Reverend Hubbard smiled. "I'm glad that Paul told you about our church here. We're happy to have you."

They traded a few more pleasantries about their church connections while Grace sipped her coffee and tried not to appear as if she were staring. She guessed that he was a few years older than she was. There was something slightly mischievous about the expression on Joseph Hu's face, as if he were containing himself in response to

Reverend Hubbard's and Mrs. Woo's commentary on their mutual acquaintances and, then, the differences between San Francisco and Shanghai weather at this time of year. (San Francisco, he allowed, was much more pleasant in late summer.) Grace had nothing to contribute to the conversation, so she stayed quiet. She didn't know this Paul, and she'd never been to Shanghai, though she knew it was supposed to be glamorous. In fact, just that morning in the *Chronicle* she had seen a story about two rival Shanghai actresses, said to be so beautiful that they somehow brought about the downfall of Manchuria to Japan. She hadn't had time to finish reading the article, and she considered mentioning it in case Joseph had seen it, but she couldn't work out how to insert it into the discussion. Besides, the fellowship hall seemed the wrong place to bring up such a scandalous story.

After a few more minutes of banal conversation, Reverend Hubbard excused himself to continue on his rounds, and Mrs. Woo invited Joseph to join her and Grace. Grace was sure he would politely decline—a man like him surely had more important things to do— but he agreed without hesitation, and soon the three of them were seated together in the corner, sipping their coffees.

"Reverend Hubbard said you are a nursing student?" Joseph said, turning to Grace.

"Yes. Up at Parnassus," Grace said. They talked about her nursing program for a few minutes while Mrs. Woo watched the two of them cannily.

"Tell me about your family, Mr. Hu," Mrs. Woo said when they came to a pause. "Your father—he is a . . . ?"

"He is a professor at Nan Yang College in Shanghai."

Grace imagined a mandarin wearing a round cap and sporting a long white beard, but then she chastised herself; he probably wore modern suits like Joseph.

"And you are the oldest son?" Mrs. Woo asked.

Joseph nodded. "I have two younger brothers and two younger sisters."

"Are any of them in the United States?"

"No. It's only me right now. But my younger brother Arthur hopes to come over in the next year or two."

"To study medicine as well?"

"Perhaps. He is also considering engineering." Joseph gave Grace a brief glance, and once again she suspected that he was containing himself. She began to think he might enjoy discussing scandalous Shanghai actresses more than his brother's educational goals.

"Ah. And are you here on a Boxer scholarship?"

Joseph smiled. "No, I'm afraid I am not."

"Some other scholarship, then?" Mrs. Woo pressed.

Grace shot Joseph a pained smile as Mrs. Woo continued to question him about his financial situation, but Joseph either didn't mind or he was doing a good job of pretending. It turned out that his travel to the United States was supported by a scholarship from a Presbyterian mission in Shanghai, which explained why he had come to the Chinese Presbyterian Church today. But his tuition was privately funded, which meant Joseph Hu's family was probably well-off. Grace thought again about glamour, about Anna May Wong in *Shanghai Express*, her seductive silk gowns and coy dark eyes wreathed in cigarette smoke. She'd liked the film a lot when she saw it a few years ago, though she couldn't admit that at church. (Her mother refused to see it because their Chinese minister condemned it as immoral.) But Joseph's family was likely extremely respectable and had nothing to do with the dramatic world of warlords and fallen women depicted onscreen. She felt a slight disappointment at the self-inflicted puncturing of her fantasy.

Mrs. Woo turned to Grace and said, "Miss Wing, you are the oldest daughter in your family, aren't you?"

"Yes," Grace said, though Mrs. Woo knew this already.

"Grace is the star of her family," Mrs. Woo said to Joseph. "Not many girls graduate from college, and even fewer enter nursing school."

"Mrs. Woo, you're flattering me."

"But it's true. Mr. Hu should know he is speaking with one of San Francisco's smartest young ladies."

Mrs. Woo beamed at the two of them, and Grace was both embarrassed and a little pleased by how obvious Mrs. Woo's matchmaking attempts were. "I've only tried to make my parents proud," Grace said, attempting humility.

"And I'm sure they are," Joseph said.

Did he sound admiring or amused? Grace wasn't sure.

Mrs. Woo abruptly said, "Oh, look at the time! I must go and see Mrs. Leong before she leaves today. It was wonderful to meet you, Mr. Hu. And, Miss Wing, thank you for your medical advice."

Grace and Joseph both stood as Mrs. Woo rose to leave, and then they looked at each other, holding their empty coffee cups awkwardly, and Joseph said, "Well, now that you know everything about me, do you feel safe sitting down with me alone?"

She saw the corner of his mouth twitch and thought, *He's definitely amused now.* "Of course, let's sit," Grace said. He made her a little nervous, but in a pleasant way.

They took their seats again, and she put her empty cup and saucer on Mrs. Woo's abandoned chair, and Joseph set his down beside it. She glanced around the fellowship hall, where the rest of the congregation was milling about with their coffees and sandwiches. None of them seemed to be looking at her and Joseph in their corner, but Grace had the feeling that everyone knew they were there.

When she turned back to Joseph, his expression had changed to one of curiosity.

"You said you came here only a few months ago," Joseph said. "Where did you move from? Not China?"

"No, Santa Barbara. I was born there."

"An American girl," he said. The corners of his eyes crinkled as he smiled.

"我係唐人,"[1] she said in Cantonese, a little pertly.

"你們老家在哪裡?"[2] Joseph asked in Mandarin.

"你話咩話?"[3] Grace asked. She did not understand.

His smile turned regretful. "I'm sorry, I don't speak your dialect."

She knew only a little about the Chinese scholars who came to America to study. They were mostly from Shanghai, usually from well-connected or wealthy families, and they didn't mingle much with the American Chinese—at least not the American Chinese that Grace knew. Joseph was the first such student she had spoken to directly, and she found him difficult to categorize. He didn't fulfill her image of a mandarin; he was too young and too Westernized. Nor did he seem American, exactly, though he spoke English with hardly a trace of an accent.

"How are you liking San Francisco?" he asked her. "Do you miss Santa Barbara? I've never been there. Is it far?"

"It's a few hours south on the train," Grace answered. "It's warmer than San Francisco, and of course I miss my family."

"How many brothers and sisters do you have?"

"Only two. Two younger brothers. We're a small family because my father died when I was eleven."

"That must have been hard for your mother."

1. I'm Chinese.
2. Where is your hometown?
3. What did you say?

"She's a strong woman. She took over running my father's export-import store in the little Chinatown there, and I helped her until my brothers were old enough to do more, and now they run the store with her."

"What does your family store sell?"

"A little of everything. Products from China—we have to serve the local population. You know, dried vegetables, herbs. Medicines. Some chinaware, silks, everything." Grace fell silent, wondering if she was boring him. The store had always bored her.

He gave her an encouraging smile, and asked, "Do you want to go home after nursing school, to continue helping with the family business?"

Grace couldn't imagine going back to work in their store. She had barely escaped by getting into nursing school. "I'll have to see what my mother needs," she said diplomatically. "Will you go back? To China?"

"Of course. China needs Western-trained doctors. And engineers and architects—and nurses, too. We're in a difficult situation right now, as you probably know."

She nodded sympathetically, though her knowledge of China's current situation was minimal. She knew that Japan was constantly threatening invasion, and the Chinese government, led by Generalissimo Chiang Kai-shek, was struggling to fight back. China had always seemed both impossibly distant and uncomfortably near to her, a land of silk-robed emperors in ancient palaces, but also of hardscrabble villages that lived on in her mother's stories. *We didn't have running water*, her mother said when Grace complained about their family store's leaky plumbing. *We slept six to a bed*, her mother said when Grace wished for her own bedroom.

"Have you ever wanted to go to China?" Joseph asked.

"Maybe, to visit my mother's family." There had been a time

when Grace's mother constantly lamented being separated from her family, but in recent years she had given up the complaints. Grace wondered if she had forgotten them, or if she had resigned herself to a kind of exile.

"When you finish nursing school, your skills will be in high demand in China," Joseph said. "Many Chinese people need modern medical treatment."

Grace had never considered this possibility. She had a sudden vision of herself in a modern hospital somewhere in China: bright and clean, with Chinese patients lying serenely in white beds. She was wearing a white nursing cap and rolling a tray of medicines down a pale green hallway.

"Is that what you will do?" she asked. "Go back and treat patients?"

"I hope so. Also I want to use my training from here to train other doctors in China—those who can't afford to come to America for medical school."

He sounded so selfless, so upright. She was ashamed of her earlier desire to bring up Shanghai actresses. Their conversation continued in a stilted fashion, moving into and away from China, medicine, and San Francisco, the way so many first conversations went, but neither of them attempted to escape from it. She found him fascinating, and the way he thoughtfully asked about her interest in nursing was flattering. She also liked the little creases around his eyes when he smiled at her. It made her skin tingle; she wanted him to smile at her again.

Later that afternoon, when she returned to the nursing students' dormitory, she remembered the article about the Shanghai actresses.

She went into the living room to see if the Sunday *Chronicle* was still there. It had been read by now, and the sections were loosely scattered across the console table beside the door, but she found the article quickly. It was the cover story of the *Sunday Magazine* ("Such a Row in China Over the Two Rival Movie Queens"), illustrated with photographs of two women gazing seductively at the camera. One of them wore a striped Chinese dress and was seated on a pouf, her legs crossed with one hand draped casually over a knee. The other was smiling at the camera with darkly painted lips and arched brows. Coiling between the two photographs was an illustration of Chinese men fighting, presumably over the actresses; they had slanted eyes and slashes for eyebrows that made them look comically menacing.

The caption beneath the illustrated melee declared: "It all started when Miss Cheng won the crown in a big popularity contest, whereupon the adherents of that radiant siren, Miss Wu, got mad—and the war was on!"

Grace sat down on the sofa to read the rest of the article. The passions stirred by Miss Wu's singing and dancing were said to have inspired Chinese military officials to ignore their duties and thus allow Manchuria to be invaded by Japan. (*That's ridiculous*, Grace thought.) This was followed by a threatening letter written in human blood (*How could they have known it was human?*) demanding that Miss Wu leave China. But the author of the article was most amazed by the idea that China, perceived as a rural backwater by most of America, had a film industry at all. (Grace rolled her eyes.) And then, in the last column, the article took an unexpected twist.

"You have no doubt heard that heroes and heroines in Chinese pictures do not kiss, as there is no such thing as a kiss in Chinese behavior." The author explained, rather slyly, that instead of kissing, Chinese women "make love with their hands" by kissing with their fingertips instead of their lips.

Grace flushed. The sensationalism—the tasteless lingering on the alluring qualities of Chinese girls—the bizarre idea that Chinese people don't kiss! Thank goodness she hadn't mentioned this story to Joseph Hu. She shuddered with embarrassment and quickly went to bury the *Sunday Magazine* beneath the other newspapers on the console.

She tiptoed upstairs to her room, irrationally worried that one of her dorm-mates would see her and know by looking at her face that she'd been reading that lurid article. And yet she couldn't stop thinking about it. It was true that she had never seen Chinese lovers kiss each other, but Chinese lovers would never kiss in public! She tried to dash the queer thought from her mind, but the feeling wouldn't go away: a sick twist in her stomach, sour as vinegar, as she contemplated Americans' prurient interest in things that should be private. What must Joseph Hu think of this country, she wondered.

She sat down at her desk to look over her notes—she had an entire chapter to review before she went to Sunday night dinner with the other girls on her floor—but she couldn't focus. Instead she thought about Joseph and his quiet self-assurance. He would never throw himself at an actress, Chinese or otherwise. There was a dignity about him that she hadn't seen in the Chinese American men who had paid attention to her.

Chinese American men were more desperate, of course, because there were so many more of them than Chinese American women due to the immigration restrictions. Grace had already had plenty of overeager suitors, and she knew she was a catch, although she'd never admit it. But a man like Joseph Hu was not limited to the small number of Chinese women in America. There was no shortage of women in China, and he was more of a catch than she was.

She saw again the modern Chinese hospital she had imagined earlier, but this time she also imagined Dr. Joseph Hu presiding over the spotless ward in his white doctor's coat, stethoscope draped around his neck. And beside him, wearing her starched nurse's uniform and taking notes on a clipboard, was Grace herself. An unfamiliar emotion swelled inside her at this image, a strangely sharp pang for a place she had never visited, for a people she resembled but did not know. As she stared blankly down at her textbook, she thought that perhaps it was patriotism, but not for America. For China.

PART II

I Enjoy Being a Girl

October–November 1954

10

ily, have you seen the pamphlet about working at the education department?" Shirley asked.

Lily was flipping through the job brochures in the filing cabinet in the back of Miss Weiland's classroom, hunting for something to write her career report about. Slipped almost slyly into a stack of brochures about government jobs was a pamphlet that offered "100 Things You Should Know About Communism in the U.S.A."

"No," Lily said as Shirley leaned against the filing cabinet. "I have this one about becoming an accountant." She hid the booklet about Communism behind it and showed it to Shirley. "Do you want it?"

"Who wants to be an accountant?" Shirley grumbled.

"It's good for math majors," Lily said, taking the two booklets back to her desk. She glanced at Kath over in the next row, but Kath had her head down taking notes from a different job manual. Lily silently slid the Communism pamphlet beneath her notebook, and opened the accounting one over it.

When Shirley returned to her seat a few minutes later, she dropped her chosen pamphlet on her desk and then swiveled around to face Lily. "Guess what happened?" she whispered.

Lily looked up. "What?"

"Louisa Ramirez is moving to San Jose and has to drop out of dance committee. She was supposed to be in charge of refreshments." Shirley sounded personally affronted.

"I'm sure you can manage without her. Maybe someone else can take over her duties."

"Someone's going to have to, obviously, but the dance is in less than two weeks. We're going to have a hard time finding someone."

Will was sitting in front of Shirley, and Lily saw him turn his head slightly, as if he were listening. She still hadn't talked to him about the dance. "Well, I could do it," Lily said impulsively.

Shirley was surprised. "You?"

If Lily were on the dance committee, she had a good excuse for not going as Will's date. "You're always asking me to join the committee. I can fill in for Louisa."

Shirley's eyes narrowed in suspicion. "Are you sure? We have a lot of work to do in the next two weeks."

"Do you want me to help or not?"

"Girls, this isn't the time for socializing," Miss Weiland said, coming down the aisle toward them. "Get back to work, please."

Shirley gave Lily a meaningful look before turning around in her chair. "Sorry, Miss Weiland," Shirley said.

"Sorry," Lily echoed. She picked up her pencil and began to take notes on accounting.

Shirley filled Lily in on the dance committee at lunch. They took their trays of ham sandwiches and butterscotch pudding over to a table at the edge of the cafeteria, so that they wouldn't be interrupted. Lily had been putting Shirley or Flora or Mary between her and Will whenever possible, so this arrangement only further convinced her she'd made the right decision to volunteer for Shirley's committee. Even the idea of lugging several giant cans of pineapple juice to the high school gym via cable car didn't seem so bad now.

But as Lily jotted down Shirley's instructions on her responsibilities regarding punch bowls and napkins, her thoughts kept circling back to the pamphlet about Communism, the Man Ts'ing, and Calvin. Shirley hadn't mentioned him since the picnic, and Lily hadn't either. She had felt constrained by her mother's admonition to tell her if Shirley was still involved with the youth group. And yet their avoidance of the subject only made her want to talk about it more.

At the end of lunch, as she was returning her tray, she gave in to temptation and said to Shirley, "Can I ask you something?"

"Sure, what?"

Shirley looked curious as Lily drew her into a corner of the cafeteria behind one of the concrete pillars. This one was covered with signs advertising the Spook-A-Rama dance and the Girls' Athletic Association's bowling league.

"Did your parents talk to you about the Man Ts'ing?" Lily asked.

Shirley tensed up. "Yes. They told me not to go to any more of their picnics." She paused, looking around to make sure no one could hear them. "I got the idea I shouldn't talk about it. It seems like you did too. Why are you bringing this up now?"

Lily didn't think she should tell Shirley that the FBI agents had been fishing for information about Calvin, but she wanted to warn Shirley about him somehow. "I thought you really liked Calvin?" Lily said, trying to sound doubtful.

Shirley scowled. "So what if I did?"

"You're not going to—if he's part of that group, you can't—"

"My parents lectured me for half an hour about how the government would put us in camps just like the Japanese if they thought we were Communists," Shirley whispered angrily. "I'm not stupid."

"I didn't say you were," Lily said, bristling. "I was only asking."

The cafeteria was almost empty now, but Shirley kept her voice low as she added, "It's all a lie, anyway. Will and Calvin wouldn't be involved with the Reds. It's ridiculous."

"Are you sure?" Lily asked. "How well do you know Calvin?"

Shirley's eyes narrowed. "As well as you do. And we've both known Will forever. I just can't believe . . . Do *you* believe they're . . . Communists?" She whispered the last word.

"No, of course not, but my mother said it's not only about that. They're using Communism as an excuse to deport us." Lily didn't know if she should tell Shirley that the G-men had taken her father's naturalization papers. Shirley's family had their own issues with citizenship; her father had come to America with false papers after the 1906 earthquake.

Shirley's face went pale, but she said, "The immigration people are always awful to us. But nobody's going to get deported. We're Americans."

The bell rang, signaling the official end of lunch, and they started to move automatically toward the cafeteria's exit.

"I'm glad you joined the dance committee," Shirley said unexpectedly. "But you didn't have to do it to avoid Will."

"That's not why I did it."

"You don't have to lie," Shirley said. "I wouldn't have forced you to go to the dance with him."

This surprised Lily so much she didn't know what to say.

Shirley paused at the cafeteria door and gave her a sad sort of smile, adding, "See you at dance committee later."

In her room that night, Lily pulled the Communist pamphlet out of her book bag and climbed into bed. It was organized into a hundred questions, starting with, "What is Communism?" The answers depicted a system in which every freedom was stripped from the individual. It warned that "groups devoted to idealistic activities" such as American Youth for Democracy secretly worked to recruit unsuspecting people to join the Reds. Communism would take your home, your bank account; it would outlaw all religion; you wouldn't even be allowed to have friends of your own choosing.

On and on it went, depicting a ruthless international organization that brooked no dissent and was bent on undermining every American value. It should have been terrifying to read, but the drumbeat of horror after horror somehow muted its effect. Lily skimmed through the questions more rapidly, until number ninety-five caught her attention: "What is Communism's greatest strength?"

The response was oddly provocative, even stirring: "Its secret appeal to the lust for power. Some people have a natural urge to dominate others in all things."

And then, in italics on a separate line: *"Communism invites them to try."*

She knew the pamphlet was presenting Communism as an immoral lust for power, but perversely, perhaps, she found this last warning inspirational. Four words seemed to rise up off the page in whispers: secret, lust, natural, *try.*

She lay back against her pillow, letting the booklet fall on her chest so that it rose and fell with the motion of her breath.

Tomorrow, she decided, she would invite Kath to go with her to Thrifty Drugs. She had to show her that novel.

11

ily spun the rack of tawdry paperbacks again, then began to flip
through novel after novel, hunting for the provocative cover of
Strange Season. The blonde (that had to be Patrice) in her negligee on the floor; the brunette (Maxine, with dark eyes) above in her
sultry black gown. Lily was aware of Kath beside her, watching, and
she said, "It's been here for weeks. I thought it would still be here."

Kath pulled a book from the next rack over—a detective novel
with the silhouette of a corpse on the cover—and asked, "What was
the title? I'll help you look."

"*Strange Season.*"

Kath put the detective novel back and started to look through
the other books. When Lily had finished with the romance rack she
moved on to science fiction, wondering if it had been mistakenly
placed there, but at last she had to admit defeat.

"It's gone," Lily said, sighing. "I suppose someone bought it." She
couldn't imagine who might have had the nerve to put their money
down on the counter. Someone very bold.

"What was it about?" Kath asked.

When she decided to show the book to Kath, Lily hadn't considered the possibility that it would be gone. She had hoped the book
would do the work of voicing the questions she wanted to ask, but
without it, she was back where she had started. She was faced with a
choice now: She could explain what the book had been about, or she

could lie. Kath was watching her expectantly, and there was something in her expression that made Lily hope that perhaps she already knew the book, but Lily told herself that was wishful thinking. In all the time they had spent together, all those walks down Columbus, they had never brought up the Telegraph Club or Kath's friend Jean. Not once. Lily wanted to believe that the total absence of those topics signified their importance, but it probably meant nothing.

She felt queasy, and Kath reached out and touched her arm.

"Are you all right?" Kath asked.

Kath's fingers pressed lightly against Lily's upper arm. She saw both concern and curiosity in Kath's eyes. They were grayish blue, like the sky covered by a scudding sheet of rainclouds.

Lily backed away into the corner between the science fiction rack and the rear wall of the store, and Kath followed her. They were quite alone now, and above them the fluorescent light buzzed as if a mosquito were trapped inside the bulb.

"It was about two women." Lily's mouth felt so dry she might choke on the words. "That book, *Strange Season*. It was about two women, and they fell in love with each other." And then she asked the question that had taken root in her, that was even now unfurling its leaves and demanding to be shown the sun: "Have you ever heard of such a thing?"

Kath's eyes widened briefly, and then she looked down at the floor and over at the science fiction rack and back at Lily, who felt her heart thudding like a drum, her blood rushing through her veins and turning her skin pink as she waited for Kath's response. An eternity seemed to pass; the heat of the fluorescent light on her head was like an artificial sun; the cash register at the front of the store rang like an alarm bell.

Finally Kath said one soft word: "Yes."

They left Thrifty Drug Store and walked down Columbus, away from Chinatown and North Beach, toward the Filipino restaurants and groceries of Manilatown. The afternoon sunlight caused the shadows to slant eastward, downhill, as if pointing them forward, and as they walked, Lily told Kath more about what she had read.

"They kissed each other," she reported, and saying it out loud was thrilling; it made her blush. And yet she couldn't say the word the book had used to describe those kinds of girls: *lesbian*. The word felt dangerous, and also powerful, as if uttering it would summon someone or something—a policeman to arrest them for saying that word, or even worse, a real-life lesbian herself. She glanced at Kath sideways and asked, "Have you ever known any girls . . . like that?"

They stopped at the next intersection. Kath looked very grave. Her face was quite pale, except for two burning spots right below her cheekbones, as if she had misapplied rouge with rough fingers. She said quietly, "My friend Jean. She's . . . like that."

"The one who took you to the Telegraph Club?"

Kath nodded. "They're all like that, there. Well, except for the tourists—and even then, maybe."

The light had turned green, but they hadn't moved. They were at Pacific, across from the International Settlement, marked by a neon sign topped with colorful flags that arched over the street. Beyond that were signs for the Sahara Sands and Gay 'N Frisky nightclubs, and a giant naked female leg kicked out from the roof of the Barbary Coast club like an obscene invitation. Lily looked away self-consciously as she imagined what went on in there.

Behind them a man whistled. "Hello, girls!"

Lily stiffened.

"You two looking for some fun?" And now he was beside them, a middle-aged man in a banged-up fedora, looking like an out-of-work accountant.

"No, thank you," Kath said. She stepped closer to Lily, nudging her to keep walking, but the light had turned red again, trapping them against the traffic.

He leered at them. "You're a little far from home now, aren'tcha? I love a little China doll, I do."

Lily grabbed Kath's hand and pulled her westward along Pacific, back toward Chinatown.

"Nothing like a little affection between girls—always makes my day!" he said, laughing.

Lily heard another man nearby laugh too, as if he had been watching the whole exchange, and her face burned with shame. Even if those men were horrible, she and Kath had been talking about that very thing, and it felt as if this were some kind of judgment from on high. She walked faster and faster as if she could outrun the shame, until Kath dragged at her hand and said, "Stop—Lily—slow down."

There was Grant Avenue, hung with red lanterns, smelling of roast pork and raucous with Chinese vendors hawking their wares, and Lily felt a rush of relief: here was home. She halted on the corner and let go of Kath's hand.

"I'm sorry," Lily said immediately. "We had to get away."

They were blocking the sidewalk, and Lily stepped to the side, Kath following her. They stood together in awkward silence. Lily wanted to continue their conversation, but back in Chinatown, she couldn't. It felt as if a muzzle had been fastened on her the instant she returned.

"Maybe I should go home," Kath said.

"Oh, not yet." Lily was afraid that if Kath left now, they would never return to the subject that had drawn them together. "Let's— let's go to Fong Fong's and have ginger ice cream."

Kath seemed surprised, but she quickly agreed. "All right."

Lily broke into a relieved smile. "It's this way," she said, and she linked her arm with Kath's and led the way.

12

As they walked through Chinatown, Lily saw the familiar streets with new eyes, and she wondered what Kath thought of her neighborhood. She noticed her looking up at the painted balconies and pagoda rooflines, the red paper lanterns and the gilded or crimson signs thrusting out over the street like pushy Chinese shoppers. Did Kath like it? Or did she find it overwhelming and strange? Kath's face gave little away. She seemed more focused on keeping up with Lily than gawking at the sights.

There were obstacles on the sidewalk to navigate around too: buckets of iced fish lined up in pearlescent rows; bushels of green-and-white bok choy and mounds of gnarled ginger roots; tourists gaping at the glistening roast ducks hanging on hooks in the deli windows. And through it all there was a cacophony of smells and sounds: bitter herbs mingling with sweet buns; the quick, harsh Cantonese of shopkeepers making deals; the rank background stench of yesterday's seafood.

Lily was self-conscious about the smells in particular; she knew that Caucasians wrinkled their noses at the unfamiliar odors. When she spotted Fong Fong's candy-cane-striped awning a block away—like an all-American beacon between Chinese restaurants and souvenir shops—she hurried Kath toward it as if it were an oasis. She swept ahead and gallantly opened the door for her. Kath seemed a little amused by her behavior, but she entered the soda fountain without comment.

Inside, booths were packed along the right wall, and a long marble-topped counter with stools ran across the back. Behind the counter, soda jerks in white aprons and striped caps concocted ice cream floats and chop suey sundaes topped with fruit and sesame cookies. Lily spotted an empty booth toward the back, and she rushed to claim it, sliding into one of the bench seats as Kath took the one across from her.

Lily had been going to Fong Fong's for as long as she could remember, but she still opened a menu. There were hamburgers and french fries; banana splits and ice cream parfaits; Napoleons and other pastries that could be ogled in the glass case up front.

"What should I get?" Kath asked.

"Ginger ice cream," Lily said promptly.

Kath was looking around the soda fountain as if fascinated, her gaze lingering on the mural of the gingerbread man on the wall behind the pastry counter. "This place is something."

Lily looked around too, taking in the shining stainless steel cases and the polished marble countertops, the Chinese waiters and soda jerks in their spotless white aprons and striped caps. She felt proud of the place; it made Chinatown seem modern and American. "Do you like it?" she asked. She'd never been to Fong Fong's with a Caucasian.

Before Kath could answer, the waiter arrived to take their order, speaking English with a thick Cantonese accent. For a brief, humiliating moment, Kath didn't understand him. Lily had to interpret, and it made her wonder if she should have brought Kath here. Her pride twisted abruptly into embarrassment.

After the waiter left, she hurriedly changed the subject and asked, "Are you going to the Spook-A-Rama?"

Kath shrugged. "I don't know. I don't really like dances."

"I don't either, but I have to go because of Shirley. I joined her dance committee."

"Why?" Kath asked, as if it was a bizarre decision.

Lily sighed and glanced behind her; she didn't see anyone she knew in the room. "Because it was the only way I could get out of going with Will Chan as his date."

"Sounds pretty dire," Kath said dryly.

Lily pretended to scowl at her. "So will you come to the dance?"

A funny look crossed Kath's face; Lily couldn't tell if it was surprise or reluctance.

"I have to set up the refreshments but I don't think I'll have to work the whole night," Lily said, in case Kath had thought they wouldn't be able to spend any time together.

Kath blinked, and then she smiled slightly. "I wouldn't know what to wear."

It took Lily a second to realize that Kath was joking, and then they were both laughing, and somehow Lily couldn't stop—she had to clutch her stomach to contain herself as the waiter delivered their matching stainless steel dishes of ginger ice cream.

Kath picked up her spoon and took a bite, and her eyes widened in surprise as she tasted it. "This is good!"

"I know." Lily knew she sounded smug, but she didn't care. She spooned up a bite too. The cold, sweet ice cream was studded with small bits of candied ginger.

"I'll go to the dance if you'll come with me to a G.A.A. meeting," Kath said.

"What do they do at a meeting? Calisthenics or something?" Lily said doubtfully.

"No, we don't do calisthenics. It's usually tennis or bowling. It's fun! Miss Weiland is the G.A.A. teacher. It's a great group."

"I'm not so good at tennis or bowling. Well, I've never gone bowling—"

"What?" Kath looked shocked. "You have to come."

Lily spooned up another bite and let it dissolve slowly on her tongue before responding. "I wish there was a girls' science club or something. I suppose I could join the regular science club, but it's all boys. I wouldn't want to be the only girl."

"What do they do in science club?"

"I imagine they do all sorts of things. Chemistry experiments, or taking apart engines, or . . . you know what I'd really like to do?" Lily leaned forward excitedly. "I want to build a model rocket. I saw an ad for a model rocket kit in *Popular Science* once—it didn't look that difficult—but the trick is, you need someplace to set it off."

Kath's eyebrows rose. "What do you mean?"

"Well, it's powered by a carbon dioxide canister, so it'll launch into the air." She grew thoughtful. "I suppose it's a lot like a firecracker, so maybe I could just set it off in the street."

"Sounds dangerous," Kath said.

From her tone, Lily knew Kath was teasing her, and she felt a little flush of pleasure. "Oh, it's just a little thing," Lily said, pretending nonchalance. "Nothing like a real rocket. I hope I can see a real one someday."

"Where would you see one?"

"I'd have to get a government job. I've planned it all out already. First I'll go to Cal and major in math. My aunt Judy did her master's degree in math there, so she knows all the professors. I might need to go to graduate school, but I'm not sure. If I don't need to, I'm going to get a job as a computer at the same place Aunt Judy works. They design rockets there, although she can't tell me much about it because it's top secret. I've read all about rockets already. They already know how to build rockets that could go into space—well, they have theories about how it would work, but they need to develop better fuels to reach the right speed to leave the Earth. I think they're going to develop these fuels really soon, though."

"How soon?" Kath asked, scraping the bottom of her ice cream bowl.

"Probably within a couple of decades. I'm sure we'll be sending rockets up into space then. And we can put automatic instruments on board to send back measurements, and maybe even take photographs! It'll take longer to send people into space, though. We have to design ships that can withstand potential meteor strikes and maybe even create artificial gravity, because otherwise people will just be floating around the ship."

"Floating? Why?"

"Because there's no gravity in space. I suppose it must be a little bit like swimming, except with no water. How strange that would be."

"Is it safe for humans?"

"I don't know. Perhaps! Isn't it exciting?" Lily beamed.

Kath returned her smile, then shook her head slightly. "All right. I'll go to the dance, but you have to come bowling."

"Deal," Lily said, and extended her hand across the table as if they were making a business agreement. Kath reached out to shake it, but when they touched, it didn't feel like a business agreement at all. Lily suddenly remembered a scene early in *Strange Season* when Maxine took Patrice's hand to study her manicure and said, *What lovely fingers you have.*

She snatched her hand out of Kath's, and then tried to cover up her self-consciousness by taking her last bite of ginger ice cream. She wanted to ask Kath another question—she wanted to ask her *the* question—but she couldn't. All around her, the laughter and chatter and tinkling sounds of spoons against sundae glasses reminded her of where she was. This bright, clean restaurant in Chinatown that smelled of sugar and cream was not the place to ask, but Lily felt as if her thoughts must be written in plain English on her face. *Are you like the girls in the book too? Because I think I am.*

13

Preparations for the Spook-A-Rama began hours before the dance was officially scheduled to begin. One of the girls on the dance committee had borrowed her parents' car to run errands, and Lily persuaded her to drive them to the nearest grocery store to pick up pineapple juice and 7-Up, pretzels and heavy bags of ice.

Back at Galileo, Lily raided the home economics supply closet for punch bowls, then carried them through the underground tunnel that connected the main building with the gym, passing the girls' locker room on the way. The door was propped open, and inside she saw Shirley's baby-blue party dress on a hanger hooked over the edge of a locker door, like the shell of a girl floating in midair. Lily was already wearing her dance outfit, a black rayon skirt with a short-sleeved pink cotton sweater. The skirt already had water marks on it from the dripping ice she'd lugged into the gym. She hoped it would dry before Kath arrived.

Inside the gym, Shirley was supervising the decorations. The committee girls had already hung the space with lime-green streamers, cut-out ghosts, and skeletons made of white butcher paper. They'd pasted on clusters of sequins for eyes, which gave the ghosts and skeletons a glazed-over look. Shirley had probably been aiming for whimsical, but Lily found them a little disturbing. Now the girls were pinning letters that spelled out SPOOK-A-RAMA onto the wall beneath the football pennants. They were cut out of aluminum foil into the wavy forms of a horror movie title. A small stage with a band was set up in front of the silvery letters, and Lily recognized a couple of the band members from school.

The refreshment table was on the far side of the gym, and as Lily headed over with the punch bowls, she began to worry that Kath wouldn't come to the dance after all, and if she didn't, did that mean something? The question made her uncomfortable, and she tried to forget about it as she mixed the punch, but she felt her uncertainty like an unreachable itch between her shoulder blades.

At eight o'clock on the dot, Shirley opened the doors. From her post at the refreshment table, Lily had a good view of the whole gym. Their friends arrived first: Will and Hanson in sport coats; Flora and Mary in pink and green party dresses. Then some boys from the football team and their dates, and then a big crowd of students all at once around eight fifteen. At first everyone mingled: the Chinese and the Italians, the Negroes and the Caucasians. The girls stood in circles as they admired one another's dresses and compared their carnation corsages. The boys moved between the refreshment table and the girls, offering them cups of punch and awkwardly hovering nearby while they got up the nerve to ask them to dance.

Lily saw Shirley flitting from one place to another, her tea-length dress floating around her in a cloud of baby blue. Shirley had saved up her money to buy that dress, and then Mary helped tailor it to fit, taking in the bust to better show off her figure. She had acquired a glittering cubic zirconia necklace and matching earrings and found some white satin gloves in the back of a Chinatown boutique. She looked like the princess of the ball, and she was reveling in it. Every so often she glanced at Lily, and once she even came over to ask if everything was all right. But she didn't suggest that Lily join her and their friends, and Lily was relieved to have an excuse to hide behind the table.

It was Shirley who made the first brave foray onto the dance floor, dragging Will with her, and soon afterward other couples followed, holding each other at regulation distance as they moved like jerky robots across the gym. The mixing and mingling was over now; the couples were all matched pairs—Chinese with Chinese, Negroes with Negroes. As Lily eyed Shirley and Will, a fragment of a memory floated into her consciousness. Hadn't his brother, Calvin, caused something of a scandal a few years ago? She couldn't remember exactly what it was, but it had to do with a girl he'd brought to a dance. Shirley would remember, because she remembered everything, but Lily didn't think that now was the right time to ask.

She glanced up at the giant clock on the gym wall beneath the scoreboard. It was already half past eight, and as the minutes continued to tick by, there was no sign of Kath. She kept the punch bowl filled and rearranged the cookies and poured out more pretzels, but there came a time when there was nothing else for her to do, and she didn't want to stand up anymore. She drifted over to the bleachers with her own cup of punch, feeling like a wallflower and trying not to stare too anxiously at the main doors.

When the band struck up "ABC Boogie," almost everyone surged onto the dance floor. The boys swung the girls out, their skirts twirling as they swirled back into their arms. There was laughter and shouting, and someone was singing the lyrics above the sound of the band, and the girls were taking off their heels to dance. Lily watched it all from her perch on the bleachers. Out of the corner of her eye she saw that she was quite alone; all of the other wallflowers had found partners or chosen to join the dance with friends. Lily crossed her arms around her stomach and pasted on an expression that attempted to declare, *I'm perfectly fine over here.*

It hadn't always been like this. Lily never used to question whether she should go to a dance, or whether she would enjoy it, or even what she would do if nobody wanted to dance with her. They'd all freely traded dance partners, because nobody was allowed to go on dates. At least, that's the way it used to be among her Chinatown friends. Now everyone knew that Hanson and Flora were steadies, although they wouldn't admit it because their parents still didn't allow it. And the kids who weren't Chinese seemed to all have girlfriends or boyfriends this year. A few of them were already engaged to be married. When had everything changed? She felt as if it had been very sudden.

As the band began another popular song, some of the dancers switched partners, and Lily took care not to meet anyone's eyes; she didn't want anyone to ask her. Instead she glanced over at the refreshment table—it didn't look like the punch needed replenishing—and around the periphery toward the main doors, where she caught sight of a girl hovering near the wall, hands clasped in front of her. Lily stood up abruptly. The girl was obscured by the dancing couples, and Lily had to climb down the bleachers to get a better look. Yes—the girl was wearing an ordinary brown skirt and a white blouse beneath her jacket—it was Kath.

Lily ran across the gym, narrowly avoiding the twirling couples, only to trip over a pair of discarded patent black heels. Kath grabbed her arm, and Lily clutched Kath's hand, and they spun through half a circle, as if they were dancing, before Lily broke away, breathless. "Let's get out of here," she said, and headed for the exit.

14

The doors to the gym slammed shut behind them, muffling the sound of the band. Lily and Kath stood on the wide landing outside; below them, concrete steps descended to the exterior door. The gym was in a building across the street from the high school, which meant there were few places for them to go: two flights down to the locker rooms, or outside into the night. Lily chose the night.

"Where are you going?" Kath called, hurrying after her.

"Anywhere," Lily said, and shoved open the heavy doors.

Bay Street was filled with fog. Aquatic Park was only two blocks away, and the scent of the ocean was thick in the air. Lily rubbed her hands over her bare arms and realized she had left her jacket inside, but she couldn't go back in—not yet.

"Let's walk to Aquatic Park," Lily said.

"Are you sure? You don't have your coat."

"It's not that cold. Or at least not that windy." She cast a glance at Kath as they began heading toward the corner. "I just need some air. I didn't realize it was so stuffy in there."

"Did something happen?"

"No. I just really didn't want to be there anymore."

They turned right at the corner, heading down Van Ness toward the waterfront. The fog seemed to swallow up all sounds, including the dull beat of their footsteps, rendering the city abnormally silent.

"I'm sorry I got here so late," Kath said. "I couldn't get away earlier."

"I'm just glad you came."

They smiled at each other tentatively, and then Lily felt a little self-conscious and had to look away. On their right, the football field behind the gym was a block-long swathe of darkness. None of the field lights were on; only the lights from the long gym windows glowed through the mist. At the end of the block, Lily looked east down North Point Street toward Fisherman's Wharf. Ghirardelli Square's giant lighted sign was like a mirage floating in the distance, the normally brilliant letters smudged by fog. In Fisherman's Wharf, all the restaurants and clubs would be brimming with light and music at this time on a Saturday night, but here in the shadows of Fort Mason, the city felt hushed and lonesome.

They continued on Van Ness in the foggy darkness. They passed a couple on the sidewalk, the woman's arm linked through the man's. She was wearing his trench coat; it seemed to swallow her shoulders, the belt flapping behind her as they walked. There was an unexpected burst of laughter, followed by the receding sounds of a conversation they couldn't make out. The fog was so thick they couldn't see more than ten feet ahead.

Lights began to come into focus. They were near the Maritime Museum, its long white submarine shape a dim curve in the night. Concrete bleachers were stacked up on either side of the museum, creating a viewing stand for the dark bay ahead. Down below, Lily couldn't see the ocean at all, but she could hear it, the waves sounding a rhythmic *shhh-shhh*, as if the ocean itself were hushing them. The fog had closed like curtains behind them. They were quite alone, it seemed, here on the edge of the water.

A foghorn moaned in the distance. Lily was cold now. She felt the damp chill of the mist against her bare forearms and face, and she shivered noticeably as the wind kicked up, whipping back her hair.

Kath took off her jacket. "Here," she said, offering it to Lily.

"But then you'll be cold. It's my own fault I didn't bring my coat."

"I have long sleeves. You take it."

Lily relented. Kath's jacket was wonderfully warm, the fabric a soft corduroy, and she buttoned it all the way up and tucked her hands in the satin-lined pockets. "Thank you," Lily said. They stood together quietly, and Lily looked out at the blackness, imagining she could just discern the faint motion of the water. She felt enveloped in a private little cocoon with Kath. She knew they were standing right out in the open, not far from the brightly lit Maritime Museum—its shadow slanted down the bleachers toward the water—but the fog made it seem as though she and Kath were hidden from view.

"What was it like when you went to the Telegraph Club?" Lily asked.

Kath didn't seem surprised. Maybe, Lily thought, she had been waiting for the question since she first told Lily about it.

"It was . . . I don't know how to describe it. I'd never seen anything like it. The performers there are sort of famous, you know. Like Finocchio's, but with women."

"Finocchio's. The one with the female impersonators?"

"Yes."

"The tourists go there. They come to dinner in Chinatown and then they go to Finocchio's. Do they go to the Telegraph Club too?"

"Some of them." Kath hugged herself against the chilly kiss of the fog. "Maybe half the audience was tourists the night we were there."

"What was the other half?"

"Women."

The ocean shushed against the sand below. The foghorn blew again. Lily asked, "Did you see . . . Tommy Andrews?"

"Yes. There was a show. Tommy Andrews was one of the performers. She sang—some of the songs had the lyrics changed."

"Like what?"

"I can't remember the lyrics. You'd know the songs. But the whole point of it was, you know, she's dressed like a man. She sings to the women in the audience. She's very . . . handsome." Kath gave a nervous, self-conscious *huff* that was not quite a laugh. "She came around to our table afterward—well, she comes around to all the tables near the stage, and the stage is so small that she comes to everyone's—anyway, Jean couldn't get enough."

Lily had imagined Tommy's performance countless times, but hearing Kath describe it aloud made her quiver with excitement. *She sings to the women in the audience*. She took a deep breath of foggy air. "Oh, I wish I could see it," she said, looking at Kath, and Kath was looking back at her with a strange expression on her face—a mix of fear and excitement. "What?" Lily asked. "What is it?"

"Well, we could go. To the Telegraph Club."

Lily was surprised. "But we're not twenty-one. Wait, how did you get in?"

"Jean got me a fake ID," Kath admitted. Then she offered, "I could get you one too."

"That's illegal," Lily said. She thought immediately of false immigration papers. What would the police do to someone like her if they found her carrying a fake ID? She curled her fingers into fists inside the pockets of Kath's coat. "I don't think it's a good idea."

"You really only need a fake ID to buy drinks. They never even asked for mine when I went."

Lily wondered if Kath's nonchalance was for show. "Then why get one at all?"

"It's just—just in case. Why don't I get one for you and then you can decide if you want to use it?"

"I don't want you to get in trouble."

"Don't worry. I'll ask Jean. She knew where to get them before." The wind ruffled Kath's cropped hair and made Lily shiver again, despite Kath's jacket. "If Jean doesn't know or can't get it, then . . . we'll figure something out."

After having the possibility dangled in front of her, the thought that it could be snatched away so quickly seemed unbearable. Again she imagined herself at the club, sitting at a small round table on the edge of the stage, Tommy Andrews singing to her.

"Oh, all right. Ask Jean," Lily said before she could change her mind. "When will you ask her?"

"I'll see her soon. She comes back once a month to visit her family. I'll talk to her next time she's back—probably next weekend."

"Next weekend! That's so soon." A thrill went through Lily. She saw Kath break into a smile, and then a shiver as the wind swept around them again. "Oh, you're cold," Lily said. "We should go back."

And just like that, their conversation was over, and the pocket of fog that had cloaked them before was moving them back up Van Ness and toward the gym, its lighted windows winking through the mist.

15

The Spook-A-Rama was still going full steam when they returned, shivering, to the warm, dry vestibule of the gym. Lily took off Kath's jacket and handed it back to her, and Kath had just put it back on when the gym doors opened and Shirley emerged, clearly searching for someone.

"Lily!" Shirley called. "There you are. Where have you been? The punch bowls need to be refilled."

Shirley came down the stairs, caught sight of Kath standing nearby, and paused a couple of steps before the bottom. "Kathleen?" she said in surprise.

"Hello, Shirley," Kath said, looking uncomfortable.

Lily was relieved that she had given Kath her jacket back before Shirley saw them. "I was just going to the bathroom and I—I ran into Kath—Kathleen."

Shirley stayed on the stairs, as if she didn't want to come any closer. "You were gone a long time."

"Well, I'm back now." From the gym, the sound of the band swelled; they were playing another lively dance number. "It sounds like everything is going really well in there," Lily said, trying to sound enthusiastic.

"Yes, it is," Shirley said. "But you should have told me before you left the refreshment table."

Lily swallowed a burst of irritation. "I'm sorry. I wasn't feeling well." It wasn't entirely a lie.

"Well, are you feeling better?" Shirley asked impatiently. "Are you coming back?"

"Of course," Lily said. There was no way to avoid it, and there was also no way to bring Kath with her; Shirley would never allow that. Lily glanced at Kath, wondering how she would communicate this to her, but Kath seemed to understand. She had buttoned up her jacket and slipped her hands into the pockets where Lily had warmed hers only minutes before.

"I'm heading home," Kath said.

Shirley said nothing.

Lily wanted to say a dozen different things, but the only thing she could say was "Have a good night." And then she turned away from Kath and walked toward Shirley, who started to go back up the stairs. Lily heard the exterior doors open and close as Kath left, and felt a breath of cold air on her legs.

Shirley paused outside the gym doors and turned back so that she was a couple of steps above Lily. "Before we go back in, I should warn you about Kathleen Miller," Shirley said.

"Warn me?" Lily said, startled.

Shirley crossed her arms, looking down her nose at Lily. "You shouldn't get involved with her."

"What do you mean?"

Shirley came down one step so that they were only a foot apart and said in a low voice, "Don't you remember what happened with Kathleen's friend, Jean Warnock?"

Lily shook her head uneasily. "What about her?"

Shirley cast a glance behind her at the doors, which remained closed, and then looked back at Lily. "Jean's queer. You don't remember? Somebody caught her in the band room last year with—" Here Shirley grimaced in distaste. "With another girl."

Lily's skin prickled. "I never heard that," she said neutrally.

"Honestly, sometimes I think you pay no attention to anything except your math homework and your space books." Shirley gave her a funny look—half motherly, half exasperated.

The criticism flew past Lily; all she could think about was the fact that Shirley knew about Jean. And then she remembered what she had half-forgotten about Calvin, who had been in Jean's class. The scandal. His junior year, he had started going steady with a girl (Lily couldn't remember her name), which was unusual enough for a Chinatown kid, but it could have been tolerated if it had been kept under the table. The scandal had been that she wasn't Chinese—she was Negro—and they'd been discovered together in Calvin's car after a dance.

Shirley was still talking. "So you should stay away from Kathleen Miller. You don't want those rumors near you."

Lily took a step up so she was on Shirley's level. "Did Calvin tell you about Jean?" Lily asked.

Shirley's eyebrows drew together. "What? It doesn't matter who told me about it. It only matters that you understand how important this is. You can't be associated with people like that."

Lily didn't respond. She felt strangely disconnected from the moment, and yet she had never been so aware of the way Shirley's forehead wrinkled when she was upset. Two little Vs had formed between her eyebrows, as if to point comically down her nose.

"If you know what's good for you, you'll make up with Will," Shirley continued. "I talked to him earlier and he's willing to dance with you. It would be a good idea—just in case anyone else saw you with Kathleen."

"I don't want to dance with him, and I wish you wouldn't talk to him about me," Lily said coolly. "And there's nothing wrong with Kath."

"'Kath'?" Shirley said with the edge of a sneer in her voice. "Do you even hear yourself? Do you *want* people to think you're friends with her?"

"Why not?" Lily asked.

Shirley looked genuinely shocked. "I just told you why. I'm trying to do you a favor."

Lily knew she was about to make a mistake, but she felt a recklessness taking hold of her. "I don't want any favors," she said curtly.

Shirley looked stunned. "Well," she said, but she didn't continue.

Lily couldn't take the words back. She wouldn't. The gym doors banged open, and a group of Caucasian students surged out—several couples arm in arm, the girls giggling. Lily and Shirley didn't know them well, and they stepped aside to let them pass. The band started playing "I'll Be True," and Lily was sure that everyone would be heading to the dance floor, but she and Shirley didn't move. She wondered if the two of them would stand there facing each other forever, each unwilling to yield, but at last Shirley gave a tiny shake of her head as if she were disappointed in Lily and went up to the gym doors.

"Are you coming?" Shirley asked.

Lily knew that if she didn't, there would be consequences. Shirley had said as much, hadn't she? Jean's queerness was contagious, like a cold, and it could be transmitted through Kath to Lily by nothing more than rumor.

"No," Lily said.

As soon as she spoke the word, a panic went through her—she shouldn't have said that—but Shirley was already opening the door and going back in. The door slammed shut behind her.

Lily took a shaky breath. There was nothing for her to do but go home, so she went to get her jacket from the girls' locker room, and left. Outside the gym she almost expected Kath to be waiting for her, but the street was empty. Only the fog moved across the pavement, silent and disembodied as a ghost.

16

On Monday morning, Lily and Eddie walked to the intersection of Washington and Grant as usual, but Shirley wasn't there to meet them. Instead Flora stood on the corner, flushed with self-importance.

All weekend, Lily had wondered how exactly Shirley would punish her for leaving the dance early. She hadn't seen Shirley at church on Sunday, and Shirley hadn't phoned to discuss the dance the way she normally would have. Lily had known that Shirley would do something, but she hadn't expected this.

"Shirley went to school already," Flora announced. "She asked me to tell you not to wait for her."

Humiliation burned through Lily, but she tried to hide it behind cool resignation. "We should get going, then, or we'll be late," she said. She was distinctly aware that Shirley had sent Flora to do her dirty work, to show by her very absence that Lily wasn't in her circle anymore.

She saw Eddie give her a curious look, but she didn't meet her brother's eyes as they proceeded up Grant Avenue. It was early enough in the morning that workers were still carrying crates of produce from the sidewalks into the markets. Lily sidestepped boxes of Napa cabbage and ginger, and narrowly missed two men carrying half a pig into a butcher shop. The skin was a waxy pink, the pig's hoof jutting out at an obscene angle as if it was about to kick her. She hurried past, her stomach clenching as if the hoof had met its mark.

As they joined their other friends on the way out of Chinatown, the surreptitious glances cast in her direction told her they all already knew. If Lily had any doubt that Shirley was giving her the cold shoulder, it was squashed when she noticed that Will wasn't waiting with Hanson. Will had gone ahead with Shirley, just the two of them.

Lily kept her head down and shoved her sweaty hands into her jacket's pockets and followed Flora and Hanson and the rest of them, pretending she didn't care. She let herself fall behind until she was trailing them all. She didn't see anything but the dirty gray sidewalk a few feet ahead of her and Flora's legs as she walked, and then she lost sight of Flora entirely and only gazed down at the ground.

At Francisco Street, Eddie turned right toward the junior high, and Lily turned left. As she trudged along the street, she allowed the gap between her and her friends to stretch until they were half a block apart, until she could only hear snatches of their conversation tossed back on the wind. Once or twice Flora glanced over her shoulder at Lily, slowing down as if she would wait for her, but she never slowed down enough, and Lily never made the effort to catch up.

When she and Shirley had been little, they had been very close. They'd liked all the same things: Smarties, which they pretended were medicine prescribed by Lily's father; *Bambi* and *Black Beauty*; and later, *Archie Andrews* on the radio. Lily had always been the Betty to Shirley's Veronica. They rarely fought, and when they did, Lily often felt like the petty one who clung to bruised feelings for too long. Shirley never held a grudge (at least, not openly) and was the generous and big-hearted one whom everyone sided with. Now Lily realized that Shirley never apologized for anything; she simply assumed that Lily would forgive her—and she did.

When Lily arrived at Galileo, there were only a few minutes left before the bell. At her locker, she saw Shirley and their friends gathered in a closed circle across the hall. Some of them eyed her as she passed; some of them whispered behind cupped hands. Had Shirley told them why she and Lily had fallen out? Had she started a rumor about Lily and Kath? The thought made her nervous, but it also made her angry.

Lily finished at her locker. Carrying her books in her arms, she turned her back on Shirley's group and headed to Miss Weiland's classroom. There was Kath coming down the hallway, carefully not looking at Lily as usual. And Lily suddenly knew what she could do.

"Kath!" she called. "Wait for me!"

Out of the corner of her eye, Lily saw everyone in Shirley's group turn their heads to watch. She saw Kath stop and look at her in surprise. Kath's gaze flickered behind her, then back at Lily.

"What's going on?" Kath asked.

"I thought we'd go to class together." Lily felt her heart beat a little too fast in her chest as she waited for Kath's response, and for a terrible moment she wondered whether she had made a mistake. Maybe Kath didn't want to be seen with her either.

But then Kath cocked her head in Shirley's direction and asked quietly, "You're not going with them?"

"No."

For a moment, Kath's expression opened. Something like hope, or happiness, passed across her face, and Lily caught her breath.

"All right," Kath said. "Let's go."

They went together, and Lily didn't look back.

17

The bowling balls were lined up on the rack like a series of planets: marbleized blue and violet, sparkling red and deep green streaked with white. Lily chose the red one for luck, because she suspected she'd be terrible at bowling, and slid her fingers into the deep finger wells.

"That one's too big for you," Kath said. "Try this one." She pointed to the smaller green one. "And don't use your fingers to lift it—it's too heavy. Carry it with both hands."

Lily was surprised by the ball's weight. "How am I supposed to throw this?"

Laughter drifted from the mixed couples group a few lanes down. Lily glanced over to see one of the men placing his hands on his girlfriend's hips, coaxing her into position while she tossed a flirtatious smile at him.

"You don't throw it," Kath said. "Come over here."

Lily carried her green bowling ball over to where Kath was standing, several feet away from the start of their lane. She could still see the flirting couple out of the corner of her eye; the way the woman leaned into the man's hands.

"Square your hips," Kath told her.

Lily turned toward her. "Sorry, what way?"

"The other way," Kath said, looking amused.

And before Lily turned on her own, Kath reached out and touched her hip, gently nudging her to face the lane. She touched her for only a second, but Lily felt Kath's hand through the fabric of her skirt like a spark on her skin.

"Now, put the fingers of your right hand in the holes," Kath said. "You're right-handed, aren't you?"

Lily blinked and tried to shift her attention to the ball. "Yes. It's so heavy."

"Hold the weight of the ball with your left. Right, like that. Now bend your knees and lean forward—but not too much! You're going to lead off with your right foot. Just walk toward the lane—keep your eyes straight ahead. Swing your right arm back—you see how they're doing it down there? Right, swing your arm and just let go— no, you don't need to throw it!"

Lily had tossed the ball heavily at the front of the lane. It smacked the polished wood with a wince-inducing crack, and then spun into the gutter.

"I told you I'm not good at sports," Lily said ruefully. "Maybe I should have just stayed with Miss Weiland's group."

Over to their left, Miss Weiland was teaching several beginners, but Kath had convinced her she could teach Lily on her own. The rest of the G.A.A. girls were split up among half a dozen lanes throughout the Loop Bowl. The group of mixed couples and a party of four men beside them were the only non-G.A.A. patrons that afternoon.

"I should have showed you first," Kath said. "Watch me this time. It's all about timing. That's what Miss Weiland says. You have to swing your arm in time with the way you walk. See?"

Lily watched Kath pick up a ball and hold it in front of her stomach. Then she started walking toward the lane, leading with her right leg as she swung the ball back with her right arm. She took four steps and slid her left foot along the polished wooden floor, extending her right leg behind her as if she were curtsying to the bowling alley, and let go of the ball. It rolled down the oiled wood and struck down half of the pins.

"That's great!" Lily exclaimed.

"It would've been better if I got them all. But I'll go again. Maybe I can get a spare."

Lily took a seat at the back of their lane to watch Kath try again. There was a pleasing rhythm to the way Kath moved, a smoothness to the arc her arm followed before she released the ball. When she slid on the fourth step, dropping low to the ground, her skirt rose up and exposed the hollows behind her knees. The sight was unexpectedly intimate, and Lily averted her eyes. The men who were bowling nearby seemed to smoke and talk more than they actually bowled, and Lily saw a couple of them eye the G.A.A. girls and grin at each other.

There was a crashing sound as Kath's ball struck the last of the pins, and she let out a triumphant whoop before returning to Lily. "You see, it's about momentum," Kath said. "You don't have to throw it down the lane. The momentum will carry it. You want to go again?"

Lily was acutely aware of the men in the next lane, and she drew Kath down on the bench beside her and whispered, "I think they're watching."

"Who?"

Lily turned her back on the men and said quietly, "Those men behind me. When you bowl, your skirt goes up."

Kath looked startled. She glanced over at their classmates, watching as they slid toward the lane and extended their legs back. Each time a girl bowled, her skirt rose up, exposing a flash of knee or thigh, and with those men watching, the ordinary motion of their bodies somehow became indecent—as if the girls were showing off their limbs to onlookers.

Kath looked down at her hands, her cheeks turning a faint pink.

"Don't pay any attention to them," she said, but she didn't suggest picking up their bowling game again.

The girls from the G.A.A. down at the far end hadn't noticed they had an audience. They were still getting their lesson from Miss Weiland, who was instructing them on the proper way to walk toward the lane. "The footwork is unhurried—you don't need to run at the lane," Lily heard her say. Her voice carried clearly in a break between the echoing, musical sounds of bowling balls crashing into pins. She watched Miss Weiland take her stance and begin her approach to the lane, her arm swinging back and releasing the ball, her right leg extending backward in that bowling lane curtsy. Miss Weiland was wearing trim-fitting khaki pants rather than a skirt, and Lily wondered if Miss Weiland had done that on purpose.

"Now, you see, you swing the ball back like a pendulum and simply let it go," Miss Weiland was saying.

Miss Weiland's bowling ball spun down the right side of the lane and then hooked toward the center, rolling right into the space between the center pin and the one to its right. The crack of collision echoed as the pins tumbled over. Lily could imagine it illustrated in a cartoon with the jagged-edged star of an explosion, and she immediately thought of rockets. "It's all physics," she said suddenly.

"What?" Kath said, puzzled.

"The bowling ball hitting the pins—it's Newton's third law. Every action has an equal and opposite reaction. It's how rockets work."

"I think you've lost me."

"Sorry. Do you want me to explain?"

"Sure."

Lily reached for her book bag and pulled out a notebook, and began to draw a diagram with a rocket and a stick figure of a human being. Kath, sitting beside her, leaned over to watch as she drew. "How do you know all this?" Kath asked.

"I've read about it," Lily said, trying to ignore the brush of Kath's knee against her leg. "And my aunt Judy has explained some of it to me."

"I'd love to go on a rocket."

"People can't go on rockets. It's too dangerous."

"Isn't that why it would be fun?"

Kath was close enough that Lily could feel the warmth from her body. "Not—not for me. I get sick when the cable car goes downhill too fast."

"I'd definitely go." Kath leaned back, her shoulder grazing Lily's. "Can you imagine how exciting it would be to go to the moon or to Mars?"

"Arthur C. Clarke says it would take about two hundred and fifty days to reach Mars. As long as a rocket can reach escape velocity, it doesn't take much more energy to keep flying all the way to Mars."

"How long would it take to get to the moon?"

"Five days or less. If we left tomorrow, we could be there by Tuesday! But we don't have the ability yet to launch a rocket that can escape Earth's gravity. And it's very dangerous." Lily tapped her pencil against her notebook, her equations forgotten. "We'd have to shield the crew—if there was a crew—from radiation. It would be much safer to send automatic instruments." She gestured excitedly with her pencil and said, "Robots!"

The pencil nearly stabbed Kath in the leg. "Careful," Kath said, laughing, and reached for Lily's hand.

"Sorry," Lily said, blushing.

Kath eased the pencil from Lily's fingers and set it down on the bench. "Let's say you invent a rocket that can do it—"

"It's a fuel problem," Lily said.

"Right, fuel. Let's say we get that right, and we can get people onto this rocket. What do you think it would be like to go to the moon?"

"Hmm." Lily still felt the ghost of Kath's hand on hers. She tried to focus. "Well, we'd need to develop space suits too. Arthur C. Clarke said they might look like suits of armor—wouldn't that be funny?"

"Why suits of armor?"

"Because of the pressure. There's no pressure on the moon, so the suit would probably have to be rigid."

"So we'd be wearing suits of armor on the moon? Like King Arthur and his knights? I guess if you meet some aliens, then you'd be prepared." Kath reached for the pencil and brandished it as if it were a sword. "En garde, aliens!"

Lily burst into laughter, and her notebook slid off her lap onto the floor. Kath picked it up to use as a shield, standing to strike a heroic pose. Lily covered her mouth, still laughing, and out of the corner of her eye she saw the group of men again. She had almost forgotten about them. Now they seemed somewhat pathetic; they were middle-aged and balding, dressed in ugly plaid shirts. There was a desperation to the way they were eyeing the girls. Whatever danger she had sensed from their attention had turned to pity, and with a burst of inspiration she stood up and went to the ball rack.

"You see, I'll show you—it's physics," she joked to Kath. There was a certain pleasure in knowing that Kath was watching her, that Kath would keep her eyes trained on Lily's body as she released the bowling ball to spin down the lane—inexpertly, to be sure—and when the ball struck only one of the pins on the left side, she shrugged. "I'm not good, but it's still conservation of momentum. The moment the ball strikes the pins is exactly like the moment a rocket launches from the ground—it's an explosion."

Kath came to pick up her bowling ball. "I think you've lost me with your analogy, but I don't think I need to know how it works. You're the one who's going to build the rockets, right?"

Lily smiled. "Right."

She stepped back to give Kath room to bowl, and also to block the men's view.

18

Kath came to Lily's locker first thing on Monday morning, her eyes bright with excitement. "I have it," she said, and Lily felt her stomach drop. All around them students were putting their jackets away, gathering their books and pencils, heading off to class. The bell would ring at any moment, and there was no time to talk about it now. "I'll show you after school," Kath promised.

All day the minutes crawled past. In Senior Goals, with Kath in the next row, time seemed to slow even further because they couldn't speak about it. She noticed Shirley, who had barely spoken a word to her since the dance, eyeing her suspiciously. She tried to suppress any trace of her impatience, but she couldn't stop her knee from bouncing beneath her desk.

By the time the day came to an end, Lily was exhausted from waiting and from keeping quiet, while Kath seemed filled with nervous energy. As soon as the last bell rang, they left school together, taking Chestnut Street up Russian Hill. At the bottom of the steps they paused to make sure they were quite alone, and Kath removed a small card from her book bag.

"I didn't think you'd have it yet," Lily said, almost afraid to look.

"Jean got it from a friend in the Western Addition. We went and saw him together on Saturday."

"How much did it cost? Do I owe you money?"

"No, don't worry. He owed Jean a favor. Here you go."

It was a little bigger than a business card, with white lettering on a dark background. The words OPERATOR'S LICENSE CALIFORNIA were printed across the top, along with the expiration date and a number. The name on the card was not Lily's; it read MAY LEE WONG. In a box on the lower right was a fingerprint, and a signature was scrawled across the bottom. It looked startlingly genuine.

"I told them you were Chinese," Kath explained. "They thought that was a good name. Is it all right?"

Lily held the card gingerly, as if it might burn her. "Whose fingerprint is that? Who signed it?"

"It's my fingerprint," Kath said. "And the guy who made the card signed it. Doesn't it look real?"

Kath seemed oblivious to the possible consequences of carrying this card, but seeing the declaration above the signature ("I hereby certify that the person described hereon has been granted the privilege of operating motor vehicles") made Lily feel queasy. She hadn't imagined it would look so authentic, and now she was certain this would doom her if the authorities discovered it in her possession. She wondered if false immigration papers could be obtained as easily.

"Is something wrong?" Kath asked. She seemed worried. "You look like—is the name wrong?"

Lily didn't want to be a spoilsport. She shook her head. "It's a little like calling me Jane Smith, but it's all right."

Kath frowned. "Are you sure? We don't have to do this if you don't want to."

A pang went through Lily. "I *want* to, I just—where's yours? Can I see it?"

Kath pulled hers out and showed it to Lily.

"'Elizabeth Flaherty,'" Lily read. "You don't look like an Elizabeth."

Kath laughed, and so did Lily, and then her nervousness began to be overtaken by excitement. "Do you really think this will work?" she asked, looking at Kath.

Those two red spots began to bloom on Kath's face again, just beneath her cheekbones. "Only one way to find out," she said. "When do you want to go?"

The newspaper clipping with the photo of Tommy Andrews was beginning to soften at the edges. Lily carefully removed it from *The Exploration of Space* and unfolded it against the book, taking care not to smudge the newsprint. She and Kath had decided to go to the Telegraph Club on Friday night, but the idea that she could see Tommy for real still felt like science fiction.

She angled the Telegraph Club ad to better catch the light from her bedside lamp. The picture was so familiar she didn't need to look at it to remember what Tommy looked like, but she still liked to look, to feel the way it tugged at something deep within her. A spark of recognition, or a glow of hope.

She lay back against her pillows, setting the clipping down beside her on her bed. She closed her eyes, trying to imagine Tommy Andrews singing to the women in the audience—to *her*—but her imagination seemed to balk tonight, as if it refused to show her this fantasy anymore because she was about to see the real thing. By the end of this week, she would be there.

When she opened her eyes, the ceiling was a shadowy dark yellow in the lamplight. The flat was quiet. Everyone had gone to bed, but she wasn't sleepy. She picked up *The Exploration of Space* and opened it at random to the chapter on the inner planets: Mercury, Venus, and Mars. She had read it before, but now she read it again, hoping that it might put her to sleep.

Clarke spent several pages on the mysteries of Venus, which

125

seemed to exasperate him. The planet was completely covered by clouds that obscured all traces of the surface. He theorized it was unlikely that Venus supported intelligent life, but he gamely speculated that if they existed, Venusians would have no knowledge of the stars until they developed machines that could fly above the clouds. Mars, on the other hand, was largely naked to the observer, and maps had even been drawn of the surface. The book included a map of Mars, which seemed to Lily almost as fantastical as a map to Alice's Wonderland. This Mars was labeled with names for places no human had ever visited: Elysium, Eden, Amazonia. There was also a color illustration of an automatic rocket that could travel to Mars. It had a spherical body mounted on several small rockets, and metallic arms that extended a satellite dish for communication as it hovered over the red planet.

There was a stage between wakefulness and sleep when she seemed to be able to direct her unconscious mind; the problem was, she could never be sure when that stage began or ended. As she drifted off to sleep, she saw the insectlike rocket crawling over the surface of Mars, which wasn't red as it should be, but was covered with swirling clouds like those over Venus. She knew she could direct the rocket closer to its destination—she had built it herself—but somehow she could never cause it to accelerate fast enough. The destination remained a silvery blur.

1942	Joseph joins the U.S. Army and becomes a naturalized U.S. citizen.
1943	The Chinese Exclusion Act is repealed.
	Grace and her family attend the parades in honor of Madame Chiang Kai-shek's visit to San Francisco.
1944	The "Suicide Squad" is formalized as the Jet Propulsion Laboratory, operating under the army.
1945	World War II ends.
	Joseph is discharged from the U.S. Army.
Nov. 16, 1945	**JOSEPH takes Grace to the Forbidden City nightclub.**
1946	Franklin Chen-yeh Hu (胡振業) is born.
1947	Judy Hu arrives in San Francisco to begin graduate school at the University of California–Berkeley.

JOSEPH

Nine Years Earlier

Organizing a night on the town was much more work than Joseph Hu imagined. By the time the children were settled with the Lums (Eddie had the misfortune to bump his knee on the edge of a packing crate, which led to tears and then a tantrum), and he and Grace had changed into their evening wear (he in his old but freshly pressed gray flannel suit; she in a navy-blue dress that he couldn't remember if he'd seen before), they were running late for their reservation. He called a taxi, which Grace protested because of the cost, but he did it anyway. She was wearing new shoes, and he could tell they were already pinching her feet. The taxi driver took the hills too swiftly, causing Grace to lurch toward him on the back seat, and the pink silk flowers she had pinned to her hair smashed into his face. She had to re-pin the flowers blindly as the car sped down Powell Street.

It was not an auspicious beginning to the night, and he was certain that Grace was noting all these little errors in her mental ledger, as if toting up harbingers of bad luck. It was one of her most Chinese traits, something that surprised him when he first discovered it, not expecting to find such Old World superstition in an American girl.

When they arrived at the Forbidden City, the nightclub's red neon sign cast a devilish glow over the scalloped awning advertising the "All-Chinese Floor Show." Joseph helped his wife out of the taxi and she gave him a pained smile, as if she was trying to brush off the unfortunate beginning to their night.

Inside, they stopped at the hat check first, where a young Chinese woman dressed in a red-and-gold cheongsam took their coats and his hat. Then they passed through a circular archway decorated with sinuous dragons on a sky-blue background and entered the front bar, where the ceiling was painted with fluffy white clouds and patrons were ordering drinks from the Chinese bartender. Joseph went to the maître d', who checked their reservation and handed them off to a waiter, who took them through another archway (it was decorated with matching dragons) to a white cloth-covered table on the edge of the rectangular dance floor. The experience was like a ritual or a ceremony, Joseph thought, amused, and now that they'd gone through three doorways (four if you counted the taxi door) and circumnavigated the ceremonial performance space, they sat down at their table for two and opened their menus to make a freighted choice: American Deluxe dinner or Special Chinese?

He saw Grace reading the menu with consternation, and when he examined the menu himself, he understood immediately. The Special Chinese dinner sounded terrible; it was all egg foo yung and chop suey. "I think we should have the American one," he said. "I'd like to have the steak."

Her expression relaxed and she nodded, folding the menu and setting it down. "Of course, steak it is."

He glanced around the restaurant as they waited to make their order. There was a small stage for the band, and Chinese paintings of beautiful maidens hung on the walls. Cocktail waitresses were coming around with trays of drinks: mai tais and Singapore slings, zombies and tropical punches. When their waiter arrived, Joseph ordered a rum concoction called the Flying Tiger solely for its name; he had known one of those pilots during the war. When the drink was delivered, he was disappointed to discover it was 70 percent crushed ice with a smattering of pineapple on top. Grace liked it more than he did, so he offered it to her and ordered himself a mai tai.

The dinner was a well-oiled machine: each course delivered in succession, the waiters swooping through the restaurant almost like dancers, their wide round trays held high overhead before they descended to table level. The couple at the table beside them had ordered the Special Chinese dinner, and the smell of sweet and sour sauce wafted over to Joseph as he cut into his steak. Wielding his knife and fork reminded him, suddenly, of surgery in a tent out near the Burma Road, and for a moment he stopped eating. He saw again the makeshift surgical table where the soldier was lying, dosed with morphine, and the ragged flesh of the man's arm where it had been punctured with shrapnel from a Japanese bomb.

He blinked and saw his steak again, sitting in a puddle of thin brown juice, and he raised his eyes to his wife, who was chewing her own first bite. "How is it?" he asked, though he still felt partially enmeshed in his memory (the clang of the scalpel against the metal tray). He wasn't sure why the memories came when they did; he wondered what triggered the neurons in his brain to fire. How incredible that electricity surged through his nerves; how strange that they called up these fragments of memory.

"Are you all right?" Grace was saying.

Joseph blinked again and lifted the piece of steak to his mouth. It was salty and well marbled with fat that left a rich smear of beef flavor on his tongue. He chewed and swallowed. He took a sip of his mai tai, tasting the sugary rum cut with the acid of lime juice. "Of course," he said.

"I wish your family could come for New Year too," Grace said. Her mother and brothers were coming for the week; they'd stay at a hotel in Chinatown, since there was no space in their two-room apartment.

"Don't worry yourself about it." There was no possibility of his whole family coming all the way from Shanghai. At least, not yet.

"I only worry about you."

"You don't need to." He wished she would drop the subject.

"How can I not? The war was one thing, but now—who knows how long this situation will drag on?"

"The Communists have acknowledged that the Nationalists are the legitimate leaders of China. I believe that Chiang and Mao both have the best interests of China at heart."

She looked skeptical. "I don't know who to believe."

"Believe me. Besides, America has too much to lose if China doesn't stabilize. We won't let it happen. And then we'll go back."

"I've never been."

She had never met his parents, only his younger brother Arthur, who was his sole family representative at their wedding.

"Then you'll go for the first time. We'll bring Lily and Eddie to meet their grandparents. You'll see. This situation won't last forever." He smiled at her, projecting a confidence that he almost believed.

"If you say so," she said as the band struck its first notes, but she sounded doubtful.

They turned to look at the band; to Joseph's surprise, they were all Caucasians. And then a trio of Chinese women dressed in diaphanous veils emerged, arms raised and fingers gracefully extended, to twirl across the dance floor. The show had begun.

Their seats were quite good. When the dancing girls swept past, they came close enough that Joseph could smell their sweet, floral perfume. Their bodies were barely covered by those sheer veils. Every time they spun, the gauzy fabric floated free to give a glimpse of what lay beneath: muscular limbs, smooth white skin, youthfully firm breasts. They were not as alluring as the dancing girls he'd seen in Shanghai before he'd come to America (he allowed that he'd been younger then and probably more impressionable), but they carried themselves with an appealing, straightforward energy. They were almost wholesome, and he wondered whether Grace approved. She had always had a Puritanical streak in her, which he attributed to her American upbringing.

The girls were followed by a number of singers. There was a tall, broad-shouldered woman with a husky voice, billed as the Chinese Sophie Tucker. There was a tall, broad-shouldered man with slicked-back hair and an easy smile, billed as the Chinese Frank Sinatra. They were all good, Joseph thought, or at least they were good enough, and their being Chinese made up for the rest. He particularly enjoyed the Mei Lings, a duo of dancers who evoked Fred and Ginger in their lifts and dips around the dance floor. They had some real elegance.

Joseph glanced across the table at Grace to see if she was enjoying herself. She was watching the show with an easygoing expression as the Mei Lings swirled past. He realized, slowly, that he hadn't truly looked at Grace tonight until this moment. He'd catalogued the silk flowers in her hair (slightly crooked now due to their earlier encounter with his face), the V-neck dress she wore, her new pumps, but he hadn't seen past the surface. Sometimes he felt as if he never saw past the surface anymore; it was safer to look at the world with a detached, clinical eye.

When he first returned from the war, there had been an awkwardness between them. The years they had been apart had distanced them from each other. Though he had been eager to see his family, he realized the moment he set eyes on them (fresh off the navy ship, the dock crowded with weeping wives and shrieking children) that they had been frozen in his memories, and now Grace and Lily and Eddie looked strangely unfamiliar. Eddie had been reluctant to approach him at first, because he didn't remember his father. It had been Grace who pushed him forward encouragingly; it had been Grace who took Lily to greet him.

Now, as the all-Caucasian band played a waltz for the Chinese dancers, he looked at his wife. He had always thought she was pretty, but her prettiness had softened over the years. The line of her cheek, which she had rubbed lightly with rouge, was plumper now. She was both the same girl he'd met a decade ago and undeniably changed, and for the first time in a long time he felt a kind of ache for her. It wasn't the yearning he would have felt as a young man long separated from his lover. It wasn't a simple physical desire. It was thoroughly unscientific, this feeling that was overtaking him, as if his body was belatedly acknowledging how far apart they had been for so long, and his mind was finally catching up.

He had missed her.

Ever since he returned from the war, he'd felt as if part of him were still back in China, but he wasn't there anymore. Those army hospitals had been long dismantled; those boys he treated had returned to their homes—or at least they were beyond suffering. And here he was now: in this gaily colored and dramatically lit nightclub in America, sitting across from his American wife. The music was loud and brash; the smell of perfume and cigarettes lay heavy on the air. He lifted his mai tai to his lips and took another sip of his drink, the condensation dripping down the side of his hand like an electric shock. *Wake up. You are here.*

Grace turned to look at him. He put down his glass and reached across the table for her. She was surprised, but she put her hand in his.

PART III

I Only Have Eyes For You

November 1954

19

Friday night, after her parents had gone to sleep, Lily turned on her lamp and got out of bed. Ever since she and Kath had decided to go to the Telegraph Club, she had thought endlessly about what she should wear. She had only a vague idea of what one wore to a nightclub, and she wished that she could consult Shirley. Even if Shirley didn't really know, she had instincts about these things.

Shirley would probably tell her to wear something daring. A form-fitting, low-cut blouse tucked into a wiggle skirt or a strapless party dress with a gauzy shawl over it. Not the black rayon circle skirt Lily had planned to wear or the boring white blouse with its Peter Pan collar, or the girlish blue short-sleeved dress she'd been keeping in reserve just in case. They were all terrible: unfashionable and unattractive and *wrong*.

Shirley would also tell her that looking her best began with a proper foundation—the right girdle and bra and stockings—and Lily was sure that nothing she had in her dresser was right. Her mother had bought her a new bra that fall, but she knew that Shirley would say it was the wrong shape. As she wriggled into her panty girdle, she contemplated her selection of stockings, and realized that none of them were sheer enough. She wore them to church, not to nightclubs, and they were thick and plain. Nonetheless, she rolled them up her legs and fastened them to the girdle; she wasn't going to go to the

Telegraph Club wearing bobby socks. That would definitely make her look like a schoolgirl. She hoped, at best, to be mistaken for a young secretary, or a college coed.

Shirley would take her time with her hair, setting it in rollers expertly and fixing the curls in place with a pretty comb or hairband. Lily's hair had never held a curl well—despite even Shirley's efforts—and although she'd taken her bath a little early so that she could set her hair, it had only been a couple of hours. Not long enough. As she pulled on her slip, the rollers snagged on the nylon fabric, and she had to struggle to delicately maneuver the slip over her head without ripping. She was half blinded by the slip, which also restricted her arms, and a sudden burst of anger exploded within her. She hated her clothes and hated her hair and hated, most of all, her uncertainty about everything she was doing.

Was she really going to do this?

She finally managed to free her slip from her head and began to pull the rollers out as fast as she could. In the mirror she saw that the curls were already loosening and wouldn't hold their shape. She glanced at the clock; she was supposed to leave the house in less than half an hour. If she didn't hurry, she would be late, and if she was too late, Kath would leave. They had agreed to wait for each other on the corner of Columbus and Vallejo for five minutes, and if the other hadn't arrived by then, they'd walk around the block and wait another five minutes. If they were still waiting alone by half past eleven, they'd give up and go home. They'd made their plan just in case, although what the case was had never been verbalized. It was some nebulous fear better left unsaid.

The throb of her heart was so strong it frightened her. The anger that had reared up inside her was replaced, now, by a growing panic. She had never done anything like this before. Getting up in the middle of the night, sneaking out—it was unprecedented. Lily Hu didn't do these things. She pulled the last roller out of her hair and dropped it into the basket, and almost as if she were rising out of her body she saw herself in the mirror like a stranger.

Her face was so pale, but two red spots burned on her cheeks, making her look like a porcelain doll. Her lips were almost purple, and the lower lip—she had been chewing on it as she freed her hair—seemed unusually, even obscenely full. Her hair was tousled into loose black waves, and the strap of her pink slip was sliding off her right shoulder, revealing the cups of her white cotton bra, reminding her of Patrice in her negligee on that book cover. Her chest flushed, and color crept up her throat and into her face.

If Lily Hu didn't do these things, the girl in the mirror surely did.

And she would definitely be late if she didn't get dressed.

A new energy flooded into her—a recklessness that gave her courage—and she impulsively put on her newest slim gray skirt instead of the black rayon. She put on the white collared blouse and a blue cardigan. She pulled her hair back with two clips, leaving some of the waves free in the back. She reached for the red lipstick that Shirley had helped her pick out at the Powell Street Owl Drugs. And she put on a soft beret, arranging it carefully over her hair. Finally she dropped her lipstick into her handbag along with the fake ID, put on her coat, and turned off the light.

The flat was silent but for the sound of her own breathing. When she went to the pocket doors to press her ear to the crack, the floorboards creaked, making her freeze momentarily in case her parents had heard, but only silence followed.

She gradually became aware of the sounds that filtered in through the window: car engines purring up the street; the occasional shout of laughter that reminded her it was Friday night in Chinatown; the clang of a cable car. When she was convinced that everyone in the flat was asleep, she opened the door and crept down the hall, shoes in hand. She felt her way down the dark stairs, and at the bottom, she unbolted the front door. It stuck. She had to tug more forcefully, and the hinges emitted a squeak, like the mew of a kitten. She twisted around to peer up the stairs, hoping that she hadn't woken her parents. She saw only darkness.

She counted to sixty, trying to breathe silently and slowly. Finally she stepped out onto the front stoop in her stockinged feet and pulled the door shut, locking it behind her. She was hot with nerves, and the concrete steps were blessedly cold beneath her warm feet as she descended to the street. The bumpy sidewalk dug sharply into her soles, but she was afraid to make the slightest noise beneath the front window, where her parents' bedroom was located. She didn't put on her shoes until she was halfway down the block.

She had never been out this late on her own, perhaps never even in the company of her parents. The Chinatown streets were lit by tall neon signs advertising CHOP SUEY and NOODLES, and the pagoda rooflines of many buildings were outlined in white lights. The sidewalks were lively with people coming to and from cocktail bars, most of them Caucasians, with the ladies in fur stoles and the gentlemen in fedoras. Laughter and music spilled from the Shanghai Low, and the smell of deep-fried food wafted through the air. She hadn't realized so many people would be out at this hour, and as she passed the Chinese man working at the corner kiosk she kept her head down and walked quickly, afraid he might recognize her. When she reached Broadway and crossed over to Columbus, she relaxed a little. North Beach was just as lively—it was Friday night, after all—but there were fewer Chinese to see her.

The escape from Chinatown left her buoyed; she wanted to laugh, but at the last moment she suppressed it out of fear that someone would notice a solitary girl laughing on the sidewalk, and it came out of her in a wheezy giggle. That sobered her up quickly, and suddenly

Columbus Avenue seemed very large and possibly dangerous. Men passed her, their faces obscured by hats, while women clicked by in their heels. Her shoes began to pinch, and as she approached the corner where she and Kath had agreed to meet, she worried that Kath wouldn't be there.

At Columbus and Vallejo, nobody was standing beneath the streetlight. Lily slowed down, hoping that Kath would appear soon. She looked northeast toward Washington Square, searching for a sign of a girl coming through the dark, but she didn't see Kath. Lily stopped about ten feet from the corner, afraid to be spotlighted. She slid her hands into her jacket pockets and glanced around warily. When they'd discussed their plan, they'd had the sense to know it wouldn't feel safe to linger alone on a street corner in the middle of the night, but now Lily realized that five minutes was far too long. Every passing man seemed like a threat. She moved toward the wall of the building on the corner, hiding herself in its shadow. She glanced at her watch, wishing that the minutes would pass faster. She eyed a couple walking down Columbus toward her; the woman's arm was linked through the man's. As they went through the light from the streetlamp, the woman turned her face up to him, smiling. She looked so relaxed, so certain and natural. Lily shrank back against the side of the building and felt ashamed of what she was about to do.

She began to second-guess their whole plan. She began to calculate how long it would take to scurry home through Chinatown and up the block to her building. She studied her watch again, angling it so that she could read the slim hands, and when she looked up, Kath was standing beneath the streetlight, looking around expectantly.

Lily exhaled in relief. "Kath," she said, stepping away from the wall.

Kath came out of the light and met her on the dark edge of the sidewalk. "Are you ready?"

"I don't know," Lily admitted.

"Do you want to go home?" Kath asked, concerned.

Now that Kath was here—really here, scarcely a foot away from her—the doubt that had risen inside her was held back by something stronger. She wanted to see Tommy Andrews. She shook her head. "Let's go."

20

The Telegraph Club's white neon sign was smaller than Lily had expected, and it glowed over a circular awning that was also printed with the name of the club. Beneath the awning, half-lit by the nearby streetlamp, was a black door, and in front of the black door stood a person whom Lily initially thought was a short, stocky man in a suit, but soon realized was a woman. Lily had seen people like her before (she had always noticed; they had drawn her eye magnetically, somehow, in a way that made her pulse leap), but never in this context: as if it were natural, and even expected, to be dressed this way.

"You girls sure you're in the right place?" the bouncer asked.

Lily felt for her fake ID in her handbag, wondering if she should take it out.

"I've been here before," Kath said. "We're sure."

The bouncer gave Kath a little grin, and waved them inside with a flourish. "Well then, welcome back," she said cheerfully.

Relieved, Lily followed Kath into the club, avoiding the bouncer's gaze. The black door opened into a narrow, dimly lit space. Lily didn't know where to look at first; she wanted to see everything, but she was afraid to stare. There was a mirrored bar on the left where patrons sat on stools. There was barely enough space on the right for Lily and Kath to pass in single file. Lily was struck most forcefully by the smell of the place: a mixture of booze, perfume, sweat, and cigarette smoke. As she followed Kath down the side of the room, she noticed some of the women turning their heads to look at her, their eyes reflecting the globe lights hanging above.

At the end of the bar, the narrow space opened via an archway into a wider room—perhaps three times as wide—and in the center rear was a tiny stage where a spotlight shone upon a solitary microphone. At the back of the stage was an upright piano, and a woman in a boxy suit with a poodle haircut was seated on the bench, placing her hands on the keys. All around the stage were little round tables, and each one was filled. Kath pulled Lily toward the side of the room and found a small empty space between a table and the wall. The pianist began to play, and the room, which had been lively with conversation and laughter, began to hush.

The rear of the stage was covered by a black curtain, and Lily wondered if someone was going to step out from behind it. She had been waiting for this for so long that these last few moments seemed interminable. She quivered in her shoes as she gazed at the stage, at the people seated near the edge—she was jealous of their proximity to that microphone—and at Kath, who was watching the stage just as she was. Then there was a murmur behind them, and all the people packed into their section turned toward the archway.

Someone was making their way through the crowd.

Lily couldn't see the person clearly, only the motion of others making way, like a wave, but she followed the ripple and turned along with her neighbors as that person strolled through the audience, and finally stepped onto the low stage and into the spotlight.

Lily knew that this was Tommy Andrews, male impersonator. She knew that the entire point of the show was the fact that the performer was not a man. Someone nearby whispered, "Is that really a woman?" And Lily squirmed with embarrassment, because that question led her to imagine what Tommy's body looked like under her suit, and that seemed so disrespectful—like those men who had leered at them at the bowling alley. Lily felt a queasy, self-conscious confusion. It was wrong to stare, and yet Tommy was onstage, and they were supposed to look. It would be rude not to watch, so she did.

At first Tommy stood with her back to the room while the pianist continued to play, and the notes began to coalesce into a melody that Lily recognized. The spotlight gleamed on Tommy's short hair, highlighting the way it was cut sharp against the nape of the neck, right above the white collar that was crisply framed by a black tuxedo jacket. Tommy pulled the microphone toward her mouth, with her face still turned away from the audience and toward the black curtain, and began to sing the first lines to "Bewitched, Bothered, and Bewildered."

The voice that emerged was pitched low and husky, like a jazz singer with smoke on her breath. A faint gasp went through the audience as if people were surprised, but Lily knew it wasn't surprise. It was acknowledgment of how immaculate the male impersonation was, how shockingly well staged. The contrast between Tommy's voice (especially when it rose smoothly to the higher notes) and silhouette (legs spread and shoulders cocked) was deliciously scandalous. Lily felt her heartbeat thrumming in her chest as she watched; she was afraid to blink; she was afraid to miss the moment she sensed coming closer—and finally, there it was.

At the end of the first verse, Tommy spun around with a cocky smile on her face, and the audience burst into applause so loud it drowned out the rest of the verse.

The black-and-white photograph in the *Chronicle* had been a poor imitation of reality, smudged and blurry. It had left out all the important details: the sheen of pomade on the waves of Tommy's hair; the precise folds of her black bow tie; the gold signet ring on her pinkie finger as she cupped the microphone close to her mouth. It had given no sense, Lily now realized, of Tommy's physicality. The way she stood, the way she moved—her swagger—so like a man and yet—

It was that *yet* that made Lily's skin flush warm. The knowledge that despite the clothes that Tommy wore, despite the attitude that invited everyone in the room to gaze at her, she was not a man. It felt unspeakably charged, as if all of Lily's most secret desires had been laid bare onstage.

Tommy didn't change the lyrics. The song was languid and liquid, with a hint of jaded self-reproach as if Tommy were confessing that she had fallen in love against her wishes. Hearing her sing to an un-named "him" while dressed as a man was a sensation. The audience whistled at her, and she winked at them, so sure of herself it made Lily's face burn.

She didn't want Tommy ever to stop. She could stand there in the hot crowd, craning her neck to see around the heads of those who had been lucky enough to get a table, gazing at Tommy in her tuxedo, forever. She had heard the song before, of course, but never like this, never the way Tommy sang with a purr in her voice that felt like she was whispering directly in Lily's ear.

Lily's blouse clung to her damp skin, and she became increasingly aware of the press of people around her and the heat that rose from their bodies. The air was close and smelled more strongly than ever of cigarette smoke and alcohol, and the undercurrent of perfume now seemed shockingly intimate, as if she were nuzzling the necks of all the women here.

And all of a sudden it was almost painful to watch Tommy on-stage. She had to look away as if she were a drowning person surfacing for air. She saw that there were some men in the audience—husbands with their wives or girlfriends, seated in a clump on one side of the room as if they had huddled together for safety. The men seemed to be having a good time, applauding and grinning, giving each other approving glances as if to congratulate themselves on their adventurousness. The wives and girlfriends were more mixed in their expressions. One looked absolutely mortified and could barely keep her eyes on the stage; one leaned forward with a broad smile, occasionally giving her husband a smirk. The smirk was so thick with suggestion that it made Lily queasy, even though she didn't understand what it meant. The not knowing made it worse; it opened a Pandora's box of implication, and yet she was painfully aware of her own naïveté. She couldn't even imagine what that woman wanted, but she was certain it was shameful.

Beyond those couples, most of the audience was women, and some of those women were dressed like men. None as finely as Tommy, but some wore ties and vests, while others wore blazers with open-collared shirts. Some women were done up for a night on the town in cocktail dresses, with sparkling earrings and necklaces around their pale throats. There were a few Negro women seated together, but Lily was the only Chinese girl in the room. That meant there was no one from Chinatown to recognize her, but it also made her stand out all the more.

She shrank back as far as she could, and when her foot touched the wall, she realized she could inch back a tiny bit more until she was entirely pressed against the wall, and Kath was half a foot in front of her, partly blocking her view. Now she felt safer, and when the song ended and the room burst into applause, she took off her jacket and draped it over her arm. Her blouse was damp where she had sweated through the back, but at least she was cooler.

Kath glanced at her and asked, "Are you all right?"

Lily nodded, but there was no time for her to elaborate, because Tommy was starting another number. This one was livelier, and it involved her stepping off the stage and flirting with the women seated around the perimeter. Lily was extra glad, now, that she was hidden against the far wall. She had dreamed about Tommy visiting her table, but now that she was in the room the possibility of that attention felt distinctly alarming. Instead she held her breath as Tommy perched on the edge of each table she visited, smiling down at the woman she had chosen and joking with the man nearby. She seemed utterly comfortable with what she was doing, as if wearing a man's suit and flirting with women were the most normal thing in the world. She leaned toward a blushing woman in a low-cut green dress, singing "You're Getting to Be a Habit With Me," then turning to her male partner and adding, "Not you, sir."

The room broke into laughter at the aside, and Lily laughed along nervously, even though she was afraid she didn't get the joke. She had wanted so desperately to come here, but the reality of the Telegraph Club was not what she had imagined. In her imagination, Tommy Andrews had been a lone, pure figure who could be admired from a cool distance. She had not been this swaggering creature who sauntered over to strange women and kissed their hands, who strode back onstage and surveyed the room like a king looking over his realm. In her imagination, Tommy had been like a matinee idol— sweet-faced and tender. In reality, Tommy was a woman made of flesh and blood, and that frightened Lily most of all.

21

At the end of Tommy's set, the audience loosened up, stood and stretched, moved toward the bar or away from it. Kath spotted several women deserting a table nearby. She quickly claimed it, and Lily followed.

Kath looked around excitedly and asked, "What did you think?"

"I'm not sure." Lily heard the strained self-consciousness in her voice and wished she had said something different.

Kath looked at her then—really looked at her—as if trying to decipher what was beneath Lily's words. Lily awkwardly dropped her gaze, studying the scarred wooden surface of the table. The votive candle at the center flickered within its red glass cup, and Lily imagined she could feel the heat from it radiating out in invisible waves.

"If you want to leave, we can go," Kath said.

Lily looked up at her friend in surprise. Kath had taken off her coat, and Lily noticed for the first time that Kath wore a collared shirt with its top button undone.

"I don't want to leave," Lily managed to say, and Kath nodded, and they sat there for a moment as the bustle around them went on: women carrying beers across the room; wineglasses ringing together; someone wondering loudly when Tommy's next set would begin.

Two women suddenly appeared at their table, and one of them

asked, "Are you using these two chairs? Do you mind if we take them?"

"No, go ahead," Kath said, and the two women sat down, pulling their chairs back and away slightly to give them some room. One of the women was wearing a blazer and collared shirt, and her hair was cut boyishly short, but in a style that could be called feminine if she put on a dress. The other woman was wearing a blouse and a skirt, her hair waved and fastened with a silver barrette; she didn't look much older than a high school senior.

Kath scooted her chair closer to Lily and asked, "Do you want something to drink?"

"We can't," Lily whispered, turning her head away from their tablemates.

"I'll get you something. I mean, Elizabeth Flaherty will." Kath grinned.

"I don't want you to get in trouble," Lily said, worried.

"It'll be fine," Kath assured her. "I'll be back in a minute. Tommy's second set won't start for a little while."

And then Kath got up and left her there, sitting with the two strange women who had their backs half turned to her. Lily took a shallow breath, holding herself very still as if that might render her invisible. The women at her table were talking about a movie they'd seen recently; it sounded like a French film, and Lily wondered where they had seen it. They seemed quite absorbed in teasing out the nuances of the movie—it appeared to be about a schoolgirl—and though Lily didn't allow herself to look in their direction, she listened quite attentively.

When Kath returned with two glasses of beer, the women made room for her to slide into her seat, and the one in the blazer took that as an excuse to say, "We haven't seen you here before, have we? I'm Paula, and this is Claire."

Kath introduced herself and shook Paula's hand. "I've been here before with my friend Jean Warnock. Do you know her? She's at Cal. This is my friend Lily."

Paula and Claire extended their hands, and Lily shook them awkwardly, as if they were all men, while Claire said, "I don't think I know Jean. What's her major? I'm at Cal too."

Lily took her glass of beer—it was cold and slippery—and lifted it to her lips so that she wouldn't have to talk. It tasted frothy and a little like soapy water, but it was cold and went down more easily than she anticipated. Claire and Paula and Kath were all talking about Jean now, and Lily thought she had avoided their scrutiny until Claire said, "We don't see many Orientals around here. Do you speak English?"

Lily blinked. "Of course I do."

Claire didn't seem to hear the umbrage in Lily's voice. "Do you know Mary Lee? She runs the Candlelight Club down the block."

They all looked at her expectantly, and she swallowed. "No, I don't know her." The name Mary Lee was so common it seemed as fictional as her false identification. "What's the Candlelight Club?"

"It's a tiny little place," Claire said. "Very friendly."

"If you like this place, you'll like the Candlelight," Paula said, and raised her glass. She was drinking beer too. "Cheers to new friends," she added, and Kath smiled and knocked her beer glass gently against Paula's.

Lily raised her glass too, because it seemed to be the thing to do, and as it clinked against Kath's, a bit of beer spilled over the lip, running coldly over her fingers. There was nothing to wipe her hand on, and nobody seemed to be paying attention to her, so Lily held her hand down at her side, letting the beer drip from her fingertips onto the floor in the dark.

Tommy Andrews was late for her second set, and the rumor was traveling around the club that she might not return that night. The stage room remained dark, and the husband-and-wife couples had all left but one—the one with the woman who had smirked at Tommy's performance. Kath continued to talk with Paula and Claire; it turned out the movie they'd seen, *Olivia*, was quite famous in Europe but had just opened in the United States in a few select theaters. It was set in a girls' boarding school where several of the female students and teachers had suggestive relationships with each other.

"In one scene they even kissed," Paula said, sounding shocked.

"Not really," Claire said, shaking her head. "The teacher kissed one girl on her eyes. Her eyes!" She laughed as if this was ridiculous.

Lily drank her beer and stayed quiet. She had never drank an entire beer by herself before, and as her glass emptied she began to relax. She felt a little warm, but not unpleasantly so. The Telegraph Club lost some of its strangeness; the darkness started to feel friendly. The girls were friendly too. Claire and Paula tried to include her in their conversation; it wasn't their fault that Lily felt as if she had nothing to say. After they'd exhausted the subject of *Olivia*, they talked about playing in a local softball league and driving up to Marin County to see the redwoods. Lily didn't want to tell them about her weekends: helping her mother run errands around Chinatown, going to church on Sundays, occasionally seeing the Cathay Band perform or cheering on the YMCA basketball team. She thought of Shirley working at the Eastern Pearl, folding hundreds of napkins over and over, so that they might be used to wipe the mouths of Caucasians. And then she looked around the Telegraph Club and felt as if she had rocketed herself to another planet; it seemed so far away from home.

Still Tommy did not return to the stage, and Kath asked if anyone wanted another round of beers. Lily realized she needed to go to the restroom, and when she stood to excuse herself, Claire said, "Are you going to the girls' room? I'll come with you. I'm dying! Paula, get me a drink while I'm gone, will you?"

Claire headed off and Lily followed her through the room. Just to the right of the archway, Claire veered into a dim passage that Lily had overlooked when she first entered. It turned into a hallway that ran toward the rear of the building, and on one side was a stairway lit by a single yellow bulb at the top, exposing a grimy whitewashed wall. Claire wobbled a bit on the stairs, grabbing for the railing, and Lily felt the wooden bar rock slightly beneath her own hand. At the top of the stairs, a narrow hallway ran along the side of the stairwell toward the front of the building, and half a dozen women were lined up outside the door to the restroom. Claire took her place at the end of the line, and Lily followed suit. Some of the women glanced at them briefly; others looked a little longer, particularly at Lily. She shrank back against the wall and wished she was invisible.

"How long do you think the wait will be?" Claire asked the woman ahead of her. "Is it moving?"

The woman, who was dressed in pants and a blazer, said grimly, "One of the toilets is stopped up. It's slow."

Claire groaned. "I shouldn't have waited so long to come up here. The line always kills me. You'd think they'd give us the men's room too."

The men's room was through one of the doors down the hall, though Lily hadn't yet seen a man come or go from it.

"Go ahead and try it," the woman said with a grin. "No one'll stop you."

Claire laughed. "I'm not dressed for it, honey." She turned to Lily and said, "Your friend downstairs—Kath? She said she's been here before but you're a new one, aren't you?"

"Yes."

Claire leaned her shoulder against the wall and said companionably, "When I first came here—oh, two years ago now, can you believe it?" She paused a little in wonder, and then went on: "I had no idea what this place was. I was beyond shocked. I grew up in San Mateo, you know, and we only ever came up to San Francisco for shopping or special occasions. Where are you from?"

"Chinatown."

A toilet flushed, and someone down the line let out a faint cheer as the women edged forward.

"Chinatown, of course." Claire gave her a conspiratorial smile, but Lily didn't return it. Claire's smile faltered a bit before she rushed on. "I mean, there's nothing like this in San Mateo. And then I found this place and—wow, it was like the clouds parted and I had arrived at the promised land." Claire laughed a little.

Lily noticed some activity at the end of the hall, and she looked past Claire to see whether someone had left the bathroom. The door to a different room had opened, and a blond woman emerged; she wore a tight powder-blue sweater tucked into a charcoal pencil skirt, and red high heels. Directly behind her came Tommy Andrews, still dressed in her tuxedo and black tie, her hair as gleaming as ever. She was smoking a cigarette, and the smoke trailed after her in a thin white stream.

As she passed the line of women, she greeted some of them by name. "Frannie, hello. How's Midge? Haven't seen you in a while, Vivian."

Meanwhile the blonde preceded her, a faintly worried look on her face, until she caught sight of Claire, who was waving at her as she said, "Lana! Lana, how are you?"

Lana's worried expression turned to pleasure. "Claire! It's so good to see you." They embraced, barely two feet away from Lily, and she caught a whiff of Lana's floral perfume.

Claire and Lana were talking in excited whispers, and all the while, Tommy came closer. She was shorter than Lily expected, but the way she held herself made her seem tall. She was waiting behind Lana now, because the hallway was narrow enough that she couldn't pass, and her eyes were sweeping over Claire, and then over Lily and beyond her—and back again, curiously. Lily felt Tommy's gaze as if it were a breath on her face. Goose bumps rose on her skin.

Tommy said, "I have to get back downstairs. Sorry to break it up, girls."

Lana gave Claire an apologetic look before saying to Tommy, "This is Claire, don't you remember? I haven't seen her in weeks."

Tommy nodded at Claire, giving her a quick grin. "Hello again, Claire."

"Hello, Tommy," Claire said, placing a strange little emphasis on Tommy's name. Tommy leaned toward her and they kissed each other on the cheek, as if they were old friends, though Lily saw the little flare of pink on Claire's face as she pulled back. "Come and find me, Lana," Claire said. "I've got a table downstairs with Paula. We should catch up."

"Will do," Lana said, and then continued toward the stairs.

Tommy was passing right in front of Lily now. She kept her gaze fixed downward, and so she saw the neatly pressed crease of Tommy's tuxedo pants, the satin stripe running liquidly down the side, the shine of her black shoes. They were men's shoes, oxfords. Tommy paused in mid-stride and said, "We don't see many Orientals around here." And then: "Does she speak English?"

Lily looked up straight into Tommy's eyes; they were brown and creased at the edges in a little smile. Lily's heart pounded, but her voice seemed to have left her.

"She's with me," Claire said. "This is Lily."

Tommy nodded to her with a slow grin, and then raised her

cigarette to her mouth and inhaled, the ember at the tip glowing red. "Hope you're enjoying the show, China doll," Tommy said, and then followed Lana down the stairs. A fragrance trailed her—not the sweet floral perfume that clung to Lana, but something warmer, a little spicy.

There was a faint roaring in Lily's ears. She was vaguely aware of the other women gaping at her; some were giggling, others openly curious. Claire was saying, "Look, she's stunned! The poor girl."

"I'm fine," Lily said automatically, and tried to laugh it off, but her own laughter sounded false, and soon enough the other women lost interest, because the line was finally moving more quickly. Downstairs, the piano began again; Tommy's second set was starting. Lily couldn't make out the melody through the roaring in her ears; everything sounded muffled, even the flushing of the toilet. Claire had been pulled into conversation with the woman ahead of her, who was intrigued that Claire knew Tommy. "Well, it's Lana I know, really," Claire said modestly.

Finally, there was the door to the bathroom. Claire went in as another woman came out, brushing past Lily to hurry back downstairs. At last it was Lily's turn, and she stepped into the bathroom and found that there were only two stalls, and one of them had a handwritten sign taped to it that read OUT OF ORDER. She went into the one that Claire had vacated—Claire was washing her hands at the sink—and the stall smelled of urine, but Lily had no choice but to use it. She hovered above the seat so that she wouldn't have to touch it.

When she was finished, she pulled the chain on the tank and water plunged into the bowl. She straightened her blouse and skirt and stockings, and as she reached for the latch on the door she noticed that all sorts of messages had been graffitied on in pen, or scratched through the beige paint. FOR A GOOD TIME CALL JOANIE, someone had written, and beneath that a different hand had added: JUST

DON'T CALL BEFORE NOON. There was a heart scratched above the handle of the stall door, and inside the heart were two names: NANCY + CAROL.

A swell of applause rose from downstairs. She hurried out to wash her hands, and then found Claire standing in the hallway, smiling at her cheerfully.

"You didn't have to wait," Lily said, surprised.

"I wouldn't leave you up here alone. You looked a little lost back there."

There was only kindness in her voice, and Lily felt overwhelmed by it. "Thank you," Lily said.

Claire shrugged it off. "Let's go. Tommy's second set is usually better, because it's after the tourists leave."

Lily followed her back down to the stage room, where Tommy was singing in the spotlight. When they returned to their table, Kath leaned close to her and said, "I was getting worried! I got you another beer."

The idea of drinking another one seemed scandalous to Lily, but she didn't want to be impolite, and she could practically hear Shirley saying, *Don't be such a square.* "Thanks," she said to Kath, and picked up her glass. The beer was cold, and with each sip it became easier to watch Tommy onstage, to laugh and applaud when the others did. Perhaps it was because the initial shock of seeing a woman impersonate a man was wearing off, and she knew a little about what to expect now. Or perhaps it was because the tourists had mostly left, as Claire predicted, and the audience was almost all women. The club felt looser now; it felt lighter, as if finally Tommy was among friends. The one or two men remaining in the audience could be overlooked at last, and Tommy did overlook them.

Lily thought that Claire was right: Tommy's second set *was* better than the first. She changed the lyrics to the songs she sang now, and the changes were so direct that Lily could hardly believe what she was hearing. *When a beautiful lady like you / Meets an irresistible gay girl like me.* The rest of the audience wasn't as surprised, though; or if they were, it was a delighted kind of surprise, because they laughed to hear it.

Tommy flirted shamelessly with a woman in a green dress seated at a table near the stage with two other women, and the woman in the green dress loved it so much Tommy brought her onstage to serenade her with "Secret Love." This time Lily was fairly certain Tommy hadn't changed a single word, and Lily was struck by how duplicitous a song could be, as if multiple languages were hidden within the lyrics. Tommy ended her set with a rollicking rendition of "Keep It Gay," and when it was over, she sauntered offstage and back to the bar, and the way some women shook her hand or slapped her shoulder, it was obvious that they knew her.

Afterward, Lily assumed it was time to go home, but when she looked at Kath, she didn't seem to be in a rush. Lily touched her arm and asked, "Should we go?"

"We can if you want. They'll tell us when last call is, and then we'll have to leave, anyway."

"What time is it?"

Kath held her watch closer to the votive candle, angling it to catch the light. "About half past one."

Claire had gotten up as soon as Tommy's set was over, and now she returned with Lana and two glasses of wine in tow. They pulled over an extra chair, and Claire introduced Lana all around—"We met Kath here tonight, and you remember her friend Lily"—and the question of leaving seemed to fade. Lily finished her beer and wondered whether Tommy would join them. It began to seem inevitable, and her pulse quickened as she imagined what might happen. Tommy would drag a chair over and sit down, taking out her pack of cigarettes; she would offer them around, and Lana would accept one. There would be more beers, and more conversation that Lily didn't quite understand, and all the while she would have to work hard not to stare, not to gaze at the way Tommy's hair was artfully slicked back with that little wave, or the way her collar pressed intimately against her throat.

A shout went around the room—"Last call!"—and several women got up to go to the bar and buy their last drinks of the night, while others headed to the hat check.

"We should go," Kath said.

Lily nodded, and realized with a mixture of disappointment and relief that Tommy wasn't going to sit with them after all. She put on her coat, and she and Kath said goodbye to Claire and Paula—Lana politely shook their hands—and then they began to move through the emptying stage room toward the narrow bar area. Tommy was walking toward them, carrying two tall glasses of beer, and for a heart-stopping moment Lily thought Tommy was bringing one of them to *her*—but then Tommy passed her by briskly, a whiff of her cologne floating behind her. Lily turned her head to follow Tommy's progress; of course she was going to meet Lana and Claire, and there was Paula standing up to take one of the beers. Lily felt Kath's hand on her arm, and Kath said, "Are you coming?"

"Sorry." Lily followed Kath down the length of the bar, past women still nursing their final drinks, and through the black door and onto the sidewalk.

The cool night air was welcome after the smoky, stuffy interior. Women were standing in little clumps outside the club, lighting up cigarettes and talking, prolonging their nights out. Someone said there was an after-hours club a couple of blocks away; someone else suggested heading to Chinatown for some late-night chow mein. Lily glanced at her watch in the light of a streetlamp as she and Kath walked away from the club; it was two o'clock in the morning, and all the neon signs on Broadway were still ablaze. Men and women were emerging from the other clubs on the street, some of them stumbling drunk, others squealing with laughter. The entire city seemed to be awake, living a second life she hadn't known existed until now. When she and Kath reached the intersection where they had to part ways, they paused on the edge of the sidewalk to avoid the other pedestrians.

"I'll see you on Monday," Kath said a little awkwardly.

"See you Monday," Lily replied. She thought she should say something more, but she felt inexplicably shy—as though she hadn't just spent more than two hours with her friend in a nightclub full of gay women. Even the thought of those words made her nervous, and she was sharply aware that there were people all around them, and she was only a block away from Chinatown.

Kath turned to leave, and at the last moment Lily reached out to touch her arm. "Thank you for taking me," Lily said.

"You're welcome," Kath said.

The traffic was a moving river of red and white and yellow lights reflected in miniature in Kath's eyes. She smiled. Lily looked away self-consciously. Someone honked repeatedly, and a black car careened up Columbus, and the pedestrians nearby shouted at the driver to watch out.

"Good night," Lily said, stepping back.

"Good night," Kath said.

Lily forced herself to turn away and walk home.

She kept to the shadows of Grant Avenue as much as she could, walking quickly through the pools of light that spilled out the doors of the Sai-Yon all-night restaurant and the Far East Café. Her fingers were steady when she quietly unlocked the front door of her building; she was utterly silent as she slipped off her shoes and carried them up the stairs. The flat was hushed and dark and so quiet she could hear the faint sound of her brothers breathing as she passed the cracked-open door to their bedroom. The door to her parents' room was closed, and she tiptoed past quickly.

She rolled the pocket doors to her room shut behind her. She left the light off. She unzipped her skirt and thought, *This is what I wore the night I met Tommy Andrews.* She unbuttoned her blouse and felt the lingering traces of dampness in the armpits where she'd sweated. Normally she would air it out on the laundry line or put it in the wash, but she couldn't do that in the middle of the night. She unrolled her too-thick stockings and peeled off her girdle and unclasped her bra; the toes and creases and seams were all a little damp, too. It was incriminating: the residue of her body on these bits of fabric. She knew she should find it revolting, but she didn't; somehow she felt triumphant. It was proof that she had been to the Telegraph Club and breathed its warm, perfumed air.

She folded her clothes in the dark and gently laid them in the bottom dresser drawer. She felt for her nightgown and put it on, the pink polyester sliding cool as water over her warm skin. Her bed creaked slightly as she lay down and drew the covers up to her chin. She closed her eyes, but she wasn't at all sleepy.

She remembered the way Tommy had leaned the microphone stand over in one hand, the spotlight making her signet ring sparkle. She remembered the curl of Tommy's lip as she smiled at the woman in the green dress while she sang "Secret Love." And she remembered the hint of cologne she had smelled on her; there had been an edge to it that felt distinctly, confusingly masculine. It sent a giddy thrill straight through her—as if Tommy had run a fingertip right up her spine. She lay in her bed for quite some time trying to catch that scent again, as if she might call it into existence out of the sheer force of memory.

22

Saturday afternoon, Lily nodded off over the kitchen sink, her hands gone slack in the warm soapy water.

"You've been staying up too late reading again," her mother said.

Lily started, her hands jerking up and splashing water over the counter and the front of her blouse. One droplet flew into her eye, and she raised her hand up instinctively, causing dirty liquid to trickle down her wrist and into her sleeve. Her mother silently held out a dish towel.

After blotting her face and blouse, she returned to the dishes, fishing the rag out from beneath the stack of rice bowls. Behind her, Eddie was seated at the kitchen table doing his homework. Her mother was putting away the lunch leftovers, and down the hall she heard her father talking to Frankie. No one seemed to be able to tell what she had done or where she had gone Friday night, even though she felt as if it must be written on her forehead. It gave her the disorienting feeling that perhaps she had imagined the whole thing.

(The graffiti on the bathroom door—*Nancy + Carol*. Who were they?)

Sunday morning at church, she worried that someone would surely know she had stepped outside the bounds of her life as a good Chinese daughter. What if someone from the neighborhood had seen her Friday night?

(The Telegraph Club's black front door, swinging open to reveal that long narrow bar, the glowing lights overhead like distant moons.)

But she got through the church service and the potluck lunch without a single person mentioning they had glimpsed a girl who looked like her crossing over to North Beach in the middle of the night.

Monday morning, Shirley was the same as ever, maintaining the cool politeness she'd instituted since the dance. Shirley's obliviousness stung the most. There had been a time when Shirley noticed every new thing about her: a hair ribbon, a rip on her sleeve, shadows under her eyes if she hadn't slept well. Shirley barely looked at her now.

Only Kath knew. When Lily saw her at school, she felt a quick excitement go through her, and Kath's pale face colored. (Tommy's eyes half-closed as she crooned into the microphone she held to her mouth.) Of course, Kath said nothing about it. They sat in the same row in Senior Goals and listened in silence as Miss Weiland announced that there would be a standard air-raid drill later that week. Lily eyed Shirley, who had taken a seat across the room near Will, and it seemed as if Shirley could feel her attention, because she raised her head and met Lily's gaze.

Shirley's eyebrows drew together as if she were puzzled, and Lily thought, *Maybe she can tell.* How could she not? She was surprised by the strength of her yearning to have Shirley detect a difference in her—as if that would make her experience real.

(Tommy in the hallway by the bathroom, cigarette between her fingers as she looked at Lily with that tiny smile in her eyes.)

Shirley broke the gaze, and the moment passed. Lily felt deflated. Miss Weiland was distributing pamphlets about nutrition for their next Senior Goals unit. On the glossy cover was an illustration of an all-American family: a blond mother, a dark-haired father, and a blond girl and boy with freckled cheeks and wide blue eyes. They sat at a kitchen table set for dinner, where a reddish-brown meatloaf rose from a platter decorated with pineapple slices, and a pat of yellow butter melted on a mound of mashed potatoes in a green bowl. Lily had only ever eaten meatloaf in the school cafeteria, and the thought of its salty, slick interior made her queasy. She flipped the pamphlet over so that she didn't have to see it.

The wind whipped at Lily's hair as she and Kath walked home. They had made a habit of walking up the Chestnut Street steps together; fewer students took this route, so they could talk without being overheard.

"Did anybody notice you were gone?" Kath asked.

"No, I don't think so. Did your sister notice?"

"No. Peggy was asleep when I got home. You had fun, didn't you?"

There was a tentative quality to her question that surprised Lily. "Of course."

"I wasn't sure. You were pretty quiet the whole night."

"I didn't really know what to say," Lily admitted. She still didn't. She had wanted to talk about it with Kath all day—to comb through what had happened and what had not happened the way she and Shirley would have dissected a YWCA dance. But now, as she and Kath walked together through the cloudy, windy afternoon, she felt the same strange shyness that had gripped her after they left the club on Friday night.

"The first time I went," Kath said, "I was a little . . . overwhelmed, I guess. Jean told me it was the same with her. It's like you've been told about chocolate your entire life but you've never tried any, and then all of a sudden someone gives you an entire box, and you end up eating all of it, and you feel sick." Kath shot her a quick glance. "You just have to get used to it—to having chocolate more often."

They had arrived at the bottom of the steps, and Kath fell silent as they both started climbing. That morning when Lily got dressed she had come across the blouse she had worn to the Telegraph Club, folded in her bottom dresser drawer. When she started to move it out of the way she caught the faint odor of cigarette smoke, and then something else. She pulled it out and pressed her nose to the cloth, where she smelled the bar itself—a stale, boozy scent. (Standing against the wall of the club, plucking the fabric of her blouse away from the sweat on her back, the air thick with the exhalations of all those women.) She should wash the blouse before her mother discovered it, but she couldn't bring herself to put it in the laundry basket. She wanted to preserve it like a piece of evidence.

It wasn't like chocolate, Lily thought. It was like finding water after a drought. She couldn't drink enough, and her thirst made her ashamed, and the shame made her angry.

At the top of the stairs, she paused and turned to Kath. "I want to go again," she said.

She watched a smile rise from Kath's mouth to her eyes. The corners turned up. Her lashes, Lily noticed, were light brown.

An understanding seemed to bloom between the two of them. It felt like a coin dropping into one of the automated dioramas at Playland's Musée Mécanique, and a mechanized scene was now about to play: miniature women on circular paths would begin to move toward and around each other, as if in a dance.

"Then we'll go again," Kath said.

Lily smiled back at her, feeling a surge of happiness, and together they continued up the crest of Russian Hill.

They had only gone half a block when Kath reached into her book bag. "I almost forgot." She pulled out a magazine. "I saved this for you. My brother had it, and he didn't want it anymore, but I thought you might like to read it."

Kath was holding out an issue of *Collier's* magazine. The front cover was a painting of several strange-looking spaceships flying in formation toward a red planet. The headline asked, CAN WE GET TO MARS? IS THERE LIFE ON MARS?

Lily felt a sudden tightening in her chest. She took the magazine from Kath's outstretched hand. "Thank you. I can't wait to read it."

23

At fifteen minutes past ten o'clock on Wednesday morning, the fire alarms went off. Lily's heartbeat thundered up into her throat at the sound, until Miss Weiland waved her hands and shouted, "All right, all right, you knew this was coming. Everyone go in order to your places—in order! Do not run!"

It was the air-raid drill. Lily had completely forgotten about it. Last summer there had been a citywide one, involving mock evacuations and what seemed like hours of ambulance and fire truck sirens crisscrossing the hills. In the newspaper the day after, Lily had read that 169,000 imaginary San Franciscans perished in the wake of a fictional atomic bomb that had struck at Powell Street.

Now everyone got up, abandoning their notebooks and pencils, and headed for the hallway. High school students were too large to duck and cover under their desks, so they'd been told to go as far from exterior windows as possible, and to lie facedown on the floor, covering their heads and necks with their hands. Teachers had to do the drill too, and it was always disconcerting to see them dropping down like the students.

Lily followed her classmates into the hall and found a space on the floor, lying down and folding her arms over her head. If she smashed her elbows over her ears, it dulled the shrieking of the alarm a little, but it was an uncomfortable position, with her forehead and nose pressed against the polished concrete, and it was hard to breathe.

The first time she'd been forced to endure an air-raid drill had been in first grade; she still remembered because it had frightened her so badly. Their teacher had told them they had to practice hiding in case the Japanese attacked, and she remembered trembling beneath her desk at Commodore Stockton while several of her classmates cried for their mothers. She'd had nightmares afterward, but she didn't remember the details, only her mother waking her up in the middle of the night and saying, *You're dreaming, you're dreaming.* The drills continued year after year, although the enemy who might attack them changed. Japan was vanquished but Korea and China might invade, and now it was the Soviets who could drop atomic bombs. She had secretly welcomed their potential Soviet invaders, because at least she'd never be mistaken for a Russian.

Now she turned her head, even though she knew it was against regulations, and rested her head on her folded arm. Shirley was lying beside her, facedown. It was a surprise, because Shirley hadn't been anywhere near her in the classroom, but it also seemed entirely normal and familiar. Lily remembered lying on the floor with Shirley during other drills in other hallways, and somehow it was right that they would do this one together, too.

Under the blaring of the alarm, Lily moved her foot and nudged Shirley's leg. Shirley turned her head too, and they looked at each other. There was something funny about it: their faces mashed against the floor, their hands flimsy protection against potential radiation. Shirley's face twitched into a small, ironic smile, and she mouthed, *We're doomed.* Lily swallowed a giggle, and the alarms went on and on so loudly that Lily thought she would go deaf, and what was the point of this, anyway? The specter of nuclear annihilation was still frightening if she truly thought about it, but over the years she had learned not to think about it and to dismiss the drills as useless. If the Soviets did drop atomic bombs on San Francisco, Lily suspected they would all die, regardless of whether they knew how to hide in a hallway.

She made a face at Shirley, as if they were children, and Shirley had to stop herself from laughing too. Eventually Shirley turned her face to the floor again, and so did Lily, because they sensed the teachers coming by with their clipboards to check that everyone was doing as they were told. And finally—suddenly—the alarms cut off. The silence that followed seemed to ring for a good long while, eventually leaving a dull buzzing noise in Lily's ears. They weren't supposed to move yet, not until the teacher designated as their Civil Defense leader came to tell them the drill was over, but people were beginning to shift, turning onto their sides, lifting their heads to see what the delay was.

At last a voice came over the intercom, announcing, "All clear! All clear! Stand up and remain in place for roll call. Stand up and remain in place for roll call."

Lily scrambled to her feet. Her arms were stiff from where she had held them over her head. Shirley was brushing off her skirt, muttering about how needlessly loud the sirens had been. Lily saw Kath farther down the hall, stretching her arms above her head. And there was Miss Weiland, hurrying toward them with her clipboard. "Mr. Anthony De Vicenzi," she called.

"Here!"

"Mr. De Armand Evans."

"Here."

"Miss Lilian Hu."

"Here," Lily answered.

"Miss Shirley Lum."

"Right here!" Shirley said.

"Miss Kathleen Miller."

"Here."

Lily glanced over at Kath and wondered how they had become separated, because they'd been sitting right next to each other in class before the alarms went off. What if there had been a real bomb, and she had lost track of Kath in the rush to evacuate? The thought was disquieting; she felt an urgent need to go to her.

"Lily, will you come by the Pearl tonight?" Shirley said.

Startled, Lily said, "Tonight?"

"Yes, I'm working. Come over?"

Everyone was trooping back into Miss Weiland's classroom. Lily was still caught in the unexpected panic that had buzzed through her at the idea of being separated from Kath. But Shirley was looking at her expectantly, as if they were still best friends, and in her confusion Lily said automatically, "All right."

"Good. I'll see you later." Shirley waved as she went off to her seat on the other side of Miss Weiland's classroom.

"What was that?" Kath asked, falling into step beside her.

Lily was relieved to see her and flustered by her relief. It had only been an air-raid drill—everyone was fine. She replied, "Shirley invited me over. I guess she wants to talk."

She and Kath went back to their seats together, where they had left their notebooks open, sentences half-finished.

It was a slow night at the Eastern Pearl when Lily arrived. Shirley made room for Lily to pull up a stool beside her at the cash register, and she offered her tea and wa mooi. It all seemed so normal that Lily felt as if she had entered an alternate dimension—one where she and Shirley had never had a falling-out.

It felt nice, Lily reluctantly realized. She had missed the comforting, familiar scent of fried noodles and the sound of Shirley's mother barking orders in the restaurant kitchen. Maybe she had missed Shirley too.

"Look at that woman over there in the corner booth," Shirley said in a low voice as Lily settled onto her stool. "I think she's got to be a nun on the run."

Lily glanced at the woman in question. She was dressed all in black with a tiny netted hat on her head, and she was seated alone in front of her plate of chow mein. "Not a nun," Lily objected. "She's a widow."

"She's too young to be a widow. She probably fell in love with her priest and had to flee her nunnery to avoid scandal."

"If she only had feelings for the priest, she didn't need to flee," Lily pointed out. "She could just keep them to herself. If she fled, she must have had an affair with him."

Shirley looked delighted. "Yes! He's probably quite handsome, this priest. He's the Clark Gable of priests. No, he's too old for our nun—what about Rock Hudson? The Rock Hudson of priests. Don't you think he's handsome?"

"Of course," Lily said. "But isn't he a little *too* handsome to be a priest?"

Shirley's eyebrows arched. "There's no such thing. Why? Who do you think is the right amount of handsome to be a priest?"

"Oh, I don't know. I don't think she's a nun."

"Come on, play along. Who would be your handsome-but-not-too-handsome priest?"

Lily had the sudden sensation she was being tested. "Maybe . . . I don't know, Jimmy Stewart?"

"Too old," Shirley said decisively. "Do you really think he's handsome?"

"I suppose."

Shirley gave her a skeptical look. "Clearly you don't. Who, then?"

There was an edge to Shirley's tone that made Lily a bit defensive. "What does it matter? I think she's a widow. Her husband—he was probably ugly. Maybe she killed him and is running away to avoid the law."

"All right," Shirley relented. "Why did she kill him? Too ugly?"

Lily ignored Shirley's smirk. "He was horrible to her."

"This is becoming tragic."

"Sorry," Lily said. "I'm out of practice."

Shirley popped a wa mooi into her mouth, going quiet while she chewed it, and Lily wondered if she was going to bring up the reason Lily was out of practice with their game. But after Shirley spit out the pit, she said, "We've been friends for so long, Lily. Let's not forget that during our senior year."

Lily couldn't decide if this was an apology or an underhanded way for Shirley to blame Lily for what had happened between them. She took a sip of tea to avoid responding immediately.

"Truce?" Shirley said.

It wasn't an apology, then. But if Shirley was offering a truce, she was also admitting it wasn't all Lily's fault.

"Truce," Lily agreed, and she was rewarded with one of Shirley's most charming smiles.

"Good." Shirley reached for her hand and squeezed it. "Now, let's make this more interesting. I'll allow that she's a widow, but she has to have killed her husband for a more interesting reason. Maybe he was a Soviet spy!"

The woman in the corner booth lifted a forkful of wide rice noodles to her mouth with a gloomy expression. A woman alone in a restaurant was unusual. She must have gone through something traumatic, something that had separated her from everyone she loved. What if she had fallen in love with someone she shouldn't? Another woman, perhaps, like the girls in that movie, *Olivia*. Paula or Claire had said one of those teachers had committed suicide at the end of that movie. The woman in the restaurant needn't have killed anyone at all to be part of a tragic love story.

"Lily, what do you think? Are you listening?"

Lily blinked and took a sip of tea. "Yes, he must have been a spy," she said. But the game felt wrong now. She was relieved when the woman in black paid her bill and left.

24

Thanksgiving brought lowered skies and cold, drenching rain. Lily normally enjoyed Thanksgiving—it was the one day of the year that her mother cooked American food, which always seemed like a novelty—but this year she felt trapped by the gloomy weather. As she helped her mother peel chestnuts and chop onions and laap ch'eung[1] for the glutinous rice stuffing, her thoughts returned over and over again to the Telegraph Club.

She and Kath had decided to go again on Friday night. Jean was coming home for the holiday weekend, and Kath wanted Lily to meet her. Lily couldn't remember much about Jean from school, and she was curious about what she was like. Kath often spoke of her in such admiring tones, as if Jean had been a heroic explorer of new worlds, but Lily remembered Shirley's disgust at Jean and what she'd done in the band room. Lily knew it was ungenerous of her, but she couldn't help thinking that Jean must have been stupid, to let herself be discovered like that. She should have known better.

"Are you finished yet?"

Lily nearly dropped the knife as her mother's voice cut through her thoughts.

"Pay attention," her mother admonished her. "I need to start frying that laap ch'eung. Hurry up with that last one."

Lily bit back a sigh and returned her focus to the narrow red links

---

1. Dried sausage.

of dried sausage. When she was finished, she took the whole cutting board to her mother, who had already begun frying onions in the cast-iron pan. Her mother slid in the laap ch'eung in and gave it a stir.

"Bring me the mushrooms," her mother said, gesturing to the bowl on the kitchen table.

The telephone rang on the landing. She heard running footsteps as one of her brothers sprinted down the hall to grab it, and then Frankie yelled, "Papa! It's Aunt Judy!"

Aunt Judy didn't come up to San Francisco for Thanksgiving, since it was only a couple of days and Uncle Francis's family was much closer to them in Los Angeles, but she always called long distance. She would talk to her brother—Lily's father—first, and then the phone would be passed around to all of the children. As Lily waited for her turn, she washed off the cutting board and knife. The rain was still dripping down the kitchen window, and she hoped that it would stop before Friday night. She wondered if she should wear the same skirt and blouse to the Telegraph Club. Would anyone notice if she did? She wished she had a new dress to wear—something as fashionable as the dress that Lana Jackson had worn. Would she be able to pull off a dress like that? She was dimly reflected in the kitchen window, and she scrutinized her figure critically. She didn't think she had the necessary curves.

"You're daydreaming again," her mother said.

"Sorry," Lily said. She dried off her hands and brought over the glutinous rice, which had to be mixed into the pan of laap ch'eung and mushrooms, and then seasoned with salt and soy sauce. It would be stuffed into the turkey, which was waiting on the kitchen table behind them. Lily's mother had rubbed salt all over the skin earlier, and now as they approached with the stuffing, Lily thought the bird looked particularly naked, the breast glistening and bare. Her mother dipped her hand into the pan of glutinous rice and inserted fistfuls of it into the turkey cavity, holding the bird in place with her other hand. There was something disturbing about it, and Lily was relieved when her father appeared in the kitchen doorway and said, "Your aunt wants to talk to you."

Out on the landing, Lily sat down on the bench beside the telephone table and lifted the heavy black receiver to her ear. "Hello? It's Lily."

"Hello, Lily," Aunt Judy said. Her voice sounded a bit fuzzy over the line from Pasadena. "How's school?"

Lily dutifully reported on what she was learning in Advanced Mathematics, the only class her aunt was truly interested in hearing about. "Oh, I also wanted to tell you," Lily said, "that a friend of mine gave me an issue of *Collier's* with an article in it by Wernher von Braun about going to Mars." She had never before mentioned Kath to anyone in her family, and a flush of happiness rose inside her.

"I've seen it," Aunt Judy said. "We were passing that issue around at JPL. I've seen him too, Dr. von Braun. He was at the lab recently."

"Really! What was he doing there?"

"I don't know. And if I did, I couldn't tell you," Aunt Judy said teasingly.

"In the article Dr. von Braun said that we won't be able to go to Mars for a hundred years—not until the mid-2000s. Do you think he's right? Can't we go before then?"

"Oh, we'll go before then," Aunt Judy said confidently.

"When? How soon?"

"Well, we won't go in that massive spaceship he envisions. He's a brilliant scientist, of course, but it's impractical to start with such a huge endeavor."

There was an unusually formal tone in Aunt Judy's voice as she described Dr. von Braun as a brilliant scientist, as if she were reading from a press release. Lily wanted to ask what her aunt truly thought of the former Nazi scientist, but before she had the opportunity, her aunt continued, "We'll send unmanned rockets first, probably within your lifetime. And there are other things we can do much sooner."

"Like going to the moon?"

"Yes, but even before that we'll need to go into orbit. That will happen very soon, I think."

"How soon?"

Aunt Judy laughed. "Well, I can't say exactly. But 1957 will be the International Geophysical Year. It will be a great opportunity for research and exploration. Peaceful exploration. You know, there were a few other issues of *Collier's* that got into some of that—a moon colony and space stations. I'll try to find them and send them to you."

Aunt Judy turned the conversation to Thanksgiving dinner (she was bringing hsin-jen tou-fu[2] to Uncle Francis's family), and end-of-semester final exams, and then she asked, "Tell me—this friend who gave you the issue of *Collier's*. Who is it? You've never had a friend who's interested in these things, have you?"

Lily beamed to herself, ducking her head down to hide her smile even though she was alone on the landing. "She's in Advanced Math with me. Her name is Kath. She wants to be a pilot—she's even been in an airplane before."

"Is she new this year?"

"Oh no. We've been in school together forever but never really been friends until now." She added, "Maybe because this year we're the last two girls left in math. It's us and all the boys."

"I'm glad you have an ally. I was the only girl in most of my college math classes. You'll have to get used to it if you're going to major in math or engineering, but I know you won't have any trouble."

Her aunt was always supportive like this, always confident in Lily's abilities and dreams, and now she knew about Kath—her *ally*,

---

2. Almond jelly; a dessert.

what a funny way to think of her—and Lily realized how unusual Aunt Judy was. Shirley thought Lily's dreams were ridiculous; Kath didn't tell her parents what she wanted to do because they would think she was crazy.

"Just between you and me, I think women are better than men at math," Aunt Judy added slyly. "Don't tell your uncle Francis."

It seemed like such a grown-up joke to make. Lily swelled with pride at having been allowed to hear it. "I'm sure he already knows," she said boldly.

Aunt Judy chuckled. "You're probably right. Oh, I'd love to talk more but we'll have to do it later. Go and get Eddie, will you?"

Later in the kitchen, as Lily peeled potatoes under her mother's direction, she wondered again about the tone in Aunt Judy's voice when she talked about Dr. von Braun. Last Chinese New Year, when Aunt Judy and Uncle Francis had been visiting, they stayed up late talking with Lily's parents about China and the Communists. Lily had gone to bed by then, and she knew they all thought she was asleep because they'd never have discussed these things in the living room if they suspected she could hear them. Her parents hardly ever mentioned politics; even when they mentioned China they didn't address its Communist rulers.

Uncle Francis brought up von Braun first. He seemed especially rankled by the welcome that the American government had rolled out for the former Nazi. "He worked against us in the war," Uncle Francis said in a low, tight voice. "He should be in prison, not given free rein over the army's missile project. And yet there he is—free! While Dr. Tsien is under house arrest."

Lily hadn't understood the whole story the night she overheard Uncle Francis, but later on she'd learned that Dr. Hsue-shen Tsien was one of the cofounders of the Jet Propulsion Laboratory, and he worked for the American military during the war even though he was a Chinese citizen. Now that China had been taken by the Communists, he had fallen under suspicion and was accused of spying.

"I believe the American government is doing its best," Lily's father said.

"How do you know that?" Uncle Francis asked. "Dr. Tsien is a good man. He does not deserve this. It's not fair."

"It's not about fairness," Aunt Judy said. "It's about fear. They're afraid of Dr. Tsien, because Communist China stands independent and could still have a claim on him. Nazi Germany is gone. Dr. von Braun has no loyalties left to claim."

At first it had seemed far-fetched that Aunt Judy and Uncle Francis worked at a job that put them in the same circle as the famous German scientist, but then Lily remembered her family had unusual links to other powerful people, too. Her father had a friend in Berkeley who had been some kind of Kuomintang government official before the war, and now was petitioning Congress for American citizenship. Aunt Judy had described her mother—Lily's grandmother, whom she'd never met—as an influential member of 1920s Shanghai society, who had been friendly with Soong Ching-ling, the wife of Sun Yat-sen.

The late-night conversation about Wernher von Braun and Hsueshen Tsien fell in the same category: tantalizing glimpses into an adult world that seemed completely separate from the mundane reality of her daily life. It was disorienting when that world bled into this one.

Now, back in the kitchen, the turkey was beginning to scent the air. As Lily peeled potatoes, her mother sat down across from her with a basket of green beans and asked, "How's Shirley? You saw her the other day, didn't you?"

"Yes. Her entire family's coming over for Thanksgiving dinner. They're making three turkeys."

"My goodness! I'm glad you and Shirley are talking again. You two had a fight, didn't you?"

Lily was surprised. "How did you know?"

Her mother plucked the ends off the green beans briskly, *snap-snap-snap*. "You came home from school every day without visiting her."

Lily cringed inwardly at how transparent she had been. "It wasn't anything," she said dismissively. "Just a silly disagreement."

Her mother nodded. "Girls fight, especially at your age. It's natural. I'm glad you're over it. Shirley's a good friend to you."

Her mother's characterization of their friendship irritated Lily—as if Lily should be grateful for Shirley's friendship. "What happened with Papa and his papers?" Lily asked, changing the subject. "Did he get them back?"

Her mother paused briefly in her bean snapping. "Not yet," she said. There was a finality to her tone that told Lily not to push. "You haven't had anything more to do with the Man Ts'ing, have you?"

Lily shook her head. "No."

1952 — Francis begins working as an engineer at the Jet Propulsion Laboratory.

— Judy is hired as a computer at the Jet Propulsion Laboratory.

Feb. 13, 1953 — **JUDY takes Lily to the Morrison Planetarium at the California Academy of Sciences in Golden Gate Park.**

— Fighting ends in the Korean War.

1954 — The San Francisco Police Department launches a drive against so-called "sex deviates," raiding gay bars and other known gay gathering places.

— The U.S. Senate condemns Joseph McCarthy.

JUDY

Twenty-Two Months Earlier

Judy Fong climbed out of the taxicab and held the door open for her fifteen-year-old niece. Lily looked slightly anxious, but Lily often looked that way; Judy sometimes worried that Lily thought too much. She closed the taxi door and joined Lily on the sidewalk while they waited for Francis, Judy's husband, to finish paying the driver.

The long driveway in front of the California Academy of Sciences was thronged with cars, their headlights creating a moving sea of light in the early evening darkness. It reminded Judy of another night, years ago in Chungking during the war. She had stepped out of the building that served as her college dormitory to see a seemingly endless convoy of vehicles rolling down the dark streets, their headlights like lanterns floating down a river. They were Chinese army trucks with soldiers packed inside, rifles in their hands. She had stood there on the front step of the dormitory until she grew stiff with cold, silently watching the young men peering out the backs of their trucks, their eyes reflecting the headlights.

Francis bounded up onto the sidewalk beside her and took her arm, slipping it through his. "Ready?"

She emerged from her memory with a start. "Yes," she said. Sometimes, the past seemed to slide directly over the present, and when she came back to herself, the world she lived in now seemed like a fantasy.

The three of them turned to face the museum. The California Academy of Sciences, with its tall columns lit by white spotlights, was as grand as a Greek temple serenely overlooking Golden Gate Park. Judy couldn't see the dome of the Morrison Planetarium from their vantage point, but she knew it rose from the roof just beyond the front facade of the building. Everybody had been talking about it since it opened last fall. It was said to be the most up-to-date planetarium in the country, maybe even the world, and tonight it was their destination.

"Let's go," Francis said, and led the way up the steps.

The interior of the planetarium was round, with the pale dome arcing high overhead, and all the seats circled the giant mechanical projector in the center of the room. Supported on two massive tripods, it looked like a cross between a robot and a huge, legless insect—or perhaps a robotic insect. There were dozens of lenses on it that resembled eyes facing every direction. Each lens would project a certain star or cluster of stars onto the dome.

Francis was enthusiastically explaining the whole setup to Lily as they made their way to their seats on the far side of the planetarium. "It was all made here at the Academy by American scientists," Francis said, "so they didn't have to source anything from German manufacturers behind the Iron Curtain. They learned about optics during the war when they ran an optical repair shop right here in the museum."

Judy checked to make sure that Lily wasn't simply feigning interest, but her niece seemed quite engaged.

"What did they repair?" Lily asked.

They arrived at their seats, and Judy entered the row first, checking the numbers against their tickets. They had good seats—far enough away from the center to be able to see almost all of the dome without craning their necks too much.

"I heard they repaired thousands of binoculars," Francis said. "For the navy."

"Did you ever use binoculars?" Lily asked.

Francis was in China during the war too, and sometimes Judy wondered if they had ever been in the same place at the same time. She and Francis had discussed it, of course, but it was hard to determine for sure. She asked him, on one of their early dates, if he would have even given her a second look had he seen her in China. Here in America, there weren't so many Chinese women her age, but in China, the ratio of men to women was normal. He had given her a rather tender look and said, "Of course. I would have noticed you anywhere." She blushed at his words, and shortly afterward, he kissed her for the first time.

Francis was explaining to Lily that he did remember binoculars in his unit—he had been an engineer in the army—but he didn't know if any of them were repaired here in San Francisco. "Wouldn't that be something if they were?" he mused, as if taken by the idea.

The beginning of the show was signaled by the gentle crescendo of violins as recorded music began to play. The lights shifted, and now black cutouts of San Francisco's skyline became clear all around the periphery of the dome. Everyone leaned back to gaze at the pale glow above, and the projector became a fantastically alien creature silhouetted against a darkening sky.

Stars began to emerge, one by one. Judy shivered as the dome deepened to black, and the stars became so numerous they created a sparkling, depthless universe above. She felt as if she were sinking back into her seat, falling into the gravity well of the earth. And then, as the stars above her moved, depicting their nightly journey across the cosmos, she felt as if she were moving with them. Her stomach lurched and she had to close her eyes for a moment against the motion, but the allure of the vision was too strong, and she opened them again and marveled at the sensation that gripped her. There was no up; there was no down. She was floating, suspended between earth and sky.

A small white disc appeared. It was only the size of a pencil eraser, and then the size of a quarter, and slowly, bit by bit, its true face emerged.

"Welcome to the moon," the lecturer said as the audience gasped. "We are using state-of-the-art imagery here. This photograph, which we will be exploring in detail, comes directly from the Lick Observatory. You'll be seeing parts of the moon that very few men have seen before."

The moon grew in size; it hung above them in a giant black-and-white orb. Huge circular craters dotted the landscape. There were blinding white patches and deep, dark shadows.

"The moon is a world of extremes," the lecturer continued in his hushed, deep voice. "In the harsh light of the sun, the temperature can easily rise to two hundred degrees Fahrenheit, but simultaneously, in those darkest areas, it can be as cold as two hundred degrees below zero."

Judy glanced at Lily while the lecturer spoke. Her niece's face was illuminated by the bright moon above, which was reflected as a tiny black-and-white sphere in her eyes. Her mouth was open slightly. She looked like someone seeing a new world for the first time.

"The surface of the moon might be covered in dust. But we can't be certain about it until we send someone there to check. Someday, man will be able to travel to the moon in a rocket ship. Once he has reached the surface of the moon, he'll be able to drive a golf ball a hundred miles with one stroke because the gravity is so light. He'll be able to jump a dozen feet into the air if he wants. He will feel light as air."

Judy reached for her husband's hand. He laced his fingers in hers as they sat together beneath the projection of the moon. She felt an exhilarating distance from the Earth, and yet a comforting closeness to these people she loved. Francis, with his warm hand in hers; Lily, with her awe-stricken face beside her. *I am here*, Judy told herself silently. *This is San Francisco.*

After the show, Judy felt light-headed and a bit wobbly on her feet. She linked her arm with Lily's as they joined the crowd leaving the museum; everyone seemed a bit wobbly after their trip to the moon and back.

"Do you think that man is right?" Lily asked as they jostled their way outside. "That we can fly to the moon in a rocket ship?"

"It's a long way off, but yes," Judy said.

Lily's face brightened. "How long?"

"Years," Judy said. "What do you think, Francis?"

"I don't know. Thirty, forty years? Certainly within your lifetime, Lily."

Outside the museum, they walked across the wide plaza toward the steps that led down to the street, where taxis waited at the curb. Car engines rumbled to life in the parking lot beyond, their headlights illuminating people walking through the crisp night air.

"Would they really be able to jump so high on the moon?" Lily asked.

"Well, the gravity is much lighter there," Judy said. "I'm sure I could calculate how high a man could jump." Judy considered the math and laughed. "Oh, it would be funny to see!"

"They could hop on the moon," Francis said. "Like a giant bunny rabbit." He reached the sidewalk and began to hop down it awkwardly, flapping his arms as if he were a seagull.

Judy laughed. Francis was so childlike sometimes; she thought it was his Americanness coming out. "That's not how it would look!" Judy chided him. "It would be much more graceful."

"Like what?" he challenged her. "Show me."

Judy saw several bystanders surreptitiously watching them. "Oh, Francis, I can't—"

"Why not?" he called. "Come on, there's plenty of room."

Judy shook her head, but she slipped her arm out of Lily's and handed her purse to her niece. "Hold this," she said. Then, before she could second-guess herself, she elevated her arms as if she were a ballet dancer and lightly leaped across the sidewalk. "Very little gravity," she called over her shoulder. "Light as a feather!"

Judy saw Lily break into laughter. She saw Francis's face, surprised and overjoyed all at once. He leaped after her, and when he caught up, he enfolded her in his arms. She let out a giggle as she pretended to push him away, but after a second she relented and allowed him to hold her.

Francis was bold, and he kissed her gently on the lips. "My moon lady," he said under his breath.

In China, she would be embarrassed to be kissed by her husband in public, but this was America. Things were different here.

PART IV

Chinatown, My Chinatown

December 1954

25

Jean Warnock came striding out of the darkness beside Kath, smoking a cigarette, wearing a blazer and slacks, her hair cut short and a smirk on her mouth. Her eyes raked Lily up and down once, twice, and then she extended her hand and said, "Lily? I'm afraid I don't remember you."

Lily was a little affronted, but she shook Jean's hand. It was limp, as if her handshake hadn't yet caught up to the clothes she was wearing. Lily squeezed back more forcefully than necessary, as if to prove a point. When she released Jean's hand, she said, "You must be Jean." She refrained from adding, *I don't remember you either.*

"That's right." Jean attempted a wink. "Let's go. Kath's been telling me you two met a couple of girls there last time."

"It wasn't like that," Kath protested.

Lily fell into step slightly behind them, because the sidewalk wasn't quite wide enough to allow all three of them to walk abreast. Lily noticed, to her surprise, that Kath had put on slacks too. Lily wondered if she should have done the same, but the only pair of slacks she owned were cropped at mid-calf, as if for a day at the beach, not a trip to a nightclub.

With Kath and Jean walking ahead of her, almost like a shield, Lily felt freer to look around and take in the other people out at this time of night. It was mostly couples, but there were also young men walking singly or in groups toward the lights of Broadway and the

International Settlement. Sometimes one of the men eyed Kath and Jean, and once Lily noticed a man give them a sneer, but they didn't notice Lily. She was grateful to walk in the other girls' shadow.

At the Telegraph Club there was a couple talking to the bouncer, who said something Lily didn't catch, but which resulted in the man pulling out his wallet and handing over a few bills. The bouncer took the money and folded it into her jacket pocket, then held the door open for them with a flourish. From inside the club the sound of conversation and laughter escaped out onto the street in a brief, rising wave before it was snuffed out by the door. Jean and Kath approached the bouncer next, and Lily wondered if they would have to pay—she began to reach into her handbag for the money she had brought to pay back Kath for the beers—but Jean said, "It's been a while, how are ya, Mickey?"

Mickey did an exaggerated double take. "Jean Warnock! Back for Thanksgiving?"

"That's right. How's the show?"

"As good as ever," Mickey said. "This your friend? Oh, I remember you."

"I'm Kath. And this is my friend Lily."

Lily came forward hesitantly, feeling out of place among these three girls in blazers and slacks. "Hello."

Mickey grinned at her. "Welcome back, doll." Mickey opened the door and gestured them inside with a miniature bow directed at Lily, as if she were an empress.

"Thank you," Lily said self-consciously. She followed Jean and Kath through the black door into the dim, narrow bar, and the smell of the club struck her again—cigarettes and beer and perfume and sweat. In the stage room, the tables were nearly full, but they'd arrived slightly earlier than last time, and Jean spied a table in a corner, half obstructed by a black pillar. There were only two chairs, but Jean insisted that Kath and Lily take them, because she was going to the bar first and would return with drinks. Lily wasn't sure if she should offer to pay. It felt wrong for Jean and Kath to pay for her, but it also felt awkward to insist, as if she were among Chinese people arguing over a restaurant bill. It was loud in the club, and she'd have to shout through the noise—and then it was too late to offer because Jean had already left to go to the bar.

Kath had barely taken her seat before she jumped up again and darted across the room to grab a third chair, maneuvering it back to their table for Jean. Kath sat down again and said, "Hope Jean gets back before the show starts."

Lily had her purse on her lap, and she opened it and pulled out a couple of dollars. "I brought money." She held it out to Kath, who seemed surprised. "For the beer. I owe you from last time."

Kath waved it off. "No you don't, it was on me."

Lily suspected that she had more pocket money than Kath, but there was a hint of pride in Kath's tone that suggested she wanted to pay. It was confusing but also flattering, and as the spotlight came on and the pianist began to play, she let her hand sink down to her lap, still holding the money.

This time she knew what to expect, but that knowledge didn't blunt her anticipation. Instead it seemed to magnify it: the slow electric thrill that built from deep inside herself as she heard the opening bars of "Bewitched, Bothered, and Bewildered." When the murmur from the back of the room began, she turned in her chair to search through the dimness for Tommy Andrews's dark-suited figure. When she finally appeared, her face coming into the light for a transitory moment, Lily caught her breath. And then as she stepped onto the stage, her back to the audience, Lily felt that sweet, warm buzz spreading over her skin as if a charge were rising from her very pores.

When Jean returned with the drinks, Lily barely noticed. Unlike her first visit to the club, when she had squirmed with worry that someone might notice her, tonight she allowed herself to look, to sink into the looking, until all she saw was Tommy. Tommy's hands as she adjusted the knot of her black tie, the gold signet ring glinting in the light. Tommy's mouth, surprisingly pink and pretty, as she sang with a tiny smirk into the microphone. Tommy's dark eyes, lazily half closed or winking at a girl in the front row. The more Lily watched, the more she began to pick out the tiny feminine details that had eluded her last time. Tommy's face was smooth and softly rounded; her hands were small and slim. And beneath the starched white shirt and tailored tuxedo jacket, Lily detected the slight swell of breasts. That made Lily's face burn, and for a moment she had to lower her gaze to the table, where she saw the glass of beer Jean had bought for her. She reached for her drink and was startled to discover that she was still clutching her money, now crumpled and limp from her sweaty grasp. She smoothed out the damp dollar bills under the table, replacing them in her purse, and then picked up the beer. She took a trembling sip of the cold, faintly bitter liquid, and then another, and when she raised her eyes back to the stage she could watch again.

Lily leaned toward the mirror in the women's bathroom, raising her lipstick to her mouth. Behind her, the door to one of the two stalls opened and a woman in a slim purple V-neck dress emerged. She carefully balanced her handbag on the edge of the sink before she turned on the taps to wash her hands. She caught Lily's eye in the mirror and smiled. "I like that color on you," she said.

"Thank you," Lily said shyly.

"Where'd you get it?"

"At Owl Drugs, on Powell."

The woman dried her hands on the rotating towel. "What's the name of the color?"

Lily capped her lipstick and peered at the bottom. "Red carnation."

"I'll have to look for it." The woman reclaimed her handbag and took out her own lipstick, while Lily slung her purse over her shoulder. "See you down there," the woman said.

"See you," Lily said as she left. She felt buoyed by the brief encounter, as if she'd been admitted to a club she hadn't known existed. As she passed the line of waiting women in the upstairs hallway, she didn't mind so much if they gave her curious looks.

Downstairs in the stage room, Jean and Kath had met a couple of other women during the break between Tommy's acts. They had pulled up two more chairs and drawn into a loose circle around the little table. Lily's seat was still empty, and when Kath saw her she waved her into it, saying, "Jean ran into some friends from Cal."

Jean made the introductions. Sally was the girl in the green-and-white shirtdress, and Rhonda was the one in the lavender sweater and gray wiggle skirt. They were both brunettes who wore their hair almost identically, but Sally wore hardly any makeup, while Rhonda had a lush, dark red mouth, and eyelashes so long Lily thought they must be false. Jean seemed to be paying Rhonda quite a bit of attention, flattering her and offering to buy her another drink even though she hadn't finished her gin and tonic. Sally, meanwhile, went back to her conversation with Kath. They appeared to be discussing something they'd both seen on *Toast of the Town* the other night, an act involving two little girls and a dancing monkey. Lily hadn't seen the show and had nothing to add to the conversation, and the buoyancy she'd felt earlier began to dissipate. Kath, on the other hand, seemed very free and easy talking to Sally, leaning forward slightly, smiling as she sipped her beer. When Jean offered around a pack of cigarettes, Kath even took one, though she held it stiffly, barely smoking it. She miscalculated the trajectory of the ash when she flicked it toward the ashtray, and a gray cinder dropped onto the scarred surface of the table, breaking up and scattering like crumbs.

There was a hubbub on the other side of the room, and for a moment all of them turned to watch as a couple got up—the wife was wobbly, and her husband had to put his arm around her waist to keep her steady—and after the couple had departed, Rhonda turned back to the table and her gaze fell on Lily.

"There's a girl in my psychology class from Chinatown. Helen Mok. Do you know her?" Rhonda asked.

"No. I don't think so."

Rhonda lifted her cigarette to her mouth, the filter stained red from her lipstick. As she exhaled she said, "I've even seen Helen around here once or twice."

Lily felt a twinge of excitement at the idea of another Chinese girl at Telegraph Club. "Really?"

Rhonda nodded. "I don't think she comes here anymore though. I haven't seen her in a while."

"People come and go all the time," Sally said.

"Just like these bars," Rhonda said. "This place has been around for a while though. I wonder how much the owner's paying the cops."

Lily's eyes widened, but nobody seemed surprised by what Rhonda had said—not even Kath.

"I heard that the Five Twenty-Nine Club might be starting up a Saturday night show with a new male impersonator," Sally said. "Have you ever been there?"

"I heard it's all hookers and dykes, and you can get bennies there under the table," Jean said with a grin.

The words shocked Lily, but Jean said them as casually as one might say *girl* or *boy* or *aspirin*. She fought the urge to look over her shoulder.

Rhonda merely shrugged. "Sometimes it's fun to have a little sleaze with your night out, but they better watch it if they don't want to get raided."

They laughed, and Lily forced herself to laugh too, though she wasn't sure what was funny about it. Lily glanced at Kath, who looked almost exhilarated by what was being said, and Lily was ashamed of her own prudish reaction. The last thing she wanted was to behave like her mother. She shuddered inwardly. She tried to relax and drank more of her beer.

"What do you think of Tommy Andrews?" Sally asked. "I think she's pretty classy."

"Classy onstage, anyway," Rhonda said archly.

"What's that supposed to mean?" Jean asked. "Do you know her?"

"Not well. I know *of* her. She was with a friend of mine last year—before the femme she's with now—I forget her name."

"Lana Jackson," Lily said, and they all looked at her in surprise. Their attention made her nervous, but she tried to pretend as if all of this—the club, the conversation, these strange women with their strange slang—was entirely normal. "I met her last time we were here, in the bathroom line."

"Well, what do *you* think of Tommy?" Rhonda asked, tapping her cigarette against the ashtray.

"I guess I think she's . . . talented."

Jean snickered, and Lily went red.

"Don't tease her," Sally said. "She's just a baby." Sally looked at Lily empathetically. "Don't worry about it—Jean's barely out of diapers herself. We've been right where you are." She cast a frown at Jean, who raised her hands.

"All right, sorry, I didn't mean it." Jean smiled at Lily in a more friendly way. "I like Tommy too. I want to know where she gets her suits."

"They're obviously custom. Would you wear one?" Rhonda asked, cocking her head at Jean.

Jean laughed. "I can't afford it." She glanced across the table at Kath. "I think you'd like one."

Kath seemed taken aback. "A suit?" She shook her head. "Where would I wear it?"

"Oh, you'd find a place," Rhonda said, shooting an appraising kind of glance at Kath. "I can see it."

Kath looked uncomfortable. "Nah. It's not my style."

"Not yet." Rhonda sounded amused. "I can see them coming a mile away, those baby butches." Her voice was honeyed, teasing.

Kath was holding another half-smoked cigarette in her hand, and now she raised it to her mouth and took a shallow puff on it, the smoke emerging in a cloud rather than a stream. She shook her head, but there was a hint of a smile in her eyes, and Lily realized she was trying to hide the fact that she was pleased. Rhonda had apparently paid Kath a compliment, and Lily felt an electric clutch in her belly as she recognized it, *butch* like a blue ribbon awarded at the county fair, *baby* like a promise.

Kath's gaze flickered briefly to Lily, and then she tapped her cigarette against the ashtray, and this time she didn't miss.

26

ily, what are you doing today? I don't have to work!"

Shirley's voice vibrated through the telephone line with what Lily felt was excessive energy for just past eight o'clock in the morning. Dramatic music came down the hall from the living room, where her brothers were watching *Tom Corbett, Space Cadet*, the tinny notes crescendoing in an explosion as a rocket presumably blasted off. Lily rubbed a hand over her eyes and answered, "I have a trig problem set. Why?"

"Do it tomorrow. Let's go somewhere."

"Where?" Lily stretched the telephone cord out as far as she could to look through the window in her brothers' room, but the curtains were still drawn. "Is it going to rain?"

"No, it's perfectly nice. It's probably going to be sunny. Come on, I have to get out of Chinatown."

There was an undercurrent of urgency in Shirley's voice that surprised Lily. "I have to ask my parents. When do you—"

"Meet me on the corner in an hour."

"But where do you want to go? I have to tell them—"

"Tell them we're going to Aquatic Park. I'll see you soon!" And she hung up.

"I don't really want to go to Aquatic Park," Shirley admitted as they walked down Grant Avenue. "It's too close to school. We're there every day."

"Where do you want to go?" Lily asked. "The Embarcadero?"

The sky was overcast, and the flat gray light muted the reds and golds of Chinatown, giving them an ashy tint. The shopkeepers were opening their storefronts, unlocking their doors and poking their heads out to frown up at the sky, wondering whether it would open up on them.

"Let's go to Sutro's. We can see the Seal Rocks! And they have that museum, don't they, that's free?"

"Sutro's! That's so far."

"I have all day." Shirley gave a little skip of excitement. "Do you have to be back soon?"

"No." The wind caused Lily's skirt to flap against her shins. She suspected it would be freezing out by Ocean Beach, but there was a franticness to Shirley that told her she had made up her mind, and Lily knew there was no use arguing.

They took the B-Geary streetcar all the way to the end of the line, rolling through the Western Addition and past Fillmore and across the wide lanes of Divisadero. In the Richmond District, the avenues began their orderly march to the Pacific, each block lined with nearly identical houses painted in pastel shades or covered in cream-colored stucco. The farther west they went, the more space each house claimed. At first they'd been shoulder to shoulder with their neighbors, but eventually small plots of land began to separate them, so that each house was granted its own driveway and tiny bit of lawn. Out here the marine layer hadn't yet burned off, and clouds of mist drifted over the streets, phantomlike, as they were pushed about by the wind.

Shirley had brought a cloth bag with her, and she opened it on her lap to show Lily its contents: a takeout box from the Eastern Pearl containing chue yuk paau[1] and faat ko,[2] a couple of apples, and a paper sack of fortune cookies. Shirley pulled one out and cracked it open. The message, printed on a tiny slip of white paper, read, *You will be prosperous and lucky.* Shirley made a face and broke the cookie into pieces, offering some to Lily.

Lily took a piece and popped it into her mouth, crunching on the slightly sweet fragment. As they passed Twentieth Avenue, she said, "My mother wants to move out here."

Shirley had tied a green-and-pink-patterned scarf over her hair, and it was dimly reflected in the window. "Do you think you will?"

"I don't know. I don't think my father wants to move so far from the hospital."

Shirley didn't respond. She seemed pensive, her earlier excitement extinguished, and Lily wondered what she was thinking. They hadn't talked—really talked—in so long; she was a little afraid that she no longer knew how to talk to Shirley. Avenue after avenue went by; they were at Thirtieth, and Thirty-Fifth, and soon they would have to get out and walk the rest of the way.

"I don't think my parents will ever move out of Chinatown," Shirley said at last. "They can't." There was a tension in her voice, as if she were holding something back.

"Sure they could. Maybe they don't want to."

"What are they going to do? Open a restaurant out here?" Shirley was dismissive.

"They could still keep the Pearl open, and just live out here."

"No. It's too expensive. They can't afford it." Shirley looked at Lily. "Your parents could though. Why don't they?"

Lily was taken aback. Shirley's tone was almost accusatory. "I don't know."

---

1. Pork meat bun.
2. Steamed cake.

"They could get out of Chinatown. I don't know why they don't." Shirley turned to look out the window, but from the expression on her face, Lily knew her friend wasn't enjoying the view at all.

Point Lobos Avenue descended in a dramatic curve from Forty-Eighth Avenue all the way to Cliff House, perched on the edge of the land, before it swept south toward the long stretch of Ocean Beach. Fog still shrouded the Pacific, but it was a Saturday, and cars already lined Point Lobos as Lily and Shirley trooped down the sidewalk into the wind, toward Sutro's. The building rose up like a cinema just before Cliff House, with the word SUTRO'S standing in giant letters over the angled front overhang. Beneath it two windows flanked a row of glass doors, and over one of the windows a placard declared: IF YOU HAVEN'T SEEN SUTRO'S . . . YOU HAVEN'T SEEN SAN FRANCISCO.

"It's too foggy to see the Seal Rocks," Lily said. They walked past the Sutro's entrance to peer over the waist-high wall at the ocean, which crashed rhythmically against the jagged rocks along the shore.

"The fog will clear out," Shirley said, but she sounded doubtful.

Down below, the glass-covered pavilions of the old Sutro Baths were visible through the mist like a faded photograph. A gust of wind nearly ripped off Shirley's scarf, and she set down her lunch bag to tighten the scarf beneath her neck.

Ahead of them Cliff House was lit up through the fog, and Lily saw a family of four climb out of their Buick and head into the restaurant, the mother clutching her scarf over her hair just as Shirley was. As the doors closed behind them, the wind snuck up beneath Lily's skirt, whirling it around her legs and causing her to shiver.

"Oh, let's go inside. This is awful," Lily said, as the wind whipped her hair into her eyes.

"I kind of like it out here," Shirley said, but she relented at the look on Lily's face.

Inside Sutro's, they climbed the central stairway to the gallery overlooking the ice-skating rink. Signs posted all around the perimeter advertised the many attractions awaiting them: DOLLS OF THE WORLD and VICTORIAN ART and SEE ITO NOW! In the gallery, children were banging at the Goalee game, causing it to ring and ring and ring, and others ran back and forth, freed from their parents temporarily as they sought out the other coin-fed games. Several tables were covered by gaily striped awnings as if they were outside, but the daylight coming through the glass atrium roof was weak and gray. Down in the ice rink, the lights were on as if it were nighttime.

"Let's get some hot chocolate," Lily said. "I'm so cold still." She bought two paper cups of hot chocolate from a cart, and then she and Shirley found a bench overlooking the ice-skaters and sat down.

Carnival music played throughout the vaulted building, and Lily watched the skaters below attempting to move in time to the music. Only a few were actually good: a girl in a fluttering skirt that swirled out as she spun; a boy who leaped up and then landed, arms flung out for balance. Lily was surprised that more people didn't crash into each other. She had never skated herself and imagined she would be terrible at it.

"Don't you ever wish you could be like them?" Shirley asked, turning her cup of hot chocolate around in her hands.

"Like who? The skaters?"

Shirley nodded. "They just go out there and—look! That one fell over. Oh, he's getting up. He's terrible. I think he just wants to hold on to his girlfriend."

They watched for a while longer in silence. The hot chocolate was powdery and not quite mixed together. Lily tried to swirl hers around in her cup, but it didn't make much of a difference.

"I mean, don't you ever wish you weren't Chinese." Shirley spoke in a low voice, as if she were afraid to say it. "You wouldn't have to live in Chinatown, and you could do anything you wanted. You could go ice-skating anytime."

Lily looked at her friend; she had a slight scowl on her face as she watched the skaters. "We could go ice-skating if you want," Lily said.

Shirley took a sip of her hot chocolate. "No. I don't want to. That's not what I mean. It's just . . . ice-skating is so silly. Why would anyone do it?"

"For fun?"

"Exactly. For fun."

Shirley sounded bitter, which was unlike her. "Is something bothering you?" Lily asked. "Did something happen?"

Shirley shrugged, as if she were trying to slough off the black mood that had fallen over her. "No, nothing. I just get tired of the . . . the smallness of Chinatown, you know? Everybody knows everybody, and they're always poking their noses where they don't belong, and you can't do anything just for fun."

Lily wasn't sure how to respond. She took the last few sips of her hot chocolate. It was too sweet now, and sugar coated her tongue like sand. Shirley was right; Lily felt those constraints too. And yet she also felt protective of Chinatown. She didn't want anyone to disparage it—not even Shirley. When they were children, Chinatown had seemed wonderfully free to Lily: a neighborhood full of friends, with shopkeepers who would give her candied fruit and lumps of rock sugar. Of course everyone knew each other; it was like a densely packed little village, and her father was the well-respected village doctor. It was safe. Outside Chinatown was a different story. Everybody knew the boundaries. You stayed between California and Broadway, went no farther west than Stockton, and no farther east than Portsmouth Square. It wasn't until junior high, when she had to walk through North Beach to go to school, that Lily became comfortable with leaving Chinatown. Even then, she heard stories about Italian boys who beat up Chinese kids who made the mistake of wandering off Columbus Avenue.

"I want to go to New York," Shirley said abruptly. "Or Paris. Maybe London—or Honolulu! One of my cousins lives there. Anywhere but here. Don't you want to go somewhere?" She looked at Lily then, challengingly, and Lily suddenly wondered if Shirley somehow knew about the Telegraph Club.

"Oh, I don't know." Lily bent to set her empty cup on the floor at her feet, which allowed her to look away.

"You do. You want to go to space." Shirley gave a half laugh, unable to hide the trace of condescension in her tone.

Lily bristled. "Why did you want to me to come out with you today? Did you just want to pick on me?"

"Pick on you!" Shirley humphed and finished her hot chocolate, swallowing her own grainy dregs with a grimace. "I just wanted to get away for a few hours, that's all. Look, I'm sorry. I've been a lousy friend, I know it. I'm sorry. Forgive me?"

The sudden turnabout took Lily aback. She wasn't sure whether or not to believe her.

"Come on, let's go walk around. There's a whole museum in here, isn't there? Let's go." Shirley got up and reached for Lily's reluctant arm to drag her to her feet. "Come on. Be my friend today, okay? I need a friend."

Beneath Shirley's joking tone was something urgent, even a little desperate. Lily saw her friend's eyes gleam for an instant as if she were forcing back tears. Abruptly she dropped Lily's arm, picked up Lily's empty cup, and went to toss it along with her own into the trash can nearby. When she returned she had a contrite expression on her face, and Lily had to give in because she had known Shirley her entire life, and this was the first time Shirley had asked for her forgiveness.

27

Sutro's Museum was full of what some people would call junk: a lineup of horse-drawn buggies straight out of the Old West; a collection of Egyptian mummies in their ancient carved coffins; dioramas of ghost towns that would come to mechanized life with the drop of a few pennies. In one room there was a life-size mannequin of a Japanese woman called Mrs. Ito. She looked subhuman, crouching on the ground with one half-bared arm pointing to the side, her head balding and faintly apelike.

Lily and Shirley approached her dubiously. She had been carved out of wood and painted, and Lily wondered if she had been based on a real woman, and if so, what woman would have consented to have this mockery made of her.

Several Caucasian children were peering at the statue while their mothers stood behind them talking to each other. One of the little boys pointed at Shirley and Lily and announced, "Mommy, they're like Mrs. Ito!"

One mother had the grace to look embarrassed, but another said, "How wonderful! Excuse me, girls, are you Japanese? Would you talk to my boys?"

Lily froze.

Shirley grabbed her hand to pull her away, calling over her shoulder in a false accent, "No speak Engrish, sorry!"

Once they were outside the room they fled, running through the

Dolls of the World display—Lily was sure there were some terrible Chinese dolls there—and back up to the gallery overlooking the skating rink as if they were being chased. The running made the whole thing funny rather than awful, and when they reached the Marine Deck, where a long line of windows overlooked the ocean, Shirley said snidely, "鬼佬,"[1] and Lily laughed, even though it wasn't really funny.

Telescopes were mounted every few feet in front of the windows to enable visitors to zoom in on the Seal Rocks out in the ocean. The marine layer had finally lifted, and the rocks were now visible offshore. Shirley went to one of the telescopes and peered through, then glanced over her shoulder at Lily. "Come look—you can see the seals."

Lily put her eye to the viewer and squinted, twisting the scope until the rocks came into focus. She saw a few seals lying on the rocks, their glossy brown bodies displayed on the steep-sided island. One of them raised its head, and Lily saw its catlike whiskers as it swung around before diving sleekly back into the water. Beyond the Seal Rocks, the Pacific stretched out wide and gray, flecked with whitecaps, until it disappeared into the cloudy horizon. It felt as if they had come to the edge of the world—or at least as far from Chinatown as possible without leaving San Francisco—and those lounging seals were entirely unconcerned with petty human dramas.

A family came clattering loudly onto the Marine Deck, and Lily glimpsed the boys out of the corner of her eye. She thought they might be the same ones from the Mrs. Ito display. Beside her, Shirley was slinging her lunch bag over her shoulder and buttoning up her coat. "I'm hungry. Do you want to go eat lunch?"

"All right." Lily stepped away from the telescope and the two of them left the Marine Deck, purposely ignoring the family. Lily felt their eyes on her back all the way to the exit.

---

1. Foreign devils; derogatory.

They decided to take their lunch up to Sutro Heights Park, which overlooked the ocean. Lily bought two bottles of Coke from a vendor on the way. At the top of Point Lobos Avenue, the main gate to the park was flanked by two giant stone lions; inside, the road was lined with palm trees that waved their fronds in the wind.

Though Lily saw a few people wandering down the paths, the park was mostly deserted. She glimpsed the remains of concrete statues half-hidden in the shrubs. There was a fallen deer, its antlers broken, and the curve of a stone woman's breasts, one plump arm extended. She and Shirley walked all the way to the old parapet that circled the site of Adolf Sutro's Victorian mansion and found a bench facing the chain-link fence at the edge, right above Cliff House. A few tourists were taking photographs, but they weren't prepared for the chilly day, and after they left, shivering, Lily and Shirley had the view of the ocean to themselves.

Lily opened their Cokes while Shirley opened the takeout box. Lily selected one of the chue yuk paau and took a bite. The steamed bread was a pleasingly light contrast to the salty, savory minced pork filling.

"I don't know why you'd want to be Caucasian," Lily said. "You'd have to eat American food all the time."

"They can eat this food," Shirley said as she picked up a bun for herself. "We sell it to them!"

"You don't sell them these—they only eat the ch'a shiu[2] ones. Normally they eat—what do they eat?—creamed corn or something? Or tuna casserole!"

Shirley hid her mouth behind her hand while she laughed. "Meat loaf!"

"Liverwurst sandwiches!" Lily made a face.

---

2. Barbecue pork.

"Chicken à la king! What is that, anyway?"

"Some kind of chicken dish, with a cream sauce? I think I ate it at the school cafeteria once."

"Once they had creamed spinach, do you remember? It was this slimy dark stuff swimming in milk." Shirley made a sound of disgust.

"Why do they always put their vegetables in cream?"

"Well, I do like ice cream."

"That's not the same." Lily took the last bite of her chue yuk paau and wished she had some ginger ice cream to finish things off. "Do you want to split that other baau?"

"Sure. Don't forget there's also faat ko."

"Oh, yum." Lily reached into the box and broke off a spongey piece of sweet steamed cake.

"I wish I'd brought some taan t'aat,"[3] Shirley said.

"Mmm. Or tau sha paau."[4]

"You like those. They're not my favorite. I like the lin yung paau."[5]

Lily took another sip of her soda, the sweet bubbles fizzing on her tongue. She was full and content, and when the wind wasn't blowing, it was almost pleasant here. She watched the changeable gray of the ocean as it swelled and sank; the white lacelike foam that swirled on top like cream; the pummeling waves that crashed against the iron-colored rocks. It was constantly changing, yet always the same.

Shirley passed her a fortune cookie, and she cracked it open to pull out the white slip of paper. She popped a piece of the cookie into her mouth, chewed, and then read the fortune aloud: " 'Perseverance brings good fortune.' "

Shirley opened hers and read: " 'To know when you have enough is to be rich. Lao Tzu.' "

Lily crunched on the rest of her cookie and thought about the

---

3. Egg tart.
4. Red bean paste bun.
5. Lotus seed paste bun.

two messages. "They contradict each other. Don't they? Mine says to keep going, and yours says to know when to stop. Or maybe they work together?"

"They're just for tourists. They don't make sense." Shirley let her fortune go, and they watched the small piece of paper flutter into the air. It was caught by a wind current that lifted it over the chain-link fence before shooting it down toward the Pacific.

Impulsively, Lily got up to toss her fortune over the fence after Shirley's, as if the vast ocean were a wishing well. She leaned against the cold metal railing to watch the slip of paper twirl on a long draft down toward Cliff House until it vanished from view, too small to see. Something was under construction near the south end of the building. Trucks and winches had been left there, along with giant bales of thick wire. A Caucasian boy, perhaps five years old, was standing outside the construction zone, holding on to the hand of his mother, who was holding on to her hat.

"Lily."

She turned around. "What?"

"I'm going to enter the Miss Chinatown contest." The wind plucked at the edge of Shirley's scarf and tugged it loose from her hair, and she reached up to tuck it back in place. She seemed very calm, as if she hadn't announced an extraordinary thing.

Lily came back to the bench and sat down. "Why? This morning you said you wanted to get away from Chinatown. This is . . . the opposite."

Shirley dropped her eyes to her lap, where she had balanced the takeout box. "I didn't mean it—what I said this morning. Not really."

"Only partly."

Shirley closed the box and set it on the bench beside herself. "I just hate the Chinatown gossip, that's all. And I decided that if they're going to gossip, why not give them something to talk about?"

Lily studied her friend; Shirley crossed her arms defensively and wouldn't meet her eyes.

"What gossip?" Lily asked.

"What does it matter?" Shirley said defiantly.

At that moment the wind knocked the empty fortune cookie bag onto the ground and blew it across the pavement toward the fence. Shirley jumped up and ran after it just as the takeout box skittered toward the edge of the bench. Lily grabbed it before it tumbled onto the ground. Shirley returned a moment later with the crumpled paper sack, then opened her cloth bag so they could stuff the garbage inside.

The act of chasing down their trash had dissipated some of Shirley's tension; now she seemed looser limbed, or at least, resigned. "Anyway," she said, "George Choy came by the Eastern Pearl the other day to ask my father to sponsor the beauty pageant, and he said I should enter—Mr. Choy did—and I thought, why not? I'm just as pretty as last year's winner, and they never get enough girls to enter, and it would be good for business. If I enter, the Eastern Pearl will get plenty of advertising at the New Year festival."

A few years ago, the contest had been moved from the Fourth of July to Chinese New Year, and it had gotten bigger every year. The winner was expected to lead the New Year parade.

"I think I have a good chance of winning," Shirley said. "Don't you?" During her speech, Shirley's posture straightened; she ran a hand over the green-and-pink scarf covering her hair; and at last she cocked her head and gave Lily an almost coquettish smile.

"Well, yes," Lily said. If anyone had a good chance of winning the Miss Chinatown pageant, it was Shirley. And yet there was an unexplained sadness beneath Shirley's bravado, and Lily wasn't sure how to ask about it. Instead she said, "What do you have to do to enter?"

"I have to submit an application, and there's a small fee, but I can pay for it out of my savings. And then I have to get sponsors—I'll ask my parents, of course, and maybe some of our neighbors. Mr. Wong's imports store would be good, because I could wear their jewelry, right? And I was wondering if maybe you could help me."

"Me? How?"

"The Miss Chinatown contestants have to sell raffle tickets. I think most of the girls who enter have people helping to sell them—sort of like a support committee." Shirley gave Lily a small, modest smile. "I was hoping you'd head my support committee."

Lily was puzzled. "Why don't you ask Flora or Mary? They're better at that sort of thing."

"Because you've been my best friend for as long as I remember." A flush crept up her cheeks. "Not Flora, and not Mary. I want to do this with you."

A warm tenderness bloomed inside Lily; it felt the way a bruise ached when pressed. Shirley scooted over and linked her arm through Lily's and laid her head on Lily's shoulder, and Lily smelled the faint scent of Shirley's Breck shampoo.

"This is probably our last year together," Shirley said wistfully. "You could be anywhere next year. What if you get into college in Pennsylvania?"

"Pennsylvania!" Lily's uncle Arthur, her father's younger brother, had gone to medical school there, but Lily had never wanted to go so far away. "I'm not going there."

"Why not? If you got a scholarship—and you could—you would go. I've known you'd go somewhere ever since we were kids. You've always been the only one who was definitely going somewhere. Even if you just go to Cal, you won't be *here* anymore."

Shirley sounded so terrifyingly certain, and her certainty made Lily feel guilty, as if she had been planning her escape from Chinatown since childhood. As if she had always planned to leave Shirley behind. "You might not be here either," Lily said, hoping that the words would sound true. For good measure, she added, "Aren't you going to college?"

Shirley sat up, withdrawing her arm from Lily's. "I'm not the college type—or did you forget?"

Lily was embarrassed. "I'm sorry, I didn't mean—"

Shirley waved her hand to stop her. "I'll probably go to City College, but it's not going to make a difference. I'll have to work at the Eastern Pearl anyway, at least until I get married. That's what Rosie did. This is my last year of freedom, and I'm going to make it one to remember." She turned to Lily, a determined look on her face. "I know we've had some disagreements this year, but this is our last year. Let's do this together."

On the B-Geary back to Chinatown, they discussed their plan. Shirley would submit her application in the next two weeks, after persuading her parents and Mr. Wong next door to sponsor her. Lily would ask her father if the Chinese Hospital could sponsor her in any way, or at least allow her to sell raffle tickets there. Shirley needed to get a cheongsam for the contest, as well as an American-style evening dress, and she needed to practice her speech and determine how best to do her hair. And over Christmas, they would sit down with their friends and strategize over how to sell as many raffle tickets as they could.

Shirley wanted to make a list of what she had to do, so Lily found a stray newspaper on an empty seat, and Shirley borrowed a pencil from a woman seated across from them. As Shirley scribbled notes, Lily saw a small story about a construction project at Cliff House. There was an illustration of a "sky tram," which looked like a single streetcar hanging by a thick wire, that would travel between Cliff

House and Point Lobos, just past the old Sutro Baths. Once it opened next year, visitors could pay twenty-five cents to ride out to Point Lobos and back.

Lily realized the construction she had seen from Sutro Heights must be related to this sky tram. She wondered whether anyone would pay to ride this short, useless loop. The same view could be seen from the shore, for free. Would it be worth the cost to dangle above the rocky cliffs and salt spray, to get twenty feet closer to the Seal Rocks? The passengers would simply be going back and forth, and when they stepped out at the end of the trip, they wouldn't have gone anywhere at all.

28

t was as if Shirley had flipped a switch, and Lily was suddenly back in the clutch of their group of friends. In the weeks after the trip to Sutro's, Shirley monopolized almost all of Lily's free time. She had to accompany Shirley to fill out the Miss Chinatown application; she had to meet with their friends to form their Miss Chinatown committee; and those committee meetings inevitably turned into gatherings at Fong Fong's where the boys joined them. Even Lily's walks home after school had been claimed; Shirley almost always looked for her now.

That meant Lily had less time to spend with Kath, and as the days turned into weeks, Lily felt increasingly out of sorts. At first, being back in Shirley's good graces had been comfortable and familiar, but it didn't last. Aunt Judy had sent Lily another issue of *Collier's*, and the articles in the magazine made Lily wonder if she should major in aeronautical engineering in college, instead of math. She thought about talking to Shirley about it, but she knew that Shirley wouldn't be interested, and she might even be resentful of Lily's aspirations. When she was younger, Lily had accepted the differences between her and Shirley, because they had been the same in all the important ways. But now their differences seemed so vast, maybe even insurmountable. She wondered if she would have felt this way if she hadn't become friends with Kath.

And yet, as the end of the semester crawled ever closer, Lily began to worry that a distance was growing between her and Kath. She was understanding when Lily couldn't walk home with her, but after several cancellations, she stopped waiting for Lily after school. Of course, they hadn't been friends for very long; perhaps their friendship was simply shrinking back to the way it was before. Kath had her own friends, including the G.A.A. girls she ate lunch with, although Lily had gotten the impression that her closest friends, like Jean, had graduated last year. Lily wondered if Kath was going to the Telegraph Club with them, and the thought raised a strange jealousy in her while another part of her sank into a fatalistic gloom. The only thing she could conclude was that she didn't understand how her friendship with Kath worked, but whatever was happening—or not happening—felt wrong.

By the last day of school before Christmas vacation, Lily hadn't really talked to Kath outside of class since early December, though Kath was still perfectly friendly to her during school. Lily hoped to find Kath before the Christmas assembly, but there had been no time that morning, and then she was almost late to the assembly itself. Miss Weiland was waving at her to hurry as she rushed through the doors into the auditorium.

"Lily, over here!"

Shirley was down near the front of the auditorium, in the third row near the middle. As Lily made her way down the aisle, she finally saw Kath. She knew Kath saw her too, because their eyes slipped past each other almost furtively. Lily wanted to go over to Kath right now, but she couldn't. She had to edge through Shirley's row, bumping against knees while apologizing, to the seat that Shirley had saved beside her. Their friends were all here too; there was Flora sitting smugly on Shirley's left, with Hanson beside her, and Mary looking unusually sour-faced.

As Lily sat down, Shirley said to her, "We're going to my house after school, not Flora's. You're coming, right?"

"Of course," Lily said, but she was still thinking about Kath. She had to find her after school; otherwise she wouldn't see her until after Christmas break.

The assembly began with the choir singing Christmas carols before the sophomore class's Nativity scene. Lily twitched in her seat, worrying about whether she had somehow made Kath angry by reconciling with Shirley. It was clear that Shirley didn't like Kath, and the feeling was probably mutual. Or maybe Lily had done something wrong the last time they'd gone to the Telegraph Club. She remembered sitting silently at the table and listening to Jean and that woman Rhonda saying all those things she hadn't understood about dykes and paying the cops. Maybe Kath was embarrassed to be seen with someone as naïve as Lily. The thought made her shrivel up inside, certain that she had ruined their friendship.

After the Nativity scene ended, the dance club trotted onstage in their pink ballet slippers to the music from *The Nutcracker*. The girls in their pink tutus twirled with varying skill, kicking up their legs exuberantly as they spun. Each time they kicked, their tutus flew up, exposing their black leotards beneath in brief dark flashes. Lily had seen the dance club's *Nutcracker* routine every Christmas throughout high school, but this year she was newly aware of what she was watching. The girls' legs and the shadows between them; the curves of their thighs and calves; the cleavage made visible by their low-cut leotards. The dancers must have always looked like this, but Lily felt as if this was the first time she truly saw them: the weight of their bodies; their aliveness and the warmth of their pink skin. A couple of boys in the row ahead of Lily whistled and hooted, and when a teacher came down the aisle to shush them, Lily dropped her gaze to her knees as if she had been admonished herself. There was a difference between those boys' whistles and what she had been thinking, but she wasn't sure why or how. She only knew she felt caught, and her face flushed. She was glad the auditorium was dark.

Her mind flitted back to the club, remembering Kath's pleased expression after Rhonda had called her a baby butch. Lily had understood that at a gut level; she had seen it not only in Kath's hint of a smile but in the way she held her body. Almost like Tommy.

"I'll meet you at your locker in a few minutes," Lily told Shirley as they left the assembly.

"We have to go soon," Shirley said. "What do you have to do?"

"I have to go get something," Lily said vaguely, and slipped away before Shirley could further question her. She had seen Kath heading down the hall toward her locker and she wanted to catch her before she left, but the crowd seemed to be purposely getting in her way. Every time she dodged one person, another seemed to pop up in front of her, and by the time she reached the locker, Kath was nowhere to be found. Frustrated, Lily spun around, searching for her, and at last she spotted Kath going toward the main doors. She rushed after her and finally caught up, reaching for Kath's shoulder.

"Kath!"

She turned in surprise.

"I have to talk to you." Lily's hand slid down Kath's arm. She took Kath's hand and pulled her toward the edge of the hall as she sought out a quiet place. It was a zoo, with everyone rushing to pack up and leave. Lily saw the half-open door to the supply room just past the main office, and she tugged Kath after her, not stopping until they were inside with the door closed, the sound of the students' exodus abruptly muffled.

The room was little more than a closet, longer than it was wide, and barely wider than the door itself. The walls were lined with shelves; the shelves were stacked with reams of paper and manila folders and boxes of pens and pencils. Overhead a flat fluorescent light panel reminded Lily of the back corner of Thrifty Drugs—she hadn't been there since the last time she went with Kath—and she realized she was still holding Kath's hand. She let go. Her palm was sweaty.

Kath stood with her back to a wall of file folders, looking a little confused. "What's going on?"

Lily spoke in a rush. "I wanted to catch you before Christmas— I'm sorry I've been so busy lately. Shirley's taking up all my time with Miss Chinatown."

"I know," Kath said. "You told me."

The fluorescent light made Kath's pale skin look even paler and turned her blue eyes into a faded gray. Kath had cut her hair, Lily realized. Not to an extreme; it had just been a trim, but it was more closely shaped around her head now. Lily could see how Kath could comb it differently, and it would make her look almost like a boy. The thought was surprising, and as if Kath could read her mind, she slid her hands into the pockets of her jacket and shifted her posture, almost like a boy.

"Has something changed?" Kath asked. "Are you running for Miss Chinatown too?"

Lily's eyebrows shot up. "Me? Oh no. I'm no beauty queen."

Kath smiled a little. "I don't know about that."

Lily's face heated up. She looked past Kath's shoulder at the stacks of manila folders and bit her lip. She couldn't remember what she had wanted to say anymore. She thought wildly of Rhonda and the *Nutcracker* dancers and her awareness of Kath's sudden boyishness—or had it always been there?

"What's going on?" Kath asked again. "Is something bothering you? I know you've been busy lately . . ." Kath gave her an uncertain look.

"I'm sorry," Lily said awkwardly. "I feel like—like something's wrong. Is something wrong? Between us?" She twisted her hands together, her flushed face going even hotter.

Kath gave her a funny look, wariness combined with surprise. "I don't—why do you think something's wrong?"

"Is it because of Shirley? She's very demanding, and I don't want you to think that I don't want—don't want to be your friend." Lily flinched at her clumsy phrasing.

Kath shifted, readjusting the strap of her book bag, and her wariness seemed to increase. "To be honest, she doesn't seem like that good of a friend."

"She's my best friend," Lily said, and then sighed.

"Okay," Kath said. It sounded like a question.

"It's just that I've known her my whole life," Lily said, trying to explain. "I don't—I can't—it's not easy to—to be around her sometimes, but I can't turn my back on her. It's our senior year." She didn't know how to make Kath understand the way Shirley had always been there; the way Lily knew Shirley always would be there, even if Lily went away to college and Shirley stayed in Chinatown. Lily would always have to come home. "It's our last year together here." Lily realized she was quoting Shirley back to Kath.

"So, what are you saying? You're going to be busy until after Miss Chinatown's over?" Kath frowned and shook her head. "I guess I don't understand. I thought we were—" Kath cut herself off, sounding frustrated.

"No, that's not what I'm saying. I . . ." Lily trailed off. It was as if the English language had failed her. She couldn't find the right words for this dammed-up feeling inside, as if she were denying herself something absolutely vital, and she didn't know why.

And then, abruptly, she realized this had nothing to do with Shirley at all.

She missed Kath. She missed having Kath to talk to, yes, but she also missed having Kath listen to her. Rockets to the moon didn't seem so far-fetched when Kath listened to her. She made previously unimaginable things seem possible.

She had wanted to ask Kath when she could go back to the Telegraph Club, but now she felt as if she had made everything worse, and she stared down at the floor miserably.

"Maybe I should go," Kath said quietly. "I feel like I'm making you upset."

"No, I'm doing this all wrong," Lily said. A rush of longing came over her. She needed to fix this. To *show* Kath what she couldn't say.

Lily reached out and impulsively took Kath's hand in hers. Kath started, but then she let Lily hold her hand.

Lily knew immediately that this was different. It wasn't like grabbing Kath's hand to pull her into the supply room. Instinctively, Lily ran her thumb across Kath's palm, feeling the swell of Kath's flesh and the delicate thread of the vein in her wrist, the fluttering of Kath's pulse beneath her fingertip. She heard Kath catch her breath.

"Let's go to the club again," Lily said softly, looking at their joined hands. She had never noticed before that Kath's skin was so white that it made her own look almost golden brown.

There was a pause, just long enough that Lily's heart began to sink, and then Kath said hesitantly, "Do you . . . do you think you'll have any time over Christmas break?"

"I'll have time!" Lily looked up in excitement, and Kath's fingers tightened over hers. "When do you want to go?" Lily asked.

Kath looked like she didn't quite believe her yet. "Jean wanted to go New Year's Eve, but it's too expensive. There's a cover charge. I asked her if she wanted to go on December thirtieth instead."

"What did she say?"

"She hasn't decided yet. I was going to ask you if you wanted to go, but I didn't know if . . . Do you want to go then?"

Kath's hair was short enough that Lily could see the tips of her ears now, the pinkness of her skin darkening, like color coming into a rose. Lily knew she was blushing too, but for an exhilarating moment, she didn't care.

"Yes," she said. "Yes."

29

When Lily was younger she'd thought of Shirley's house as a marvelous kind of maze. All of the rooms, large and small, were crowded with Chinese knickknacks: jade statues in all sorts of nooks; ink-brush paintings of faded yellow and brown landscapes; silk hangings and screens shoved into the back corners. Over the years, various members of Shirley's extended family had lived there—uncles and aunts, grandparents and visiting cousins—but now it was only Shirley's immediate family. Since Shirley's older sister, Rosie, had gotten married and moved out, there were only six of them occupying the two floors above the Eastern Pearl.

Today Shirley led Lily, Flora, and Mary into the living room on the third floor. Its windows overlooked Sacramento Street, and Lily and Shirley had spent many an hour leaning out those windows, surveying the activity on the street below and keeping an eye on who came to the restaurant. It was too chilly for the windows to be open today, though, and Shirley had to turn on the lamps for light. It was a formal room, outfitted with a set of rosewood Chinese furniture and a trio of Ch'ing dynasty vases on the mantel over the cold fireplace. A family altar was set up in one corner, with small black-and-white photos taped to the wall above the bowl of half-burned incense sticks. The faint, sweet scent of incense lingered in the room, above the aroma of fried noodles that always clung to the Eastern Pearl.

Today's task was to work together on Shirley's speech. Mary

shuffled through her notes while Flora proudly reported that her father was going to buy a couple of hundred raffle tickets.

"That's wonderful," Shirley gushed. "You have some competition, Lily."

Lily was startled. "I do?"

"I'm sure the hospital board will buy a thousand tickets," Flora said smoothly.

Mary almost smiled, but hid it by reaching for some of the dried cuttlefish that Shirley had poured into a bowl on the coffee table.

Shirley opened her notebook. "All right. What should I say in my speech to the judges? It's supposed to be about why I'm the right candidate to be Miss Chinatown."

"Well, why do you want to be Miss Chinatown?" Mary asked.

"Because you're ambitious?" Lily suggested.

"She can't say that," Flora objected. "She has to be modest."

"Because you're beautiful," Mary said.

"She can't say that either," Lily said. "What did they say last year? Miss Chinatown has to be good, serene, and industrious. Well, you are industrious." She popped a strand of cuttlefish in her mouth; it was chewy and salty and fishy, with a slight spicy bite.

Shirley batted her eyelashes. "I'm serene as well!"

"Then you'll just have to lie about the good part," Lily said.

"I'm perfectly good!" Shirley said.

"Depends on what you mean by good," Mary joked.

Lily laughed while Shirley pretended to be hurt. Flora held a hand over her mouth as she giggled.

"I heard that Donna Ng is dancing at the Forbidden City now," Mary said, eyes wide to show she was scandalized by the rumor. Donna Ng had been last year's runner-up.

"I heard Miss Chinatown Los Angeles is auditioning for movies," Flora said.

Shirley struck a pose in her chair, head tilted back as if she were gazing into the distance. "Do you think I should audition for a movie?" she asked.

"Yes!" Mary said.

"There aren't very many movies with Chinese girls in them," Lily said. "Not here anyway."

"You could go to Hong Kong," Flora suggested.

"Well, first I'll try Hollywood," Shirley said confidently. "I bet they would cast me."

The light from the standing lamp was perfectly positioned to shine directly onto Shirley's face, almost like a spotlight. And Lily found it quite easy to imagine her on the silver screen. Shirley relished attention, but she also knew how to turn that desire to be looked at into something coquettish and somehow flattering to the person who was looking.

Then Shirley broke the pose and crossed one leg over the other, bobbing one slippered foot up and down in the air. "Come on, girls, what should I say?" she asked, leaning over to grab several strings of cuttlefish. She chewed on them like an old Chinese woman who didn't mind the fishy stink that would cling to her afterward.

"I know," Lily said, and everyone turned to look at her. "You want to be Miss Chinatown because this is your home. You grew up here, you love this place, and you want to help represent it to the rest of America."

Shirley was scribbling down what Lily said. "Yes, exactly. That's perfect." She smiled at Lily and added, "I'm so glad you're here."

It was the first time anyone had acknowledged, even obliquely, that for a little while, Lily had been gone. Flora and Mary looked at her a bit guiltily. Lily took some more cuttlefish.

On Christmas Eve, Frankie played a shepherd in the Christmas Nativity tableau at church. He had acquired a fake brown beard and tied it around his head with kitchen twine. Due to his role, Lily and her family had to arrive at church early. While she waited outside the sanctuary with Eddie and her father—her mother had gone off with Frankie—she wondered whether Kath was attending a mass at Saints Peter and Paul. She wondered if Kath was thinking about her. What if they were thinking of each other at the same time? The idea made her pulse quicken.

It wasn't long before friends began to arrive, and she had to pretend she was glad to see them. First, her father's colleagues from the Chinese Hospital and their families, and then a group of students from China who were studying at Cal and wanted to be introduced to her father. She had to shake their hands and speak to them in her terrible Mandarin. At last, everyone dispersed among the pews: Lily with her father and Eddie; Shirley with her family across the aisle; the Chinese students at the back. Her mother slid in next to Lily a moment before the choir began to sing, and Lily raised her eyes to the altar to watch.

She fidgeted as young Joseph and Mary took their places. Her coat was laid over her knees and it was too much like a blanket. She tried to fold it up, but she elbowed her mother in the process. "Sorry," she whispered, and her mother frowned as she took the coat and folded it for her as if she were a little girl.

Lily glanced across the church at Shirley, who was watching the tableau with a blank expression on her face, as if her mind was elsewhere too. Lily realized that Shirley had changed her hair. She had done it subtly, but somehow she had combed it back and pinned it in a way that made her look older, more sophisticated. There was something in Shirley's posture—shoulders back, head lifted—that reminded Lily of Lana Jackson.

Instantly Lily remembered the smell of the Telegraph Club, the sound of the piano and glasses knocking against the table. Her thoughts turned to Kath and the last time she'd seen her; the feel of their hands twined together; their promise to meet on the night before New Year's Eve.

No one in this church knew she had been to the Telegraph Club or that she would go again. No one. The thought was disorienting, as if she had lived a second life in a separate dimension, and she had to curl her fingers over the hard wooden edge of the pew in order to remind herself of where she was.

One of the children was reading from the book of Luke in a high, childish voice: "And she gave birth to her firstborn son and wrapped him in swaddling cloths, and laid him in a manger, because there was no place for them in the inn." Young Mary—a Chinese girl in a brown peasant-style dress with a blue cloth over her hair—carefully set a swaddled baby doll inside a wooden manger lined with hay. Someone had built that manger years ago; Lily recognized it from Christmases past.

Lily had played the part of a shepherd once in the Christmas tableau, when she was about nine or ten. She had been the only girl to play a shepherd, and in fact she had argued her way into the role, because Shirley had been cast as Mary and that was the only role for a girl. She remembered saying to the Sunday school teacher: "It's not fair if Shirley's the only girl in the play!" The teacher relented and told her that she could be a shepherdess, but Lily insisted that she was a shepherd, just like the boys. She had been so proud.

Now she wondered, a bit tensely, if it had meant something. Had Kath also played a shepherd in her church's pageant? She suddenly envisioned all the women she had met at the Telegraph Club as little girls, every one of them dressed up as a shepherd boy or even a wise king, boys' robes hiding their dresses, false beards covering their girlish faces.

The shepherds were moving across the front of the sanctuary, surrounding Mary and Joseph and the baby doll Jesus. Frankie was gripping his shepherd's crook fiercely, completely invested in his role. Lily noticed that none of the shepherds were girls this year; they were all boys.

1937	Japan invades China.
1940	Edward Chen-te Hu (胡振德) is born.
1941	United States enters World War II.
1942	Joseph joins the U.S. Army and becomes a naturalized U.S. citizen.
1943	The Chinese Exclusion Act is repealed.
Mar. 25, 1943	**GRACE and her family attend the parades in honor of Madame Chiang Kai-shek's visit to San Francisco.**
1944	The "Suicide Squad" is formalized as the Jet Propulsion Laboratory, operating under the Army.
1945	World War II ends.

GRACE

Eleven Years Earlier

Chinatown was thick with flags and streamers and flowers: red, white, and blue American and Chinese flags; long red ribbons fluttering from lampposts; white-petaled apricot blossoms with their soft pink hearts blushing in polished windows. Madame Chiang Kai-shek was visiting San Francisco, and the sun itself seemed to glow with particular warmth to mark her arrival, slanting between the buildings to gild every flag and streamer in golden light.

Grace Hu had caught the fever that gripped the entire city. Earlier that morning she staked out a spot on Grant Avenue between a corner kiosk and a lamppost to watch China's first lady process through Chinatown. Grace's mother had dragged an empty crate onto the curb and sat there with two-year-old Eddie perched on her lap, miraculously calm for the moment. Lily, who was six, leaned back against Grace as they waited. That afternoon, Lily would join thousands of Chinatown's children in a parade through Civic Center, and Grace would march with her, one of dozens of volunteer mothers who would corral the children through the city. Now, Grace imagined, was the calm before that storm.

"佢話佢好虛弱," Grace's mother said. "無論佢走到邊度, 都有白車跟住佢。"[1]

---

1. They say she is very frail. She has an ambulance following her wherever she goes.

"但佢一定要好堅強先可以橫跨美國演講,"[2] Grace said. "為中國佢會忍受一切。"[3]

Grace's knowledge of her mother's Cantonese dialect was limited to what was spoken at home. She couldn't always fully understand when her mother talked about politics, but she knew her mother well enough to hear the cynicism in her tone. She was about to ask her what exactly she meant when Lily interrupted.

"Mama, when will she get here?" Lily asked.

"Soon," Grace said.

"But you said that a long time ago," Lily complained.

Grace laughed and squeezed her daughter close, and as Lily squealed half in protest, half in laughter, Grace bent down and said, "Any minute now. Any minute!"

Eddie heard the anticipation in her voice and reached for her, his little fingers spreading wide. She tickled his pink palm with the tip of her finger and smiled as he giggled. Watching her son laughing on her mother's lap made her realize she didn't want to squabble with her mother about Madame Chiang. She wanted to enjoy the day.

Her husband had joined the U.S. Army a year ago, and today was the first day she had felt optimistic about the war. She was sure that Madame Chiang's tour of America could only bring greater American support to China in its struggle against imperial Japan. She felt a distinct pride that her husband was part of the effort. Though he couldn't tell her much about what he was actually doing, she knew that he had been sent to China, and that he was working to save the lives of men from both of his countries: his homeland and his new, adopted nation.

At last Grace heard the rising roar of the crowd heralding Madame Chiang's arrival at the gates of Chinatown. Grace's mother

2. But she must be very strong to endure this tour across America.
3. She will endure whatever she needs to endure for China.

stood, lifting Eddie in her arms so that he too could see the approaching motorcade. Those in the crowd were waving their flags excitedly. Their cheers drowned out the sound of the motorcade's engines, and everyone leaned forward in unison, yearning to catch a glimpse of the one woman who had come to embody all of China.

It was rumored that Madame Chiang might get out of her limousine and walk along Grant Avenue, and as the car rolled up the street, everyone waited for her to do just that, but she didn't stop. The dark-suited secret service men walking alongside the motorcade only gazed grimly back at the spectators from beneath the brims of their fedoras. But finally there it was—the limousine bedecked with flags, the polished fenders and windows gleaming in the sunlight. Grace urged her daughter to stand on the wooden crate so she could see China's first lady.

Grace spotted the flutter of a white handkerchief from the back seat—Madame Chiang was waving at them, but she didn't get out of the car. Everyone was saying that she must be too exhausted; and besides, she was about to go visit the leaders of Chinatown at the Six Companies headquarters. There was no time to linger here, greeting the ordinary Chinese of America. They should cheer louder, so she would know that the American Chinese supported her. Grace reminded herself, not for the first time, that Madame Chiang was practically half American, having been educated in the United States. She clung to this idea as the motorcade disappeared and was followed by the St. Mary's drum corps, beating a merry rhythm just as if it were Chinese New Year.

"Mama, I thought the parade was this afternoon," Lily said.

"There is another one this afternoon. This one is to welcome Madame Chiang to Chinatown."

"Two parades! In one day?"

"Yes, two parades."

"This madame must be very important."

Grace smiled at her daughter. "Yes. She is a very important Chinese woman, indeed."

The disadvantage of being part of a parade, Grace realized, was that one didn't get to see the rest of it. But the historic moment must be appreciated, she told herself, as she marched back and forth to keep an eye on the twenty restless children she had been charged with supervising. Her group was but one of dozens, adding up to what she had heard was thousands of children. They were all dressed in traditional Chinese clothes, ranging from colorful caps tasseled in gold to white silk pajamas embroidered with pink flowers. Lily and her friend Shirley wore matching sky-blue silk trousers and mandarin-collared jackets with yellow frog buttons. They were as enraptured with their costumes as they were with the importance of their endeavor: representing the young Chinese in America. The responsibility, imparted to them by Grace and the other mothers, seemed to rest lightly on their slim shoulders. They were simply thrilled to be gathered together with their friends beneath a clear afternoon sky on what should have been a school day.

When it was finally their time to join the parade, Grace lined up her charges and led them toward Civic Center. The crowds that lined Polk Street were thirty, forty people deep; Grace couldn't see where they ended. As they neared City Hall, the cheering became thunderous, and she could feel the excitement rattling her bones, as if an earthquake were shaking the confetti-covered streets.

They said that Madame Chiang was watching the parade from the balcony above the entrance to City Hall. Grace gazed up between the columns and saw tiny people there, but she couldn't recognize anyone. She didn't even see the white flash of Madame Chiang's handkerchief, which she must surely be waving at the masses gathered below her.

Grace noticed a plane flying overhead, the groan of its engine swallowed by the cheering crowd. It pulled a wide white banner painted with a dark circle. The sight of it caused a sudden drop in her mood. It was a warplane towing a target sleeve out to the ocean, where it would be used for machine gun practice by navy pilots rehearsing their attacks against the Japanese. She wondered if Madame Chiang saw it, too.

When the Lums invited the Hus to join them for dinner at their home after the parade, Grace was grateful to accept. The day had been exhilarating but exhausting, and she didn't want it to end by taking the children home to their small, dark apartment.

Grace had often secretly envied the Lums. There was something very appealing to her about their large, boisterous family, with many generations and cousins all living together above their restaurant. And she admired the ease with which Ruby Lum, Shirley's mother, managed the entire household. There was a time, before Lily was born, when Grace had thought she would move to China with Joseph and be part of his family, as was proper for a Chinese wife, but the Japanese invasion of Shanghai had scuttled those plans. Sometimes she was still resentful about it. Instead of taking her rightful position in Joseph's family as the wife of the eldest son, she had been relegated to this faraway city alone. She knew she should be grateful to her mother for moving in with her to help with the children while Joseph was in the army, but she struggled to find her gratitude. She felt as if she had somehow moved home again, like a penniless widowed daughter, even though the situation was the opposite.

She could never let Joseph know she felt this way. To think that she would envy the wife of a restaurant owner—even a successful one!—over her own position as the wife of a Stanford-educated doctor. In China, Joseph's family would outrank the Lums, but here in America, Grace wasn't sure the same social stratification applied. People treated Joseph with respect to his face, but Grace knew that to many of Chinatown's residents—all those old bachelors crowded six to a room—Dr. Joseph Hu was an uppity Shanghainese who didn't speak their language.

All of this crossed her mind as she followed her mother up the stairs to the Lums' living room. She wondered what Madame Chiang would think of the Lums. Their home was cluttered with Chinese furniture and paintings, but it was a pleasant sort of clutter, speaking to the family's success. Lily and Shirley were already running back to the room Shirley shared with her sisters, and though Grace told them to be quiet, she knew they wouldn't listen. Eddie was fussy, and he took some time to settle down for a much-needed nap. By the time Grace returned to the living room, Ruby had already had food brought up from the restaurant downstairs. On the dining table were platters of fried noodles, water spinach, and braised fish. Rosie, the oldest Lum daughter, carried in a stack of bowls, a dozen flat-bottomed spoons and a container of chopsticks, and Ruby brought a tureen of pork bone soup from the family's small kitchen.

The dinner was casual and loud. Rice wine was poured, and the older men of the Lum family (the younger ones had enlisted in the army) started to talk very brashly about the war—how America would send airplanes and guns and soldiers and bombs, how the Japanese would be slaughtered as ruthlessly as they had slaughtered the Chinese.

Ruby and Grace shared a skeptical glance that turned into a smile, and then Ruby gestured for Grace to move with her to the sofa. One of the restaurant's waiters had brought up a basket of steamed custard buns, and they each took one along with a cup of tea over to the quieter half of the living room, sitting near Grace's mother.

"Do you think they're right?" Grace asked, eyeing the men. "Will America really send all that aid to China?"

Ruby shrugged. "Who can tell? The president has said he would, but so far America has not lived up to its promises."

"If anyone can persuade President Roosevelt to help China, Madame Chiang can," Grace said. "Have you seen the way the newspapers cover her? They love her."

"They love the woman she presents to them."

"You think she's putting on a false front?"

Ruby shook her head. "Not false. Practiced. Prepared. She's so American—that's why they love her."

"They love her because she's beautiful," Grace's mother said.

The men burst into laughter over some joke that Grace didn't hear; it was jarring in the wake of her mother's statement. Grace said, "She's intelligent too."

"Of course she is," Ruby said. "She's intelligent enough to make sure she's beautiful. Oh, I know you like her, Grace. I like her too. But she's still a woman. Can she really persuade all those Caucasian men to help China? They might love her, but I'm not so sure they love China."

"They love it more than Japan," Grace pointed out. Out of the corner of her eye she glimpsed Lily running into the living room, and she called out, "Lily! No running!"

Lily slowed down, but then Shirley grabbed her hand and tugged her toward the windows at the front of the living room. The curtains were still drawn back, and the red-and-white neon of the Eastern Pearl's sign glowed through the glass. Shirley dragged a low ottoman over to the window and climbed on top of it. Lily followed, and

Grace was about to warn her daughter to be careful when she realized what they were doing. Standing on the ottoman, the windowsill was at the girls' waist level, and they leaned against it as if it were a balcony. They each clutched a white restaurant napkin in their right hands and waved them at the dark street below.

PART V

Lush Life

December 1954–January 1955

30

Kath was alone when Lily met her on their designated corner the night of December thirtieth. "Jean's not coming," Kath said as soon as she saw Lily. "She's saving up for tomorrow night. It's going to be a big show apparently."

"I'm sorry you won't get to see that," Lily said, though she felt a twinge of relief at Jean's absence.

"It's all right," Kath said. "I'd rather go tonight."

Lily wondered if that meant Kath would rather be here with her than with Jean, and she felt a brief flush of excitement. She fumbled with her scarf, re-wrapping it around her neck. The night was foggy and downright cold, and gusts of wind kept tugging the scarf loose.

"How was your Christmas?" Kath asked as they started walking toward the club.

"I got a handbag," Lily said. She hadn't intended to sound so glum, but the glumness was unintentionally funny, and both she and Kath broke into laughter.

"You didn't want one?" Kath asked.

"I guess I didn't," Lily said. "What did you get?"

They discussed Christmas for a little while longer, and then they had to stop talking as they crossed Broadway, taking care to avoid a clump of men going in the opposite direction. When they arrived on the other side, Lily said, "I've been thinking how strange it is that I never used to do this—and now it seems almost normal." She paused. "Not exactly normal, but you know what I mean?"

"I know."

"Isn't it strange that nobody in our regular lives knows about it? That they think we're at home asleep?"

"Well, you don't want them to know, do you?"

"No," Lily said quickly. Of course she didn't want anyone in her regular life to know. The very thought of it was horrifying. No, it was better to do this in secret.

At the club, there was a short line waiting outside. Mickey was working again, but she didn't recognize Lily at first, so she had to unwind her scarf and say, "I've been here before."

Behind her a woman said, "Is that you, Lily?"

She turned around in surprise, and a petite woman in a belted raincoat came forward and said, "It's me, Claire. Remember me?"

Lily shook Claire's hand, and then Claire shook Kath's hand too. Claire was with Paula again—Lily remembered her—and the four of them went into the club together, finding a table on the left side of the stage room near the back.

This time, a waitress in a black cocktail dress with a little white apron tied around her waist moved between the tables, taking orders and delivering trays of drinks. "Hello, girls, we have champagne on special tonight," she said when she arrived at their table.

"Let's have a round for all of us," Paula said. "It's on me."

It took several minutes for the waitress to return, and while they waited, they talked about the upcoming show: whether Tommy would do any new numbers, and whether she should retire any of her standards.

"She's been here for a while—at the Telegraph Club, I mean," Claire said. "Several months at least."

"I'm surprised Joyce has kept her on for so long," Paula said.

"She must be bringing in the business," Claire said. "How many times have we been here? Half a dozen at least?"

"Who's Joyce?" Kath asked.

"Joyce Morgan. The owner," Paula said. "She's usually behind the bar."

"Where was Tommy before?" Kath asked.

"The Paper Doll, maybe?" Claire said. "I never saw her there."

"She used to park cars for a living," Paula said. "Over at that parking lot by Columbus."

"Can you imagine?" Claire said, laughing. "Having your car parked by the likes of Tommy Andrews."

"I don't think she was going by Tommy Andrews back then," Paula said.

The waitress returned, carrying four coupes of champagne on a small round tray.

"Happy early New Year," Paula said, and they all raised their glasses and carefully clinked them together to avoid spilling the liquid.

Lily took a tentative sip. It was sour and a little flat.

Paula grimaced. "I don't think this is French, but it'll get the job done."

Claire said, "Oh, Paula!"

The pianist came out then, and the spotlight snapped on, and they all fell silent as they waited for the show to begin. Lily drank her cheap champagne too quickly, and by the time Tommy Andrews stepped onstage, she was light-headed and a little too warm, as if summer had bloomed inside the club and wrapped her in its lazy heat. She didn't mind at all.

At the break, Claire and Paula went up to the bathroom, and when they returned, they had Lana Jackson in tow. Lana had been drinking a martini, and when the waitress returned to take new orders, Lana greeted her by name—"How's your night going, Betty?"—and asked for another. Paula and Claire ordered martinis too, and Lana suggested that Betty simply bring a pitcher for the table.

Kath said, "I'll just have a beer, thanks."

"What about you, miss?" Betty asked Lily.

"Just a beer, thanks."

"You don't look like a beer drinker," Lana said, lighting a cigarette. "You sure you don't want a martini?"

"I've never had one."

Lana's darkly penciled eyebrows lifted, and she smiled at Lily before she looked at Betty. "The China doll will have a martini too."

Lily wasn't sure if she should feel flattered or insulted.

Lana offered her silver cigarette case around the table, and Claire said, "I'll take one. Did you hear about Ruth Schmidt?"

"Ruthie from San Mateo?" Lana said.

"Yes. Have you heard?"

"No, what happened?"

Claire leaned into the lighter that Paula held out for her, inhaling quickly. "She told me some G-men asked her to be an informant."

Lily—and everyone else—stared at Claire in surprise.

"An informant!" Lana exclaimed. "I thought she was working over at the shipyard."

"Yes, as a typist. But apparently the feds think her new boyfriend is a pinko."

Lana's eyebrows rose again. "Really? You mean little Marty Coleman? The car salesman?"

Claire laughed. "The shoe salesman. Yes. The feds think he's involved in a Communist organization, and they want her to spy on him for them. I told her she should throw him over for a real woman."

The word *Communist* was jarring to Lily, as if someone had

thrown a rock through a glass window, but the women at the table continued talking and smoking as if nothing had happened.

"I thought they were done with that kind of snooping now that McCarthy's out," Paula said.

"Apparently not," Lana said.

Claire blew out a stream of smoke impatiently. "You'd think they would avoid asking Ruthie to be an informant, given her past association with homosexuals." She said the word *homosexuals* sarcastically, as if it were a joke, but the word still sounded obscene to Lily.

"Do you really think the feds know?" Lana asked doubtfully.

"Oh, they know all right," Claire said. "She said I should be on the lookout in case they came to interview me, because they told her they knew about us."

"You didn't tell me that," Paula said, startled.

"It doesn't matter," Claire said casually, but there was a tension in the way she brought the cigarette to her mouth and drew on it, deeply. "I'm a nobody. I work in a dentist's office. No Russians could possibly be interested in anything I do."

Lily was increasingly bewildered by the conversation. These women were talking as if it were all a good joke, and yet there was an undercurrent to their tone that suggested something darker. She wanted to ask for more details, but she didn't think she had the right. She barely knew Claire; she barely knew any of these women. She glanced at Kath, who had a slightly puzzled expression on her face as if she didn't really understand either.

The waitress returned with their drinks, and Lana scooted her chair out of the way so that Betty could set down the pitcher of martinis, four cocktail glasses, and a beer. "It's on the house," Betty said.

"Thanks," Lana said. "Say, what are you up to after the second act tonight? We're having a little party up at our place. You want to join us?"

"I'm supposed to go out with Cheryl," Betty said.

"Bring her." Lana smiled archly. "Tommy loves Cheryl."

Betty laughed and shook her head. "If by love you mean hate. No, but thanks, doll. I'll tell Cheryl you said hello."

"You do that," Lana said, and then Betty had to leave to attend to another table.

Lana poured the martinis, then raised hers in a toast. "Cheers!" she said as she clinked her cocktail glass against Claire's.

Lily did the same, holding hers carefully to avoid spilling the clear liquid. The drink smelled astringent, practically medicinal, and when she took a tiny sip, it was sharp on her tongue and a shock to swallow, like cold fire. She wasn't sure if she liked it or not.

"You should come too, Claire," Lana was saying. "All of you should come over after the show. It would be lovely to have some new faces around. I'm getting a little tired of Tommy's friends." She said the word *friends* dryly, sharing a knowing look with Claire.

Lily wondered what Lana meant. She wondered if the invitation to her party truly included her and Kath, and then she began to hope that it did.

31

After the second act, Tommy came through the crowded room with an entire bottle of the cheap champagne and pulled up an empty chair between Lana and Claire, who made room without being asked. Lily caught Claire looking around a little self-consciously, as if she knew others in the club were eyeing her proximity to Tommy and wondering who she was. Lana called Betty over to clear away the empty glasses and bring over fresh ones. As Tommy reached over to pour champagne, her cologne drifted toward Lily. The scent was heady, like being drunk on a leather sofa. It made Lily's skin go warm.

Tommy sat back in her chair, lit a cigarette, and downed a coupe of champagne in one gulp. "That stuff's terrible," she groused. "I'll have to tell Joyce not to serve it tomorrow night."

"It's on special," Lana said in a bored tone of voice. "I think she's trying to get rid of it."

"So she's pawning it off on me and my fans? Of course, gotta save the best for Miss Rita Rogers." There was a jealous sting to her words, and Lily wondered who Rita Rogers was.

Kath leaned over to her and said, "I'm going up to the bathroom. Come with me?"

Lily didn't want to leave the table now that Tommy had arrived, but there was a look in Kath's eye that made her get up. When they reached the dim hallway that contained the stairs going up to the bathroom, Lily caught a glimpse of a woman slipping into the shadows beneath the stairs. She stared for a moment, confused. The woman's body was moving in an unusual way—her shoulders were bent forward, her head dipping—and all of a sudden Lily realized the woman wasn't alone. There was another woman with her beneath the stairs, the edges of her skirt visible around the other woman's legs. They were pressed together, their heads close. Lily couldn't see exactly what they were doing, but she had a good idea.

She hurried after Kath, who was already standing in the unusually short bathroom line. Kath must have noted her flushed face because she asked, "What happened?"

"Nothing," she said, flustered.

Kath seemed a bit tense. "Do you want to go over to Lana's with everyone?"

Lily tried to put the image of those two women out of her mind. "Do you think they really meant to invite us?"

"I don't know. Maybe." Kath's forehead furrowed as she glanced up the line and then back at Lily. "If we go, it'll be late. When do you need to get home?"

Kath had never been concerned about getting home late before. Lily looked at her more closely, but couldn't read the expression on her face. "Well, it's already late," Lily said. "Who's going to notice if I'm a couple of hours later? But what about you? Do you want to go?"

Kath's shoulders hunched slightly. "Only if you do."

"Well, yes. I don't really want to go home. Do you?"

Kath seemed to be holding something back. "I guess not."

Lily was about to ask what was wrong, but they had reached the bathroom door and it was Kath's turn to go in, so Lily was left standing in the hallway. By the time they were both finished, the moment had passed, so Lily said nothing.

They went downstairs together, and at the bottom she looked behind her at the alcove beneath the stairs, but it was empty. Back at their table, Tommy and Lana and the others were all standing up and putting on their coats, getting ready to leave. Lana saw her and Kath, and said, "We're walking up to Telegraph Hill. Are you coming along?"

Kath plucked their jackets from the backs of their empty chairs, handing Lily hers. "Sure, we're coming. Thanks."

They spilled out onto the sidewalk, a group of half a dozen. Lily kept close to Kath, and they followed the others up a side street that was cut with stairs it was so steep. When they started out from the club they had been talking gaily, laughing and joking, but as they proceeded through North Beach their voices grew hushed. Lily lost track of where they were going. All around them the neighborhood slumbered, a world removed from the noise and music of the night-clubs a few blocks away. They finally arrived on a flat block just below Coit Tower, which was lit up at the top of Telegraph Hill like a beacon. Someone took out a ring of keys, and Lily heard a crunch as a key turned in the lock of a three-story building. A light was switched on and spilled out, yellowish, onto the front stoop.

"Come on in!" Tommy called back, and they all crowded through the doorway, into the front hall, and through a second door on the right into a first-floor apartment.

At first, Lily got the impression of a jumble of different dark lumps everywhere, but as Tommy and Lana went around switch-ing on the lamps, the lumps resolved themselves into a long rust-colored sofa, and a set of black lacquered Chinese chairs like the kind that were sold to tourists in the Grant Avenue shops. There was a Mission-style coffee table, an octagonal end table like something out of *Arabian Nights*, and a medieval-looking bench by the door where Lana told everyone to leave their coats. Past the living room was a small dining room with a white Formica-and-chrome dinette set and an antique mirrored buffet, on top of which were clustered several bottles and cocktail glasses. Lana went through to the kitchen, announcing that she would bring back a bucket of ice, while Tommy disappeared down the hall, loosening her tie.

Lily left her coat on the bench with the others and wandered over to the rust-colored sofa; above it were several framed photos hung in a somewhat haphazard order. There were a couple of snapshots of Tommy standing with other male impersonators on a busy street; Lily thought it might be in front of the Telegraph Club. There was a picture of Tommy with her arm around Lana, the Golden Gate Bridge in the background. Tommy was wearing a sweater beneath an unbuttoned jacket, a cigarette drooping out of her mouth. Lana had a polka-dotted scarf tied over her blond hair and wore a trench coat and sunglasses. They were both reluctantly smiling, as if the photographer had been scolding them into doing it.

And centered over the sofa was a large glossy picture of Tommy Andrews that Lily recognized as the original of the headshot that had been printed in the *Chronicle*. Seeing the photo on the wall was somehow shocking: here she was in Tommy Andrews's apartment. Tommy Andrews! She had gazed at her photo in the paper—*this* photo—countless times, and now she was in this woman's home. It was as if time had stuttered, and she was back in the Eastern Pearl surreptitiously tearing the ad from the paper. She could still hear the dull ripping sound, the crumple as she folded it. She felt detached from her body, and when she closed her eyes for a moment she might have been floating, untethered from the earth's gravity.

She heard the sound of a record falling into place, the scratch of the needle as it struck vinyl. The song "Black Magic" began to play, and she felt her knee pressing against the edge of Tommy's sofa. She opened her eyes and turned around, feeling a little dizzy. She hadn't finished her martini—it had been too strong for her—but perhaps the champagne she had drunk earlier was still affecting her. She didn't know how to act in a place like this—and where was Kath? She couldn't see her anywhere.

From the dining room, Lana announced that she had made a Spanish sangria and asked who wanted cocktails. There was a proprietary air to Lana's behavior that made Lily realize this wasn't Tommy's apartment—it was Tommy *and* Lana's. They lived here together. She sat down on the sofa, feeling like an idiot. The cushion was too soft, pulling her into an unexpectedly intimate embrace. More people arrived—they seemed to be mostly women, a few in Levi's with their cuffs rolled up—and she began to worry about where Kath had gone, but at last she spotted her emerging from the kitchen, carrying two wineglasses. Relieved, Lily waved at her, and Kath came to the sofa with the drinks.

"It's sangria," Kath said, handing her a glass of red liquid. "There's fruit in it. I didn't think you'd want another martini."

"Thank you," Lily said.

Kath sat down beside her, and the softness of the sofa caused them to bump together. Kath nearly spilled her drink and apologized, but before she could scoot over Claire reappeared, carrying a martini. When she sat down the cushion sank toward her, and then Paula arrived, and everyone had to squeeze together to make room. Finally the four of them were seated properly, with Lily's right leg and hip and shoulder pressing close against Kath's warm left side. Lily sipped her drink; it was sugary and sweet, and filled with bits of canned pineapple and mandarin oranges.

One of the women in Levi's sat down in the Chinese chair next to the end of the sofa near Lily. She was dressed like Marlon Brando in *The Wild One*, with a leather jacket and thick-soled black boots, and her short dark hair was combed into a pompadour, shiny with pomade. She had a round face and brown eyes, and she gave Lily and Kath a frankly curious look and said, "You two are new, aren't you? I'm Sal."

Lily and Kath clinked their glasses with hers. "Lily."

"Kath."

"Did you come from the club?" Sal asked. "How was the show tonight? I missed it."

They talked about the Telegraph Club for a few minutes—or Kath and Sal did, while Lily sipped her drink and tried to pretend as if she went to these sorts of parties all the time. Over in the corner by the record player she saw two women laughing, one woman's arms looped around the other's neck as if they were about to start dancing.

"We don't see many Orientals around here," Sal said to Lily. "Do you speak English? Where are you from?"

Lily stiffened. "Chinatown. I was born here."

Sal looked impressed. "You don't even have an accent. That's amazing."

"I was born here," Lily said again, a bit more sharply.

"I thought all the Orientals in Chinatown only spoke Chinese."

"No." She hoped that her short tone would make Sal drop it.

"Hey, Patsy," Sal called across the room, "there's an Oriental over here—where'd you meet that other one? Over at Blanco's?"

Lily was grateful for the sofa then, for allowing her to sink back; if only she could sink through it to the other side, where it would hide her from their scrutiny.

Patsy turned out to be a redhead in a red-and-white-checked dress that reminded Lily of a picnic blanket. She came over and perched on the arm of Sal's chair, while Sal's arm snaked around her small waist. "Hello, I'm Patsy," she said, extending her hand.

Lily sat up with some effort and shook Patsy's hand reluctantly.

"Where was that?" Sal continued. "Blanco's? Is that where you saw that girl?"

Patsy leaned against Sal's shoulder. "I've never been to Blanco's. That place is for Filipino dykes. What do I look like?"

Sal laughed and squeezed Patsy's waist, causing her to squeal. "Where was it then? I swear it was recent—you said there were gay girls there."

"The Forbidden City," Patsy said promptly. "Have you ever been there, hon?" She looked at Lily.

"No," Lily said again.

There was a commotion over in the dining room, and a moment later Tommy entered the living room with a martini in one hand, scanning the faces as if she were searching for someone. Tommy had taken off her tuxedo and put on gray flannel pants and a blue collared shirt with the top button undone. Of course, Lily realized, the tuxedo was a costume, and now Tommy was at home. And yet she still carried herself the same way, as if her onstage persona was barely more than a gloss over her real life.

Sal yelled, "Terry! Over here!"

Lily didn't know who Terry was, but when Tommy saw Sal, she came over to join them, pulling over the other Chinese chair. Patsy smiled at Tommy and lifted her face for a kiss, and Tommy obliged, planting one on her cheek. "You look good, Pat," Tommy said, and then reached over to shake Sal's hand. "It's been a while. Glad you could make it."

"Thanks for the invite," Sal said. "Sorry I can't make it to your show tomorrow night—my budget's kinda tight."

Tommy shrugged and sat down, placing her martini glass on the coffee table. She pulled out a pack of cigarettes and lit one. "So's mine."

"You could make some extra bucks with those fans of yours," Sal said, grinning. "Remember that dame who followed you up to your dressing room?"

Tommy looked bitter. "If she figured out I'm actually a woman, she would've called the cops." She shook her head. "How're things with you?"

"Good. We were just talking about the Forbidden City, since you have an Oriental guest here."

Sinking through the couch wasn't enough, Lily thought. She wished she could sink all the way through to China. At least then she'd blend in.

Tommy's eyes flickered from Sal to Lily. "Yeah, the China doll's been to my show a few times. You like it, sweetheart?"

Lily's face burned, and she felt Kath tense up beside her. "Of course," she forced herself to say politely, reminding herself she was Tommy's guest. "It's wonderful."

Tommy grinned. "Wonderful." She sat back, crossing her legs, and took a deep drag on her cigarette. "You know, I heard the Forbidden City had a male impersonator once."

"Really?" Lily said warily, but she was interested in spite of her discomfort. "When?"

"A few years back," Tommy said. "Maybe during the war? I can't remember, it was before my time. But I've heard about her—she did herself up in a suit, like Marlene Dietrich, Gladys Bentley. Not exactly the same as my gig, but I wonder what happened to her. I heard she was good."

The praise, delivered in such an offhanded tone, curled through Lily as if Tommy had offered her a personal compliment. She couldn't imagine a Chinese woman putting on a show like Tommy's, but she was immediately proud of her. She wanted to ask more about her, but Lana came into the living room looking for Tommy.

"There you are—you slipped right past me," Lana said. "Where's the tonic?"

Tommy had to get up and go back to the kitchen, and Patsy and Sal sat quietly for a moment, smiling fixedly at Lily and Kath, before Patsy got up and took the chair that Tommy had vacated. Lily raised her glass to her mouth and realized, to her surprise, that she had finished her drink.

"Let me get you another," Kath said.

"I don't need another," Lily said, but Kath didn't appear to hear her. She stood up abruptly, causing the sofa cushion to heave like a wave, and took both of their glasses—Kath's was empty too—off to the kitchen. Lily felt the distinct absence of Kath next to her, as if part of her own body was suddenly missing.

"How long have you two been an item?" Patsy asked after Kath left the living room.

Lily was taken aback. "Me and Kath? We're—we're not."

Patsy gave her a hint of a knowing smile. "Oh, my mistake."

Embarrassed, Lily glanced around for something to distract her and caught sight of the couple by the record player again, still gazing into each other's eyes, and another couple beyond them sharing a single chair while they sorted through records. The room was full of couples, Lily realized. How naïve had she been to not notice this until now? No wonder Patsy thought that she and Kath were . . .

She dropped her gaze to her lap, stunned. Perhaps Patsy had seen something in her and Kath—just as Lily had seen the other pairs and known they were not simply friends. The thought made Lily's heart race.

Someone put "Shake, Rattle, and Roll" on the record player, and Patsy jumped up, declaring, "I love this one. Come on, Sal, dance with me."

Sal objected for a second, but it was obvious she wanted to say yes, and she allowed Patsy to drag her into the small empty space between the coffee table and the kitchen door, where they began to dance. A moment later Claire and Paula got up from the couch to join them, leaving Lily alone at last.

How long have you two been an item?

Her face was burning. Out of the corner of her eye she saw Paula's hands on Claire's waist, Claire's fingers sliding down Paula's arms, laughing at each other as they swiveled their hips in time to the music. She saw Patsy in Sal's arms; she saw Sal spin Patsy away from her and back again, her skirt flaring out. She had never seen two women dance together like that before, as if they were a man and a woman.

And then Kath appeared in the doorway behind the dancing couples, holding two more glasses of sangria, and though Lily didn't allow herself to meet Kath's eyes, she was sharply aware of her approach. There was more room on the sofa with Claire and Paula gone, so Kath didn't need to sit so close to her now. She took a seat about a foot away and handed Lily her sangria. The cushion sagged under her weight, and Lily braced herself so that she didn't slide toward Kath as she took the wineglass. Patsy's question rang in her head, like someone pressing a doorbell over and over again.

How long?

Lily felt as if she should say something to Kath, but everything she could say or do now seemed impossibly weighted. Her head was fuzzy; she was a muddy mess of panic and wonder. The sofa felt like a trap. She had to escape.

"I have to find the bathroom," Lily said abruptly. She set her sangria glass down on the coffee table and lurched to her feet. The room seemed to shift beneath her.

"Are you all right?" Kath asked, reaching out to steady her.

She felt Kath's fingers brush her arm, and she pulled away skittishly. "I'm fine," she said, and hurried out of the living room, narrowly missing Paula's elbow as she swung Claire around.

The kitchen was filled with people she didn't know, and she couldn't see Lana or Tommy anywhere. "Where's the bathroom?" she asked one of the women, who pointed to an open doorway at the back of the kitchen.

She stepped through into a dim, empty hallway, where she saw a door with a crack of light beneath it that she assumed was the bathroom. When she knocked, someone called, "Just a minute!"

Lily stepped back to lean against the wall. The sound of the record player and the laughter from the living room was muffled here, and the dimness made her feel invisible at last. The hallway continued on a short distance to her right, where another door was halfway open. A soft golden light spilled from the room, and she saw a pair of black oxfords abandoned on the floor in front of a dresser.

It was only a few more steps to the end of the hall, and she didn't have to enter the room to look inside. There was a double bed, covered by a nubbly green blanket, and a nightstand with a yellow lamp. Beside the dresser was a half-open closet door; Tommy's tuxedo hung on a hanger hooked over the edge. Inside the closet, more suits nestled right next to several dresses—Lana's clothes. On top of the dresser, a handled metal tray contained an assortment of cosmetics, and a couple of black bow ties lay limply beside it.

From what Lily could tell, this was the only bedroom in the apartment, and Lana and Tommy shared it. She glanced over her shoulder at the bathroom door, but it was still closed. She took a shallow breath and stepped into the room. She was acutely conscious of the double bed behind her as she moved toward the dresser. Behind the satin bow ties, propped against the speckled mirror, was an old-fashioned sepia-toned postcard of a man in a tuxedo. She leaned closer: no, the person was identified as "Miss Vesta Tilley." She wore a top hat and held a cigarette between her lips, and she had a mischievous light in her eyes.

Lily reached out to pick up the postcard, but before she touched it, a door creaked and there was a light step on the wooden floor.

"Hello there."

Lily spun around to face the door, and there was Tommy, hands in her pockets, studying her. "I'm sorry, I—I didn't mean—"

Tommy came into the room. "Looking for the bathroom? It's down the hall."

"Yes, I was—I'm sorry." She started for the door, but Tommy was in her way and she didn't move, and Lily had to stop. Tommy looked amused at first, and then her amusement turned into something more like curiosity.

"How old are you?" Tommy asked.

Lily trembled. "Twenty-one."

Tommy came toward her. It was only a few steps; the room wasn't very large, and now Lily smelled her cologne again, and her stomach clenched as if in anticipation or in fear—she wasn't sure which. Tommy smiled at her gently, the kind of smile one gave to calm a nervous child, perhaps, and said, "Twenty-one going on sixteen, I think." Tommy closed the distance between them and lifted her hand to Lily's face, cupping her cheek in her palm, turning her face up to hers.

All of her senses rushed to that tender spot where Tommy's warm hand was touching her, her fingertips softly pressing against her neck, her thumb running lightly but deliberately over her mouth.

"Sweet sixteen." There was a honeyed tone to Tommy's voice, a low dip to it that sounded like a secret.

Lily felt as if Tommy was onstage again. Her voice and her touch and the way she was looking at Lily: a performance that she had slipped into effortlessly, like water.

For a moment—an excruciatingly long moment—Lily was sure that Tommy was thinking about kissing her. Silky heat ran through her like a river. She swayed on her feet—as if she were standing on the deck of a ferry in the Bay—and Tommy gave a brief, breathy laugh.

"You're drunk, sweetheart."

"No," she whispered. Tommy's finger still nudged against her lips.

"Yes." Tommy withdrew her hand almost reluctantly.

"I'm not sixteen." Lily felt, dazedly, as if she had to make that clear.

"You sure?" Tommy smiled a little—almost flirtatiously. "You shouldn't be in here, doll," she said gently. "You better go back to your girlfriend."

Lily felt as if she were sinking, as if the floor were tilting dangerously. But even in her state, Lily knew who Tommy meant. "She's not—we're not—" Lily said, and immediately felt as if she had betrayed Kath.

Tommy raised her eyebrows. "Does she know that, sweetheart?" She stepped toward the door and made a flourish as if to show Lily out of the room. "After you."

32

Kath was still sitting on the sofa. She was holding a wineglass half full of sangria in one hand, the other hand resting on her thigh, her fingers loosely curled up as if something had recently been pulled out of her grasp and she hadn't yet noticed.

When Lily saw her, she felt a fresh pang of embarrassment. She had been so stupid. If she had been so obvious to everyone else, Kath must surely know, and she had never said a thing. That could only mean that Kath didn't—

She couldn't even think it. She had to leave. She needed to go home.

Lily began to skirt the edge of the living room, going around the dancing couples, and caught Kath's eye on the way. Kath rose from the couch immediately, nearly spilling her drink. She righted it just in time and set it on the table, heading toward Lily to meet her at the bench where everyone's coats made a multicolored pile.

"What's wrong?" Kath asked.

"I have to go," Lily said at the same time.

"Did something happen?"

"I just need to go home," Lily insisted. She glanced down at her wristwatch, which enabled her to look away from Kath. "It's three o'clock already."

"All right. I'll go with you."

"You don't have to."

"You can't walk back alone."

"I don't want you to go out of your way."

"It's not."

"You really don't have to bother," Lily said as she dug through the coats.

"Are you sure you're all right?"

One of the coats—a blue wool peacoat—tumbled to the floor, and several others cascaded down after it. "I'm fine," Lily said, bending over to grab the fallen coats. She was mortified by her encounter with Tommy, but she wasn't about to tell anyone what had happened—especially not Kath. "If you want to come with me, then come with me. I just can't stay here anymore."

It was awkward after that, but Kath wouldn't let her walk home alone. Kath helped her find their coats, which were near the bottom, and when Lily dislodged hers at last, an envelope fluttered down to the floor. She bent over to pick it up; it was addressed to someone named Theresa Scafani. She shoved it back into the pile. Kath had pulled Lana away from a group of dancers to say good night. Lily wished she hadn't done that, but now here she was, beaming at them with her face flushed from dancing.

"Thank you for coming," Lana said, and reached out and took Lily's hand in hers.

"Thank you for inviting me—us," Lily said.

"You'll be safe heading home?"

"Yes, we'll go together," Kath said.

"Good. Be careful, girls."

As Lana went back to the dancing, Lily saw Tommy emerge from the kitchen, a cigarette in her mouth and a cocktail glass in one hand. Tommy's eyes met Lily's, and a little smile passed over Tommy's face—that same flirtatious smile from the bedroom—and Lily turned away and headed for the door.

She went so quickly that Kath had to rush after her. "What's gotten into you?" she asked as Lily plunged out onto the street.

"I'm just tired." Lily crossed her arms against the foggy chill and began to walk away from Lana and Tommy's building.

Kath tugged at her elbow. "That's the wrong way."

Lily stopped and looked up. She was walking directly toward Coit Tower, which was still illuminated in the dark. She glanced around in confusion and realized she had no idea where she was.

"It's this way." Kath gestured in the opposite direction.

They went back past Lana and Tommy's building. The living room window was curtained, but through the cracks Lily saw light and movement, and the faint sound of music leaked out into the night. At the end of the block, Lily saw the street sign—Castle Street—right before they turned steeply downhill. They hadn't gone much farther before Kath reached for her arm and said, "Wait—wait."

Lily felt Kath's hand slide down her arm and lodge around her wrist, then around her fingers, pulling her to a halt.

"What happened?" Kath asked. "I know something happened."

The streetlight was behind Kath, so Lily couldn't see her face clearly, but she could hear the concern in her voice and, beneath that, the hurt that Lily wouldn't tell her what it was. Lily wasn't sure she understood it herself, this combination of burning embarrassment and outright fear. Those strange women at the party seemed to see her much more clearly than she saw herself, and it was disorienting—as if her body were not her own, but capable of acting without the conscious direction of her mind, which was screaming at her to let go of Kath's hand, to go home as fast as she could, to crawl into her bed and pull the covers over her head and forget about this entire night, forget about Tommy Andrews and the Telegraph Club and all those women who looked at her and saw that she and Kath were . . . what?

"Did Tommy do something?" Kath asked, her voice hardening.

"She thinks I'm a child," Lily said, the words bursting from her mouth before she could stop them. Tears sprang to her eyes. "I'm so stupid."

"No," Kath said, stepping closer to her, still holding Lily's hand. "You're not stupid. Do you . . . do you have feelings for her?" Kath whispered.

"For Tommy?" Lily wanted to laugh, but she had started to cry and her laughter came out of her in a choked sob. "No, I have feelings for *you*." Her words came out too loud—they seemed to reverberate in the empty street, and she forced her voice into a whisper as she said, "Everybody can tell. Even Tommy! I'm so stupid. So *stupid*."

Kath exhaled in a startled burst.

"I have to go home," Lily insisted, trying to pull away, but Kath wouldn't let her go.

"Wait," Kath said. "Please." She glanced around nervously. The steep street was deserted, but the lights and noises of the city seemed to rise up in warning: a car engine rumbled and streetlights flickered and down the block, a lamp burned in a bay window.

Kath pulled Lily toward the edge of the sidewalk and into the shadow of a building. There was a narrow opening there, an alleyway, and Kath tugged her inside, past the reach of light from the main street. The buildings on either side shot up several stories toward the night sky, their windows all black. All sound seemed to be swallowed up here, leaving the two of them in a velvety, dark quiet.

"I wasn't sure you felt that way," Kath said, and came closer to Lily. "I mean, I hoped."

Lily's heart raced at that word and what it implied. "Really?" Her embarrassment at her own obliviousness was abruptly replaced by astonishment. It made her reel—the speed of this, the way her feelings rushed in, pushing one emotion out and shoving in another.

"I thought—I thought you were just being nice to me, I mean, you can't possibly—I'm so stupid! Don't you want someone like—like Rhonda?"

"Rhonda?" Kath sounded dumbfounded. "No, why would you think that?"

"I don't know. Because at least she knows things. I don't—I don't understand the way this works."

Kath let out another breath, a hint of laughter. "I don't either. I just know—"

She didn't finish her sentence, but she took another step toward Lily, closing the space between them. Lily could feel the warmth of Kath's body radiating off her, could smell the traces of cigarette smoke and beer on her breath, along with a new fragrance she didn't recognize, something clean and bright. It made Lily's skin tingle.

"Lily," Kath said softly.

"Don't say anything," Lily whispered. She felt as if speaking would ruin everything—then they'd have to put a name to this feeling between them, this rapidly growing heat and longing that made the sliver of air between their bodies charged with electricity. She could swear she felt the air humming.

She had never noticed before that she and Kath were the same height. If she leaned forward just a little bit, her nose would graze Kath's, and then they were touching noses gently, practically nuzzling each other, and it was funny and startling, and Lily giggled nervously while Kath let go of her hand and, deliberately, touched Lily's waist. The feel of Kath's hands sliding around her body silenced her laughter. She stopped breathing, and Kath's mouth touched hers, feeling its way in the dark. Her lips were cool and dry at first, but quickly, so quickly, they bloomed into warmth and softness. Her body was close against hers, the shape of her like a shock, her breasts and her hips and her hip bones against her, her hands pulling her closer, closer.

Lily had not known, had never imagined, how a first kiss could turn so swiftly into a second, and a third, and then a continual opening and pressing and touching, the tip of her tongue against Kath's, the warmth of her mouth and the way that warmth reached all the way through her body and raised an indescribable ache between her legs. She had to push herself closer to Kath; that was the only thought in her mind. She put her hands on Kath and slid them beneath her jacket and clutched her back, and there was an awkward fumbling as they moved in the dark alleyway together, seeking something to press against, until the wall of the building was at Lily's back and she could pull Kath into her.

She didn't know how long they kissed—not long enough—but at one point Kath drew back to take a breath, and Lily opened her eyes and saw to her right the dim glow of the street beyond their dark alley. She realized with a start what she was doing and where she was doing it and whom she was doing it with, and she knew she should feel ashamed, but all she felt was the heaving of Kath's chest against hers, and the tenderness of her lips where Kath had kissed her.

don't know why you're bothering with an evening gown at all," Lily said, flipping through an issue of *Seventeen*. "The competition only requires a cheongsam. When will you even have time to change?"

She, Shirley, and Flora were gathered around the table at the back of Flora's father's shop, waiting for Mary, who was late. They were supposed to go to Union Square to shop for Shirley's dress for Miss Chinatown, and Lily did not want to go. She wished she was with Kath instead, and if that wasn't possible, she'd rather shut herself in her bedroom alone, and remember. (The sensation of Kath's mouth against hers, her hands on her waist.)

"It's so that I stand out," Shirley said. "I'm not going to give my speech in a cheongsam. I'll wear that for the main portion of the pageant but I don't want to be like the other girls during the speech part. I want to show that I'm American, too."

Lily was only half listening; she had landed on a column at the front of the magazine titled "A Look at Tomorrow: The Challenge of the Planets." To her surprise, it was written by Arthur C. Clarke and was about the problems of outer-space travel.

"Give me that," Flora said, reaching for the magazine.

"Wait, I'm reading—"

Flora gave Lily a reproachful look—Lily thought Flora hadn't yet accepted that Shirley had welcomed her back into their group of friends—and pulled the magazine out of Lily's hands, flipping to a story on evening gowns. "This would be beautiful on you," Flora said, pointing to the photograph of a white tulle ball gown.

Shirley frowned at the small print. "Why does it cost so much?"

"We can alter something to look like that," Flora assured her.

"Where's Mary?" Shirley wondered, glancing toward the front of the shop. "We can't go without her. She knows about tailoring."

"I'll go see if she's coming," Lily volunteered. She left the back room and went out into the main shop area, passing shelves displaying vases and statues, blue-and-white porcelain and boxes of silk fans. There were a few customers in the store, but it was still relatively early on Sunday and so it was mostly empty. She opened the front door and peered out into the rainy morning, hoping to see Mary coming down the sidewalk, but she didn't see her.

Reluctantly she went back inside, but rather than rejoining Shirley and Flora, she wandered through the aisles of the store, delaying the moment when she'd be forced to have constructive opinions, again, on dresses. Flora's father's shop held an assortment of art pieces and tourist tchotchkes; there was always something funny or interesting to discover. When she had been younger, at Christmas time he would allow her to pick out a small toy from a display in the back, and now she found herself winding her way to that same corner. The rotating rack was still there, and Lily spun it slowly, examining the toys. There were matchbox-size cars painted garishly red and yellow, and baby dolls with eyes that rolled open when they were picked up. There were small boxes of jacks and dice that rattled when she handled them, and a row of green toy soldiers. And on the bottom shelf of the last side of the rack was a row of miniature jet airplanes, with plastic cockpit bubbles through which the helmeted heads of tiny pilots were visible. Lily picked one up, delighted; the plane was painted silver and white, with the United States flag on the tail, and black wheels that really spun were attached to the bottom.

The toy planes made her think of Kath. It had been three days—well, three mornings—since they had parted on the dark corner of Columbus and Broadway. They had hugged each other quickly, and Lily realized then and there that they'd never be able to kiss goodbye in public. (A tightening in her chest as she reluctantly turned away.)

They hadn't seen or telephoned each other since then, but that wasn't unusual. Lily still didn't know Kath's address or phone number. They only saw each other at school—or on the nights they went to the Telegraph Club. In retrospect, it seemed so obvious that their friendship had always carried the added weight of something that neither of them was equipped to address openly. It was easier and safer to pretend that their friendship was merely a casual one. But the time for pretending was over, and Lily was painfully aware of the responsibility that came with admitting how they felt about each other. It was risky to share this secret.

Lily turned the airplane over in her hands. On the bottom of the plane a sticker read MADE IN JAPAN. She ran the edge of her fingernail beneath it, and it lifted off so easily, as if it had barely been there to begin with. But a sticky residue remained, a trace of the plane's hidden origin.

She heard Shirley and Flora break into laughter at the back of the shop. She put the airplane back on the shelf and went to rejoin her friends, walking past an American woman in a camel-colored coat who was examining a display of marked-down jade figurines.

"Excuse me," the woman said, "can you help me with these?"

"I don't work here," Lily said.

The woman was middle-aged and wore horn-rimmed glasses through which she gazed short-temperedly at Lily. "Can you find someone who does?"

Taken aback, Lily said, "Of course." She went to find Flora's father, who was behind the jewelry case on the other side of the store, taking an inventory of unsold Christmas items. "Mr. Soo, there's a lady over there who wants someone to help her," Lily said.

Mr. Soo looked over the top of his black-framed glasses at Lily. "Where?"

She pointed, and he huffed and went off to find her. Lily paused for a moment in front of the Christmas leftovers, her gaze drawn to the wall behind the jewelry case. It was a notice board where advertisements for Chinatown events were posted: a hodgepodge of Cathay Orchestra concerts and YWCA charity raffles and Christmas potlucks for the needy. On the right side was a poster that Lily couldn't remember seeing before, emblazoned with a large dark headline: PLEDGE OF LOYALTY. She went around the jewelry counter so she could read what was printed below:

1. *We Chinese-American citizens pledge our loyalty to the United States.*
2. *We support the nationalist government of free China and her great leader, President Chiang Kai-shek.*
3. *We support the United Nations charter and the efforts made by the United Nations troops who are fighting for a united, free and independent Korea.*
4. *The Chinese communists are the stooges of Soviet Russia. Those who are invading Korea are the Chinese communists, not the Chinese, peace-loving people of free China.*

The paper was slightly yellowed, and by the thumbtack holes in it, Lily realized it must have been hanging there for some time, hidden beneath other posters. The bottom third of it was mostly obscured by an ad for a New Year's Eve concert. Curious, she unpinned the concert ad, and beneath it she read: "Pledged by patriotic members of the Chinese YMCA and YWCA, 1951."

She had been in junior high school then. It was only a few years ago, but it felt much longer, as if she had been an entirely different person than she was now. She barely knew Kath then, and only as one of the few girls in her math class. She hadn't yet secretly skimmed that book in the back of Thrifty Drugs. She hadn't yet gone to the Telegraph Club or Lana and Tommy's apartment—or stopped on the way home in a dark alley and kissed a girl. (The way her body had fit against Kath's; the exquisite ache it had caused.)

Behind her the shop door opened, the bell jingling, and she heard Mary's voice. "Shirley? I'm sorry I'm late!"

Lily spun around, irrationally certain that someone had read her mind, but she was quite alone. There was Mary hurrying through the store, her hair windblown and the umbrella she was carrying damp from rain, and there were Shirley and Flora emerging from the back room, pulling on their coats. Lily had to force herself to go meet them, tamping down the hot, panicky feeling that bubbled inside her, as if something sordid might spill out of her against her will.

"What took you so long?" Shirley asked Mary.

"My brother was sick this morning, and my parents— Oh, forget about it," Mary said. "Let's just go!"

34

Shirley pulled a dress out from an overstuffed rack in the juniors section of Macy's bargain basement. "This is the one," she declared. Lily came over from the rack nearby as Shirley held it against herself. "What do you think?"

It was two pieces, instead of one: a pale blue halter-neck blouse tucked into a matching full skirt, and accented by a wide darker blue belt. "It's pretty," Lily said, "but I thought you wanted a strapless dress?"

Flora came over with an armful of wraps. "You have to try it on. It's very Hollywood."

Shirley glanced around. "It's my size. Where are the dressing rooms?"

The vast windowless space was crowded with bargain hunters drifting from giant bins of marked-down sweaters to spinning racks of dresses in odd sizes. Lily couldn't see the dressing rooms anywhere, but she did see a Macy's employee folding blouses at one of the nearby bins.

Shirley saw her too, and said, "Lily, will you go ask that woman?"

Lily knew Shirley was sending her because she didn't want to go herself and risk facing an unfriendly salesgirl; they often seemed to doubt that any Chinese had the money to pay. Lily didn't want to go either, but she wanted to argue with Shirley even less, so she straightened her shoulders and approached the woman.

"Excuse me, miss, where are the dressing rooms?" Lily asked politely.

The woman turned toward her. "They're on the far side. Let me take you—"

Lily froze in surprise, because it was Paula. Not Paula the way she had looked at the Telegraph Club, in her blazer and slacks, but Paula nonetheless. Her short hair was done in a feminine style now, and she wore a tan shirtdress along with her Macy's smock and identifying name tag, which read MISS WEBSTER. Lily knew that Paula recognized her too, because she saw it in Paula's slight widening of her eyes, which was followed almost instantly by a shuttering of her expression—as if she had drawn on a mask. The idea that Paula from the Telegraph Club had a job as a Macy's salesgirl was astonishing. Was Lily supposed to acknowledge that she knew Paula? And if she did, would Paula acknowledge that she knew Lily? Lily was immediately certain that it was dangerous for them to do so. The midnight world in which they had met did not belong here in the brightly lit public afternoon.

She and Paula looked at each other for what felt like a very long moment, but was probably no more than a few seconds. Then Paula dropped her gaze to the blouse she was folding and said formally, "Let me take you to the dressing room."

"It's not for me. It's for—" Lily gestured to Shirley, who was still standing behind her at the rack with Mary and Flora.

Paula nodded. She finished folding the blouse and headed over to Shirley, not even looking at Lily. "Do you need a dressing room, miss?"

"Yes," Shirley said. "Where is it?"

"Please follow me," Paula said.

Shirley, Flora, and Mary followed Paula across the floor, and Lily trailed after them nervously. She began to worry that Paula would say something, that she would ask about Kath or why they had left the party so abruptly. She hung back a little when they reached the dressing room, allowing her friends to go in ahead of her. It wasn't as nice as the dressing room in the junior miss department. This one had no carpet on the floor, and the mirrors were smaller and chipped in the corners.

"May I help you with anything else?" Paula asked, after Shirley had been installed in her small dressing room.

"No, thank you," Shirley said. She caught sight of Lily standing outside, behind Paula, and added, "Lily, come in with us—I need all of your advice on this."

Paula silently stepped aside for her, and in that moment Lily understood that Paula wasn't going to say anything to suggest that she knew her, and Lily wasn't going to say anything, either. The invisible walls of their two different worlds would slide right back in place, and they would return to their separate lives without comment. As Lily squeezed into the dressing room, she saw Paula escaping back into the bargain basement without a backward glance.

The encounter had left Lily feeling uncomfortably vulnerable, as if her most intimate secrets could be exposed at any moment, and the tiny room provided nowhere to hide. The four of them barely fit inside, and Lily had to stand with her back against the door. Shirley was undressing and handing each article of her clothing to Flora to hold carefully. It was Mary's job, apparently, to help Shirley put on the dresses, which meant Lily didn't know why she was there at all, because the only thing she could do was watch.

She and Shirley had undressed in front of each other countless times before in changing rooms or bedrooms, and there had never been anything lewd about it. Lily had sometimes been self-conscious about her body, but Shirley had always been very matter-of-fact, openly comparing their measurements as they grew up and excitedly sharing every new development with Lily—the first bra she bought, the first period she got. In fact, the first time Lily got her period, over a year after Shirley started, she'd asked Shirley how to use a sanitary napkin. Her mother had given her the supplies, but Lily hadn't understood her instructions, and it was less embarrassing to ask Shirley how to manage the pins and gauze and belt. Shirley had knelt before her on the floor of her bathroom and practically put her hand between Lily's legs to show her. It had been awkward but also exciting, because it meant that Lily had finally caught up with her friend.

All of this meant that Lily shouldn't be self-conscious to see Shirley undressed. She knew what Shirley's body looked like, and it didn't attract her. But now she was aware of bodies—their physicality, their possibility—in a way she hadn't been before. (Kath's body pressed against her, taut and soft all at once.)

She couldn't look at Shirley until she had the dress on. And then she couldn't help but notice the soft rise of Shirley's breasts over the cups of the bodice; the way they shifted when she twisted back and forth, trying to see every angle in the mirror. The back of the dress dipped low, revealing Shirley's bra; she'd have to get a different one if she wore that dress. It also revealed the naked expanse of her back, the bones of her spine like a map for someone's fingers. (The feel of Kath's back beneath her hands, through the fabric of her shirt; how she'd wanted to touch her bare skin.)

"I don't know about this one," Shirley was saying. "I think it's a little too . . . *flashy*, you know?"

Mary giggled, and Flora did too.

"What do you think, Lily?" Shirley asked.

Lily swallowed. "You're probably right. Maybe try the two-piece one?"

Shirley nodded. "Yes. Mary, can you help me out of this?"

And then the dress was coming off again as she raised her arms and Mary pulled it up, up over her head. Lily dropped her eyes to the floor, where she saw Shirley's stockinged feet on the ground. The black seams had twisted off the center of her calves, but she did not volunteer to help straighten them.

Walking home from Union Square later that day, Lily wondered if she'd run into Paula again—or maybe Claire, or even Sal. She realized, with a jolt, that the city must be peppered with women who frequented the Telegraph or similar clubs; women who watched performers like Tommy Andrews, made friends with each other, made girlfriends of each other. At each intersection she cast skittish glances at the women waiting for the light to change, wondering if she was one of them too, or her, or her.

35

inally, it was the first Monday back at school after Christmas break. Lily had been inordinately nervous about seeing Kath again, but when the moment arrived—there she was, standing at her locker in an ordinary-looking skirt and blouse—it was disappointingly anticlimactic. The hallway was full of rushing students and teachers, and the fluorescent lights shined bright overhead, erasing the tiniest possibility of romance.

Then Kath met her eyes from ten feet away, and a blush colored her face, and Lily's skin went hot as she remembered the way Kath had held her in the shadows of that alley.

They couldn't talk about it in school, of course, except in the most coded of ways. When Kath greeted her, she asked, "Are you . . . all right?"

There were a thousand questions hidden within those words. Lily clutched her books close to her chest as if to cage herself behind them, and answered, "Yes. I'm fine. How are you?"

A smile flickered onto Kath's face, and her eyes darted behind Lily for a moment. Lily knew that Shirley was back there somewhere, and Kath seemed to swallow her smile before she said somewhat formally, "I'm fine also."

They had to separate then. "I'll see you in class," Lily said.

Kath nodded, and at the last possible moment, she turned away.

After school, they walked home together, but it was nothing like the way it used to be. Lily was extraordinarily conscious of every time they touched: Kath's elbow brushing hers as they left Galileo; the back of Lily's hand grazing Kath's hip when they stopped at an intersection. She was even more aware of the undulating space between them, like an invisible barrier that could not be crossed—not in public.

"I can't stop thinking about it," Lily said nervously. "About what happened."

Kath glanced at her shyly. "I can't either. I can't stop thinking about you."

Lily glanced around to double-check that no one was in hearing range. "How long—how long have you known about . . . the way you are?"

"I don't know. I guess I've always known I was . . . different. It didn't seem like a surprise when I figured it out."

They crossed Polk Street on Chestnut, heading for the stairs up Russian Hill. It was cold today; the air was damp and the wind constantly tugged at Lily's hair.

"What about you?" Kath asked. "How long have you known?"

"I'm not sure. Maybe a long time, in some ways. But not very long for real. Not—not until you." Lily glanced sidelong at Kath.

"I'm glad I could help," she said, smiling.

Lily laughed, and then shivered. She wasn't sure if it was the wind or Kath's smile that did it. "Do you remember that day in Senior Goals when you said it wasn't strange that I wanted to go to the moon?"

"I remember."

"I think that was the first day I really noticed you."

"Took you that long?" Kath teased her.

"Maybe I'm a late bloomer," Lily said tartly. "Why, when did you notice me?"

Kath shot her a grin. "You really want to know?"

"Yes!"

"Well . . . last year, you helped me with a geometry proof. You probably don't remember. You do this thing where you . . ." Kath trailed off, looking a little shy.

"What? What do I do?"

"You chew on your lip when you do a difficult math problem," Kath said. "It's cute."

Lily's face went red, and she laughed. "I'd better stop that in college, or no one will take me seriously."

When they reached the stairs they started up side by side, and sometimes as they climbed they bumped against each other, accidentally on purpose. Lily's arm against Kath's; their hands knocking gently together; their fingers almost linking.

Right before they reached the top, Kath said very softly, "I want to kiss you again."

A jolt went through Lily—she had to stop to catch her breath—and Kath stopped too, and they turned to look at each other. The wind had gone still, and Kath's hair was blown sideways across her forehead as if someone had tousled it with their fingers. Lily could look at Kath forever, but looking was not enough. She wanted nothing more than to touch Kath, but the space between them seemed to buzz warningly. They were on top of Russian Hill now, on top of the city itself, completely exposed.

"Where?" Lily asked. "Where can we go?"

The last stall in the girls' bathroom on the second floor had a full-length door, but every girl knew about it and tried to use that stall when she was on her period. There was a shadowy corner under the stairs to the gym by the locker rooms, but anyone could walk past and see them. And then Lily remembered the home-economics storage closet on the third floor, which had a key that Lily knew about from her time on the dance committee.

Several days passed before Lily was able to get the key. Preparations for the Miss Chinatown contest were ramping up (there were barely three weeks to go), and after school Lily had to help sell raffle tickets at the Chinese Hospital, or at Flora's father's store, or at the Eastern Pearl. Figuring out a way to evade Shirley's various demands felt like running an obstacle course, but Lily was afraid to deny her too openly and raise her suspicions.

Finally, on Thursday after school, Lily met Kath outside the home economics kitchen, where she pulled the key off the pegboard over the sink, and then led the way to the unmarked door down the hall. Lily checked to make sure that the hallway was deserted before she unlocked the closet, and then she and Kath quickly ducked in, pulling the door shut behind them.

It was cramped and dusty and hard to see. The only light came from the crack beneath the door, and Lily immediately bumped into a stack of metal bowls that made an awful racket. "Sorry!" Lily whispered.

"Careful." Kath reached for her hand to pull her away from the bowls, and it was the first time they had really touched since that night in the alley.

Lily suddenly felt strangely shy. Kath was so close. She couldn't see much beyond the dim outline of Kath's head and shoulders. The storage closet smelled faintly of pineapple juice, and Lily heard the sounds of the school in the background. Distant doors slammed shut; voices rose and fell indistinctly; footsteps came briskly down the hall toward them and then, thankfully, went past. The closet didn't lock from the inside, of course; anyone could open the door and find them. She was conscious of her own hand becoming slippery in Kath's.

"Are you okay?" Kath whispered. "You seem . . . tense."

"No, I . . ." *Tense* was not the right word. Terrified, maybe.

Almost a week had passed since their first kiss, which had been so surprising that it almost felt accidental. Today was no accident. They had planned to meet here, in this closet, to keep this secret. They knew what could happen if they were discovered; Jean had shown them.

For one awful moment Lily wanted to flee. She could open the door right now—she could say this was all a mistake—she could feel the relief waiting for her out in the hallway, and perhaps Kath sensed this because she asked, "Are you changing your mind?"

Her voice was thin and vulnerable, and it made Lily ashamed. "No," she whispered, and she took a step closer to Kath. Her mouth was almost touching her own; she could feel the heat of her breath on her lips. She could smell the fragrance of Kath's skin; it raised goose bumps on her arms. She gently pulled her hand from Kath's and deliberately, lightly, placed her hands around Kath's neck as if they were about to dance. She heard the inhale and exhale of Kath's breath in the darkness, and then Kath slid her hands around Lily's waist and leaned forward to kiss her.

It felt different this time—weighted. They were making this choice together, and Lily felt the seriousness with which Kath touched her. Her mouth questioned her with each kiss: *Is this what you want?* And Lily tried to say *yes* in the way she pulled Kath close to her, the way she caressed the fine soft hairs on the nape of Kath's neck, the way she pressed her breasts against Kath's body.

Yes.

36

On Friday, Kath pulled Lily aside after math class, her fingers briefly—electrically—curling around Lily's arm. As students rushed past them in the hallway, Kath said, "Miss Weiland is taking the G.A.A. bowling next Wednesday."

"You want to go bowling again?" Lily said, surprised.

"No. Her classroom will be empty." Kath glanced behind Lily and leaned slightly closer so that she could whisper. "Meet me there on Wednesday? Fifteen minutes after school. The door locks."

On Saturday, Shirley called Lily at home.

"Are you still going to the hospital to sell raffle tickets today?" Shirley asked.

"Yes, why?"

Shirley sighed heavily. "You don't need to bother. One of the other Miss Chinatown contestants convinced some of the Six Companies' board members to buy thousands of them all at once. I'm not going to beat her."

"What? That's not fair," Lily said.

"Flora said I'd win with my speech," Shirley said gloomily.

Lily doubted that, but she wasn't about to make Shirley feel even worse. "It's going to be fine," Lily said, trying to sound positive. "I could still go to the hospital—maybe Papa will help me get the hospital board to buy a bunch."

"Two thousand?" Shirley said doubtfully.

Lily winced. "Maybe not that many. But you never know. Do you want to come with me?"

"No, I can't. Thank you for what you've been doing, really, but I'm not going to win by selling tickets."

After Lily hung up, she lingered for a minute on the landing, wondering whether she should call Kath. Her afternoon was free now that she didn't have to go to the hospital for Shirley. Before she could lose her nerve, she went back to her room to retrieve her math notebook, where Kath had written down her telephone number a few days ago. Lily had done the same in Kath's notebook, but neither of them had called the other yet.

She ran back to the telephone and dialed with nervous fingers. Each rotation of the dial seemed to take forever, but at last she heard the call go through and begin to ring. She imagined the telephone in Kath's house coming to life, but it rang and rang, and nobody answered. Finally Lily hung up.

"Who were you calling?"

Lily started, and turned to face her mother in the kitchen doorway. "Just a friend—Mary," Lily said, and instantly wished she hadn't said a name.

"Are you still going out to sell raffle tickets this afternoon?" her mother asked.

"Yes," Lily lied.

"Will you stop by Dupont Market for me on your way back? I need some ginger and your father needs more coffee."

Her mother held out a five-dollar bill, and Lily took it wordlessly. She was afraid her mother would realize somehow that she had lied, but her mother simply went back into the kitchen, leaving Lily standing by the phone.

After lunch, Lily walked up Grant Avenue toward North Beach. She turned onto Jackson Street and went into a few of the shops, idly looking through display cases full of cheap jewelry. She had no real plan for the afternoon now that she didn't have to go to the hospital, but she was filled with a restlessness that made her twitchy and anxious. In one store she found an inexpensive rhinestone comb and impulsively bought it, thinking that she might wear it to the Telegraph Club one night, for Kath to see.

The thought lodged in her like a hook, and she began to consider what else she could buy. A new dress, perhaps. New stockings—grown-up ones. A new bra—and that made her imagine Kath seeing it, which made something clutch in her belly.

She went north, going into a couple of Chinatown boutiques and finding nothing she liked, and then continued past Broadway, up Columbus and into North Beach. The cafés were lively this afternoon, and as she walked past their big glass windows she looked inside at couples sipping espressos and nibbling on Italian pastries. Boys and girls, men and women, smiling at each other or talking animatedly, hands touching, unafraid to be seen together. She felt a growling jealousy in the pit of her stomach at the unfairness of it.

Before she knew it she had arrived at Washington Square Park, and she crossed Columbus and stood at the edge of the grass. It was chilly, and not many people were lingering outside. She catalogued them one by one: Caucasian man and woman; three Caucasian men (maybe Italian) smoking on a bench; two older Negro women walking slowly together; a Chinese girl of about ten with a woman who was probably her mother, holding her hand. Lily had been hoping she might see Kath, but there was no sign of her.

She glanced at her watch. It was time to go to Dupont Market and then home. She turned back toward Chinatown and decided to walk down Powell before cutting across to the grocery store. At the intersection of Powell and Green Street, she stopped to wait for the traffic before crossing, and on the corner diagonal to her a car pulled up to the sidewalk. The car was familiar, but she wasn't sure why until the passenger door opened and Shirley got out.

Lily almost raised her arm to wave at her, but something stopped her—perhaps the furtive way Shirley was moving, the way she drew her hat down as if to hide her face. But Lily would know Shirley anywhere; she had gone with her to pick out that powder-blue coat she wore. It had been her favorite purchase of the last year. Shirley came around to the driver's side of the car, and the window there rolled down, and a man's face appeared in the opening. Lily recognized Calvin Chan with a faint shock.

Shirley bent down to Calvin and kissed him. A smile crossed his face, and he reached out of the car and put his hand on her waist, drawing her down for another kiss. The way Calvin touched Shirley—the way they lingered over their kiss—sent a shiver of recognition through Lily. (Before she and Kath left the home economics closet, their fingers linked until the last possible moment.)

When Shirley finally pulled back, she was smiling too.

The street was clear by now, but Lily didn't move. She continued to stand on the corner, watching as Shirley waved goodbye to Calvin and hurried down Powell toward Chinatown. Calvin turned his car toward Columbus. Shirley didn't glance back in Lily's direction. She didn't see Lily at all, but Lily saw the jaunty way she walked, head up and shoulders back, carefree.

On Monday, Lily watched Shirley closely, but Shirley seemed the same as ever, except with a renewed determination to win the Miss Chinatown contest. She regaled Lily and their friends with her plan to rework her pageant speech, which she would practice at a full dress rehearsal on Friday night. Lily and Kath had plans to go to the Telegraph Club on Friday night, too, but she agreed to the dress rehearsal; it would be over before it was time to meet Kath.

On Tuesday, Kath left a note in Lily's locker. They'd begun leaving each other messages after Christmas break—only a few lines long and never signed. Lily knew she should wait to read them in private, but she was always too impatient, and today was no exception. She unfolded it inside her locker, angling the metal door so that she had some privacy. Kath had small, neat handwriting, and the note was short and to the point. *Can't wait till tomorrow.*

Lily smiled. She pulled out her pencil and wrote beneath it: *Me neither.* She folded it back into a neat square, and in math class she slipped it into Kath's hand, her fingers brushing like feathers against Kath's palm.

On Wednesday, it rained. All day it tapped against the windows like a drumroll. After school, Lily dawdled at her locker, straightening up her books, putting on and then taking off her coat, glancing impatiently at her watch.

Finally, it was time. She walked to Miss Weiland's classroom alone, and when she arrived, it was unlocked and deserted. Rainy afternoon light came through the half-closed blinds, casting pale stripes across the floor. She went to one of the windows and looked out; it had a view of the courtyard. She was there for barely a minute before she heard footsteps, and when she turned around, she saw Kath closing the classroom door.

Lily crossed the room and reached for Kath's hand, her pulse already leaping.

"Wait," Kath said, and she first locked the door from the inside, and then went across the room to close the blinds.

Lily went to help her. When they were finished, the room was almost dark, although the thin rectangular window in the door let in light from the hallway. If anyone stood at that window and peered inside, they'd be able to see most of the classroom. Lily and Kath headed for the farthest corner, which was blocked from the window's view by the tall metal filing cabinet. Above it, Miss Weiland had pinned a travel poster depicting palm trees and a beach, with the words LOS ANGELES written across the sky.

Lily reached for Kath's hand and drew her closer, her heart racing with anticipation. She had to be at Commodore Stockton to meet Frankie in an hour and a half, which gave them barely an hour together. She already felt the minutes ticking by too fast, but part of her realized there was something delicious about prolonging this moment, this intolerable pause before they kissed. Here, everything was possible.

In the dim light, Kath's face was all shadows. She was close enough now that Lily could smell the faint trace of mint on her breath, and the light, warm scent of her skin. She brushed her nose against Kath's neck, and she wanted to bottle up the fragrance of her. She felt Kath's pulse beneath her lips, and Kath's hand cupping the back of her head, and at last, Kath's mouth touching hers.

It was still a shock to feel it: the connection between their bodies, as if it had risen from the marrow of her bones, thick and charged and sweet. Before, she had been afraid of being discovered and afraid of discovering herself, but the more they kissed, the less afraid she felt, until her fear was subsumed beneath much more powerful feelings.

She wanted to touch Kath's skin. She tugged the hem of Kath's blouse out from her skirt and slid her hands beneath it, and finally she felt the warm skin of her back, and the quiver of Kath's body as she touched her. Kath drew back briefly and reached for the buttons of Lily's blouse, asking, "Can I?" Lily helped her unbutton it, and then Kath put her hand on the bare skin of Lily's waist, and Lily closed her eyes. Kath's hand slid up over her ribs and cupped the curve of her breast, and her thumb trailed electrically over the outline of Lily's nipple through her bra. And then she pushed her leg between Lily's thighs, and Lily gasped at how it felt—the pressure and the movement there—and it was exactly what she wanted. She was astonished by the way this worked between them so instinctively, as if they had been made to do this together.

But Lily felt as if there were no time. She couldn't entirely forget that they only had an hour together. A desire for something more was rising inside her as Kath moved against her, their skirts riding up as their bodies rubbed together. It felt urgent, as if they were counting down the seconds till a bomb would explode. There was no time; they had to do this right now. And she reached for the hem of her skirt and tugged it up to her hips, and she took Kath's hand and moved it to the cleft of her body.

Kath hesitated. "Are you sure?" she whispered.

"Please," Lily said, overcome.

So Kath put her hand between Lily's legs, and Lily helped her, fumbling with her underwear. It was awkward, but when Kath's fingers touched her, they both gasped.

"Am I in the right place?" Kath asked.

"Yes," Lily whispered.

It all felt like the right place. Kath's fingers rubbed and rubbed, and it was so marvelous, so intoxicating—she'd never even really touched herself like this before—and now she was pinned against the side of the filing cabinet, and it made a dull metallic thud as her hand slapped against it.

"I'm sorry," she gasped, but she couldn't really be sorry because it was all happening so quickly, so unexpectedly, and she clutched Kath close to her as the sensations took over, her body shuddering, and she pressed her face into Kath's neck until it was over.

There was a minute in which she breathed in and out, in and out, and Kath held her gently, her head resting against the filing cabinet. Then Kath kissed her neck and shifted herself over Lily's thigh and whispered, "Can I—is this all right?"

"Yes," Lily said, and she leaned into Kath, holding her as she moved, feeling Kath's wetness slide against her leg.

It was extraordinary, Lily thought. There was nothing like this in the world. How different this was from when Lily was alone in her room. How different, and how much more: an overflowing amount of more. Kath kept rocking against her thigh, her breath ragged against Lily's cheek, and Lily stroked her hand over Kath's hair tenderly, feeling impossibly close to her. How precious she was, and how miraculous.

37

All this time, Shirley had said nothing about Calvin. Earlier, Lily might have been resentful or even jealous, but her own secret was much more important now.

On Friday night, Lily arrived at the Lums' home to find Shirley and Flora in the living room. Shirley had already put on her Macy's dress, and when Lily entered, Shirley asked, "Look what I have—do you like my earrings?"

"They're from Mr. Wong's store," Flora said.

Lily took off her coat and came closer to look at the blue drops clipped to Shirley's ears. They looked like sapphires. "Pretty," Lily said.

"They go really well with the dress," Flora said.

"What do you think, Lily?" Shirley asked, twirling around. The dress fit her well. She'd selected a gauzy pastel-blue gown with a full skirt and a Grecian-style draped neckline. She was wearing white patent leather heels and full makeup, with a crimson mouth and the corners of her eyes emphasized by a sweep of eyeliner, and she'd curled her hair and pinned it in place with a rhinestone comb. "Do I look like a good Chinese girl?" Shirley fluttered her eyelashes.

Lily sat down on the sofa and picked her words carefully. "You look like a beauty queen," she said.

Shirley pursed her lips and walked over to the coffee table, where she had left a written draft of her speech. "Well, the judges better think so," Shirley said.

"I know they will," Flora said.

They heard footsteps on the stairs, and a moment later Mary appeared, carrying Shirley's cheongsam in a garment bag. "I'm sorry I'm late," Mary said, rushing into the living room. She laid the bag over the back of the sofa and unzipped it to display the dress, which her mother, who was a seamstress, had altered for Shirley. "You should try it on to make sure it fits."

The cheongsam was sky-blue silk embroidered with white flowers, to coordinate with the Macy's dress.

"Oh, it's beautiful! But I'm going to give my speech in this dress," Shirley said, gesturing to the one she was wearing. "Let me practice in this first. Dress rehearsal! And then I'll try on the cheongsam. Here, all of you should sit down and be my audience—and my judges." Shirley moved the cheongsam over to one of the empty armchairs while Mary joined Lily and Flora on the sofa.

Shirley stood across from them, backlit by the windows, and held her speech in both hands as she gave them a bow. "Good evening, gentlemen," she began.

Flora and Mary giggled in response, because of course they weren't gentlemen. Lily managed a smile.

"恭喜發財.[1] Thank you for allowing me the honor of speaking to you tonight. I have thought carefully about who Miss Chinatown is meant to be, and I humbly hope that you will find me best suited to the task. One of Miss Chinatown's most important responsibilities is to reign over the New Year festivities as a representative of our community. The New Year festival is an ancient tradition dating back thousands of years, and yet it also celebrates the opportunity to make a new start in the New Year. Every year we honor our ancestors and thank them for their blessings, and every year we prepare our homes and families for the New Year by paying our debts and cleaning out the dust of the old year.

---

1. Congratulations and wishing you prosperity (a common New Year greeting).

"We Chinese Americans have come to this new world of America to make new lives for ourselves and our families. Miss Chinatown should represent the best of both these traditions, ancient and modern. She should honor the strength of the Chinese family and Chinese tradition, but she should also embrace the best of the new American way of life.

"I am the daughter of hardworking immigrants from Canton. I was born right here in Kau Kam Shaan,[2] and I grew up working in my parents' restaurant, where I saw how Chinese culture can be embraced by Americans. I am a daughter of the Old World as well as the New World, and I am ready to represent Chinatown as we move forward into the Year of the Sheep. I humbly present myself to you, honored judges, as an obedient and dutiful daughter of Chinatown. Thank you."

Shirley curtsied, holding her skirt back delicately as if she were a princess, and Lily, Flora, and Mary clapped.

"I think that's pretty good," Flora said. "Very humble."

"And virtuous," Mary said.

Lily wasn't sure she liked the speech. It felt like a fraud, as if Shirley were trying to flatter the judges into voting for her. "I like the curtsy at the end," Lily said.

"But do you think it's enough to win?" Shirley asked. "I didn't sell enough raffle tickets."

"You can still win," Flora declared. "You're so much prettier than the other girls. I saw the one who sold all those tickets to the Six Companies—she has a face like a cow."

"Flora," Mary admonished her. "That's mean."

"It's true," Flora insisted. "If Miss Chinatown is supposed to be a beauty queen, then Shirley should win."

"What do you think, Lily?" Shirley asked. "You're so quiet."

---

2. San Francisco; literally, "old gold mountain."

There was a subtle challenge in Shirley's tone, and Lily knew she was supposed to say something encouraging—that Shirley was the prettiest of all, that she would surely win or else those judges were all blind idiots. That was the price of admission to Shirley's circle, and Lily had paid it before. It was easy enough to continue paying it, but she didn't want to anymore. Lily realized she'd stopped wanting to pay her fee a long time ago. All she wanted right now was to get this dress rehearsal over with and go to the Telegraph Club with Kath.

"Miss Chinatown is about supporting Chinatown businesses," Lily said finally. "The judges don't care how pretty you are—the girls are all pretty enough. They only care how much money you'll bring in. You know how it works."

Flora gasped, and Mary frowned, but Shirley gave Lily a look of grudging respect.

38

When Lily got home after the dress rehearsal, Frankie was sick with a stomachache. As she waited for him to settle down and for her parents to go to bed, she watched the hands of the clock move toward and past the hour she usually went to meet Kath. By the time the flat was quiet, she knew Kath had left their meeting spot. She hoped Kath had gone ahead to the club to wait for her.

Outside, the streets were thick with fog, and she doubled her scarf around her neck. Every headlight, every streetlamp had a nimbus around it, an otherworldly glow, and the air itself seemed to press against Lily's body. It clung to her like smoke, like a cloak, making her feel as if she must be invisible. It was as if the city itself were helping to hide her.

The Telegraph Club's neon sign shivered in the distance. Music drifted down Broadway; disconnected laughter floated on the air. She was a ghost gliding through the streets. She was a fish sliding through dark waters. She was at the door of the club, and there was Mickey, who said, "Your friend's already inside."

"Thank you," Lily said, and stepped through the doorway.

The club was warm and loud and smelled as it always did of perfume and cigarettes and beer. Lily heard Tommy crooning through the speakers. The bar area, which she had never walked through alone, was a long line of women turning to look at her. She felt as if she were on display, and part of her wanted to hide, but another part thrilled to it: this being seen, as if every person who gazed at her were creating her anew.

She paused in the archway between the bar and the stage room, loosening her scarf in the warm room and scanning the tables for Kath. Every face was turned toward the stage, where Tommy stood spotlighted, singing "Secret Love." Like every time before, there were a number of couples—men and women—seated close to the stage, the women somewhere between enthralled and embarrassed, the men wearing knowing smiles. Lily wondered what they thought they knew. She was pretty sure they were wrong.

She spotted Kath seated with Jean and Jean's college friends in the leftmost corner, toward the back. Lily might not have seen her at all, because she was largely in shadow, but Kath leaned forward to light a cigarette, and the flare of the lighter drew her attention. The flame briefly illuminated Kath's face; her hair was swept back and parted on the side, like a man's. It startled Lily to see her like that, and she suddenly felt self-conscious. She was wearing her new dress, the one she told her mother she'd bought to wear to the pageant, but had actually chosen for tonight. It was tighter than the dresses she usually wore, with a lower V-neck than she was used to, although it was still quite modest. But in this room, among these women, her new dress was a declaration. If she went over to Kath and sat beside her, everyone here would know what it meant.

Tommy began another number, a lively one that involved her flirting with the women around the edge of the stage. Lily remembered how she had once fantasized about Tommy singing to her at one of those tables, and her fantasy seemed so naïve now, so silly. A schoolgirl dream. She recognized the smile on Tommy's face as she leaned down to serenade a brunette in a maroon cocktail dress. She looked so flattered, so eager.

Lily looked away. She began to weave her way toward Kath, who seemed to be looking around too. Lily thought she saw Kath put down her cigarette; she thought she saw the slightly paler shadow of her face rise up, as if she were standing. "Excuse me," she whispered, bumping into strangers' chairs, slipping around women standing at the rear of the room. When had the small stage room become so large and filled with so many obstacles? She wasn't even paying attention to Tommy's show anymore.

At last she was there, and Lily recognized the set of Kath's shoulders even though she couldn't see her face, which was only a blur in the smoky dimness. "Kath," she whispered in relief. It had only been a few hours since she'd seen Kath at school, but it felt as if days had passed.

"What happened?" Kath whispered. "I waited, but then it got too late."

Someone nearby shushed them, and Lily grabbed Kath's hand and pulled her back through the stage room and into the hallway that led to the stairs. The alcove beneath the stairs was empty, and Lily drew Kath into its shadows, her skin already flushing with anticipation.

"I'm sorry I was late," Lily said. "Frankie was sick and I had to wait till he went to sleep."

There were a few beer kegs and some wooden crates stored under the stairs, but there was just enough room for the two of them. Overhead, cracks in the stair treads let in paper-thin shafts of dim yellow light. It slanted over Kath's face as she closed the space between them and said, "I'm glad you're here," and then she kissed Lily.

"Me too." Lily kissed her back.

When they drew apart, Lily remembered that she had brought a gift for Kath, and she pulled the toy airplane from her pocket. "This is for you," she said.

Kath held it up to examine it in better light. "What's this for?" She sounded surprised.

"It made me think of you."

Flora's father had assumed it was for Lily's youngest brother, and she hadn't corrected him. She had wanted to put it in a box and wrap it, but she didn't have the right size box, and the only wrapping paper at home was left over from Christmas. Now, seeing Kath holding the bare little toy plane in her hand, she was embarrassed.

"It's nothing," Lily whispered. "It's all right if you don't like it."

Kath spun the wheels and smiled. "I like it." She slipped the airplane into her pocket and slid her hands around Lily's waist again. "Do you want to go out to the show?"

"In a minute."

"Just a minute?" Kath teased her.

Lily laughed. She pulled Kath closer; she felt her smiling mouth against her own. Lily remembered the sight of that other couple beneath the stairs, and it was as if time had folded upon itself and she couldn't tell if she was herself or someone else. How many girls had stood beneath these stairs, kissing? Lily envisioned a long line of girls like them cocooned in this dark pocket of beer-scented air.

A shout suddenly went up from the bar, and the lights flashed in the hallway, startling them apart.

Tommy abruptly stopped singing. The pianist halted in mid-phrase, and then Tommy's voice came over the speakers: "I'm sorry to say we're calling it an early night, folks." Voices rose at once in confusion and surprise, and the lights flashed again, repeatedly.

"What's going on?" Lily asked. She glanced out into the hallway, which continued past their alcove beneath the stairs, and ended in a closed door.

Someone came running down the short hallway from the bar and went directly past them, knocking into Lily's shoulder. They opened the door at the end and plunged through, and just as Lily was stepping out from beneath the stairs, more women came—dozens, all of them, it seemed—heading pell-mell for that door.

Kath grabbed hold of a stranger's arm and asked, "What happened?"

The woman was in a suit; she dragged her arm away and called over her shoulder, "Cops! The club's being raided!"

Lily was still holding Kath's hand, and Kath squeezed her fingers as she peered down the hall at the door. It was a back exit. "Come on," Kath said. She tugged Lily into the hallway, joining the exodus. Lily could smell the fog seeping inside.

Kath abruptly halted and dragged her out of the way. "Wait—I left my coat."

The panic of the crowd was contagious, and Lily's only thought now was escape. "Can't you leave it?"

Kath shook her head. "My identification's in the pocket. You go ahead. I'll meet you out there."

"Isn't it fake? Just leave it!" Lily wouldn't let go of her hand.

"I forgot to leave my real one at home. I have to get it. You go—meet me on our corner, okay?" Kath squeezed Lily's hand once more, and then Kath went back down the hall, going against the tide of women, leaving Lily alone.

A woman brushed past her, advising, "You better get out of here, unless you want to get caught."

Heart pounding, Lily followed everyone else outside and into a narrow alley. It was very dark, and it smelled like urine. Up above, the buildings loomed black against a cloud-covered night sky. Only a few windows were lit, and Lily was reminded of how late it was. Everyone emerging from the Telegraph Club seemed to be heading to one or the other end of the alley, and Lily went to the left—she thought that way was Columbus Avenue—but when she emerged onto a side street she didn't recognize, she stopped. She looked back down the alley. The open door cast a rectangle of yellow light onto the ground, illuminating a puddle of rank liquid that several women splashed through as they ran out of the building. There was no sign of Kath.

Voices came now, loud and insistent. Men's voices—and then men in uniform, wielding flashlights.

Lily fled across the unfamiliar street. There was a group of men there, standing and smoking in the shadow of a building. The embers at the ends of their cigarettes seemed to float in the air like tiny red eyes. They had probably seen her lingering in the mouth of the alley, and she ducked her head nervously, realizing she'd lost her scarf somewhere.

She kept moving, even though she didn't know where she was going. She was approaching light and noise, but she kept her gaze lowered toward the stains and spots on the sidewalk, the darker shadow of the gutter running like a river beside her.

The street was short and ended in a wide avenue—she had found Broadway again. To her left was a kaleidoscope of blue and white lights, rotating like a Playland ride. A white neon sign hung from the side of the building closest to the lights: THE TELEGRAPH CLUB. With a jolt, she realized that several police cars were parked outside the club. A clump of women stood near the awning, huddled together as if for safety. A policeman stepped away from one of them, and Lily didn't understand what she was watching at first. It was only when the woman turned, her arms positioned unnaturally, that she understood that the policeman had handcuffed her.

She spun around immediately and headed for Columbus Avenue. In her quick glimpse of the handcuffed women, she didn't think she had seen Kath. Maybe she had gone down the alley in the other direction. She might already be on Columbus. Lily quickened her pace. The traffic screamed past her and someone was laughing too loud; men tossed burning cigarettes onto the curb like tiny missiles to dodge. Someone called after her, "Slow down and smile, sweetheart!" She ignored him; she was almost there. She could see their corner in the distance.

But no one was there when she arrived. The streetlamp was shining on an empty sidewalk.

She wasn't sure how long she stood there, shivering. It felt like hours. When she saw a police car cruising down Columbus, she shrank back into the shadows, but she knew she couldn't wait there all night. With a desperate, sinking feeling, she turned toward home and resolved to call Kath first thing in the morning. She would understand why Lily hadn't stayed on their corner.

When she got home, she tried to be as quiet as possible, but she was clumsy from the cold and stumbled on the stairs. The door to her bedroom stuck and she had to force it—with a rumble—to open.

The silence afterward was unbearable. She heard the creak of bedsprings, the squeal of her parents' bedroom door.

She rushed to undress, shoving her clothes under her bed and pulling on her nightgown so fast she nearly tangled herself in the sleeves. She accidentally stubbed her toe against one of the bed's legs and couldn't suppress a yelp of pain. Tears smarting at her eyes, she climbed into her bed and pulled up the covers just in time—her father was sliding open the door, saying, "Li-li, are you all right?"

She rolled over, pretending to be sleepy. "Yes, Papa."

"Couldn't sleep?"

"No."

He came in and sat on the edge of her bed, switching on her bedside lamp, and she had to turn over to face him, schooling her face into emptiness. He placed a warm hand on her forehead. "You're a little hot."

"I'm fine. I just couldn't sleep."

He studied her for a moment, and she willed herself to look normal—sleepless, maybe, but normal—and she must have succeeded, because he eventually removed his hand. "All right. Well, if you're not feeling well in the morning, let me know."

"I will."

"Good night." He turned off the lamp and left, sliding the pocket doors shut.

1950 — Judy Hu marries Francis Fong.

— Lily attends the third annual Chinese American Citizens Alliance Independence Day Picnic and Miss Chinatown Contest.

1951 — Dr. Hsue-shen Tsien is placed under house arrest on suspicion of being a Communist and a sympathizer to the People's Republic of China.

Aug. 12, 1951 — **JUDY takes Lily to Playland at the Beach.**

— In *Stoumen v. Reilly*, the California Supreme Court rules that homosexuals have the right to public assembly, for example, in a bar.

1952 — Francis begins working as an engineer at the Jet Propulsion Laboratory.

1953 — Judy is hired as a computer at the Jet Propulsion Laboratory.

— Judy takes Lily to the Morrison Planetarium at the California Academy of Sciences in Golden Gate Park.

JUDY

Three and a Half Years Earlier

The Opium Den diorama was located on the left side of the Musée Mécanique at Playland, just past one of the mechanical fortune-tellers whose eyes rolled each time a coin was dropped into the machine's slot. Judy had seen the Opium Den before, and though she'd been horrified the first time, it had never struck her with such disgust before today.

That morning, as she and Francis prepared to pick up Lily, Frankie, and Eddie for their long-scheduled Saturday outing, she had tried to convince Francis that it was too cold for a trip to Playland. "It'll be foggy and windy," she had said. "Let's take them somewhere indoors instead."

But Francis had resisted. "The boys want to go to the Fun House, and Frankie wants to ride the roller coaster for the first time. I promised them I'd take them there last month."

So they had piled into Francis's Mercury and driven out to Playland at the Beach. Judy watched Francis take Eddie and Frankie to the wooden roller coaster while Lily wandered off to the Musée Mécanique to feed pennies into the automated dioramas. As a child, Lily hadn't liked the rides very much, but she could watch the miniature figurines processing through their painted wooden worlds for hours, thrilled by the tiny, orderly details. Lily was fourteen now, and Judy suspected her interest in those mechanized marvels had waned, so she followed her niece inside to wait for her.

There was a bench a few feet away from the Opium Den, and Judy sat down there, pulling a paperback out of her purse to read. It was *The Martian Chronicles* by Ray Bradbury, which she'd borrowed from Francis, who had a taste for science fiction. She thought some of the novels he liked were terrible, but she was enjoying this one. She couldn't focus on the story, though. From her vantage point it was hard to avoid noticing each time the Opium Den whirred into life, and children seemed to be endlessly feeding it coins.

The diorama wasn't very large, maybe two feet wide by one foot deep, but it contained a number of weird creatures that twitched or jumped when the machine was running. It depicted an underground opium den populated by figurines with slanted eyes, ghostly skin, and blank expressions, possibly intended to represent men in the throes of opium-induced euphoria. In the back of the den, a Chinese man lay in an alcove in the wall, jerking up and falling back over and over again. A disturbing figure with a skull-like face descended into the den from a stairway on the right. To the left, a door sprang open to reveal a hanging skeleton. And most bizarrely, a giant cobra popped out repeatedly from behind a fringed curtain in the back.

Children loved the Opium Den—they especially loved to giggle and point at the cobra—but the more times Judy saw it, the more it repulsed her. The cobra, with its bulbous head and thrusting motion, seemed obscene. And the opium addict in the rear alcove bouncing up and down was humiliating. He was powerless, unable to escape this mechanized depiction of a real-life tragedy.

"How long do we have to stay?" Lily asked, sliding onto the bench beside her.

"Lily! Finished already?" Judy said. She had been so absorbed in her anger over the diorama that she hadn't noticed Lily approaching.

Lily's gaze followed Judy's over to the Opium Den, and she frowned as she watched the repeated humiliation. "I hate that one," Lily said.

"Me too," Judy said. "Let's go. We don't have to stay here."

Sometimes Judy felt a deep and burning anger at her adopted country, and she never knew what to do about it. She had come to America for an education and had intended to return home, but first she had met Francis and then the Communists had taken over and now, unfortunately, she couldn't leave. America had given her so much in the four years since she arrived, but it also regularly reminded her of how it saw people like her.

"Where are we going?" Lily asked, running after her.

"Let's go to the beach," Judy said, opening the door.

"What about Eddie and Frankie and Uncle Francis?"

Judy glanced at her watch. "We agreed to meet at the Fun House at three o'clock. We have forty-five minutes. Come on—I want to see the ocean."

Judy had fallen in love with Ocean Beach the first time she saw it almost four years ago, right after she first arrived in San Francisco. That had been a chilly day, too, and she remembered the wind whipping her hair against her face as she climbed over the sand dunes.

It wasn't a warm and sunny beach like the ones in travel guides. It was cold and vast like the Pacific Ocean, which roared in on wild, foam-crested waves. She loved Ocean Beach because when she stood here she could finally grasp, in her bones, how large the Pacific was. She could almost see the curve of the earth on the ocean's horizon—or she imagined that she could—and it gave her a physical sense of how far away from home she had traveled.

Yes, she truly had come that far. No, she really wasn't going home anytime soon.

There was a strange sense of freedom in those thoughts. They left her free to be here, in this place, right now.

The ocean was gray today and blended almost seamlessly into the sky at the horizon. She remembered her passage across that ocean, sixteen days on a converted American troop transport ship in a second-class cabin with several other young Chinese women. She had spent so much time with those women, and yet now she barely remembered them. She wondered if they ever thought about her: studious and quiet, head down in her math and English-language books the entire voyage. She was sure they had thought her strange.

Now Judy watched Lily walking away from her down the hard-packed sand near the edge of the waves, looking for seashells. Lily went past a clump of seaweed that had washed ashore. It looked like a mass of dark green snakes tangled together, and when the water rushed back over it, one tail jerked back and forth like the cobra in the horrible Opium Den.

Just like that, Judy remembered the snakelike twist of blood and tissue in the toilet last April, when she had miscarried. It had been so early in the pregnancy that she had barely begun to accept it herself. She and Francis had been married for ten months, and it was time to start a family—everyone said so—but she had been reluctant to go to the doctor to confirm that she was pregnant.

Afterward, she secretly wondered if her reluctance had doomed the unborn baby. She had been planning to apply for Ph.D. programs in mathematics when she got pregnant. She'd dreamed of continuing her studies, not having a baby.

She had been overwhelmed by guilt. She still was. How could she have been so careless? She should have gone to the doctor earlier. She should have known, somehow, that something was wrong. It was probably her fault for not paying closer attention to her body. She'd always been lost in thought, in numbers and patterns and theorems.

She'd always been an oddity, not like normal girls who cooed over babies and put all their heart into planning and preparing and waiting for them. She wasn't one to coo; she never had been. Perhaps that meant there was something wrong with her, and her body had known that and had rejected motherhood.

In some ways, the guilt was more painful than the miscarriage.

She lifted her eyes from the snaking seaweed and sought out Lily, down the beach. She started to walk toward her niece. She felt shaky, the way she always did when she remembered that awful time last spring. She wondered when it would pass. Sometimes she caught herself fearing that it never would, and then she told herself that she was being melodramatic. She had experienced horrors during the war that she learned to forget.

(That woman torn open on the side of the road after the bomb; the shine of her organs.)

"Lily!" she called, deliberately pushing away those thoughts.

(Her father nailing planks over the windows, blocking out the daylight.)

Lily heard her and turned around, waiting for her to catch up. Lily was so fortunate. To live in the same country she had been born in, to have never experienced war on her doorstep.

"What did you find?" Judy asked.

Her niece held out her hand and revealed a purple-and-black mussel shell, perfectly empty, with a bone-white interior.

"All the good shells are crushed today," Lily said. "There was only this."

She raised her arm and threw it back into the ocean, but it landed lightly on the foam-crested wave that was rolling back to shore, and the water ushered the shell right back to them, depositing it at their feet.

They walked back to Playland side by side, staying on the hard-packed sand as long as possible until they had to strike off over the shifting sand dunes. Judy took one last look at the horizon, imagining she could see over the edge and across those thousands of miles of open water, all the way to the harbor in Shanghai.

When they reached the amusement park, she saw Francis before he saw them. He was standing outside the Fun House, laughing, as Frankie and Eddie tugged long strands of cotton candy from the spindle he held in his hand. Judy knew, somehow, that Eddie was about to turn around and raise a handful of the bright pink candy and wave it vigorously at Lily as he saw her—and he did—and Lily waved back, smiling.

似曾相識, Judy thought. The sensation of having already met someone, or what the French called *déjà vu*, the feeling of having already seen something. There was probably a scientific explanation for it, but the older she got, the more she was inclined to give in to the feeling that these moments were glimpses into a world greater than this physical one. It was as if there were cycles that repeated themselves over and over, but most people never saw the repetition; they were too deeply enmeshed in their own path to see.

In one cycle, she had already experienced this day at Playland, and part of her brain remembered it. Did that mean that she had always been destined to come here, to this city in this land so far from her home? She slid her hand into her pocket to feel the mussel shell, which she had picked up out of some kind of vague superstition. If the ocean had tossed it back to them, that must mean they should take it. All these signs, she thought, pointed to this moment, and then this one, over and over again.

PART VI

Secret Love

January 1955

39

The headline on the front page took up the entire width of the newspaper that Lily's father was reading: TEEN-AGE GIRLS 'RECRUITED' AT SEX DEVIATE BAR. Lily felt all the blood rush to her head as she saw it. The toast she was chewing turned dry as dust in her mouth, and she had to choke it down with a sip of coffee.

The story didn't seem to make much of an impression on her father. He finished the article he had been reading and folded the paper back on itself, hiding the front page, then glanced at the clock over the stove. It was eight twenty-six on Saturday morning, and he was on duty at the Chinese Hospital that day.

Lily had barely slept last night, lying awake waiting for morning so that she could call Kath. It was almost an appropriate hour now, but the closer she got to dialing Kath's number, the more nervous she became.

Lily's mother was packing up her father's lunch and saying, "You're sure you can pick up a roast duck? I don't have time. We have to clean the flat."

"Yes, I told you I will."

"And you'll be back before Judy and Francis arrive?"

"Of course. They're not due in until eight o'clock tonight."

"Mama, when do the firecrackers start?" Frankie asked.

"At midnight, but you'll be in bed."

"Why can't I go see them?"

"There will be more tomorrow. They'll be going off all week."

Eddie, who had been crunching through his bowl of Sugar Frosted Flakes, said, "Lily, what's wrong?"

She had stopped eating her breakfast. She picked up her piece of toast again and forced herself to take another bite. "Nothing."

Her father looked at her over the edge of the newspaper. "You're not feeling sick?"

"No."

"Good." He dropped the paper on the table and stood up. "I'd better go."

"Why did you ask if she was sick? Are you sick, Lily?" her mother asked.

"No."

"She was up late last night," her father said. "I thought she might have caught what Frankie had."

"I'm fine," Lily said.

Her father picked up his lunch from the counter. "I'll see you tonight."

Lily got up and dumped her half-finished piece of toast in the trash before her mother could notice she hadn't eaten it all.

"Lily, I need you to stay home today with Frankie," her mother said. "I have a lot of errands to run."

"I don't need her to stay with me," Frankie said. "Eddie can stay with me."

"Eddie has to do his homework, and you're still recovering. Lily will be here. Wait—when do you need to meet Shirley?"

"Not until six. The judging happens at seven but we have to get there an hour early."

"That should be fine, but make sure to eat before you go. I won't have time to make you dinner."

"I know."

"Will you go and strip the beds, please? I need you to start the laundry this morning."

"Yes, Mama."

But Lily hesitated before leaving the kitchen; the newspaper was sitting on the corner of the table, abandoned. She wanted to grab it, but before she could make her move, her mother sat down at the table and picked up the paper, flipping directly to the society columns in the back. Lily watched her for a moment, wondering if she'd go back to the front page, but she didn't.

Lily had to wait until her mother left before she could use the telephone. By then it was late morning, and she could barely contain her anxiety. After making sure that Eddie and Frankie were in the living room, she went to the telephone and nervously picked up the heavy black receiver, dialing Kath's number from memory. There was a click in her ear, and then the call connected. The *brr-brr* sound repeated over and over as she stood there waiting for someone to pick up, but no one did. After ten rings, she hung up, her heart racing.

She dialed the number again.

Once more she counted ten rings; once more there was no answer. This time when she hung up, she sank down onto the bench. She felt dizzy with worry. She told herself that the fact that there was no answer didn't mean anything. Maybe they were just out—her own mother had gone out—perhaps everyone in Kath's family had gone out, too. She briefly imagined the whole family at the market, or going to the park, or—

She suddenly remembered the newspaper article, and she jumped up and went back into the kitchen. She found the *Chronicle* in the trash can, the edges dampened by coffee grounds. She shook it off as well as she could and unfolded it. The front page was wet in the lower right quadrant, but the headline was still crisp and shockingly large.

TEEN-AGE GIRLS 'RECRUITED' AT SEX DEVIATE BAR

Police raided a North Beach bar known as the Telegraph Club Friday night, after receiving tips that the bar has long been a hunting ground for "gay" types that use the establishment to recruit teen-age girls into debauchery. The club, located at 462 Broadway, has been under secret investigation for months. Inspector J. L. Herington of the San Francisco Police reports that at least a dozen teen-age girls have been seduced by older women into a vice academy, in which they were introduced to marijuana and Benzedrine, and encouraged to attend secret parties after hours at the homes of sex deviates.

On the testimony of several teen-age girls interviewed at the Youth Guidance Center, warrants were issued for the woman owner of the Telegraph Club, Joyce Morgan, and Theresa Scafani, who performs at the club as a male impersonator under the stage name Tommy Andrews. Both women were arrested and charged with contributing to the delinquency of minors, and Scafani was charged with lewd conduct.

Inspector Herington related a sordid story of abominable acts that are in some cases unprintable, involving high school girls ranging in age from 16 to 18, many from good families. "There was a pattern," Inspector Herington explained. "Girls would go to the Telegraph Club to see a nightclub act, and once they were there they would be plied with alcohol and invited for dates by older women who were sexual deviates.

Once a girl was ensnared, she would recruit her friends from school."

At first, the girls would think it was a "lark," Inspector Herington said. But soon, some of the girls started to wear mannish clothing and were known as "butches," emulating the older women who had seduced them. These sexual deviates took the lead in inviting unsuspecting teen-age girls to private apartments in the North Beach and Telegraph Hill neighborhood, where marijuana cigarettes were offered, and Benzedrine, known as "bennies," were for sale.

The story continued on page five and included a sensational account of a cluttered flat in North Beach, reportedly the home of Telegraph Club owner Joyce Morgan, where a stash of marijuana had been found next to a detective novel. Although several teen girls were mentioned, none were named. Lily read the story several times, both hoping and fearing that she had missed Kath's name, but it wasn't there. Each time she read it, the story seemed more bizarre. It was as if the reporter had taken the truth and distorted it into a pulp novel. Reading it made her feel as if she had been splattered with something filthy, and no matter how hard she scrubbed, she would never come clean.

She crumpled up the newspaper and shoved it back into the trash, sick to her stomach. She poured herself a glass of water and then she couldn't drink it, instead standing half frozen with panic while she stared blankly out the window. All she could think about was Kath. She remembered her beneath the stairs at the Telegraph Club, the darkness a cocoon around them as they kissed, the sound of Tommy singing in the background like an old record on repeat. She needed to find out what had happened to Kath.

She ran back into the hall, picking up the telephone and dialing

Kath's number again, but again there was no answer. She hung up in frustration, unsure of what to do. She wished she knew Kath's address, so she could go there and wait for her to come home— and then she spotted the corner of the telephone book on the shelf beneath the phone. She pulled it out and knelt down on the floor, flipping to the page for Miller, and ran her finger down the numbers, searching for Kath's. About halfway down the page she found it. She grabbed a pencil and tore off a piece of paper from the notepad by the phone, scribbling down the North Beach address.

The front doorbell pealed loudly. Lily started and dropped the pencil, which immediately rolled beneath the telephone table. She bent down to retrieve it, but the doorbell sounded again, and there was an impatient edge to the repeated rings.

Eddie poked his head out of the living room at the end of the hall. "Lily? Are you going to get the door?"

She gave up on the pencil and scrambled to her feet, discombobu-lated and tense, thinking irrationally that it must be the police. "Stay in there with Frankie," she told her brother.

"Why?"

"Just go!"

His eyes widened in surprise, but he retreated, glancing back at her worriedly. As the doorbell rang again, Lily went downstairs. At the bottom she put her hand on the deadbolt and called out, "Who is it?"

"Lily? It's Shirley. Let me in."

Confused, Lily opened the door. Shirley stood on the front step carrying her purse and a garment bag.

"What are you doing here?" Lily asked. "Is something wrong with your dress? I thought I was supposed to meet you at the judging."

"I just picked up my dress at the cleaners. I need to talk to you."

There was something strange about the expression on Shirley's face. "About what?" Lily asked. She wondered if Shirley's parents had found out about Calvin.

"Can I come in?"

Lily let her in, and Shirley started up the stairs. Lily closed the door and followed. "Did something happen?" she asked.

Lily heard Eddie saying hello to Shirley, who responded briefly. At the top of the stairs, Shirley took off her shoes and set down her bags. "Are your parents home?" she asked.

"No."

"Let's go in the kitchen."

"Why? What's wrong?"

Lily went after Shirley into the kitchen, and Shirley shut the door. She went to the kitchen table as if she were about to sit down, but then she seemed to think better of it and paced over to the sink, arms crossed.

"I don't know how to say this," Shirley began.

"Say what? Is your family all right?"

"They're fine. This is about—it's about you." Shirley lowered her gaze as if it pained her to look at Lily. "Someone saw you last night— this morning, very early—leaving a nightclub in North Beach. It was raided last night for— Honestly, I can't even bring myself to say it. I told them it was a mistake because what would you be doing at a place like that? But they insisted it was you. It wasn't you, was it? Tell me it wasn't you."

Lily had to sit. At first, she hadn't quite believed what Shirley was saying, but slowly—too slowly, and then suddenly as if an explosion had gone off that only she could hear—she understood.

Shirley knew.

"—told him you're not like that. I've known you since we were children! I would know if you were like that, but you're not. Lily, why won't you say anything? It wasn't you, was it?"

She realized all at once, in one great overwhelming rush, how incredibly stupid she had been—how naïve, how ridiculously foolish—to think she could go to the Telegraph Club time after time without consequence. Perhaps once—if she were extremely careful—but she had gone several times. She had left her home in the middle of the night and walked right down Grant Avenue—Grant Avenue!—past restaurants and shops owned by people who had known her since she was born. She hadn't even bothered to hide her face. She had blithely assumed that in North Beach, surely, no one would recognize her. She had conveniently, recklessly, overlooked that she would be a lone Chinese girl on Broadway at two o'clock in the morning, as conspicuous as she could possibly get. The danger had always been there, but she had chosen to ignore it, and now here was Shirley, looking at her—pleading with her—to lie about where she had been.

Lily knew that she should lie. She should tell Shirley what she wanted to hear. Perhaps whoever had told Shirley hadn't told anyone else, and if she denied it, Shirley might be able to put an end to this gossip; but as soon as that thought arose, she knew it was already too late. Word traveled lightning fast through Chinatown.

"Who saw me?" Lily asked.

Shirley was noticeably startled. "What does it matter?"

"I want to know. Who saw me?"

Shirley frowned. "Wallace Lai. One of Calvin's friends."

Of course.

Shirley asked, "Are you saying he was right?"

Lily didn't answer. She didn't have to. She saw the knowledge pass across Shirley's face like a ripple on a pond. Her expression hardened and turned cold as she averted her eyes from Lily, as if she couldn't bear to look at her.

"Why would you go to a place like that? Were you there with Kathleen Miller?" Shirley spoke Kath's name bitterly.

Lily bristled. "What does it matter?"

"She was arrested last night."

Lily felt as if all her breath was knocked out of her. "What? How do you know?"

"One of Kathleen's neighbors is on the dance committee, and she called to tell me. The police went to Kathleen's house this morning. The neighbors all know."

"Is she at home now? Is she all right?" She wanted to shake the information out of Shirley.

"I don't know," Shirley said primly. "Are you and Kathleen . . ." Shirley glanced briefly at Lily, and in that quick, skittish look, Lily saw disgust. "Never mind, I don't want to know. I came here to tell you this because I'm your friend—or at least I thought I was before I found out you've been lying to me. And lying about something so—so unnatural. I can't believe you would do this. Did Kathleen do this to you?"

There was accusation in her tone, but also a hint of hope, as if Shirley would forgive Lily for everything as long as Kathleen had made her *do this*. It rankled. Lily was the one who now averted her eyes. Shirley never believed that Lily could do anything on her own. Shirley always thought of Lily as a follower, and perhaps Lily had never given her any reason to doubt that, until now.

"Kath didn't do anything to me," Lily said.

"Of course she did. She's—she's kwai lo.[1] Chinese people don't go to places like that. Chinese people aren't like that. I can see that you're confused. They must have done a number on you—oh, I'm so angry at them for doing this to you!"

"Nobody did anything to me," Lily insisted.

"Don't you understand?" Shirley came over to the table and pulled out a chair, sitting down and facing her. "Lily, you have to snap

---

1. Foreign devil; derogatory.

out of it. Obviously they brought you there against your will—or they were seducing you or—I don't even want to think about what they'd want with a Chinese girl. It's disgusting. But you can fight it. Don't let this ruin your life. Kathleen Miller's out of the picture now that she's been arrested—thank God for that—but you need to admit to your mistakes. Maybe it's not too late for you and Will. I can talk to him."

As Shirley went on about talking to Will and how he still had feelings for her and how this must be a phase, Lily's heart beat faster and faster. She had to bend over and put her head in her hands while she took several deep breaths. Below her on the wooden floor was a scattering of crumbs that must have fallen from her toast, hours ago. She thought, inanely, that she had better clean that up before her mother returned.

"I'll talk to Wallace Lai too," Shirley continued. "I'll tell him it was all a mistake, and he can tell whoever else he told that it was a mistake."

"Stop it," Lily said, her words muffled by her hands.

"Unfortunately he wasn't alone when he saw you. Some others might already know, but I told Calvin to tell Wallace that you weren't like that. I told him—"

"Stop it!" Lily stood up, pushing her chair back violently. The legs screeched across the floor.

"Lily—"

"Nobody made me go there," Lily said angrily. "Nobody forced me to do anything. I went there because I wanted to. I don't want to go on any dates with Will Chan, and you know he doesn't want to have anything to do with me! We are not going to be double-dating with Calvin and Will—isn't that what you want? I know you're dating Calvin. I saw him drop you off in North Beach."

Shirley's face went white. "What does that have to do with this?"

"You said I was lying to you. You were lying to me too."

Shirley, who had been gaping up at Lily, got to her feet. "If you know so much, you know why I kept that to myself."

"Because he's a Communist."

"He's not a Communist! Don't be a child. He's not a Communist—he's an American with a right to go to whatever meetings he wants to go to. There's nothing wrong with Calvin. I love him." Shirley's face flushed as she spoke, her voice rising. "But there's everything wrong with that nightclub. And with Kathleen Miller. The shame you will bring on your family—"

"Shame?" Lily interrupted. "You know what's worse than shame? Being deported."

Shirley flinched.

"You can believe whatever you want about Calvin, but it doesn't matter if he's really a Communist as long as the government thinks he is one. Did you know the FBI interviewed my father about him? Did Calvin tell you? They wanted my father to say Calvin was a known Communist, and he wouldn't, so they took his citizenship papers. My father is in danger because he was protecting your boyfriend! If they deport my father because your boyfriend wants to be an American who can go to meetings— You're being so stupid!"

Lily was breathless with anger; it had spilled out of her in one hot rush.

Shirley's face shut down immediately. All emotion fled from it as if she had turned into a mannequin; even the two red spots on her cheeks looked painted on. She took a quick, sharp breath. "If that's what you think, we have nothing left to say to each other. I don't think you should come with me to the Miss Chinatown judging anymore. I can't have someone like you there. You should know that your parents are going to find out. Everyone's going to find out because Wallace Lai's a gossip, and if you won't even bother to deny it, I can't help you. I tried. I told you last fall—don't you remember?—I told you about Kathleen Miller. I warned you, but you didn't listen. I've been trying to watch out for you." Shirley's voice betrayed her with the slightest hitch. There was a sudden brightness in her eyes that she blinked away. "Obviously you didn't appreciate it," Shirley said, and started for the door.

Once, Lily had admired the way Shirley sailed through the world with such confidence, as if she wore an impenetrable armor that protected her against all slights, real or imagined. Lily had envied Shirley that armor, but now she saw that it was an illusion, and those who possessed the right knowledge could pierce it at will. Lily knew Shirley better than anyone; she could wound her thoughtlessly, and she had.

I love him, Shirley had declared. Love was the justification for all her secrets, but it also made her vulnerable. And Lily understood. She suddenly felt horrible.

"Shirley, wait," Lily said. She reached for Shirley's arm as she passed, pulling her back.

The expression on Shirley's face stopped her cold. It was plain repugnance. Shirley's eyes dropped to Lily's hand, and she pulled away.

Horrified and humiliated, Lily said, "You can't think—"

Shirley didn't look at her. "I think you should stay away from me from now on."

Lily almost laughed. "Oh my God. You think—I've *never*—" She fell silent, her face burning.

Shirley marched to the kitchen door and yanked it open, going to collect her things from the bench on the landing. Lily didn't move; she couldn't believe what Shirley had implied. The silence between them seemed to pulse. Lily heard every thump and slide as Shirley put on her shoes, every rustle as she slung her garment bag over her arm. And then suddenly Shirley came back into the kitchen doorway. She was pulling something out of her purse, holding it out to Lily.

Her scarf. It dangled from Shirley's hand like a brown woolen snake, the fringed end discolored as if it had been dragged through a gutter.

"This is yours, isn't it?" Shirley said.

At the end of the scarf a cloth tag had been sewn onto the wool, and a name was embroidered on it in white thread: L HU. Lily had done it herself. She remembered missing her scarf after she fled the club, but it had seemed so inconsequential at the time. She felt faint.

"Wallace found it on the street," Shirley said. "He brought it over to Calvin this morning. I told them there had to be a mistake, maybe someone stole it, but—" Shirley shook her head. "I thought I should bring it back to you, so at least they don't have it."

When Lily said nothing, Shirley tossed the scarf onto the nearest kitchen chair and left.

As she descended the stairs, Lily distinctly heard the crunch of the key in the lock; she heard the creak of the hinges as the front door opened; and then she heard her mother's voice.

"Shirley! What brings you here?"

In the pause before Shirley answered, Lily was fatalistically certain that Shirley was going to tell her mother the whole story right then and there, but Shirley merely said, "I came by to talk to Lily about Miss Chinatown. She's not coming tonight."

"But I thought—what happened?"

"It's just better this way. I'd better go."

Lily imagined her mother giving Shirley a puzzled look. She imagined Shirley avoiding that look and quickly making her last few steps down the stairs, and a moment later, the door closed behind her. Hurriedly, Lily grabbed her scarf from the chair and went to hang it on the coatrack on the landing. She heard her mother's footsteps slowly ascending, and then she came into view, carrying two white bakery boxes. She placed the boxes on the bench as she removed her coat and shoes.

Lily was standing nervously outside the kitchen. A paralyzing anxiety had overtaken her, making her head throb.

"What's going on?" her mother asked calmly. "Did you and Shirley have another fight?"

Lily remembered that Aunt Judy and Uncle Francis were arriving that night, and Uncle Sam was bringing his entire family tomorrow morning. The thought of them all converging on the flat now—they would be here the entire week, for the New Year festivities—made the throbbing in her head even worse, so that she had to reach out and clutch the kitchen doorframe to keep her balance.

"Are you all right?" her mother said.

She squeezed her eyes shut for a moment, taking a shallow breath in a futile attempt to tamp down her rising panic. *Wallace Lai's a gossip.* There was an unmistakable threat in what Shirley had told her, and she realized that she had two options: she could wait for the gossip to spread through all of Chinatown until her parents found out, or she could tell them herself right now. She didn't know how long it would take for the rumors to spread, but given that it was New Year week, they would probably spread quickly—and it was likely that her whole family would be here when they heard them. The idea of facing her uncles—oh God, her grandmother was coming, too—

She could barely breathe anymore. She felt nauseated, and her mother asked, "Are you sick? Maybe you do have what Frankie had."

"No," she said, but she didn't resist when her mother came over to her and led her by the arm back into the kitchen—right past the spot where Shirley had looked at her as if she were a pervert.

"Sit down," her mother said, and Lily obeyed. Her mother placed a cool hand on Lily's flushed forehead, and went to get her a glass of water. It was the same glass she had tried to drink earlier, and the sight of it paradoxically calmed her because it seemed so ridiculous. Everything was moving in circles. She couldn't get out of the kitchen; it was only the person she spoke to who changed. Here was her mother sitting down across from her, reaching for her hands and chafing them as if she were frozen. She felt the rub of her mother's wedding ring against her skin, and her mother's face swam into focus, her brown eyes full of the sharp worry of love, and Lily thought, *You will never look at me like this again.*

40

ily went to the trash can and retrieved the crumpled-up newspaper. She brought it over to the kitchen table and spread it out, smoothing down the wrinkled, wet corners. The right half of the front page was ripped, and the letters of the headline were smeared, but the story was still readable.

"What is this?" her mother asked.

"I was there last night. At the Telegraph Club. Shirley came over to tell me that someone saw me." Lily sat down again and waited, lowering her gaze to her hands. The ink from the newspaper had stained her fingertips gray.

"I don't understand. This story has nothing to do with you."

"I was there," she repeated. "I don't know how else to tell you," she added a little desperately.

Her mother pulled the newspaper toward her and leaned closer to read it. When she turned the page to read the second half of the story, Lily closed her eyes. The ticking of the clock over the stove sounded like a countdown. She felt almost as if she were floating untethered from her body. She wasn't all here—she couldn't be.

"You're not in the story," her mother said, sounding very far away.

"No, but I was at the club," Lily said. "Wallace Lai saw me outside."

Where had he seen her? She remembered the men on that side street, their glowing cigarettes.

"You couldn't have been anywhere near that place," her mother said. "You were at home last night, asleep!"

Lily opened her eyes. Her mother's face was pale beneath her powder; she looked unnaturally white.

"I went out," Lily said. She was sure her own face was bright red; she felt the blood rushing to her head as she spoke. "I went to that club. Wallace Lai saw me there, and Shirley came to tell me. Everyone's going to know soon. I thought I should tell you first."

Her mother's gaze dropped down to the newspaper again. There was an ad for ladies' hosiery on the page next to the second half of the story, with an illustration of a woman's legs dressed in sheer nylons. The ad seemed deliberately obscene to Lily, and as if her mother agreed, she closed the newspaper and flipped it over.

"It must have been a mistake," her mother said tightly. "You're a good Chinese girl. Whoever Wallace Lai saw—it wasn't you."

Lily felt as if she were stuck on a broken track in a diorama, as if she were not herself but merely the figurine of a Chinese girl that kept jerking back to the beginning rather than continuing through her miniature world. It was clear that if she agreed with her mother—and Shirley—if she would only tell them what they wanted to hear, then she could move forward on her prescribed path. But that would mean erasing all her trips to the Telegraph Club; it would mean denying her desire to go at all. It meant suppressing her feelings for Kath, and at that moment, her feelings seemed to swell inside her so painfully that she was terrified she might burst. Was this what it felt like to love someone? She wished she could ask Shirley how she had known.

Her mother was waiting for her to say it had been a mistake, but Lily couldn't do it. "No," she said. Her voice sounded ugly to her ears, but it relieved some of the pressure building inside her. "He didn't make a mistake," she insisted. "I was there."

"Lily, you don't know what you're saying."

"I know exactly what I'm saying," she said, frustrated.

"You're saying you were at this—this club for homosexuals?"

Her mother's voice rose on the last, shocking word. Lily had never heard her mother say it before. All she could do was nod, and her mother's face went even paler.

"Why?" her mother demanded.

"I wanted to go," Lily said. It felt like making an obscene confession.

Her mother shook her head. "You've been influenced by someone— who? It can't be Shirley. You wouldn't do this on your own."

"I did," Lily said. Her eyes grew hot.

"You're a good Chinese girl, Lily. I don't understand. What would make you go somewhere like this?" Her mother looked so confused.

Lily took a trembling breath. "I—I think I'm like them."

Her mother's eyes widened. "You think— No. You're not. You've never even had a boyfriend! You'll grow up and marry and realize that this was all a mistake, a temporary—"

"It's not a mistake," she protested.

"Lily. 胡麗麗!"[1] her mother cried, saying her full name in Mandarin the way her father did. "What has gotten into you? If only one person saw you outside this club—we can deal with it. You're young. You'll find a boyfriend in college. You won't go to that place again, and you'll forget about it right away. Do you hear me?"

"You're not listening to me!" Lily cried. "I'm like *them*."

It wasn't Lily who was the figurine in a diorama; it was her mother. Her mother was going round and round on that track, hearing only what she wanted to hear.

Her mother stood up, snatching the newspaper off the table and crumpling it in her hands. She threw it into the trash again. "There

---

1. Hu Li-li.

are no homosexuals in this family," she said, the words thick with disgust.

Her mother's chest heaved, and Lily saw that her hand was now stained with newsprint just like Lily's. In the trash can, the newspaper itself was slowly coming uncrumpled; it was unfurling as if it were a living thing, the words *sex deviate* screaming across the room.

"You are young," her mother said harshly. "You aren't even eighteen years old yet. Sometimes girls have these ideas when they're younger—before they meet their husbands. Girls love their friends and mistake that for the love they'll have for their husbands. It only becomes an illness when you won't let go of the idea. We'll tell your father. He'll be able to help you. You won't tell your aunts and uncles about this. You won't say a word to your grandmother. Do you hear me? Everyone knows you're a good Chinese girl. This is just a mistake."

The more her mother insisted it was a mistake, the more certain Lily was that it wasn't. Perhaps that was the most perverse part of this: the inside-outness of everything, as if denial would make it go away, when it only made the pain in her chest tighten, when it only made her emotions clearer.

"It's not a mistake," Lily said miserably.

Her mother strode across the kitchen and slapped her.

Lily jerked backward, shocked. Her mother hadn't hit her in years—since she was eight or nine—and she instantly felt like that child again, cowering in fear of another strike. With the terror came a crippling guilt and the belief that she must have done something awful, that she deserved this punishment.

She raised a hand to her stinging face; tears sprang into her eyes. Her mother looked both horrified and horrifying, her pale face suddenly blotchy with red, her brown eyes bright with anger.

"There are no homosexuals in this family," her mother spit out again. "Are you my daughter?"

The tears spilled hotly from Lily's eyes. She turned away from her mother and fled from the kitchen. In the hallway she saw Eddie and Frankie standing uncertainly outside the living room.

"Lily?" Eddie said.

She didn't answer him. She put on her shoes, but her fingers couldn't work the laces properly. She clutched the railing as she stumbled down the stairs. She heard her mother calling her—no, she was calling for Eddie, telling him to stop—and then she was at the front door. She wrenched it open; she stepped outside and down onto the sidewalk. She was crying freely now. The air was misty and wet. She didn't know where she was going; she only knew she had to go away.

41

There are no homosexuals in this family.

Grant Avenue's red-and-gold banners celebrating the Year of the Sheep sagged damply overhead, dripping on Lily as she crossed the street. A group of boys pushed past her with their arms full of unlit firecrackers, shouting and laughing.

There are no homosexuals in this family.

Portsmouth Square was ahead. She wished she had put on a coat, and her canvas shoes were getting wetter with each step, but she couldn't go back.

Kath had been arrested. Lily's stomach clenched.

There are no homosexuals in this family.

She kept walking. Past the International Hotel, past the gaudy lights of the International Settlement. The neon sign for the Barbary Coast nightclub, built in the shape of a woman's naked leg, glowed through the dusk, advertising DANCING GIRLS.

Are you my daughter?

Lily went left along Columbus, walking quickly in an effort to warm herself up, and then she came to Broadway, and down the street she saw the lighted sign. The letter *l* in the word *Club* was on the fritz, blinking out every so often as if it were tapping out a message in code.

In a daze, she angled across Broadway, narrowly missing a taxi that honked at her as it swerved around her. She slowed to a halt in front of the club. She noticed for the first time a small window to the left of the door. It was filled in with glass blocks so that she couldn't see inside, but it must overlook the end of the bar. She began to take in the other details around her: the stained concrete beneath her feet, blackened in spots as if people had stubbed out countless cigarettes on the ground. The faint smell of alcohol and smoke, like a bitter perfume, hanging in the chilly air. A layer of filth seemed packed onto the lower extremities of the building's wall, which was covered in a dirty stucco that once might have been white, but had turned gray-ish brown over time. A particularly disgusting puce-colored patch spread over part of the wall beneath the glass-block window. The black door itself looked like it had come out of a fire, sooty and beaten, and there was a small white sign affixed to it.

She had to walk right up to it to read it in the gray light: CLOSED BY ORDER OF THE SAN FRANCISCO POLICE.

She shouldn't have been surprised by the notice, but she was. She realized that she had stupidly thought she might go to the club—that Mickey might open the door for her, that someone might help her, or at least allow her to sit there while she figured out what she was going to do. Abruptly she became aware that she was standing right in front of the club on the sidewalk in full view. Once again she was putting herself in danger of being seen.

She turned away in a panic, not caring where she was going as long as she put distance between herself and anyone who might know her. She went uphill, racing up the steep sidewalk, and at the top she was forced to pause to catch her breath. When she raised her eyes and saw the nearest street sign, she was startled to discover it was the street that Kath lived on.

She had completely forgotten about that scrap of paper with Kath's address, but she remembered the details: 453 Union Street. It couldn't be far.

Kath's house was a three-story building with a central entrance and bay windows stacked up on either side. In the cloudy afternoon, a lamp glowed in a first floor window, but the top two floors were dark. She went up the stairs to the entryway and looked at the three doors, examining the nameplates beside each buzzer. There it was on the right: MILLER. She raised her finger to press the button.

It sounded distantly inside the building—too distantly to be attached to the first floor with its lighted window.

No one answered the door.

She pressed the buzzer again, and leaned forward to listen carefully, but no one was coming.

She retreated down the steps and stared fiercely at Kath's building, as if that would conjure her out of thin air, but of course it did not. In the first floor window she saw an old woman looking out at her suspiciously. She couldn't stand here forever. The woman would call the police.

Lily turned her back on the building and continued downhill, walking aimlessly into the heart of North Beach. The neighborhood was a maze to her; some of the streets turned into dead ends, while others culminated in steep wooden steps climbing up the side of Telegraph Hill. Eventually she went all the way up to Coit Tower, joining the tourists who gathered at the overlook to gaze out at the misty city. She lingered there for some time, her mind going as numb as her feet, and then she went into the gift shop to lurk in the warmth. She used the public restroom and pretended to consider buying a miniature Coit Tower, but when the clerk started walking past her repeatedly, she left.

Maybe you should go home, she thought, but immediately recoiled from the idea. She couldn't face her mother—her father—the entire family. *There are no homosexuals in this family.*

She headed downhill, taking random streets, until she emerged in Washington Square Park. She remembered that sunny September afternoon again: Kath's legs stretched out on the grass; the cold sweet sorbetto; the wooden spoon scraping against her tongue.

The memory hurt almost physically. She went to the nearest bench on the edge of the park and sat down.

She felt hopelessness creeping upon her. The fog was rolling in; it seeped through her thin cardigan and blouse and crawled beneath her cotton skirt to settle on her skin. No matter how much she rubbed her hands along her upper arms, she was still cold. Washington Square Park was quiet. The afternoon was darkening into dusk, and few people were out, but she gradually became aware of the presence of others. There was the lumpy shape of someone stretched out on a bench not so far from her; it had been motionless when she arrived, but after some time it twitched, startling her. Then the shape seemed to ripple and roll, and she realized it was a man shifting over onto his back. He was sleeping there, exposed to the chilly air. He didn't even have a blanket.

The sound of glass rattling against metal caused her to look to her right. Someone was rooting through the trash can. They were wearing a long woolen coat beneath a blanket that kept slipping, its ragged edges trailing on the damp ground.

She crossed her arms and legs, hugging herself closer, trying to ignore the fear that was rising inside her. She called up the memory of Kath's mouth against hers as they kissed beneath the stairs at the club. *Last night.* If she closed her eyes, she could still feel Kath there.

She heard footsteps coming from her left. They slowed down, and then someone sat on the bench beside her. She blinked her eyes open as a man said, "Nay ho, little girl."

He was lanky and scraggly looking, with an unshaven chin and a stink about him, and she realized he was trying to speak to her in Chinese.

The fear she had been trying to keep at bay flooded through her. She jumped up and ran, and she heard him calling after her, laughingly, "I'm not gonna hurt you, China doll. Just saying hello. Nay ho, nay ho!"

Her skin crawled and she ran faster, leaving the park behind as she fled uphill. Coit Tower loomed in the distance. She remembered leaving Tommy's party with Kath that night, Coit Tower a candle behind them as they emerged from Castle Street.

Castle Street. Lana and Tommy lived there at number forty-something.

The idea was so startling, and it felt so right that she almost laughed out loud. But her relief was short-lived; she suddenly remembered that the *Chronicle* had said Tommy had been arrested. She was probably in jail.

But Lana might be there, and Lana would know what to do.

Lily glanced up at Coit Tower, trying to remember where it had been in relation to Lana's apartment. North Beach wasn't that large, but it wasn't her neighborhood. At the next corner store, she went inside and asked the man behind the counter where Castle Street was. He gave her a funny look, but he also gave her directions, and then she headed up the steepest part of Green Street, passing slivers of dark alleys on her left—one of them might have been the one that Kath had pulled her into—and then there it was.

She turned onto the block and started studying the building numbers. She was afraid she wouldn't recognize Lana's building, but when she came to it, she was certain. She remembered the front stoop and the way the curtains hung over the window. Light shone through a crack in the curtains. Someone was home.

She hesitated. There were plenty of reasons she shouldn't knock on the door. Lana barely knew her. She would be a virtual stranger showing up like a beggar on her front step. And if Tommy was in jail, this had to be a terrible time for Lana. The wind whipped around her, plastering her fog-dampened hair across her eyes so that she had to scrape it aside with freezing fingers.

She had nowhere else to go.

She climbed the three steps and found the button labeled JACK-SON and pressed it. She heard it ring. Just when she was about to try peeking through the crack in the window curtains, the door opened.

There was Lana, her blond hair pulled back in a ponytail, dressed in slim blue checkered pants, a pink sweater, and a pair of red-and-gold Chinese slippers.

Her penciled eyebrows rose in surprise. "You're that girl from the club—Lily, isn't it? My goodness, you look like a drowned kitten!" Lana glanced behind her at the empty street. "Well, you'd better come in."

42

Take off that sweater—you'll catch a cold," Lana said. "And leave your shoes there. I'll bring you a blanket."

There was a gently compelling quality about Lana, and Lily felt a sense of relief in surrendering to her orders. She peeled off her cardigan and took off her wet shoes and socks, putting them in front of the electric heater. Lana returned from the bedroom with a crocheted purple-and-white blanket, which she wrapped around Lily's shoulders. She stepped back and gave Lily an appraising look, as if she were examining a rather sad work of art, and said, "Take a seat. I'll make you something hot to drink."

"You don't have to," Lily said.

"I'll just reheat some coffee."

Left alone in the living room, Lily sat down on the rust-colored sofa, tucking her cold feet under the edge of the blanket.

"Do you want cream and sugar?" Lana called from the kitchen.

"Yes, please."

A pile of unopened mail on the coffee table bumped against a dinner plate stained with the remains of what looked like scrambled eggs. A half-filled ashtray squatted nearby, along with a smudged wineglass, a half-empty bottle of wine, a table lighter in the shape of a nude woman, and a pack of Lucky Strikes. The record player was standing open on the octagonal table in the corner, and a few records were leaning against it on the floor. Only one lamp was turned on, giving the living room a warm, golden glow. It felt different than it had the night of the party—cozier, more like someone's home—and when she remembered Sal and Patsy dancing together in the small open space between the bench and the kitchen door, it seemed like a strange fantasy.

Lana emerged from the kitchen carrying a mug of coffee, and when she handed it to Lily, she said, "I added a little whisky. I think you need it."

"Thank you." Lily sipped the coffee hesitantly. It was hot and sweet and left a pleasant warmth in her stomach.

Lana took a seat across from Lily. She reached for the Lucky Strikes and pulled one out, holding it between her lips while she thumbed the lighter. A flame shot out of the nude woman's head. "This was a gag gift from one of Tommy's friends," Lana said. "It's awful, isn't it? At least you don't have to squeeze her breasts to get it to work. I've seen one of those too." She put the lighter back on the table and pulled the ashtray closer to herself. "Sorry for the mess. It's been quite a day. But I think it's been one for you too."

Lily cupped her hands around her coffee mug. "I'm sorry to barge in on you uninvited."

Lana waved her hand, the cigarette trailing smoke. "I have a feeling you wouldn't be here unless you had to be." She leaned forward to pour some wine into the smudged glass, then sat back, kicking off her slippers to tuck her feet up beside her, and took a sip. "Do you want to tell me what happened?"

It turned out, to Lily's surprise, that she did want to tell her. The living room felt so intimate, and Lana seemed like someone who had heard everything and would be surprised at nothing. Lily found herself spilling out the whole story, from the moment she left Kath at the Telegraph Club to her confrontations with Shirley and her mother, to her chilly trek through the city to Lana's front door.

"Do you think I should have done what my mother wanted?" Lily asked when she came to the end. "She kept saying that it was a mistake—as if everything would be fine as long as I called it a mistake. But that would be a lie. I don't want to lie about it, but I can't help thinking it would be easier if I did."

Lana had listened quietly the whole time, smoking while Lily talked. Now she stubbed out the end of the cigarette in the ashtray and said, "If you lie about it, it'll make it easier in the beginning, but your mother will never trust you again. Because she'll know you lied to her. And every time you speak to her she'll wonder if you're lying—even if you're talking about what you had for dinner, and especially who you went to dinner with. It's better to be true to yourself than give her a reason not to trust you."

Lily took another sip of her coffee. Maybe the whisky was working because she felt more at ease now, as if the clenched fist inside herself were loosening. "But she doesn't trust me anyway," Lily said.

"No, she trusts you. She's having a hard time right now because you're not what she expected. But we're never what our parents expected. They have to learn that lesson." Lana gave a short laugh. "My brother and I both taught our parents that lesson, and they didn't like it with either of us. He was supposed to grow up and become a lawyer, just like Daddy, but instead he decided to go to New York to become an actor. They thought for sure it meant that Russ—my brother—was a homosexual, but it turned out I was the homosexual, and they didn't like that either."

"Did they—do they still not like it?"

"Oh, they're coming around. It helps that Russ married a lovely woman and they have a beautiful little boy now. They're still working their way around to me. At least they write to me now. For several years they didn't."

"They write to you—you mean they're not here?" Lily asked.

"No, in Detroit. That's where I grew up. I moved here when I was seventeen because I heard San Francisco was friendly to people like me. Russ said our parents were afraid I'd become destitute and end up working the streets." Lana spoke dryly, but when she reached for the cigarettes again there was a touch of nervousness to her movements. "They're happy I have a steady job now. Maybe if I looked like Tommy, they'd give up on me, but they keep hoping I'll meet the right man. My mother tried to set me up on a date last week with a banker here who's the cousin of one of her bridge partners. They won't give up."

Lily looked down at her coffee. "My mother said there are no homosexuals in our family."

"Maybe there aren't, but there might be a lesbian."

It was a terrible joke, but it seemed so painfully funny to Lily in that moment. To think that she was sitting in Tommy Andrews's girlfriend's living room, hearing her life story! And then the reality of her predicament came crashing back down, and it wasn't funny anymore. Here she was, in a near-stranger's home, with nowhere to go.

The expression on her face must have been plain as day, because Lana gave her a sympathetic look and said, "You'll be all right."

"I don't know what to do," Lily said. The words came out, embarrassingly, like a plea for help, and Lana said nothing in return, only took a deep drag from her cigarette and considered her, giving her that same look from when Lily first arrived. But now Lily thought it was more as if Lana were trying to determine what to do with her: as if she were an unexpected package that had at first been interesting, but was rapidly turning into a burden.

The doorbell rang, and Lana straightened up. "That must be Claire. I forgot she was coming. Hang on."

Lana went to the door, and Lily set her half-finished coffee on the table, getting up. A moment later, Claire came in bearing a brown paper sack with a wine bottle tucked under her arm.

"I'm sorry I'm so late," Claire said. "The deli took forever."

"It's all right, and look, we have a surprise guest." Lana took the wine and the paper sack, nodding in Lily's direction.

"Hello!" Claire exclaimed. "Lily, right?" She unwound the scarf from her hair. Lily had never before noticed that it was quite red, and her face was scattered with light brown freckles.

"I'm sorry to intrude," Lily said, gathering up the blanket to fold it. "I can go now."

"Don't be ridiculous." Claire tugged off her rain boots and removed her coat. "The sandwiches are huge—you should join us."

Lily protested again, but weakly. The next few minutes were filled with the mundane tasks of taking the food and wine into the dining room, turning on the lights, bringing out plates and cutlery and glasses. Claire opened the wine and poured three glasses full, not even asking if Lily wanted one, and Lana unwrapped the two sandwiches on a cutting board. They were indeed huge. Claire had bought them at an Italian deli and said there was salami and mortadella and fontina and something else she couldn't remember, all piled onto chewy sourdough bread spread with grainy mustard and layered with pickles. Lana cut each large sandwich into three smaller ones, and brought out a bag of potato chips from the kitchen and a pile of napkins from the antique sideboard. By the time the three of them sat down at the table, Lily felt almost normal again, rather than an interloper at someone's private party. Claire claimed Lana's attention now, and they spoke in shorthand like old friends, which meant Lily didn't understand a good part of their conversation and could eat her sandwich without having to say much.

". . . even Sandy called me about it," Lana said between bites.

"Sandy! My goodness, I thought she was long gone," Claire said.

"No, just moved down to San Jose."

"She's still carrying a torch, I guess."

"Maybe. But not a big enough one to offer to help. She just wants the gossip. Parker called me too."

"Well, that's good. Can he do anything?"

"He's going to meet me tomorrow. Hopefully he'll have some ideas."

Claire took a sip of her wine, and when she replaced her glass on the table she turned to Lily, who was almost finished with her sandwich. "So, what brought you here tonight?"

"She might not want to talk about it," Lana said.

"Oh, I'm sorry," Claire said. "Did I put my foot in my mouth?"

"No, it's fine," Lily said. Haltingly she explained what had happened, while Claire watched her with growing sympathy.

"I'm sorry, honey," Claire said. "Last night was rough for a lot of us, it seems." She reached out and squeezed Lily's hand.

The touch seemed to release all her worry for Kath, which had been held at bay since she arrived at Lana's. "I have to find Kath," she said. "How can I find out where she is?"

Claire and Lana traded glances, and then Lana said, "How old is she? And how old are you?"

"Seventeen." Lily remembered Tommy asking her the same question; she remembered Tommy's thumb on her mouth, and now she blushed. "We're both seventeen."

"A little young for the Telegraph Club," Claire said gently.

Lily's blush deepened.

"I was sixteen the first time I went to a gay bar," Lana said. "I can hardly believe it now. I was so young! But this is good news—if Kath's only seventeen that means she couldn't have been arrested. She's not legally an adult. They probably took her to juvie."

"But how can I find out? I tried to call her house—I even went there—and no one was home."

"You should ask Parker," Claire said to Lana. "He would know someone."

Lana nodded slowly. "Yes. Maybe Parker could make a call. I could ask him tomorrow."

"Who's Parker?" Lily asked.

"A lawyer I know," Lana said.

"He's one of us," Claire said meaningfully.

Lily nodded, not wanting to let on her confusion. "He'll know where Kath is?" she asked eagerly.

"Maybe," Lana said. "At least he'll know how to find out."

"Do you think Joyce will get her liquor license taken away?" Claire asked.

"I hope not," Lana said.

The mood seemed to sour a bit, and Lana went to the living room to get the cigarettes and the obscene table lighter, which Claire laughed at, and then Lana and Claire lit their cigarettes and poured more wine. Slowly the conversation drifted away from the bar raid, but eventually it circled back again, as if there were no way to escape its dragnet. Lily gradually realized that Claire had come over to keep Lana company because Tommy, of course, was in jail. Parker was their lawyer friend—Lana was a secretary at his law firm—who was trying to get Tommy out, but he hadn't been successful yet. That had something to do with money, which Lana didn't like to talk about. There was another woman involved, too—someone unnamed—who had been attached to Tommy sometime in the past, whom Lana disliked. Lily felt as if she were a sort of detective, piecing together the story from bits and pieces of their coded conversation.

At one point Lana said, "Oh, why does it even matter? She's just going to get in trouble again. I should leave her." She noticed Lily then, still sitting quietly at the table, and seemed irritated. "I guess you're hearing all the secrets tonight."

"I'm sorry, I'll leave," Lily said, and scooted her chair back.

"Where will you go?" Lana asked bluntly.

"I—I don't know. Somewhere." She couldn't go home. The thought of her parents looking at her—their disapproval and disgust—made her ill. She stood, feeling woozy and warm from the wine, and went back to the living room where she had left her sweater and shoes and socks, which weren't quite dry yet. Nevertheless she sat down on the bench to put them on.

Lana came after her. "Lily."

"Thank you for letting me in—and for the sandwiches," Lily said, shoving her feet into her damp shoes.

"Stop it. Stay."

Behind Lana, Lily saw Claire hovering in the doorway, looking worried.

"You can stay here tonight, all right?" Lana said. "It's cold and wet outside and I know you're not going home."

Lily wiped at the corners of her suddenly brimming eyes. "I'm sorry."

"Stop apologizing. You haven't done anything wrong."

"This is an awful time for me to be here."

Lana raised her cigarette to her mouth and took a drag, then exhaled slowly. "Would you like some more wine?"

The living room was thick with smoke; it hung in the yellow lamplight like a fog, and Claire got up from where she had been lounging against one arm of the sofa to push up the window.

"You'll let out all the heat," Lana objected. She was lying on the floor now, her head propped up on a maroon pillow that looked like it belonged in a Turkish harem.

"And some of the smoke too, I hope," Claire said. "Otherwise we're all going to suffocate." She didn't return to the sofa, where Lily was curled up at the other end, but instead went to the record player and began to shuffle through the albums leaning against the octagonal table. "Oh, I love this one."

"What is it?" Lana asked.

"'The Lady Is a Tramp.'"

"Oh, play it. I can't get Tommy to sing that one."

Claire put the record on and then flopped back down on the sofa, reaching for her wine. They had opened a second bottle, and Lily watched the two of them become languid and loose-limbed, their laughter coming more easily. Lily had had a glass or two also; she wasn't keeping track. She felt as if the night had turned in a new direction at some point, she wasn't sure when, but as the trumpets kicked in on the song, it seemed perfectly natural for Claire and Lana to start singing along.

Afterward, Claire asked, "Why won't she sing it? People would love it."

"Oh, it's not a Tommy song," Lana said. "I've heard her sing it in the shower though. She said she used to sing it years ago, back when she was Theresa Scafani, Ingénue of North Beach."

"Ingénue of North Beach!" Claire giggled. "I wish I'd seen her then."

"Theresa Scafani was only a mediocre lounge singer," Lana said. "They're a dime a dozen, you know. There's less competition for Tommy Andrews."

"How did she pick that name?" Claire asked. "I've always wondered."

"She said she thought of herself as the long-lost Andrews sister.

Isn't that ridiculous? She wanted to sing in uniform, as if she were a soldier."

"Well, the girls would love that. Maybe she can do a number in uniform sometime."

"D'you still know that girl in the army?"

"Barbara Hawkins? No, we're not in touch anymore. Last I heard she shacked up with some nurse."

Lana laughed, propping herself up on an elbow so she could look at Claire. "She was your first, wasn't she? I remember you mooning over her. Barbara Hawkins—how funny."

Claire shot a grin at Lily. "You never quite get over your first one. Honestly, if Barb ever showed up I might go out with her again, Paula be damned."

Lana sat up, leaning against the coffee table. "Do you really like Paula? Really? She's so . . ."

"Solid?" Claire suggested, and broke into laughter. "She's good to me. She's not the dangerous type I know you go for—"

"I don't!"

"There was Nicky, and then Kate, and now there's Tommy Andrews. Do you always call her Tommy?"

"Of course."

"But isn't it a stage name? I've always thought it a little odd that you call her that."

"I've never known her as Theresa. Some folks call her Terry—Sal does. You remember Sal?"

"The dyke in the motorcycle jacket?"

"Yes. But I never knew Terry. I've only known Tommy, so that's what I call her. I think she's more of a Tommy anyway." Lana's gaze flickered over to Lily, who had been listening quietly, and said, "You look sleepy."

"I've had too much to drink, maybe."

"Who's your first, Lily?" Claire asked, turning to face her. "Your first love?"

Kath. But she couldn't say it. She thought of Shirley and how certain she'd sounded. "How am I supposed to know?" she asked instead. "What's it supposed to be like?"

Lana and Claire traded tiny smiles, and Claire asked gently, "What's what supposed to be like?"

Lily slumped back against the sofa, feeling boneless and muddled. "Falling in love, I guess."

"You'll know," Claire said. "It's unmistakable."

(How she could recognize Kath at the other end of a crowded Galileo hallway by the way she walked.)

"It's like . . . well, it's like falling," Lana said. "Falling, or floating, or sinking."

(Every time they kissed.)

"You won't know which way is up."

"It's like having a fever."

(The way the world seemed to narrow down to the tips of Kath's fingers.)

"It's like being drunk—drunk for days."

"But this is all so unspecific," Lily said. "How did you know when you fell in love with—with Barbara Hawkins, or with Tommy?"

She knew she sounded petulant, like a child, but her head was fuzzy and the smoke was swirling through the room toward the window and she didn't care. Impulsively she reached for the pack of cigarettes. It was almost empty, but Lana knocked it over to her and she pulled one out, placing it between her lips. Claire handed her the table lighter, and her thumb came to rest on the nude woman's breasts as she pressed the switch. The flame leaped up, hot and bright, and caused the end of the cigarette to sizzle. She inhaled clumsily and coughed.

"Here, take a breath like this," Claire said, demonstrating.

Lily copied her, and the smoke felt awful going into her lungs, but it also felt necessary, as if it might burn away the haze of wine and the horrible day she'd had. She exhaled, and the stream of smoke emerging from her mouth made her remember Tommy smoking in this very room on the night of the party. And now here she was, and everything important had changed.

Lana reached for another cigarette as well, and after she lit it she said, "The first time I fell in love—well, I didn't know that's what it was. I just knew I wanted to be with her." Lana glanced at Claire. "And it wasn't Nicky. It was someone you didn't know, back in Detroit. I'd sneak out of my house to be with her, and when my parents found out they—" Lana paused and gave Lily a frank look. "They didn't approve, and that's why I moved here. Falling in love makes you do things you'd never do otherwise."

The cigarette burned the back of Lily's throat. She picked up her wineglass and took another swig; the alcohol wasn't exactly soothing, but it felt grown-up.

"Do you regret it?" Lily asked.

Lana tapped her cigarette against the ashtray. "No. I will always love her, because even though we're not together anymore, she brought me here, in a way. What about you, Claire? Tell Lily about Barbara."

Claire sighed. "You sure you want to know? Barbara broke my heart. She was my first love, but I wasn't hers, and it took me a long time to figure that out. But before that, it was wonderful. She made me feel like—like I could do anything." Claire looked at Lily. "Do you know what I mean?"

Yes. But she couldn't say it. To her horror, her eyes grew hot and her face, which was already flushed from the wine, burned even hotter, and she leaned forward to stub out her cigarette in the ashtray. (Kath leaning forward in the darkness of the Telegraph Club, the ash from her cigarette crumbling onto the table.)

"Oh, honey," Claire said. She reached out and put a hand on Lily's back, as if to steady her. "It'll be all right."

Lana picked up the wine bottle and poured the last few drops into Lily's glass.

43

ily woke up to the sound of church bells. They were unusually loud, and she attempted to muffle the noise with her pillow, but the pillow was the wrong shape. She truly woke up then, and remembered that she was on Lana's sofa. Her head was resting on the Turkish pillow, a blanket was draped over her, and a crack of light shone through the curtains.

It was Sunday morning. That's why the bells were ringing.

When the sound died away, the apartment seemed abnormally silent in comparison. She couldn't remember how late they'd been up. At some point, Claire had decided to go home, and Lana called a taxi for her. It took so long to arrive that Lily began to nod off on the sofa, but at last Claire left, and Lana brought out another blanket for Lily before going to bed.

Now Lily remembered, with a pang, that Aunt Judy and Uncle Francis must have arrived the night before, while she was eating Lana and Claire's sandwiches and drinking wine and smoking. She had smoked a cigarette! She sat up too quickly, and was struck with a burst of dizziness followed by a gurgling noise in her stomach. She was starving.

She became aware of another, more pressing need, and she pushed off the blankets and got up to go to the bathroom. Afterward, when she flushed, the sound seemed as loud as an explosion, and for a second she froze, fearing that she'd woken Lana—but she heard nothing from the direction of the bedroom.

At the sink, she splashed water onto her face and used a towel she found on the bar nearby to dry off. Her face was a little pale, and the outline of a button from the maroon pillow was pressed into her left cheek, but when she ran her fingers through her hair and pulled it into a ponytail, she looked all right. She didn't look like someone who'd been up half the night after running away from home. She could barely believe that she'd done that. In the bathroom light, in this strange apartment, it all seemed unreal.

She noticed a small white hutch behind her, reflected in the mirror. It had lower cabinet doors and two small open shelves on top. Various bottles and containers were crammed onto those shelves, and though she knew she shouldn't poke around, she couldn't resist. There was a box of lipsticks and a basket of eye shadows, several lotions and a glass jar of cotton puffs. There was a selection of perfumes on a silver-plated tray: Tabu, Shalimar, Knize Ten. Shalimar smelled like Lana. She opened the Knize Ten and its fragrance, undiluted and sharp, went through her like an electric shock—that was Tommy. She put it back too hastily, making a banging noise against the silver tray.

Feeling guilty, she turned off the bathroom light and opened the door, afraid that Lana would be standing outside, but the hallway was empty. She tiptoed back to the living room, trying to ignore her empty stomach.

To occupy herself until Lana got up, Lily folded the blankets, opened the curtains, and sorted the mail into two different piles: one for Lana Jackson, and one for Theresa Scafani. She cleared away the dirty wineglasses and plates, stacked them as quietly as possible on the counter by the kitchen sink, and looked yearningly at the fruit bowl, which held two bruised apples and a browning pear. She glanced at her watch countless times as the minute hand ticked slowly toward and past ten o'clock, and finally she heard the bedroom door opening. It was a little sticky and made a brief peeling noise.

She leaped up from the sofa. She had prepared an entire speech about how grateful she was to Lana for allowing her to stay the night, but the sight of Lana in the doorway, tying on a rayon bathrobe printed with roses, made the speech die in her mouth. She realized, while waiting for Lana to wake up, that she had left her home in Chinatown with nothing: not a coat, not a single penny, and not even keys to her family's flat. She was entirely at Lana's mercy, and Lana looked exhausted and somewhat surprised to see her still there, and now did not seem like a good time to ask for anything more than she had already been given.

"Hello," Lana said blearily. "What time is it?"

"Just after ten."

Lana yawned again. "My goodness, my head is pounding. How are you? Do you need some aspirin?"

"No, I'm all right."

Lana smiled weakly. "Lucky you. Come on, I'll make us some coffee."

A little after eleven, Lana left to meet her friend Parker for lunch. She gave Lily a spare key in case she wanted to go out. "When I get back," Lana said as she put on her hat, "we can talk about what you want to do."

Alone in the apartment, Lily cleaned up the remains of their breakfast. Lana had only eaten toast, but she had given Lily some eggs to scramble for herself, and she ate them hungrily and gratefully, feeling even more like a tramp that had been taken in out of pity.

Now she carefully washed the dishes, feeling as if she should leave no trace of herself there. When she finished, she went out into the living room and sat down tensely on the edge of the sofa. The light coming through the front window was flat and dull, making the eclectic assortment of furniture look like the odds and ends they probably were. The sofa was visibly worn and threadbare in spots. The octagonal table was chipped on several of its corners, and the Chinese chairs' lacquer finish was lusterless and obviously cheap. Her mother would never have bought those chairs.

Her thoughts circled back, relentlessly, to Kath. She imagined her in a cold, cement jail cell, or led out in front of a judge, or locked into the padded room of an institution. She went to the window and peered out at the quiet street as if Kath might suddenly appear, but of course she didn't.

She had to go to Kath's house again. Someone had to be home by now, and they would know what had happened to Kath, and Lily would make them tell her.

She raced to lace on her shoes. She took the key that Lana had given her and left the apartment, locking the door behind her.

The air was cool and damp; she wished she had thought to borrow one of Lana's jackets. North Beach seemed like a foreign city around her; unlike Chinatown, the neighborhood was practically deserted, and the quiet made her feel especially conspicuous. She spotted a couple of people going into a corner store, and they looked secretive, as if they knew they shouldn't be outside.

Lily heard the snap of firecrackers in the distance. She could see them in her mind's eye: flashes of bright white light and smoke streaming upward, the paper wrappers fluttering through the air like confetti.

She wasn't that far from Chinatown. For a moment she considered going back. Today her mother was cooking a special dinner for the New Year, and she was supposed to help. But then she imagined what it would be like to return home—to be forced to ring the doorbell because she didn't have any keys, to wait for someone to open the door and let her in. She imagined the look of disappointment and disgust on her father's face, and she knew she couldn't go home.

When she reached Kath's street, she slowed down as she approached the building. The curtains were all drawn; none of the windows showed any life. Of course, it was Sunday morning. The neighborhood was deserted because people must be at church. Her heart sank at the realization, and she almost turned back, but the thought of returning to Lana's apartment with nothing to show for it seemed even worse than finding no one at Kath's home.

She climbed the front steps to the entryway and rang the doorbell. The building was quiet. After a minute, she pressed the button again. She was about to turn away when the door cracked open.

A girl peered out. She had giant blue eyes that looked exactly like Kath's.

"Are you Kath's sister?" Lily asked. "Peggy?"

The girl opened the door all the way. She was about twelve years old, with light brown hair pulled into two wavy pigtails. She looked dubious, but nodded. "Who are you?"

"I'm Lily, her friend. From school. Is she home?"

Peggy shook her head. "Your name's Lily?"

"Yes."

"She told me about you."

Lily was astonished. "She did?"

"Yes. But she's not here."

"Where is she? I've been so worried. I called the other day—" Lily cut herself off as Peggy looked past her. Lily twisted around to look up and down the block, but no one was in sight. "What's wrong?"

"I'm not supposed to tell anyone where she is."

"You can tell me," Lily said eagerly, trying to be persuasive. "You said she told you about me, so you know I'm her friend. I just want to know if she's all right."

"I'm not supposed to say anything to anyone," Peggy said reluctantly.

"Will she be coming home soon?"

"I don't know." Peggy began to step back into the house. "I'm sorry."

"Wait. Wait! If you can't tell me, can you tell Kath I came by?"

Peggy hesitated.

"Can you tell her where I am? I'm not at home. I'm—I'm at Lana's apartment. Tell her I'm at forty-eight Castle Street."

Peggy backed away again, and Lily was afraid she was going to close the door in her face, but then she returned with a small pad of paper and a pencil. "Here," she said, giving it to Lily.

Lily took the pad and scribbled down Lana's address. She wrote: *I'm at Lana's. Lily.* She handed it back to Peggy, who read it and nodded somberly.

"I'll give it to her if she comes home."

And then Peggy shut the door.

44

Lana returned carrying two bags of groceries, and Lily jumped up from the sofa to help. "Thanks, you can take that into the kitchen," Lana said, handing Lily a bag while she nudged the door shut.

When it was all put away, Lana sat down on the sofa and lit a cigarette, and said without preamble, "I saw Parker. I asked him whether your friend Kath would have been arrested, but he thinks no, because she's under eighteen."

Lily took a seat in one of the Chinese chairs. "Does he know where she was taken?"

"No, but he thinks she would have been released by now. They can't keep her, not if she didn't have a record. She didn't, did she?"

"No."

"She probably went home, if her parents let her. That's the real question."

Remembering her encounter with Kath's sister, Lily suspected that Kath's parents had not let her.

Lana observed her thoughtfully across the coffee table while she smoked. "I think Tommy's getting out tomorrow morning," she said, tapping the cigarette into the nearly overflowing ashtray. "I know you're in a tough spot, honey, but I think you'd better go before then. You can stay here tonight if you need to. Do you have a place to go tomorrow?"

Lily shrank back against the chair. "I—of course," she managed to say. "I can go . . . somewhere."

"If you don't have anywhere to go, Parker said you might try the Donaldina Cameron House in Chinatown. Do you know the place?"

Lily was painfully aware that Lana was watching her with something like pity, and the pity made her shrivel with shame. "Yes, I know the place." She tried to call up some bravado. "I'll be fine. Thank you for letting me stay here for a bit."

"Happy to. I'm very sorry for what happened." Lana put out the cigarette and stood up, stretching. "And now I'm going to take a nap. I'm still hungover from last night. You'll be all right out here? Do you want a book or anything?" She went to the octagonal table and opened the doors, pulling out a few paperback novels. "Here—they're junk really, but some of them are fun."

The covers were as lurid as the paperback romances in the back of Thrifty Drug Store. A woman in a slinky gown, her eyes downcast as a man in a fedora came after her, holding a gun: *The Final Mistress*. Two men engaged in a brawl in a dark alley while a woman in a ripped dress cowered in the corner: *Midnight Caller*.

"Thanks," Lily said awkwardly.

Lana yawned. "Oh! I'm going to go collapse. See you in a bit."

Lily listened as Lana went back through the apartment and into her bedroom, closing the door with a faint click. Her fingers tightened over the arms of the Chinese chair. Cameron House! Decades ago, Cameron House had taken in fallen Chinese women—prostitutes—but these days it was an after-school program for Chinatown kids. She imagined showing up at Cameron House, approaching the front desk in the wood-lined entryway, and asking for a place to stay. She could see the girl on duty giving her a puzzled look, lifting up the telephone to call one of the women on staff, saying, *A destitute girl's here*. No, it couldn't be done.

She knew she needed to make a plan, but her mind balked against it. Instead she moved over to the sofa and picked up *The Final Mistress*. Beneath it, to her shock, was *Strange Season*. She hadn't seen the book since the last time she'd read it in Thrifty Drugs.

She took the book over to the couch and opened it. The spine was creased, and several of the pages were dog-eared. She flipped past the scenes she'd already read, quickly becoming absorbed in the melodrama of Patrice's love life. Patrice simply couldn't accept her feelings for Maxine; Maxine called her a tease and threw a vase at her, and then apologized profusely and made love to her on the floor of her penthouse foyer. (Lily glanced up to make sure Lana was still in her bedroom when she read that scene.) Patrice's ex-boyfriend, the one who had left her at the beginning of the book, returned and begged her forgiveness. Patrice took him back and told him she'd done something crazy, then confessed her affair with Maxine.

Lily had a bad feeling about the confession. She read the scene with growing unease. Patrice's boyfriend was simply too understanding. "You've just made a mistake," he said to her soothingly. *No she hasn't!* Lily thought. But even she didn't see the surprise ending coming. On the pretext of taking Patrice out to lunch, Patrice's boyfriend delivered her to an insane asylum. The book ended with Patrice sedated in a hospital bed, whispering Maxine's name.

Lily wanted to throw the book across the room. She was so incensed by the ending that when the doorbell rang she started in surprise. She looked toward the kitchen, wondering if Lana would wake up, but when the doorbell sounded a second time, she decided she should answer it and take a message for Lana.

Lily hurried out into the building's foyer and opened the front door. To her shock, standing on the front stoop was Aunt Judy.

45

You *are* here!" Aunt Judy exclaimed, and immediately pulled Lily into an embrace. She smelled like the Ivory soap from Lily's family's bathroom, along with a trace of ginger and garlic as if she had come straight from the kitchen. The fragrance was so familiar it made Lily cling to her for an unselfconscious moment, as if she were a little girl again. Aunt Judy squeezed her back and said, "You worried us so much. What were you thinking? Nobody knew where you were!" Then she held Lily at arm's length and studied her closely. "You look all right. Have you eaten?"

Lily's eyes pricked with tears. Aunt Judy looked the same as ever; she had always been a small, thin woman in black-framed glasses, a product, she said, of spending too many hours peering at math books in dim lighting. "How did you find me here?" Lily asked.

Wordlessly Aunt Judy reached into her purse and extracted two pieces of paper. One was the scrap on which she'd written Kath's address. The other was the note she'd left at Kath's house, with Lana's address. She realized her aunt had tracked her down like a detective, and now—Lily's heart plummeted—Kath would never receive that note.

"Can I come in? What is this place?" Aunt Judy asked.

Lily stepped back to let her aunt inside. "I'm staying with a—a friend."

She saw Aunt Judy consider taking off her coat and shoes—her fingers briefly touched the top button of her raincoat—but then she seemed to decide she wouldn't be staying for long. She turned to Lily and said, "You need to come home."

Startled, Lily responded, "I can't."

Aunt Judy came farther into the living room and walked around the perimeter, taking in the furniture, the books (*Strange Season*, Lily noticed with relief, was facedown), the framed headshot of Tommy Andrews. She sat down on the sofa, and Lily saw her look askance at the nude woman table lighter. But Aunt Judy only said, "Why not?"

Lily sat down stiffly across from her. "Mama told me—we had a fight. She doesn't want me there."

"Your mother told me you had a fight, but she didn't say she doesn't want you at home."

Lily wondered if her mother had failed to explain the whole truth.

"Who is this friend you're staying with?" Aunt Judy asked.

There it was already: another opportunity to choose whether to lie. *A friend from school. She graduated last year. She lives with her brother; he's not home.* She glanced toward the rear of the apartment, wondering when Lana would hear them and emerge from her nap. No. She couldn't bring Lana into this lie without her permission.

"Lana Jackson," Lily said finally. "She lives here with—with Tommy Andrews. That's Tommy in that picture. She sings at the Telegraph Club, which the police raided on Friday night. It's a bar for ho-homosexuals. Wallace Lai saw me outside after the raid. I was there."

Her aunt regarded her expressionlessly, though her eyebrow twitched when Lily stumbled over the word *homosexual*. Why did it have to sound so obscene, Lily thought, the *x* crushed wetly in the back of her mouth.

"I see," Aunt Judy said. She seemed at a loss for words. She lowered her eyes to her hands, which she folded together tightly.

In the silence, Lily heard the ticking of a clock somewhere in the apartment. She saw the pack of Lucky Strikes and thought, wildly, that perhaps if she smoked one, her aunt would be so shocked she would forget what Lily had just said.

The door to the bedroom came unstuck with its familiar peeling sound, and Lily shot to her feet. A few moments later Lana appeared in the doorway to the living room, tying her silky flowered robe around herself, barefoot and looking like a woman who had just tumbled out of bed. "Hello," she said, looking from Lily to her aunt. "I thought I heard some voices out here."

Aunt Judy rose and went across the room, hand extended. "I'm Judy Fong, Lily's aunt."

Lana shook her hand, blinking. "Oh. I'm Lana Jackson."

"Thank you for letting Lily stay with you."

Aunt Judy was shorter than Lana, but she held herself as if she were taller. Seeing them together made Lily realize that Lana was closer to her own age than to Aunt Judy's. Lily had thought Lana was so sophisticated, but now in comparison to Aunt Judy, she seemed young and even a little naïve.

"I've been happy to have her," Lana said, but it sounded wrong— too prim. She shifted uncomfortably and looked at Lily. "It sounds like you're leaving?"

"I don't—"

"Yes," Aunt Judy interrupted. "I've come to take her home."

Lily balked. "But I told you—"

"We'll go home and discuss it with your father."

Lily paled. "I don't think that's a good idea."

Lana watched the exchange, her eyebrows rising. "Perhaps I'd better leave you to talk it over," she said, and began to back away into the dining room.

"No, we're leaving," Aunt Judy said. "We don't want to overstay our welcome. Thank you again, Miss Jackson. Lily, are you ready? Do you have a coat?"

There was an edge to her tone, as if she were hurrying Lily out of an unsavory situation, and Lily suddenly realized how Lana must look to her aunt: dressed in that clinging robe, her cleavage showing in a way that it shouldn't at this time of day, her blond hair mussed from bed and her lipstick half worn off, as if she had been kissing someone. Lily felt a rush of protectiveness toward Lana, who had taken her in despite barely knowing her, and she felt an uncharitable prickling of judgment against her aunt.

"You're not listening to me," Lily said, frustrated.

Aunt Judy's expression softened. "We were very worried, Lily. It's the New Year. Your mother has been working all day to prepare the dinner for everyone. Come home. Please."

Lily and Aunt Judy walked back to Chinatown. It was still chilly, and Lily still only had her thin cardigan to wear. When they stopped at an intersection a few blocks from Lana's apartment, Aunt Judy took off her coat and handed it to Lily, and Lily put it on, feeling like a child.

The streets of Chinatown were littered with firecracker wrappers. The shops were mostly closed to the public today, but a few tourists wandered through anyway, gawking at the calligraphy scrolls they couldn't read and peering in shop windows at mounds of dried herbs or gaudy souvenirs. Many Chinese were out on the sidewalks in their finest clothes, visiting family and friends or heading to New Year banquets at their clan or district associations.

During the war, Lily's mother had taken them to her family association on New Year, but after Lily's father returned, they stopped going. He wanted to eat Shanghainese food, and the associations were for the Cantonese from Kwangtung. "They don't cook the right food," he had complained. So Lily's mother had taught herself how to prepare his favorite dishes for the New Year dinner, and when Aunt Judy arrived in 1947, she started helping, too.

Usually Lily looked forward to the New Year dinner, but this year, she wished she could be anywhere else. She knew that as soon as she got home, she'd have to greet her grandmother and uncles and cousins and pretend that everything was normal. She'd have to obey her parents and especially her mother, who had told her, *You won't tell your aunts and uncles about this. You won't say a word to your grandmother*. It felt like a trap from which there was no escape.

A few steps away from the front door she briefly considered running away again—but where would she go? She didn't really have a choice. She might be able to spend one more night on Lana's sofa, but then what?

Aunt Judy was already taking out the key to the front door, and then she turned the knob and looked at Lily, gesturing for her to enter first.

The entryway was dim and smelled like ginger and the syrupy scent of the Shanghai-style braised fish her mother made every New Year. She already heard the voices of her brothers and younger cousins upstairs. They didn't know she was standing there at the bottom, hesitating to go back to them, where she would be absorbed back into the family as if nothing had happened. Everything she had experienced over the past forty-eight hours would be deliberately ignored.

"Lily," Aunt Judy said.

She climbed up the stairs, her heart sinking.

46

The upstairs landing was empty, but several suitcases and bags were pushed against the wall across from the telephone table.

"Go say hello to your grandmother," Aunt Judy said. "She's in the living room."

Lily took off her shoes and went where her aunt told her to go. Her brothers and cousins—eleven-year-old Jack and nine-year-old Minnie—were sprawled on the floor playing marbles. Uncle Francis and Uncle Sam were smoking by the front window, and A P'oh[1] was sitting in one corner of the sofa, observing the action. She saw Lily as soon as she entered the room.

"阿麗,"[2] A P'oh called, gesturing for her to join her on the sofa.

"Lily!" Eddie said. "Did you just get back?"

"Everybody was mad," Frankie said before Eddie shot him a quelling look.

"I'm sorry," she said to her brothers—to everyone—and then she sat down beside her grandmother, who took her hand. Her grandmother's skin was loose over her bones and dry as paper, but her grip was quite firm. "阿婆好," Lily greeted her. "幾時到咖?"[3]

"我今早到咖,"[4] A P'oh said. She gave Lily a canny look that made Lily wonder how much she knew about what had happened.

---

1. Grandmother (Lily's mother's mother).
2. A Lai; a nickname for Lily.
3. Hello, Grandmother. When did you get here?
4. I got here this morning.

"大家好擔心你啊. 千其无再咁做."[5] Her grandmother's tone was soft, but the warning in it was unmistakable.

Lily flushed. "對唔住, 阿婆,"[6] she said, lowering her gaze. She told herself she hadn't done anything wrong, but she still felt guilty.

She changed out of the clothes she had slept in. She washed her face and brushed her teeth; she combed her hair and pinned it away from her face. In the bathroom mirror, she looked like a good Chinese girl.

In the kitchen, Aunt Judy and Aunt May were chopping vegetables at the table while her mother fried nien-kao[7] on the stove. Her father was making a pot of tea, and he saw her first, his face relaxing into sudden relief.

Her mother turned. Her expression softened, but only briefly. "Come and help your aunts," she said.

Lily pulled out a chair and sat down beside Aunt May at the table, while Aunt Judy, who was about to start mincing ginger, slid the chopping board over to her along with the knobby root.

Her father placed the teapot on a small round tray along with a stack of teacups, and headed out of the kitchen. Lily thought he might say something to her—he even hesitated next to her chair—but he remained silent. A hot shame rose within her. She didn't know what her family knew, but their silence told her they knew enough.

She focused on the ginger, mincing it as precisely as she could, and eventually her aunts and her mother picked up their conversation. Each time Lily finished a task, Aunt Judy gave her another one: peel and chop garlic, then the scallions, then the water chestnuts. Every surface in the kitchen was crowded with ingredients for the

5. You made everybody worry. Never do that again.
6. I'm sorry, Grandmother.
7. Rice cakes.

other dishes that would be served: two kinds of dried mushrooms, dried lily flowers and bean thread, all soaking in separate bowls of liquid; a mound of washed lettuce air-drying in the battered metal colander; bottles of soy sauce and oyster sauce and cooking wine. A pot of lotus root soup was simmering on the back of the stove, and Lily's mother was turning out the nien-kao onto a platter, while Aunt May took a whole fish out of the refrigerator.

It was exactly like every other New Year, and it was that sameness that made Lily feel as if she wasn't all there. Her fingers were doing the work, but she could prepare vegetables in her sleep. It left her mind plenty of room to wander, and it returned over and over to those last moments in the Telegraph Club with Kath. The running and jostling through the back hallway; the flashing lights and the women shouting at her to move; Kath's hand squeezing hers before letting go.

Lily's eyes grew hot and she willed herself not to cry. She should never have let go of Kath's hand. She should have held on to her and dragged her out the back door.

Her hands trembled, and the cleaver slipped, and the blade nicked the tip of her left index finger. A droplet of blood welled up instantly, bright red. She stared at her finger in shock as the blood splashed onto the cutting board.

Aunt Judy reached for the cleaver, gently easing it out of her grasp, and said quietly, "You're all right. It's just a little cut. You'd better go put on a bandage."

There were eight dishes, plus lotus root soup and rice: poached whole chicken with ginger sauce; roast duck from a Chinatown deli; lo-han chai, a vegetarian dish traditionally eaten by monks; hsün yü, the cold Shanghai-style fish; steamed whole fish Cantonese style; the nien-kao; oyster sauce lettuce; and for dessert, pa pao fan, a steamed sticky rice filled with sweet bean paste.

Lily had been starving all afternoon—it felt like an eternity had passed since her scrambled eggs at Lana's apartment—but although the food was delicious, she had lost her appetite. Aunt Judy, who was sitting next to Lily at the makeshift table for twelve, noticed. She selected some pieces of hsün yü and deposited them in Lily's bowl, urging her to eat.

At least no one was making an effort to talk to her. Lily's mother, Uncle Sam, Aunt May, and her grandmother spoke Cantonese together at one end of the table, while Lily's father and Aunt Judy fell into Shanghainese. Uncle Francis, who had grown up in Los Angeles, stuck to English with the kids. Sometimes she caught her mother or father glancing at her, but they didn't speak to her.

She began to feel as if she had been split in two, and only one half of her was here in this living room. That was the good Chinese daughter who was delicately chewing her way around the bones in each piece of hsün yü, carefully extracting them from her mouth and laying the tiny white spines on the edge of her plate with her chopsticks. The other half had been left out on the sidewalk before Lily walked in the front door. That was the girl who had spent last night in the North Beach apartment of a Caucasian woman she barely knew. Everything would be all right, Lily understood, as long as she kept that girl out of this Chinese family.

Perhaps one day she'd get used to the way it made her feel: dislocated and dazed, never quite certain if the other half of her would stay offstage as directed. But tonight she felt as if she were constantly on the edge of saying or doing something wrong, and the effort of keeping that unwelcome half silent was making her sick. Her stomach rebelled against it, and her head hurt, and she was so tired she felt as if she were in danger of falling unconscious there at the table, her head dropping right into her bowl of rice. The image struck her as ridiculously funny, and she had to swallow hard to prevent herself from breaking into hysterical laughter.

Finally, dinner was over, and A P'oh was calling for the lei shi[8] to be distributed. Uncle Sam went out to the hall, and when he returned his hands were full of red envelopes. Minnie and Frankie both squealed as the adults laughed indulgently. Lily's father produced several lei shi from his jacket pocket; Uncle Francis went and got his from his coat; and A P'oh instructed Frankie to bring her purse from Lily's bedroom.

The red envelopes were handed out to all the children, Lily included: four each, stuffed with crisp new bills. The little ones got only a dollar in each envelope, but Lily received thirty-five dollars this year, with twenty coming from her parents. The money was a gift, but it also felt like a warning. It came with the expectation that Lily would do as she was told.

The lei shi marked the end of dinner, and Lily helped her mother clear the dishes away. Afterward, the men disassembled the temporary table and lit up cigarettes. Aunt Judy opened the living room windows to let out the smoke, and the sound of firecrackers popping could be heard coming from Grant Avenue.

Frankie ran to the window to peer outside, his brother and cousins close behind. "Can we go see the firecrackers, Papa?" Frankie asked.

It was the New Year, after all, so the adults agreed, and Uncle Sam, Uncle Francis, and Lily's father put on their jackets to accompany the children down the block. They asked Lily if she wanted to come, but she shook her head and went to help her mother and aunts wash the dishes.

---

8. Red envelopes filled with money given to children at the New Year.

When they finished, and her mother and aunts put the kettle on for tea, Lily said she would go to bed. Her mother looked at her—really looked at her for the first time all day—and Lily looked away.

"Take some blankets from my room so you can sleep on the floor in your brothers' room," her mother said.

"I'll help you," Aunt Judy said, rising quickly.

They found a quilt and the old army blanket and took one of the pillows from Lily's bed, arranging everything on the floor between her brothers' beds. She said good night to her grandmother, who would sleep in Lily's room during her visit. She brushed her teeth; she changed into her nightgown; she took clean clothes for tomorrow into her brothers' room, and closed the door. The floor felt very hard beneath her, and immediately she remembered the soft give of Lana's sofa.

She closed her eyes. She thought about the first time she had seen Lana, in the hallway of the Telegraph Club outside the bathroom, but the memory was disjointed and vague, with snatches of color and disembodied voices. It seemed so unbelievable now—the idea that she, Lily Hu, had ever snuck out of her house and gone to this homosexual club in the middle of the night. How could she ever have done such a thing? A few hours at home and the Telegraph Club seemed more like a fantasy than a real thing. This troubled her. It felt as if someone had taken an eraser to her memory—to her very self—and rubbed at it, then blown away the remains.

She tried to think back, to remember what was real. The shy look on Kath's face as she gave her that issue of *Collier's* on top of Russian Hill. The tentative softness of Kath's lips, the first time they kissed. The heat of Kath's breath on her neck as Lily held her in the corner of Miss Weiland's classroom. Lily had never felt closer to anyone in her life.

It hurt to remember these things because they reminded her of Kath and her fears of what might have happened to her. But the hurt felt real—much more real than the entire afternoon of staying silent. So she lay on the hard wooden floor between her brothers' beds and let that ache fill her.

47

ily woke before dawn. The room was dark, and she heard her brothers breathing on either side of her, their lungs rising and falling almost in unison. When they had come back the night before, they had stood over her—she had heard them but pretended to be asleep—and whispered, *Is she all right? Why was Mama so angry at her? Did she do something wrong? Shh, don't wake her.* And then Eddie tucked the blanket up beneath her chin and brushed his hand over her forehead as if he were their father checking her temperature. His touch had brought tears to her eyes, and they slid silently down her temples while he and Frankie climbed into their beds, their sheets rustling as they settled down for the night.

She didn't want to wake them, but she remembered that the flat now contained an additional five people, and she didn't want to be last in line for the bathroom. She got up as quietly as she could and snuck out of the room.

She could almost pretend it was a normal day. She washed up quickly and got dressed. In the kitchen, her mother was already brewing coffee and making porridge from the leftover rice.

"Will you set out the dishes?" her mother asked.

Lily went to the cabinet, wondering if their conversations would only be transactional from now on. She felt dull inside, like a tarnished silver bowl.

She heard little Minnie chirping from the other end of the flat as everyone else began to wake up, and soon the kitchen was crowded. It was Monday, but because it was New Year week and family was visiting, Lily's parents were taking a couple of days off from work. Eddie and Frankie still had to go to school, of course, and Lily— Lily stopped short, about to butter a piece of toast, alarmed by the thought of having to go to school. With Shirley. With everyone who must already know about her and Kath.

Thankfully, there was breakfast to distract her. Eddie and Frankie tried to argue their way out of school, but failed. Minnie and Jack tried to swallow their glee at not having to go to school themselves, but also failed. After A P'oh woke up, Lily was charged with taking her a tray of porridge and tea. When she returned to the landing to pick up her book bag, her mother appeared as if she had been waiting for her and said, "You're not going to school today."

Lily's relief was cut short by instant wariness. "Why not?"

Her father came out of the kitchen holding his coffee cup. "We need to talk."

It didn't happen right away. First, Eddie and Frankie had to be taken to school. Everyone had to finish their breakfast. Uncle Sam and Aunt May decided to take Minnie and Jack to the Chinese playground for the morning. A P'oh declared her intention to go to the Tin How Temple. Aunt Judy arrived just as they were all leaving; she said that Uncle Francis had gone to meet a friend for breakfast. Lily was sure this had all been carefully planned.

At last, the four of them—Lily, her parents, and Aunt Judy—took their seats at the kitchen table. Her mother hadn't put on makeup, and her face seemed colorless in the overhead light, her lips pressed together thinly. Her father looked more tired than usual, and he was smoking cigarettes one after another, rather than his pipe. Aunt

Judy's eyebrows were drawn together in a permanent expression of worry as she glanced around the table.

"You won't be going back to school," her mother said. "I won't have you anywhere near that girl."

Lily pretended to misunderstand. "What girl? You mean Shirley?"

Her mother's nostrils flared. "You know who I mean. I talked to Shirley yesterday—"

"You—what?"

"Shirley told me everything. About how that girl Kathleen Miller went after you. How she is a homosexual and took you to that place. Shirley told me she tried to get you to stop being friends with her, but you refused."

"That's not what happened! Shirley's lying."

"If that's not what happened, tell me what did. Don't lie to me!"

"Grace," Lily's father said. "Give her a chance. Is anything that Shirley said true?"

He seemed to have trouble looking at her. His reluctance to meet her eyes made her feel worst of all.

"Shirley doesn't like me to be friends with other people." There, she'd said it: the thing she'd been thinking practically her entire life.

"Don't be ridiculous," her mother said.

"It's true. We all know it's true. She didn't like it when I became friends with Kath."

"Then you *do* know that girl," her mother said.

"Yes, I know her, but she didn't—she didn't do whatever awful thing Shirley said. She didn't *go after me*. We—we've been in the same math classes for years." Lily looked at her aunt pleadingly. "I told her about your job, and she was interested. She wants to fly planes. She's so smart. She's the one who gave me that magazine I told you about."

Aunt Judy smiled at her gently, and Lily knew it sounded ridiculous, as if she'd had a schoolgirl crush on Kath. The thought that her parents and Aunt Judy would think that very same thing was mortifying. She didn't want them to think of her as someone who had feelings like that for anyone, girl or boy, but at the same time, characterizing her relationship with Kath as a crush was completely inadequate. It had been so much more. She wished she had realized it sooner.

"Girls don't fly planes," her mother snapped. "What did she do to make you go to that nightclub?"

Lily rubbed her hot forehead with her cold fingers, trying to ease the pressure that was building inside her. Every sentence she spoke was a choice. She had an infinite number of chances to turn back, but she refused to turn her back on Kath.

"I wanted to go," Lily said finally. Her voice was remarkably steady. "She didn't take me. I asked."

The kitchen was silent but for the ticking of the clock. Her father was staring at the cigarette burning between his fingers. Aunt Judy was gazing at her with that same worried expression.

Her mother began to shake her head, as if she could shake off Lily's words. "No. You don't know what you're saying."

"Yes I do."

"No you don't! And this just proves that you can't go back to Galileo. You can't go anywhere near that girl. I was afraid of this. Lily, if you'd only admit that you've made a mistake, we could help you get over this. We won't let you throw your life away like this."

"There are studies," her father said. "You're too young for this. This is a phase."

"There, you hear your father. It's going to pass. It may not seem that way now, but when you're older you'll understand. Lily, look at me. We looked the other way when you went to that Man Ts'ing picnic. We know you didn't mean anything by it, but this—this can't be excused. You're already on the record as sympathizing with the Man Ts'ing. If word gets out that you've been *voluntarily* in the company of homosexuals—"

Her mother looked anguished. Her arms were barricaded across her stomach as she leaned forward to make her point, deep lines grooved in her forehead. "Your father still doesn't have his papers back. Do you understand what I'm saying?"

With a twist in her gut, Lily did understand. Being linked to the Man Ts'ing was bad, but if she never had anything to do with them again, it could be overlooked. Adding in the corrupting influence of homosexuals made it exponentially worse, and not only for her, but also potentially for her father. Her behavior could further endanger him with the immigration authorities because it reflected poorly on him. She looked at him. He inhaled so deeply on his cigarette that a good inch of the paper burned away at once, and dark shadows pulled at the skin beneath his eyes. He still wouldn't look at her.

"Tell us you'll accept that you've made a mistake and we'll help you," her mother said.

Her mother was practically begging her to lie, and the temptation to give in was strong. It would be so much easier, and she didn't want to endanger her father. But something stubborn in her balked at what her mother was asking for.

She loved Kath.

It was crystal clear to her now, and it was exhilarating and illuminating and it turned everything upside down, because there was no way to resolve her love for Kath with the demands her mother was making. If she lied, she would betray Kath, and she refused to do that. But even if she could live with lying, would it make any difference in her father's situation? If he hadn't gotten his papers back, it was probably because *he* refused to lie about Calvin, not because Wallace Lai had seen her leaving the Telegraph Club. And if her father wouldn't lie, why should she?

Lily took a deep breath. "I didn't make a mistake. You can ask me as many times as you want, but I'm not going to lie." The more she spoke, the bolder she felt.

Her mother abruptly stood up, shoving her chair back with a screech. Lily recoiled.

"You ran away!" her mother cried. "You left this house and didn't tell anyone where you were going. Anything could have happened to you!"

Lily's father reached out to put a steadying hand on her mother's arm. She seemed about to say something utterly furious—her face was turning a blotchy red—but then, as if it took all her effort to restrain herself, she threw off her husband's hand and stalked out of the kitchen. Lily heard her mother's footsteps receding quickly down the hallway, and then a door slammed shut.

Shocked, Lily turned to her father. He seemed as stunned as she was, and finally their eyes met. He winced, and bent forward to stub out his cigarette. There was a long moment of uncomfortable silence. Lily glanced at Aunt Judy, who was watching her brother worriedly, but remained quiet.

Finally, Lily's father scrubbed a hand over his face and said, "There's no other choice, then. You'll go with your aunt to Pasadena to finish the school year."

Lily stared at her father uncomprehendingly. "What?"

"Your aunt and uncle have offered to take you away from here while—while things settle down," her father said. "They're making a big sacrifice to help you. They've even offered to take you down to Pasadena right away—tomorrow. There's no reason to wait. Today you should pack your things, and tomorrow you'll take the train to Pasadena. Judy thinks you'll be able to enroll in the high school there. Isn't that right?"

"Yes," Aunt Judy said. "I know this must come as a surprise."

Lily stared at her father, and then at her aunt. Her head throbbed painfully; it was the only real thing in the room. Everything her father and aunt said seemed utterly unbelievable.

"We think this will be best for you," Aunt Judy said. "It'll get you away from—from the complications here."

It would take her away from Kath. She understood that immediately; it was like a gut punch.

"This is for your own good," her father said. "You'll be safe in Pasadena."

They were afraid, Lily realized, that there would be more trouble if she stayed—trouble for herself, trouble for her father. And they wanted to make sure she wasn't here in Chinatown, inviting gossip. They wanted to hide her away until people forgot what had happened.

"I don't want to go," she said, shaking her head.

Her father looked at her bleakly. "You'll have to learn that sometimes you have to do things that you don't want to do."

Lily gazed at her father in disbelief, and then in growing anger.

"I live very close to the high school in Pasadena," Aunt Judy said. "You'll be able to walk there. Once we get home we can go right away and make sure you can enroll. If you can't, your father said it might be possible for you to finish your senior year by correspondence. And, you know, maybe we can find you a part-time job or something at the lab. You'd like that, wouldn't you?"

Lily could barely register her aunt's words. They were splitting her up from Kath.

"We want you to be happy," her father said. "You'll be free from distractions in Pasadena."

Even though she didn't know where Kath was or if she was all right, she had believed that eventually she would find out, and they would be together again. The idea that she might never see Kath again took her breath away. She felt faint; she felt as if she might dissolve into thin air.

"I'm going to call Galileo to see if you need to collect any paperwork for your transfer," her father said.

She felt Kath's hand letting go of hers again and again; her fingers sliding through hers over and over. Everything she and Kath had done could be erased so easily. It could be erased by her family pretending it had never happened. It could be erased by her parents uprooting her from her home and sending her away so that Kath would not know where she was. It could be erased because they were her parents and she was their daughter, and they loved her, and she could not disobey them even if it broke her heart.

"You should pack your things," her father said. "Be ready to leave tomorrow morning."

48

ily's father brought out an old brown suitcase and gave it to her to use. A luggage tag with an address in Chinese hung from the handle. Lily could read her father's name and the characters for Shanghai, China.

She opened the suitcase on her bed. Her grandmother's powdery scent clung to the blankets; already the room was no longer hers. She packed her clothes quickly, without looking at them. She shoved in the new dress she'd worn to the Telegraph Club two nights ago, not bothering to fold it. She tossed in her black pumps and a hairbrush. Her father came into the doorway, looking anxious. She ignored him and kept packing. She didn't want to speak to him; she didn't want to speak to any of them.

"I knew a doctor once, a woman, who was a lesbian," he said.

The sound of the word was startling, and she froze for a second, but she refused to acknowledge him.

"She was a very successful doctor," he continued. "She was Chinese too, like you."

This slowed her down for a moment, but only a moment.

"I admired her skill as a physician. But everyone knew about her personal life, and she never married. There were rumors, of course, but she lived alone. I think she still lives alone. This is what your mother and I are worried about. We want you to marry and have children. You should have a full life, not a stunted one in which you wind up alone, with no one to care for you. Remember this."

He was imagining a tragic future for her as if she were one of the strangers in the Eastern Pearl that she and Shirley liked to invent stories for. It only made her more angry.

When she didn't respond, he exhaled in resignation and left.

She continued to roughly throw her clothes into the suitcase. She thought about Lana and Tommy in their cozy if cheaply furnished North Beach apartment. They were not stunted. She thought about Claire and Paula, and the indulgent tone in Claire's voice as she described Paula as *solid*. They had full lives. She thought about Kath, and a hollow seemed to open up inside her. It had gravity; it pulled at her in a way that made her sway on her feet. She had to sit down on the edge of her bed, and suddenly she remembered the *Collier's* magazine that Kath had given her, but it wasn't on top of the stack of books that made her nightstand.

She began to unstack them, hunting for the magazine, but although she found the one her aunt had given her, Kath's issue wasn't there. She moved all the books aside in case it had fallen against the wall, but there was nothing. She looked around the room, wondering in rising panic if someone had stolen it from her, or if her mother had come into her room and thrown it away. It was only a magazine, but she had to bring it with her. Kath had given it to her.

Her book bag. She spun on her heel and rushed out of her room, running down the hall to find her book bag where she had left it on the floor beside the bench. She knelt down and unbuckled it and there it was, tucked in the back behind *The Exploration of Space*. She let out her breath in relief.

Footsteps approached from the kitchen. Aunt Judy stood a few feet away. "Are you all right?"

Her anger surged up again. If her aunt hadn't played detective and found Lily in North Beach—if she hadn't offered to take her back to Pasadena—

She rose to her feet, leaving the magazine in her bag; she didn't want her aunt to see it. "I'm fine," she said, because her aunt looked so forlorn.

Back in her room, she looked at the cover illustration of spaceships traveling toward the red planet before carefully tucking it between her clothes in the suitcase. She glanced over her shoulder, then opened *The Exploration of Space*. The photograph of Tommy was still there. She remembered Kath picking it up off the floor of the girls' bathroom and holding it out to her. For a moment, they'd both held this piece of paper, like a talisman that had called them into existence, together. How long ago that was, and yet it felt like yesterday.

Somehow, time did not stop. The suitcase was packed; her grandmother returned from the temple; Uncle Sam and Aunt May returned from the playground with Minnie and Jack. There was lunch to make—leftovers from the New Year dinner—and there was another mess to clean up. Eddie and Frankie came home from school. Uncle Francis returned much later than expected, because he had gone to the train station to exchange his and Aunt Judy's tickets for new ones that departed tomorrow—and to buy one for Lily.

Late that afternoon, Lily's parents gathered Eddie and Frankie and Lily together and explained that Lily was going to Pasadena for a while. "She'll finish high school there," her father said.

"Why?" Frankie asked.

"It's best for her," their mother said in a tone of voice that indicated no further questions would be answered.

Eddie followed Lily away from their parents and whispered, "Did something happen? I heard some things at school. I didn't know what to do."

She drew him back into his bedroom, pushing the door shut. "What did you hear?"

His cheeks went pink.

"Never mind," she said. "You don't have to say it. Do you think I'm disgusting?"

He frowned and shook his head. "Of course not. I don't care what they said. You're my sister. Should I beat them up?"

She had to take a deep breath to prevent herself from crying. "No. But will you do something for me?"

"What?"

She pulled a small envelope from her skirt pocket. It was addressed to Peggy Miller on Union Street. She wasn't sure if Kath's parents would confiscate her mail, but she thought that Peggy would pass on a letter. "Will you mail this for me?"

He took the envelope. "Peggy Miller," he said in surprise. "She's the sister of—" He cut himself off, looking embarrassed. "I heard something about her sister."

"And me?" Lily said.

He reddened. "Maybe."

"It's all right. Just—will you mail this to Peggy?"

"Well, I know her," Eddie said. "We're both in the band. She's first-chair trombone. I could give it to her."

Lily was relieved. "You will?"

"Sure."

"Don't let anyone else have it."

"Okay."

"Thank you," she said, and impulsively pulled him into a hug. After a startled moment, he hugged her back.

As they parted, she asked, "Will you tell me one more thing?"

"What?"

"Did Shirley win Miss Chinatown?"

He was surprised. "No."

"Who did?"

"Some girl from George Washington High School."

She felt an entirely ungracious satisfaction.

And then it was time to go.

The morning of her departure, all the adults pretended as if it were completely normal for Lily to be leaving with her aunt and uncle in the middle of the New Year festival. The children's questions were shushed, and they were herded away into the living room to look out the window for the waiting taxi.

Lily's mother thrust a paper bag full of steamed buns into her hands. They were still warm, and Lily realized her mother must have just run out to buy them. "Don't forget to eat," her mother said stiffly.

Lily's father carried her suitcase down the stairs and put it into the trunk beside Aunt Judy's and Uncle Francis's luggage. On the sidewalk, he placed his hands on Lily's shoulders and looked her in the eye, finally, and said, "Listen to your aunt and uncle. Call us when you get there."

Lily turned away first, angry with herself for wanting to cry.

The taxi ride to the train station was a blur. They crossed the Bay Bridge on the lower deck, heading toward Oakland, and the bay whipped past through the steel girders—water and boats and tiny crested waves. It made her queasy. She rolled down the window to catch the breeze, but it smelled of a noxious combination of exhaust and seawater. She closed her eyes and wished she was going in the other direction.

The train station was smaller than she had expected, but still confusing, with countless people rushing around with their suitcases and tickets clutched in their hands. She was embarrassingly grateful to have her aunt and uncle to guide her in the right direction. Uncle Francis lit a cigarette while they waited and paced, smoking; Aunt Judy sat on a bench beside Lily, studying the train schedule. When their train was announced, Aunt Judy jumped up and Uncle Francis put out his cigarette, and Lily followed them down the platform and onto the train. Aunt Judy gestured for Lily to take the seat by the window.

Lily had tossed a random novel from her bedside stack into her bag when she packed yesterday. She hadn't even glanced at it then, but now she pulled it out and saw that it was *The Martian Chronicles* by Ray Bradbury. Aunt Judy had given it to her. She opened it, but she couldn't focus on the words. She felt as if her mind had been turned off, and all this was happening to someone who looked like her but couldn't possibly *be* her.

After the train started moving, and after the conductor came through to check their tickets, Uncle Francis went to the lounge car for a coffee. Once they were alone, Aunt Judy turned to Lily.

"I know I'm not your favorite person right now, but I need to tell you something," she said. "Please listen."

Lily didn't speak, but she closed her book.

"I really am trying to do what's best for you," Aunt Judy said.

She put her hand on Lily's arm, and Lily tried not to stiffen in response. Her aunt's thin gold wedding ring glinted in the light from the window.

"I know it feels like the end of the world now, but it's not," Aunt Judy continued. "In a few months you'll graduate from high school, and your whole life will be ahead of you."

My life is right now, Lily wanted to retort, and she raised her gaze to her aunt's face to say it, and was stopped short by the expression there. A pleading look, straightforward and earnest. The bright bubble of tears in her eyes.

"I don't understand what you've been going through," Aunt Judy said, "but you'll just have to put up with me until I do understand."

Aunt Judy squeezed Lily's arm, and then she let go. Lily nodded slightly, just enough for Aunt Judy to notice, and it felt like wrenching a door open the tiniest crack. It was all she could do just then, and she had to turn away to look out the window to avoid seeing the hope on her aunt's face.

Lily watched the city of Oakland roll by, brick buildings and chimney stacks and the chrome glint of crawling traffic. She wondered where Kath was. She wondered if Kath could sense her, sitting here on this train as it took her away. Perhaps it was possible, if she closed her eyes and sent out her thoughts along the steel track like a message along a telegraph wire.

I love you. I love you.

The train swayed gently beneath her, and she leaned against the window to feel the cool glass against her cheek, and she was sure that Kath had heard her, she was sure.

Later, Uncle Francis returned with a newspaper that he split with Aunt Judy. Lily kept her book closed on her lap as she gazed out the window. After Oakland, they passed through suburbs and small towns, and then there was a flash of water—the end of San Francisco Bay, glittering beneath the cloud-scudded sky. The train stopped for a while in San Jose, just long enough for the passengers to stand and stretch and think about dashing into the station, and then it continued onward.

Lily pulled out the bag of steamed buns her mother had given her and shared it with her aunt and uncle. Lily raised one to her mouth and took a bite, and the taste jolted her: the caramelized edges of the meat, the fluffy softness of the bun, the savory-sweetness where the sauce had soaked, jamlike, into the dough.

Rounded green hills dotted with live oaks went by, and all of a sudden the clouds that had been dogging them since San Francisco were gone, and the sky was robin's-egg blue. A hawk soared overhead, riding a draft of wind on widespread wings.

Lily realized she had never been this far from San Francisco before, and a fleeting thrill went through her. This was the world.

One Year Later

EPILOGUE

t was only four o'clock in the afternoon, and Vesuvio's was mostly empty. Lily looked past the long wooden bar with its few patrons, past the colorful paintings hanging from the upper walls, and toward the rear of the room. A row of small tables with cane-back chairs lined the wall across from the bar, and there at the end, in a shadowy corner, she saw her.

Kath saw Lily too, and stood up.

All last year, through letters and long-distance phone calls, Lily had imagined her, but now she realized her imagination had left out all the important details. As Kath stepped out from behind the table, Lily remembered the way she stood, hands nervously hidden in her pockets. As Lily came closer, she saw the familiar, slightly shy expression on Kath's face, and the same patches of color in her pale cheeks.

"Hello," Kath said softly.

"Hello," Lily replied. They were separated by only a few feet now, and she didn't know how she was supposed to greet her. Shaking hands seemed ridiculous, and she couldn't kiss her on the cheek as if they were merely friends.

"Would you like to sit down?" Kath said somewhat formally, and pulled out a chair.

"Thank you." Lily sat down, and Kath's hand touched her

shoulder very briefly before she went back to her seat on the other side of the table.

Kath was wearing a collared shirt and trousers, and she had gotten herself a haircut—recently, Lily guessed, because it was trimmed so close against her neck. Kath still had the same delicately shaped mouth, the same long-lashed blue eyes. She smiled at Lily, and the longer they looked at each other, the deeper her smile went.

"It's really good to see you," Kath said in her straightforward way, but Lily understood the heartfelt weight of her words.

Lily couldn't stop smiling either. "It's really good to see you, too."

"How was your trip?"

"It was fine. It's not very interesting."

"I haven't seen you in over a year," Kath said. "Everything you say is interesting."

Lily's eyes grew hot. She looked down at the wooden table and saw that there were already two glasses of beer there. "Did you buy these?"

"Yes. If you want something else, I'll go to the bar."

"Oh no. This is fine." Lily picked up her glass, and Kath did the same, and they gently knocked them together.

"Happy New Year," Kath said.

"Kung hei faat ts'oi," Lily responded, and they both took a sip from their beers.

"I'm serious," Kath said. "I want to know how you are."

Lily was so nervous all of a sudden, as if she had forgotten how to talk to Kath. They had shared a lot in letters over the past year—maybe she had shared too much—but writing something down was different from meeting face to face. And Kath had always been more reserved in her letters. Perhaps she hadn't told Lily everything. What if she had met someone else? It had been a long time, and they didn't live in the same city anymore. They'd never made any promises to each other. Nothing was certain about the future.

Kath scooted her chair around the table so that her back was to the door and she was closer to Lily. A moment later Lily felt Kath's hand reach for hers under the table, lacing their fingers together as if to hold her still, right here, right now. *This* was certain.

"Lily," Kath said softly. "Tell me everything."

They talked for almost two hours. They already knew the basic details of their lives, but saying them out loud made things real. Lily had finished high school last spring and spent the summer doing fill-in secretarial work at the Jet Propulsion Lab, before starting college at UCLA in the fall. She lived in an apartment in Westwood now, with another Chinese girl, and she was studying math. She told Kath about a new class she had just started on programmable computers, which Aunt Judy thought would become important in the future.

Kath had moved to Berkeley last spring, temporarily living with Jean, but had since found an apartment in Oakland. She lived with two other gay girls; one was at Cal and the other was a mechanic. Kath had found a job working at a tiny airport in Oakland and was about to start flying lessons. She finally got her high school diploma in December, finishing it by correspondence with the help of Miss Weiland.

"Are you going to go to Cal now?" Lily asked.

"Maybe. I'm too late for this semester, but maybe in the fall."

"What about UCLA? Some really smart people go there."

Kath laughed. "I'll think about it. But . . . I don't want to give up my job. I need the money, and I just convinced my boss to train me to fix the airplanes. It's exactly what I want."

Lily felt a little bolder now. "It's not everything you want, is it?"

Kath smiled. "No, it's not."

Lily went warm all over and glanced over her shoulder at the other patrons of the bar. It had filled up since she arrived, and she wondered what time it was. She reluctantly looked at her watch. "Oh no," she said, "I have to go. I'm going to be late for dinner." She stood up, already imagining her mother's curious look and the lie she'd have to tell her.

"I'll walk you out," Kath said, standing as well.

"I don't want to go," Lily admitted.

"I don't want you to go either."

At that moment a man laughed very loudly down at the other end of the bar, and they were reminded once more of where they were. Kath said nothing more, but she helped Lily into her coat before putting on her own. They walked quickly and silently past the other patrons, who barely noticed them leaving.

Kath held the door open for her, and Lily stepped out into the city and saw that night had fallen while they were talking. The lights were on all along Columbus Avenue, and she smelled the distinct cool scent of the fog rolling in. She felt Kath's hand on her back, nudging her over into Adler Place, the narrow street between Vesuvio's and the next building. The other end of Adler Place opened onto Grant Avenue, and Lily saw the Chinatown streetlamps glowing in the distance.

"Come out with me tomorrow night," Kath said, drawing close to her.

Lily backed away into the shadow of the building, past the light that spilled out of Vesuvio's windows, and Kath followed. "I can't go tomorrow," Lily said. "It's the New Year parade."

"What about the night after?"

"Monday night?"

"Yes, Monday."

"Where?" Lily asked.

Kath was right in front of her now, but there was still a foot of space between them. Lily wanted to reach out and touch her, but she held herself back. The traffic on Columbus was barely twenty feet to their right.

"There's a place called the Paper Doll, on Union Street west of Grant," Kath said. "We can have dinner there. I can get there by eight o'clock."

"All right, I'll meet you there."

Lily didn't know what sort of excuse she'd give her parents, but right now, with Kath so close to her, she didn't care. She glanced at the lights of Columbus Avenue again, and before she could second-guess herself, she took Kath's hand and pulled her farther into Adler Place. The shadows weren't quite dark enough to hide them, but Lily had come so far—hundreds of miles from Los Angeles—and she wouldn't allow the last few inches to be insurmountable.

"Careful," Kath said softly.

But she didn't resist when Lily pulled Kath into a hug, and after a second's hesitation, Kath hugged her back. Lily buried her face in Kath's neck for one breathless moment. If she closed her eyes she might fix this in her memory always: the pulse in Kath's throat; the warmth of her body; the scent of her skin.

"I love you," Lily whispered.

A catch in Kath's breath; the ripple of it moving from her body to Lily's.

Kath drew back just enough to kiss her quickly. "I love you too."

"I'll see you on Monday," Lily said, and then she hurried away down the dark street. At the end of it, right before she stepped onto Grant Avenue, she looked back to see if Kath was still there—and she was.

She was standing in the middle of Adler Place, and when she saw Lily turn, she raised her hand in a wave. *Monday.*

Lily's heart lifted, and she waved back, and then she stepped into Chinatown. Grant Avenue was hung with red-and-gold banners welcoming the Year of the Monkey. A group of children on the corner were lighting clusters of illegal handheld sparklers. Lily raised her fingers to her lips as if to touch the last trace of Kath's mouth on hers. She felt a queer giddiness overtaking her, as if her body might float up from the ground because she was so buoyant with this lightness, this love.

1954	The U.S. Senate condemns Joseph McCarthy.
1955	Dr. Hsue-shen Tsien is deported from the United States and returns to China.
Feb. 11, 1956	**LILY meets Kath at Vesuvio Café in San Francisco.**
	The Immigration and Naturalization Service launches the Chinese Confession Program, encouraging Chinese to voluntarily confess if they immigrated to the United States illegally, leading to widespread fear of deportation within the Chinese American community.
1957	The U.S.S.R. launches Sputnik 1 into orbit.
	Kath obtains her pilot's license.
1958	United States launches Explorer 1, a satellite built by the Jet Propulsion Laboratory, into orbit.
1959	Lily graduates from the University of California–Los Angeles and begins working at the Jet Propulsion Laboratory.

AUTHOR'S NOTE

Lily Hu's story was inspired by two books. In *Rise of the Rocket Girls: The Women Who Propelled Us, From Missiles to the Moon to Mars*, Nathalia Holt introduces us to the female computers who worked at the Jet Propulsion Lab starting in the 1940s, including Chinese American immigrant Helen Ling, who went on to become an engineer at JPL and hired many more women to work there. In *Wide-Open Town: A History of Queer San Francisco to 1965*, Nan Alamilla Boyd notes almost casually, "San Francisco native Merle Woo remembers that lesbians of color often frequented Forbidden City [nightclub] in the 1950s." Both books gave me glimpses into Asian American history that has too often fallen through the cracks, and I wondered what life might have been like for a queer Asian American girl who dreamed of rocket ships, growing up in the 1950s. This nugget of an idea first became a short story, "New Year," published in *All Out: The No-Longer-Secret Stories of Queer Teens*, edited by Saundra Mitchell, in 2018. And now Lily's story has grown into this novel.

ON LANGUAGE

I made every effort to use historically accurate language in this book. For example, I chose terms about race that were widely used in the 1950s, some of which are offensive or at least outdated by contemporary standards. *Oriental*, which is now considered offensive, was applied to Asian Americans all the way through the 1970s and '80s. The term *Asian American* was not coined until the civil rights movement of the 1960s.

Lily and her family speak multiple dialects of Chinese, including Cantonese and Mandarin, and I followed historically accurate forms of writing for these languages. I chose to romanize Chinese terms when Lily and others are speaking Chinglish—that is, when they speak primarily in English but throw in a few Chinese words. I used Chinese characters when the whole sentence or the character's thoughts are entirely in Chinese.

All Chinese characters are rendered in their traditional or complex form. Simplified Chinese characters were not introduced until the 1950s and '60s in the People's Republic of China and would not have been in use in the

United States at that time. For Cantonese romanizations, I followed *The Student's Cantonese-English Dictionary* by B. Meyer and T. Wempe, published in 1935. For Mandarin terms, I followed the Wade-Giles romanization system, which was the standard for most of the twentieth century.

There are a few exceptions to these romanization choices. Place names (e.g., Kwangtung) and historical figures (e.g., Chiang Kai-shek) are rendered with their historical spellings. I also chose to use *cheongsam* to refer to the form-fitting dress with slits up both sides, first popularized in Shanghai in the 1920s. This word is a loose romanization of 長衫, which is literally the "long shirt" traditionally worn by men, not women. The term for a woman's dress is 旗袍, which would be romanized as *kei po* in Cantonese, but because *cheongsam* has become generally understood in English to mean a woman's Chinese dress, I decided to use *cheongsam*.

THE 1950S

Popular perceptions of the 1950s often center on conformity and social repression, but in reality the midcentury was a time of transition and thus a time of great cultural anxiety that was often expressed in efforts to suppress difference.

In 1952, the United States detonated the first hydrogen bomb. The Soviet Union followed in 1953, setting off atomic-age fears of nuclear annihilation—and duck-and-cover drills in schools. The Korean War had ended, though it had not been won; and China, which had been an American ally during World War II, became a Communist enemy. Senator Joseph McCarthy began his paranoid crusade against Communist infiltration in 1950, and although he was censured by the Senate in 1954 and dead by 1957, McCarthyism pervaded the decade, resulting in the deportation of Dr. Hsue-shen Tsien, a Chinese scientist who cofounded the Jet Propulsion Laboratory and had aided the United States during World War II. Once he returned to China in 1955, Dr. Tsien became known as the father of Chinese rocketry. McCarthyism also led to the so-called Lavender Scare, in which queer people were forced out of their government jobs because homosexuality was believed to be linked with Communism.

Although many people identify the 1950s with rock 'n' roll and artists like Elvis Presley, Elvis himself didn't really arrive until 1956, when "Heartbreak Hotel" was released. The pop charts of the early '50s were still topped by crooners such as Perry Como and Rosemary Clooney. Rock 'n' roll was still rhythm and blues recorded by black artists—and increasingly discovered by teenagers, who were coming into their own as an age group to be courted by advertisers and feared by adults, who depicted them as juvenile delinquents in films such as *The Wild One* (1953) and *Rebel Without a Cause* (1955). Although *The Wild One* would later become known for its homoerotic subtext, same-sex relationships were largely verboten in mainstream popular media—except in pulp fiction, which were small, mass-produced paperbacks that sold like hotcakes.

The first lesbian pulp novel, *Women's Barracks* by Tereska Torrès, was published in 1950 and sold a million copies. It was followed in 1952 by *Spring Fire*, which sold at least a million and a half copies. *Spring Fire*'s author, Vin Packer, was a pseudonym for Marijane Meaker, who would go on to write young adult novels as M. E. Kerr. Lesbian pulps were widely available in drugstores across the country, and although many were written with the male gaze in mind, plenty of lesbians also found them. Despite the publishers' requirement, due to obscenity laws, that these books end in punishment for the homosexual characters, they still created a kind of imagined community for lesbians scattered across the nation, who could read these books and discover that people like them existed.

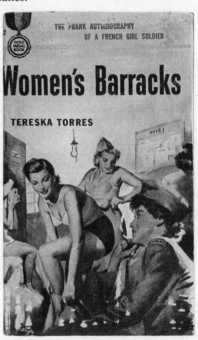

A copy of *Women's Barracks* printed in 1951. Like many pulp novels, this one was manufactured as cheaply as possible, hence the title is slightly cropped.

SAN FRANCISCO

San Francisco has long been known as a magnet for queer people. In *Wide-Open Town*, Boyd explains that although San Francisco's licentiousness was periodically quashed by anti-vice campaigns, those very efforts ironically drove attention to the city's anything-goes reputation, and "a wide range of adventure-seekers, homosexuals among them, made their way through the Golden Gate" in search of that freedom.

World War II had a major impact on queer communities in San Francisco, due to the arrival of thousands of service members—many of them gay or lesbian—who moved through the port city and were looking for nightlife and community. Minority communities in San Francisco changed during the war too, with Japanese Americans forced out into internment camps, and African Americans migrating to San Francisco to work at military bases and in the defense industries.

By the early 1950s, Chinatown was a well-known stop on the tourist circuit, and business owners leveraged white fascination with the Far East to sell them chop suey and souvenirs. The North Beach district, a traditionally Italian neighborhood that would become the heart of Beat culture in the late 1950s, was already home to multiple clubs that catered to gay men and lesbians. Sexually adventurous tourists could visit famous spots like Finocchio's (advertised as the place "Where Boys Will Be Girls"), or Mona's ("Where Girls Will Be Boys"). The Telegraph Club is fictional, but it is inspired by bars like these. North Beach abuts Chinatown, sharing several blocks along Broadway and Columbus, so those who were interested in visiting Finocchio's for a flamboyant queer-coded show could easily walk over to Chinatown afterward for late-night lo mein.

CHINATOWN AND CHINESE AMERICANS

The first Chinese landed in San Francisco in 1848, and soon afterward settled in the center of the city near Portsmouth Square in an area that would become known as Chinatown. For the next several decades, anti-Chinese bigotry tangled with demand for Chinese labor. White American entrepreneurs needed Chinese workers to build railroads and wash laundry, but white American workers resented the Chinese for taking those jobs. In 1882, President Chester A. Arthur signed the Chinese Exclusion Act, the first immigration ban in the United States targeting a specific ethnic group. It remained in place until World War II.

The sixty years of Chinese Exclusion created a bachelor society among Chinese Americans, because most Chinese women were legally barred from immigration due to the racist belief that they were all prostitutes. The vast majority of Chinese immigrants in the nineteenth and early twentieth centuries came from southern China and spoke Cantonese and its related dialects, including Toishanese. Robbed of the ability to form stable families in America, Chinese Americans formed institutions to serve communities of bachelors, such as mutual-aid societies based on family surnames or home villages. Businessmen founded the Chinese Consolidated Benevolent Association, or the Chinese Six Companies, to officially represent their interests and Chinatown.

World War II had a major impact on Chinese immigration. With Japan situated as the enemy, China—which had thrown off imperial rule in 1912 and formed a republic led by Generalissimo Chiang Kai-shek—became an American ally. Chiang's wife, Soong May-ling, aka Madame Chiang Kai-shek, was a key part of persuading America to support China against Japanese aggression. Madame Chiang was a Wellesley College–educated woman who spoke English fluently and was so adored by the American media that she appeared on the cover of *Time* magazine three times. In 1943, she embarked on a national tour to raise money and goodwill for China and became the first woman to address a joint session of Congress. After Madame Chiang's tour, Congress repealed the Chinese Exclusion Act in December 1943 and established a quota that permitted 105 Chinese to immigrate each year.

Meanwhile, the war provided an additional route to citizenship for Chinese immigrants: the military. Previously, due to Exclusion, many Chinese Americans arrived under false pretenses. After the 1906 San Francisco earthquake destroyed thousands of public documents, Chinese began to arrive with false documentation claiming that they were the children of American citizens of Chinese descent. These immigrants became known as "paper sons." When the United States entered World War II, approximately one-third of all Chinese American men between ages fifteen and sixty enlisted, in comparison with about 11 percent of the general population. Military service is not traditionally valued in Chinese culture, but perhaps one reason so many Chinese American men enlisted was because it enabled them to become naturalized American citizens, regardless of their previous immigration history.

After the war, quotas for Chinese immigrants loosened, first allowing veterans (including Chinese American veterans) to bring their wives to the United States, then extending that right to non-veteran Chinese Americans. In 1952, the McCarran-Walter Immigration Act allowed the naturalization of family members of American citizens, which enabled many Chinese families to reunify in the States. By the early 1950s, San Francisco's Chinatown had developed two distinct but overlapping populations: the aging group of bachelors who'd immigrated before the war, and a growing community of families based in the merchant class. Shirley Lum is rooted in this part of Chinatown, and her aspirations to compete in the Miss Chinatown pageant echo the broader goals of Chinatown's business community.

Actual contestants in 1954's Miss Chinese New Year Pageant. They are (left to right) Frances Fong, Margie Yee, Gloria Leong, Maye Leong, Bernice Wong and Florence Young.

Due to longstanding racist beliefs that Asians could not be true Americans, which were drawn into sharp focus first by Japanese internment and then by McCarthyism, Chinatown's leaders aimed to blunt white fears of the "other" by engaging in a quintessentially American cultural practice: the beauty pageant. Chinatown girls were selected to represent their community as models of American womanhood, spiced up with a little carefully cultivated exotic flair in the form of their dress, the cheongsam. The Miss Chinatown contest was originally held over the Fourth of July, making clear the patriotic connection, but by 1953, the beauty pageant had moved to coincide with the Chinese New Year festival. The festival and the Miss Chinatown contest were part of a broader effort to convince white Americans that Chinese Americans could assimilate and become model citizens—model minorities.

Combating racism through fitting in has never entirely worked. In 1956, the Immigration and Naturalization Service began the Chinese Confession Program, which promised forgiveness if an immigrant revealed their fraudulent "paper son" documents. However, if one confessed, that would implicate by extension their family, and sometimes the information revealed was used to deport suspected Communist sympathizers. In fact, the Confession Program snared members of the leftist youth group that Lily encounters, and ultimately revoked the citizenship of at least two of its members.

Lily's family represents a category of Chinese immigrant rarely depicted in popular culture and is inspired by my own family's experience. During the late nineteenth and early twentieth century, sons (and a few daughters) from upper class families in China sometimes came to the United States to study at American universities. The Chinese students who came to the States to study were not subject to the same immigration restrictions as laborers because of their class privilege, and they generally returned to China after completing their education. Some of them came from wealthy families; others were funded by scholarships. Many of them learned English in missionary schools in China. Although these students faced racism like all Chinese immigrants, their privileges smoothed their passage to America.

From 1937 to 1945, the Sino-Japanese War and World War II, both fought on the ground in China, limited the number of Chinese students in America, but after World War II, thousands more came in search of a modern education that they could use to rebuild their devastated homeland. However, the Chinese Civil War, fought from 1946 to 1949 between Chiang's Nationalist Party and Mao Zedong's Communist Party, got in the way. When Mao triumphed and the People's Republic of China was founded in 1949, those Chinese students were stranded in the United States, which did not recognize the Communist government until 1972. Many Chinese students were able to be naturalized, especially after the McCarran-Walter Act in 1952, but a few were deported—notably, Dr. Hsue-shen Tsien.

My paternal grandfather, John Chuan-fang Lo, came to the U.S. in 1933 to earn his Ph.D. in psychology from the University of Chicago. While there, he met my paternal grandmother, Ruth Earnshaw, who was white. After he graduated, he returned to China to teach at Huachung College. He and Ruth were married on August 5, 1937, in Shanghai, days before Japan invaded. They spent the rest of the Sino-Japanese War and part of World War II as refugees in western China near the Burma Road. In 1944, my grandmother was evacuated with the help of the U.S. military, but my grandfather remained in China until 1946, when he obtained a temporary teaching job at Franklin & Marshall College in Pennsylvania. He soon realized that he was being paid less than his white colleagues, and due to health care issues, the family needed additional income. Thus, the entire family went back to China in 1947, and were not able to leave until 1978, after I was born.

My grandparents didn't know that the Communists would take over China. I have often wondered if they would have tried to stay in the States if they had known. Lily's family, although different from mine, was loosely inspired by this question.

LESBIANS, GENDER, AND COMMUNITY

In the 1950s, the concept of same-sex marriage was largely inconceivable; interracial marriage wouldn't even be legalized across the United States until 1967. Homosexuality was categorized as a psychological disorder until 1987, and laws against homosexual sex only began to be repealed in 1962. These legal restrictions didn't mean that gay people did not exist, but being gay was not culturally acceptable, and that meant the gay and lesbian community was largely underground and had its own coded language.

Within San Francisco's white lesbian community in the 1940s and '50s, women used terms such as *butch* and *femme* in ways that could indicate gender expression and sexual preferences. At this time, gender was perceived as a predominantly binary concept. Although people certainly crossed gender boundaries and existed between them, the terminology available to Lily's community was black or white: men or women, butch or femme. Butches were lesbians with masculine appearances; femmes were traditionally feminine; and butches usually had relationships with femmes. "Butch/femme" has sometimes been misunderstood as an imitation of heterosexuality, but in *Boots of Leather, Slippers of Gold: The History of a Lesbian Community*, Elizabeth Lapovsky Kennedy and Madeline D. Davis explain: "Butches defied convention by usurping male privilege in appearance and sexuality, and with their fems, outraged society by creating a romantic and sexual unit within which women were not under male control. . . . Butch-fem roles were the key structure for organizing against heterosexual dominance."

Expressing a butch identity involved cultivating a masculine appearance, which could involve wearing men's clothing. Many cities outlawed cross-dressing in public; San Francisco's law was not repealed until 1974. As lesbian Reba Hudson relates in *Wide-Open Town*, gay men and lesbians were often harassed by police for cross-dressing in the 1940s and '50s, but women who cross-dressed would wear women's underwear, because then "they couldn't book you for impersonating a person of the opposite sex."

Cross-gender impersonation was all right, however, onstage. Male and female impersonation had long been part of theater, and it differed from what we today call drag. Impersonation was not queer-coded in its early days and was usually performed by heterosexuals. By the 1920s, however, mainstream male impersonation fell out of vogue, possibly due to changing ideas about sexuality that linked cross-gender performance with homosexuality. Male impersonation did not end, though; it continued and transformed in marginalized spaces. In 1920s and '30s Harlem, African American singer Gladys Bentley performed in menswear, and at the time she didn't hide her queer identity. When her Harlem career began to fizzle in the 1940s, Bentley went west, eventually landing at Mona's, the lesbian nightclub in San Francisco. Mona's featured other male impersonators who, like Bentley, dressed in tuxedos and often replaced standard lyrics in their songs with openly gay ones. Clubs featuring male impersonators continued to advertise in the *San Francisco Chronicle* and other publications well into the 1950s, and heterosexual tourists went to the shows seeking exotic entertainment, just as they visited Chinatown for a taste of the Orient.

The early 1950s was a period of relative freedom for San Francisco gay bars, because the 1951 *Stoumen v. Reilly* decision legalized public assembly of homosexuals in California. Homosexual acts, however, remained illegal, and as the decade wore on, police crackdowns would start to focus on homosexual activity. In September 1954, police raided 12 Adler, a bar owned by butch lesbian Tommy Vasu. Several teenage girls were also arrested, and newspaper accounts played up a scandalous cocktail of drugs, homosexuality, and cross-dressing. In 1956, a new mayor launched an anti-vice campaign to put many gay bars out of business. It's no coincidence that 1956 was also the year that the Daughters of Bilitis (DOB) was founded; this early gay rights organization aimed to provide a way for lesbians to socialize outside the bar scene.

A Mona's ad from the *San Francisco Examiner*, June 25, 1943.

The DOB and the lesbian bars described in *Wide-Open Town* seemed to be predominantly white. It has been difficult for me to find evidence of lesbians of color in this time period, although Kennedy's and Davis's research does include black women. Finding any history of queer Asian American women has been even more difficult, but tantalizing clues have surfaced in many sources. *Wide-Open Town*, of course, mentions Merle Woo, who was an Asian American activist in the 1970s and '80s, and it also mentions the existence of Filipina lesbians. Incidentally, a Filipina lesbian named Rose was the originator of the idea for the DOB, though the DOB's white cofounders, Del Martin and Phyllis Lyon, have become far better known. Arthur Dong's *Forbidden City, USA*, a documentary and accompanying book about the Chinatown nightclub, includes gay Asian American performers, but they don't speak about their experiences in detail. The Chinese lesbian that Lily's father mentions was inspired by Margaret Chung, who was the first Chinese American woman doctor and was rumored to be a lesbian who had a relationship with singer Sophie Tucker. Chung never came out. Historian Amy Sueyoshi put me in touch with Crystal Jang, a Chinese American lesbian who grew up in San Francisco's Chinatown and went to Galileo High School in the late 1950s and '60s. I also spoke with Kitty Tsui, a lesbian poet who was active in the 1970s and '80s with Merle Woo. Tsui and Jang both told me that they were often the sole Asian American lesbian in the room.

Lily's story is my attempt to draw some of this history out from the margins, to un-erase the stories of women like Crystal Jang and Merle Woo and Dr. Margaret Chung. Lily's story is entirely fiction and is not based on theirs, but I imagine that she and these real women all had to deal with similar challenges: learning how to live as both Chinese American and lesbian, in spaces that often did not allow both to coexist.

SELECT BIBLIOGRAPHY

In addition to periodicals from the 1950s including the *San Francisco Chronicle,* the *San Francisco Examiner,* and *Seventeen* magazine, some of the most useful references I consulted include:

BOOKS AND ARTICLES

Boyd, Nan Alamilla. *Wide-Open Town: A History of Queer San Francisco to 1965.* Berkeley: University of California Press, 2005.

Chang, Iris. *The Chinese in America.* New York: Viking, 2003.

Halberstam, Jack. *Female Masculinity: 20th Anniversary Edition.* Durham, NC: Duke University Press, 2018.

Holt, Nathalia. *Rise of the Rocket Girls.* New York: Little, Brown, 2016.

Kao, George. *Cathay by the Bay: Glimpses of San Francisco's Chinatown in the Year 1950.* Hong Kong: The Chinese University Press, 1988.

Kennedy, Elizabeth Lapovsky, and Madeline D. Davis. *Boots of Leather, Slippers of Gold: The History of a Lesbian Community.* New York: Penguin Books, 1994.

Lim, Shirley Jennifer. *A Feeling of Belonging: Asian American Women's Public Culture, 1930–1960.* New York: New York University Press, 2006.

Moy, Victoria. *Fighting for the Dream: Voices of Chinese American Veterans From World War II to Afghanistan.* Los Angeles: Chinese Historical Society of Southern California, 2014.

Nee, Victor G., and Brett de Bary. *Longtime Californ': A Documentary Study of an American Chinatown.* New York: Pantheon Books, 1973.

Ni, Ting. *The Cultural Experiences of Chinese Students Who Studied in the United States During the 1930s–1940s.* Lewiston, NY: The Edwin Mellen Press, 2002.

Rodger, Gillian. *Just One of the Boys: Female-to-Male Cross-Dressing on the American Variety Stage.* Urbana: University of Illinois Press, 2018.

Sueyoshi, Amy. "Breathing Fire: Remembering Asian Pacific American Activism in Queer History." In *LGBTQ America: A Theme Study of Lesbian, Gay, Bisexual, Transgender, and Queer History.* National Park Service, U.S. Department of the Interior, 2016.

Wong, Edmund S. *Growing Up in San Francisco's Chinatown: Boomer Memories From Noodle Rolls to Apple Pie*. Charleston, SC: The History Press, 2018.

Wu, Judy Tzu-Chun. *Doctor Mom Chung of the Fair-Haired Bastards*. Berkeley: University of California Press, 2005.

Yeh, Chiou-Ling. *Making an American Festival: Chinese New Year in San Francisco's Chinatown*. Berkeley: University of California Press, 2008.

Zhao, Xiaojian. *Remaking Chinese America: Immigration, Family, and Community, 1940–1965*. New Brunswick, NJ: Rutgers University Press, 2002.

DOCUMENTARY FILMS

Chen, Amy, and Ying Zhan. *Chinatown Files*. Filmakers Library, 2001.

DeLarverié, Stormé, and Michelle Parkerson, et al. *Stormé: the Lady of the Jewel Box*. Women Make Movies, 2000.

Dong, Arthur E. et al. *Forbidden City, U.S.A.* DeepFocus Productions, 2015.

Poirier, Paris. *Last Call At Maud's*. Frameline, 1993.

ACKNOWLEDGMENTS

This book would not exist without the hard work and support of so many wonderful people. I will always be grateful to my friend and fellow author Saundra Mitchell, who first gave me the opportunity to imagine Lily's story when she invited me to contribute a short story to her anthology *All Out: The No-Longer-Secret Stories of Queer Teens Throughout the Ages*. I thought that story, "New Year," was the end of it—until my prescient agent, Michael Bourret, persuaded me that it could become a novel. (It only took me three years!) My editor, Andrew Karre, gave me invaluable guidance in transforming that story into this novel, and inspired me to think outside the boundaries of what I perceive to be young adult fiction.

Thank you to my parents, Kirk and Margaret Lo, and my aunt, Catherine Lo, who provided invaluable assistance in writing the book's Cantonese and Mandarin dialogue. Thank you to Amy Sueyoshi, Crystal Jang, and Kitty Tsui for sharing their advice and personal experience when I was researching this book. Thank you to emily m. danforth, Britta Lundin, Cindy Pon, and Betty Law, who read early drafts and offered honest feedback and encouragement. I'm completely in love with the beautiful cover illustration by Feifei Ruan, who brought Lily and Kath's San Francisco to life in such a magical way.

Thank you to Julie Strauss-Gabel and the entire team at Dutton and Penguin who made this book into a real thing that readers can hold in their hands. A fuller list of the publishing professionals who worked on this book follows these acknowledgments. Although I don't work directly with each of you, please know that I think of all of you during the long process, and I thank you for the work that you do.

Last but not least, thank you to my wife, Amy Lovell, who supported me throughout the entire journey: my first reader, my cheerleader, my love.

CREDITS

DUTTON BOOKS AND PENGUIN YOUNG READERS GROUP

ART AND DESIGN
Anna Booth
Kristin Boyle

CONTRACTS
Anton Abrahamsen

**COPYEDITORS AND
PROOFREADERS**
Anne Heausler
Rob Farren
Elizabeth Lunn

EDITOR
Andrew Karre

MANAGING EDITOR
Natalie Vielkind

MARKETING
James Akinaka
Christina Colangelo
Brianna Lockhart
Danielle Presley
Felicity Vallence

**PRODUCTION
MANAGER**
Vanessa Robles

PUBLICITY
Kaitlin Kneafsey

PUBLISHER
Julie Strauss-Gabel

**PUBLISHING
MANAGER**
Melissa Faulner

SUBSIDIARY RIGHTS
Micah Hecht

SALES
Susie Albert
Jill Bailey
Maggie Brennan
Trevor Bundy
Nicole Davies
Tina Deniker
John Dennany
Cletus Durkin
Joe English

Eliana Ferreri
Drew Fulton
Felicia Frazier
Sheila Hennessey
Todd Jones
Doni Kay
Steve Kent
Jill Nadeau
Debra Polansky
Colleen Conway Ramos
Mary Raymond
Jennifer Ridgway
Judy Samuels
Nicole White
Allan Winebarger
Dawn Zahorik

**SCHOOL AND LIBRARY
MARKETING AND
PROMOTION**
Venessa Carson
Judith Huerta
Carmela Iaria
Trevor Ingerson
Summer Ogata
Megan Parker
Rachel Wease

LISTENING LIBRARY

Joseph Grimm
Orli Moscowitz
Emily Woo Zeller
Rebecca Waugh

DYSTEL, GODERICH & BOURRET

Lauren E. Abramo
Michael Bourret
Kemi Faderin
Michaela Whatnall
Kieryn Ziegler

DISCUSSION GUIDE

1. **(PROLOGUE)** What themes and tensions does Lo set up for the novel in the prologue, particularly around race, nationalism, culture, and gender?

2. **(CHAPTER 2)** When Lily returns home from the Eastern Pearl, she takes out the Tommy Andrews ad for the Telegraph Club and adds it to her other newspaper clippings. Why is this collection important to her? What does it tell us about Lily at this point in the novel?

3. **(CHAPTER 5)** Lily feels "exhilarated" after she finds *Strange Season* at Thrifty Drug Store, "as if she had finally cracked the last part of a code." What has Lily discovered about herself, and why was the pulp novel important in that process?

4. **(CHAPTER 9)** After Lily's father is interrogated by the FBI he says, "We're living in a complicated time. People are afraid of things they don't understand, and we need to show that we're Americans first." Why does he say this, and what is at stake for the Hu family? How might this experience parallel the experiences of immigrants today?

5. **(CHAPTER 12)** Lily tells Kath about her plan to work at the Jet Propulsion Laboratory, but not everyone is as supportive of Lily's dream job. How does Lily's interest in space set her apart from—or align her with—the other women in her life?

6. **(CHAPTER 15)** Shirley "warns" Lily about Kath and then rejects Lily when she doesn't come back inside at the dance. What role does Shirley and Lily's friendship play in the story?

7. **(CHAPTER 18)** Kath secures a fake ID for Lily so that they can sneak into the Telegraph Club as minors. What bothers Lily about this fake document?

8. **(CHAPTER 22)** Lo uses the automated dioramas at Playland's Musée Mécanique as a metaphor for Lily and Kath's romantic feelings for each other. What is Lo communicating in this scene, and how does she use this metaphor again later in the novel?

9. **(CHAPTER 25)** At the Telegraph Club, Lily and Kath hear women talk about being "butch" or "femme" and when Kath is called a "baby butch" Lily recognizes it is a compliment. In what other ways do Lily and Kath learn about lesbian culture?

10. **(CHAPTER 27)** In the scenes at Sutro's, Lo illustrates racial tension and racism between white and Chinese Americans after Lily and Shirley are assumed to be Japanese. What are the ways Lo does this? Why do Lily and Shirley react in the ways that they do?

11. **(CHAPTER 30)** Lily notices a difference in the way the women at the Telegraph Club talk about "the feds" and communism. What is different—or similar—about this conversation compared to the discussion Lily has with her parents about the FBI's suspicion of Chinese Americans?

12. **(CHAPTER 31)** Again, Lily experiences microaggressions when socializing with the women from the Telegraph Club; however, this time she also learns about a Chinese male impersonator, for whom she feels "immediately proud." Why does Lo juxtapose these two experiences? When else does Lily encounter racism within the lesbian community?

13. **(CHAPTER 36)** Lily witnesses Shirley getting out of Calvin's car, but she doesn't tell her parents about them. Why does she keep Shirley's secret? And why doesn't Shirley keep hers?

14. **(END OF PARTS I–V)** Lo ends Parts I–V with memories from Joseph and Grace, Lily's parents, and Judy, Lily's aunt. How do these flashback scenes function in the story as a whole?

15. **(CHAPTER 40)** When Lily's mother says "There are no homosexuals in this family. [. . .] Are you my daughter?" what does she mean? How does Lily react to this and why?

16. **(CHAPTERS 41–42)** What might have happened to Lily after she ran away from home if she had not remembered where Lana lived, or if Lana had not taken her in?

17. **(CHAPTER 47)** "And if her father wouldn't lie, why should she?" When Lily comes out to her parents, it is complicated by her father's immigration status and the cultural climate of the 1950s, and yet she refuses to lie to them. Why does she make the choices she makes?

18. **(CHAPTER 48)** "This was the world." What does Lily mean by this when she is on the train to Pasadena? How does your interpretation influence your reading of the events that follow?

Turn the page for an excerpt from

A SCATTER OF LIGHT

the companion novel to

LAST NIGHT AT THE TELEGRAPH CLUB

Set in 2013, during the summer the United States Supreme Court began dismantling the laws that restricted same sex marriage, Aria Tang West's coming-of-age story is deftly intertwined with a poignant note of closure for Lily and Kath from *Last Night at the Telegraph Club*.

My grandmother was gone by the time I came downstairs on Friday morning. Analemma was sprawled on the rug in front of the cold woodstove in the living room, and her tail thumped against the floor as I bent down to pet her. In the kitchen, Grandma had left a check for Steph on the table, weighted down with the saltshaker.

I poured myself coffee, made toast, and took it all out to the deck, where I sat in the morning sunlight and gazed at the hills. It was going to be a hot day; I could feel the promise of it in the way the sun sank into my hair. In the distance, I heard the gate opening and closing. That metal latch dropping into place.

I couldn't see Steph from here, but there was something delicious about knowing that she was coming up the hill, and if I went around the house to look for her, I could see her. From my vantage point, it seemed as if I was alone, but I wasn't. Steph was close enough that if I called her name, she would probably hear me.

I sat on the deck for a while, listening. The gardening tools were kept in a shed just below the studio, and I heard the bolt on the shed door thrown open, and then the low creak of the hinges. I heard the clanging of tools against each other, and the rumble of the wheelbarrow as it was pushed out into the yard. Thump, thump, clang. The door creaking again, closing. Footsteps and the wheelbarrow, trundling away.

Another few minutes passed, and then I went back into the kitchen. My grandmother always had a pitcher of iced tea in the fridge, and there was a bowl of lemons on the counter. It was getting hot already, and Steph would probably be thirsty. I took out the lemon squeezer and some glasses and set them on the counter along with the iced tea, long spoons, and a tray of ice from the freezer. I didn't let myself think about what I was doing; I just did it.

Analemma ran ahead of me out the front door, and I followed more slowly with the two glasses of iced tea. The hill that the cottage was built into was terraced, and the brick path wound back and forth down the hill like a Z. I heard Steph greeting Ana before I saw her, and when I rounded the bend and Steph came into view, she looked exactly as I expected—baseball cap, shorts, sleeveless tee—but it still startled me: my imagination made real.

She looked up as she rubbed Analemma's back and smiled. "Hey."

"I thought you might want some iced tea," I said, and offered her a glass.

She was wearing work gloves, and she took one off to accept it. Our fingertips brushed together. "Thanks." She took a sip and then set the glass down on the stone bench nearby.

"My grandmother gave me this to give to you, too." I took the check out of my pocket and held it out to her.

"Great." She took it without touching me, and I was a little disappointed.

"She also asked me to invite you over for lunch sometime."

"That's nice of her," Steph said as she folded the check and put it in her pocket.

"She said any day would do, as long as it was after noon."

"I'll check my schedule at work and get back to her. Is she out? Her car's gone."

"Yeah, she went to Berkeley."

Steph went to sit on the bench, taking another drink of her iced tea, and gestured for me to join her. "Did you have a good time last Saturday?" she asked. Analemma nosed around the flower bed where she had been weeding.

I sat down beside her. "Yeah, I had a great time. Thanks for inviting me."

"Anytime." She glanced sideways at me, a mischievous expression on her face, and asked, "Did Mel try to make a move on you after we left?"

"That's private," I said with hint of a grin.

"She did, didn't she?" Steph seemed to think this was hilarious. "I hope she didn't make you uncomfortable."

"Oh, no. Mel is great."

"Good." Steph drank more of the iced tea; it was almost gone already. "You doing anything this weekend?"

"No. I'm helping my grandmother go through my grandpa's old papers, but that's more of an ongoing thing."

"She never says much about your grandpa. I only know he was a professor at Berkeley."

"Yeah, he taught astronomy. I'm sorting his research papers because she's using them in her art."

"Really? How?"

"I don't know. She won't tell me."

"What did he research?"

"Protostars. I can show you if you like." As soon as I said it, I wanted to take it back. Why would Steph want to see Grandpa's research notes?

But she said, "Sure, I'd love to see it. But I have to finish up here first."

"Oh, of course. Sorry. I'm distracting you."

"Happy to be distracted."

Did I imagine that look in her eyes? A hint of pleasure. I didn't imagine the buzz I felt in my body.

"But I do have to get back to work," she added, and then she set down the now-empty glass and pulled the work glove back on, going back to the flower bed she'd been weeding.

I wondered if I should leave, but I didn't want to. Analemma had stretched out on the moss-covered brick path and was panting slightly in the growing heat.

"When did you start working for my grandmother?" I asked.

"About a year ago. She used to come to the Greenbrae Garden Center, where I work, and I'd help her there. Then she asked if I did gardening gigs outside my job."

"Were you here last summer?" My dad and I had visited last July, but Steph hadn't been around then.

"Yeah, I started in August."

She threw the weeds she had pulled into a yard waste bag. A dark bloom of sweat dampened the back of Steph's shirt, and the short strands of hair along the nape of her neck were damp too. I watched the way the muscles in her arms flexed as she worked, and then I realized I was staring and looked down guiltily. The glass in my hand was slick, and a droplet of condensation plummeted to the ground, leaving a splotch of water on the bricks.

"So—" she said.

"So—" I said.

She looked over her shoulder at me and grinned. "You go first."

"I was going to ask if you decided whether you're doing that concert in August with Roxy."

She straightened up to get the bag of fertilizer from the wheelbarrow. When she lifted it up, I tried not to look at her. The way her koi tattoos moved.

"I haven't decided yet. If I get involved again, it could be—" She shook her head. "It's just a lot."

"What do you mean? Is there drama or something?"

"No. The band gets along fine. I'm just not sure if I have time to do the band and work, and I was thinking about finishing my music degree."

"You were getting a music degree?"

"An associate in fine arts at the community college. I have one semester to go, but I don't know when I can do it." She finished pouring out the fertilizer and returned the bag to the wheelbarrow.

"What's stopping you?"

She gave a short laugh. "Money. What else?"

"Aren't there scholarships?"

"Not for community college." She knelt down and began to spread the fertilizer around the plants. "At least not as far as I know. Anyway, I don't even know if it makes sense to finish the degree. I feel like life might be a better teacher."

"My mom has a music degree. She's an opera singer. She'd say it was worth it."

Steph looked up. "Your mom's an opera singer? Like professionally?"

"Yeah." Sometimes, when people found out about my mom's job, they thought I was making it up, but that didn't seem to be what Steph was implying. She seemed impressed, which made me uncomfortable.

"Where does she perform?" she asked.

"All over," I said vaguely. "She's in Europe this summer."

Steph sat back on her heels. "Touring?"

"No, she's with an opera company. Sometimes she tours, but—I mean, the point is, she couldn't have done that without her degree. Maybe it's a good idea for you to finish yours."

Steph looked at me for a second, and then returned to spreading the fertilizer around the plants. "Yeah, maybe. Or maybe it would be more useful if I get an accounting degree." She sounded a little bitter.

"I can't imagine you as an accountant."

"I can't either, but it might have helped with the rent."

I felt like I had screwed up our conversation somehow. "Well, you should do whatever makes sense for you," I said, trying to fix it. "Whether that means you finish your degree or get back together with the band. I just feel like if you have that talent, you should go for it. Otherwise you're suppressing who you really are, and that just seems wrong."

She smiled slightly, first down at the dirt, and then over her shoulder at me. "Thanks for the words of wisdom," she said.

I flushed. "Sorry. I mean, I didn't mean to be condescending."

"You weren't. I appreciate it. It's nice when someone believes in you."

I felt that warm flush spread down my neck as we looked at each other—as she looked at me. Her eyes bright, focused. Did I imagine the slight color on her cheeks too?

"Enough about me," she said, turning back to the flower bed. "Tell me about you. You're going to college in the fall? What are you going to major in?"

"Yeah, probably either physics or planetary science."

"Really?" She sounded surprised.

"Why, you don't think girls can do science?" I teased her.

She laughed. "I never said that."

"It's just that people have assumptions, you know? Most boys take one look at me and think there's no way I could do math, even though I'm Asian. It's like their two stereotypes get crossed and they don't know how to deal with me."

"I'm not a boy," she said. She sounded amused.

PHOTO CREDITS